STARS AND SCORPIONS

THE AFTER EDEN SERIES: BOOK TWO

AUSTIN DRAGON

This is a work of fiction. Names, characters, places, and incidents are the product of the author's imagination or are used fictitiously. Any resemblance to actual persons, living or dead, events, or locales is entirely coincidental.

Published by Well-Tailored Books, California

Stars and Scorpions / After Eden Series: Book Two

978-0-9887235-3-5 (paperback)
978-0-9887235-5-9 (ebook)

http://www.austindragon.com

Book cover design by Leslie K.

Formatting by Polgarus Studio

Printed in the United States of America

For Ulin,
Enjoying the Empyrean view from above.

Foreword

"After Eden, Thy Kingdom Fall.
All Kingdoms Fall, New Kingdoms Rise."

World War III. It was inevitably going to be one of religion, this great, grim, evil war of humans, machines, and *other things* in the shadows that have never existed before. Unfortunately, neither the cause nor the outcome was within our perception, though the former should have been. No one could ever have imagined that it would not just be the third of the world wars, as that is unremarkable, but the explosion of the first global war of the Technological Age, the Tek Age—a hell we had never seen before.

Net-Dictionary

Wolf 359

1. A red dwarf star located in the Leo constellation, approximately 7.8 light-years from Earth, making it one of the stars nearest to our solar system.

2. A fictional space battle in the Star Trek Universe between the United Federation of Planets and the Borg Collective in the year 2367.

3. The opening battle of World War III in New York City on September 11, 2125. Over sixty percent of the United States of America Atlantic Oceanic Battle Fleet was destroyed by the Supreme Islamic Caliphate Battle Group on the first day.

Other terms:

Pagan: (universal or American usage) a non-believer of god or gods; one that doesn't believe in religion, often negative to, hostile to, or hateful of religion.

Jew-Christian: (American usage [by non-religious people]) a religious person, other than Muslim.

Faither: (global usage [by religious people]) a religious person, other than Muslim.

Tek World: common slang for tek-cities, tek-metropolises, or general tek-society.

Resistance: (pre-World War III)

1. [by non-religious people] government term for the network of Jew-Christian domestic "terrorists" in America.

2. [by religious people] the civilian resistance force against the militant, anti-religious American government.

Continuum:

1. (general usage) the parallel society created by and controlled exclusively by Faithers outside of Tek World.

2. (formal usage) the formal alliance of the New Protestant Order, New Jewish Continuum, New Catholic Order, Mormon Order, the African Collective, Shogun, and the Magi.

Private Letter #6487 (World War III)

{Portions of personal letter were irretrievable due to EMP weapons damage. Remaining data portions were delivered to surviving partner per official will-on-file.}

11 September 2125

Dear Hunnie-Bunnie:

{Irretrievable Data Blocks}…the end of paradise…{Irretrievable Data Block}…but to hell with the military regs. America will survive this Muslim menace. We better with those damn CHINs circling like vultures. How did we get here? It's like the Jew-Christians knew this war was coming. The President and the Emperor will be the death of this entire shiny planet! Our once great American empire. I know you and the kids are panicking over talk of the mandatory draft being reinstated, but the brass told us that it's not going to happen. I believe them. I can tell when they're mouthing administration propaganda. I don't know how they plan to assemble a million-man, non-robotic army, where they're going to get the people from, if not from the general population. I could write more, but we'll be making first battle contact soon. The guys think this will end very badly for our unit. I wonder if death hurts when you cross over. Too bad the dead can't call you via vid-phone. We could end this whole after-death debate once and for all—atheistic oblivion or religious afterlife. Either way, I hope it doesn't hurt. I'm rambling now. Time to get my game face on and send as many of those hadjis to their celestial virgins as our bombs and bullets can manage. It's killing time. I love you and the children, and if I don't make it home, remember the best of me—your partner. Peace and Semper Fi, JB.

Military Wire: John B. York, Colonel, United States of America Marine Corps, was killed on 11 September, 2125 at the Battle of "Wolf 359," Atlantic Oceanic Battle Group, World War III. He is survived by partner (hetero) and five children (unverified).

Table of Contents

THE JEWISH ORDER
(Prelude to the New Jewish Continuum)
America

Suspicions Down Under

"Atheism is hereby recognized as a religion." – Ruling of the United States Seventh Circuit Court of Appeals (pre-Rule of Law era), August 2005

"Religion is regarded by the common people as true, by the wise as false, and by rulers as useful." – Attributed to Seneca the Younger, Roman stoic philosopher, 4 BCE - 65 CE

Western Europe fell to the Supreme Islamic Caliphate in 2065. Ibiza, Spain, that tiny island in the Mediterranean off the country's Valencian coast, became the final stand of secular Spain against the Muslim invaders. There were heroic stories from every one of the twenty countries that the Caliphate seized in the war. Spanish resistance lasted longer than most of Western Europe, but it, too, lost violently. Those lucky to escape made it to whatever country would take them. Millions of secular Western Europeans fled to America, the Russian Bloc (which absorbed Eastern Europe), and Africa; but most Spaniards made it to Australia and named the city they created after that final battle for Spanish freedom.

The now thriving tek-city is home to not only Spaniards, but minority populations of Portuguese and Moroccans. It is a popular travel destination for the wealthy from the Spanish Americas—

known as Latin America a half century ago, from Mexico to the tip of South America. The most notable visitor today is the President of Mexico.

Ibiza, Australia
3:05 p.m., 27 May 2088

Stars of all colors reflect through the blackness: yellow, red, orange, blue, and white. The man looks up from his custom-made reflex hyper-scope; jet black hair, salt-and-pepper graying mustache and beard; casually dressed in an exquisitely patterned short-sleeved white shirt, tan pants, and shoes, his gold-plated e-pad clipped to his belt.

"We look at them with fascination even though what we see is an illusion," he says. "The stars may all be dead, many millions of years ago even, the light being their only offspring to remind us that they ever existed. There was a nice Mexican poem we used to sing as children about the stars."

Another man casually dressed in a black short-sleeved shirt with white pants and shoes stands next to him. "There's a Mexican song for everything," his guest says. Both men speak in Mexican Spanish with accents that reveal they are well-educated and city-born.

The guest notices something moving in one of the thick palm trees that shade the large outside patio where they stand. A bluish-gray koala bear hangs on the tree with its black clawed hands and stares at him with shimmering black eyes. Is it real or a robotic pet, or maybe a surveillance vid-cam robot masquerading? It yawns wide with its cute face and then refocuses on him. The wind blows, shifting the leaves and the shade, and for an instant it seems that there are dozens of tiny black eyes all throughout the canopy of the tree watching him. The wind blows again, and the eyes and the koala bear are gone in the shade.

The man in white and tan swings the gaze of his scope to focus on the city; though it's over five miles away, he can see the foreign delegates clearly. His palatial hillside mansion gives a beautiful 360-degree view for miles of the entire residential area of the tek-city, with its multi-colored homes surrounding the high-priced mansions littering the hillside. The towering steel and glass buildings of the tek-city's business section loom in the distance. He straightens up to directly look up at the halo, slang for a circle of drones hovering above a specific site, or, in this case, the visiting President of Mexico, the guest of the Australian President, with staffers and security detail at the home of some wealthy donor.

"The Americans, Chinese, and Muslims think there is no world outside of theirs. And we *lesser* nations do everything in our power to prove them right. A world summit without them is no summit at all," he says.

Drones come in many configurations, but the ubiquitous ones are the "globe" surveillance models, twenty-inch-diameter flying spheres in a muted silver color, used by law enforcement all over the world. The hover-tek of these sophisticated flying vid-cams is so advanced they can hover or zip around more than a hundred feet in the air, allowing the government to continuously monitor tek-cities for any disturbance, crime, or act of terrorism. In halo formation, it is said drones can monitor billions of targets in the air and on the ground simultaneously.

He looks at the second man, Augustin. "What is it that you want me to say? I'm flattered you put so much confidence in our optics tek, but it can differentiate biological from artificial. That's all." He smiles. "The androids you see in the movies are science fiction, you know. No one can make ones that can fool scanners or even the human eye. No one can, man or robot—at least not yet."

"I don't know what I'm asking exactly."

"Just that something isn't right. You've known him since we were children. My dear Augustin, sometimes machines lie and your instincts tell the truth. I have never understood why people trust machines more than their own God-given instincts."

Augustin looks away for a moment.

"Don't worry, I won't tell anyone you're religious. Only in America do they hunt religious people down like dingoes. Here in Australia, we do that only to Muslims and CHIN spies."

"Any recommendations for me?"

"I can get my people close enough to do better scans, but I know your people have already done so. What are you going to do? Instincts, no matter how true, are not the kind of proof you'd need…" He gives him a deadly serious look. "…to justify a coup."

"You mean a civil war. My people will get the samples and the evidence."

"If your suspicions are correct, all I can say is, whatever is going on, the American White House is behind it."

Long Island Expressway, New York City, New York
12:02 p.m., 4 June 2088

The real driver lies dead in the trunk.

Henry Ford didn't invent the car. He allowed every American to be able to buy one. And buy they did. Today, the car drives you. For the elite, hiring a driver remains a conspicuous status symbol. "Driving" simply means telling the car where to go, making calls, running errands, etc. A "driver" is nothing more than a "slave," slang for personal assistant, who travels along.

In the back of the silver limousine, the boss looks at his hand-watch—one of the many fashionable, wearable devices available—a silver-dollar-sized, plastic circle affixed to the back of his hand, with the time displaying in four large silver digits. A young woman sits next to him, and across from them are another two men, all busy at work on their tablets or e-pads. All four of them are dressed in some variation of a dark suit. A hard, black partition separates the back passenger seats from the driver's compartment.

Some eighteen years ago, author Ahn Droid wrote his seminal work, *We Are Borg Now*, about the merging of man and machine in modern tek-society. He wasn't speaking of bionic people or cyborgs or any other kind of cybernetic tek, though they did exist even back then, but the inability of the average tek-city dweller to be without their mechanical device of choice for even a few seconds. For most of the world's population it is the e-pad, the descendant of the smartphone of the past. The playing-card-sized device of virtually no discernible weight simply never left the side of its human owner as it did *everything*. The tablet, colloquially known as a tab, is a larger e-pad of usually seven inches by eleven inches. Droid commented that these devices, along with their near-ubiquitous ear-sets (the descendants of the old analog phone and headset) were the new mechanical appendages of the new quasi-cyber human race. This race would further evolve with ever bolder wearable and bio-integrated tek.

The boss touches his ear-set with his index finger to activate the intercom. "Driver, we need to move faster. I know it's lunch-crunch traffic, but we need to get there at least thirty minutes before our appointment."

The driver's voice sounds over the speaker. "Yes sir, we'll make it."

The boss resumes speaking in Spanish on the phone via his e-pad: "Yes, sir. We made sure to land outside any major tek-city. We're driving to the private airport now. We'll get the deep-gene samples. Yes, we won't let Centro know." He refers to Mexico's CIA, Center for Research and National Security.

The woman glances to the front of the vehicle. "The car has stopped."

The boss touches his ear-set. "Driver, why have we—"

The limousine is hit at over one hundred miles an hour by a super-truck. After skidding down the road for twenty feet, both explode.

The driver, a square-jawed man, stands on the sidewalk, watching it all happen in dark shades and a black uniform. He is taller than average, with a very thick mane of hair and a rock-hard, ultra-defined musculature. Even his large hands, with porcelain black nails, seem to be muscled.

He looks across the street and notices two young boys watching him. He purposely drove the limousine to a secluded back street. The area was supposed to be empty, but here these two boys are, out of nowhere. One of the boys was filming the explosion with his e-pad. He is now filming him.

The square-jawed man reaches into his jacket, takes out a gun, and shoots both boys dead. He walks across the street to the bodies and grabs the dead boy's e-pad. He puts it in his jacket and speaks into his ear-set.

"Send the clean-up team. Primary targets eliminated, but two additional collateral targets."

Oval Office, Washington DC
2:14 p.m., 4 June 2088

President T. Wilson stands in silhouette as he addresses his distinguished guests: the Presidents of Canada and Mexico. The two men sit attentively in facing chairs.

"I know my predecessors ignored your nations and your people. And your predecessors did the same when it came to the United States. Forget the Three Towers in New York City. As the leaders of the great North American continent, we must be our own 'three towers.' We have the duty and obligation to act as one against our mutual enemies…and sometimes, even our own mutual allies."

The Capitol Dome, Washington DC
8:34 a.m., 6 June 2089

Washington DC—the District—is neither the largest nor the showiest of the nation's tek-metropolises, but it is the embodiment of pure, unfiltered power, and there are only two other cities on the planet (Riyadh and Beijing) that can boast the same.

Unlike all the other American tek-cities, the District is obsessed with maintaining the antiquity of its landmarks. The world-famous Capitol Dome, designed by Thomas Walter, is still made out of its original cast iron and topped off by its Statue of Freedom.

The square-jawed man stares at the ivory-white Capitol Dome building. There is something alluring about it, separate from its being one of the key seats of power in the nation. Maybe it's the architecture; everything built today is so…unimaginative. People build buildings that they think the people of the future should live in. The Capitol Dome is simple, non-tek majesty.

Executive Branch, Non-Public Off-Site Offices, Washington DC
11:13 a.m., 6 June 2089

The square-jawed man sits quietly on one of the many mahogany benches lining the dimly lit underground hallway. It's been six months since the murder of the most powerful political campaign manager and "king maker" in American history, Lucifer Mestopheles (known by all as Lou), but it's *still* the talk of the District. There is no shortage of sensationalism, debauchery, and lurid gossip in this town. Even the massacre of Palestine Israel,

"Muslims exterminating Muslims," eclipsed his story only for a few days in January. Millions of them don't compare to Lou, who was instrumental in getting "God," as President T. Wilson is known among the insider power elite, into the Oval Office.

Officially, the murder remains under investigation. Unofficially, it is being blamed directly on Jew-Christians. But he doesn't believe it. The rumors run wild. It was the Muslims, either a lone, unaffiliated jihadi or the Islamic Caliphate itself; the CHINs, causing their chaos from the shadows; or even the Russian Bloc, who love doing things on a global stage just so you know they are still alive, no matter how pathetic or erratic the action. It could easily have been a random act of crime or maybe even a lovers' quarrel that ended violently. Who really knows, except the people who did the murder.

He looks at his wrist-band watch with four large red numbers on its oval dial. 11:14. *Forty-five minutes of waiting! They are never on time.* But he already knows why he has been summoned. There is a bit of commotion as doors open and people stream out into the hallway. He sits back quietly, recognizing the security and intelligence community heavy-hitters in their dark suits as they exit the conference rooms for the elevators: the assistant secretary of state for the Western hemisphere, the assistant secretary of state for the Eastern hemisphere, the deputy secretary of state for the Americas, the deputy secretary of state for Asia, the deputy secretary of state for Africa, the deputy secretary of state for Eurasia and the Middle East.

"They will see you now," a female voice says. Standing at an open door of the adjacent office is a sharply-dressed, middle-aged woman.

She leads him into the massive, now empty, conference room and then to an inner office. She motions him inside, but doesn't follow. The door closes.

"Please have a seat, sir. We're sorry to have had you wait so long," a man says.

He sits at a large desk. In a chair next to it is a blonde-haired woman who doesn't even acknowledge his presence as she taps on her tablet. He knows who she is: the director of the Homeland Defense and Intelligence Agency, the most powerful agency in America.

Presidents of years past had merged the nation's Old Homeland Security, Federal Bureau of Investigation, Central Intelligence Agency, Defense Intelligence Agency, National Security Agency, et cetera, into one supreme law enforcement, border security, anti-terrorism, counter-terrorism, and intelligence-gathering organization. It wasn't just terrorists and criminals who were scared of its size, scope, and capabilities. The fear extended to even congresspeople, senators, governors, and the media.

"Do you know who I am?" the man asks.

The square-jawed man studies him for a moment with his wild, glistening brown eyes. "No sir."

"Good. Do you know the Director?"

"Not directly, but I've seen her many times before." As head of the agency, she is simply called the same thing that the super-agency is for short: Homeland.

"I'm the President's special advisor on strategic domestic security," he says.

The square-jawed man nods. One of the perks of being President is that you can make up out of thin air whatever jobs in the White House—and with any title—you want. You can also hand them out like candy. But all world leaders do it.

"Have you been read into Project Purify?" he asks.

"Yes sir."

"What are your personal feelings toward the project?"

"I fully support it. There's religious madness all over the world with the Caliphate. The Russian Bloc, Africa, Spanish Americas, here in America. At the end of the day, the only thing the American people want from their government is safety."

"Exactly. It reminds me of the President's speech at his third inauguration. His 'Light and Darkness' speech. 'The human race is evolving into a New Enlightenment, beyond superstitions and religions. But it's much more than being irreligious. Humankind, of a future today, will finally and logically rid itself of the belief in all fairy tales, just as we did with the notion that the Earth was flat. Then the governments of the world can use their collective resources and intellect to create a great global civil society, a near-paradise here on Earth, rather than defending its people from those who would rather kill and die to go to an imaginary one in the sky.'"

The square-jawed man nods again. In politics, you adopt the "religion" of the people in power. He could care less about religious or irreligious. He is a Nihilist mercenary in the employ of the American government. He cares only about his job (violence) and benefits (money).

"Let me get directly to it. This year has not begun well for the administration. As you already understand, the most important duty of government is to protect its people, and we must never forget that. Nothing else comes even a close second, even above keeping the Grid stable and the Net forever-on. The President invests much time, energy, and resources into the protection of the American people. Heading up our domestic anti-terrorism and counter-terrorism efforts of the project was an elite team of Vampires. Or so we thought. That team has been permanently disbanded. You and your Werewolf SS team will replace them. I am told you are a star within the special ops community. We expect you not to disappoint."

One of the newer and officially recognized religions in Tek World is Vampirism; a lot more stupid, but a made-up one like all the others. A religion based on fang dental implants and permanent yellow or red contact lenses. How stupid indeed, he thinks.

"I respect the confidence being placed in me, sir, but I am already heading up another important op which has had us on continuous duty all over the globe. We're at a very critical point."

"That project has been concluded, thanks to the efforts of you and your team. It has been duly noted in your file and already recognized as an impressive success."

"Thank you, sir. May I know who the enemy foreign power directly behind the plot is?"

"The President will make that known to the American people in due course."

"I'm sorry. That was an inappropriate question."

"Not at all. Your curiosity is understandable. As for your new assignment, let me digress for a moment. In the pre-modern era, after World War Two, there was a common term used: the Cold War. It was between the two superpowers of the time, us and the empire that existed before the Russian Bloc, before Russia, called the Soviet Union. That Cold War could have, at any time, erupted into a 'hot war,' the proverbial World War Three, with the very nuclear annihilation of the planet. It never happened. Instead, one day the Soviet Union just up and collapsed without anyone on either side predicting it.

"There is a New Cold War today and the stakes are much higher. This time we have three global superpowers: us, the Muslims, and the Chinese. I never include the Indians because it's China, not India, that makes the CHINs formidable. There are two wannabe superpowers, the Russian Bloc and Australia, and two irrelevant continents, the Spanish Americas and Africa. My geopolitics professor at Harvard had a saying: 'Don't be Sue.' 'Sue' wasn't the female name S-U-E, but the initials S-U. 'Don't be SU.' In the global game of musical chairs, make sure when the tune stops playing that you're not the Soviet Union, that you're not the empire that collapses with a puff of smoke, without the least bit of warning. To that end, America must remove any unneeded domestic distractions."

The square-jawed man notices that Homeland is listening attentively, too.

The President's man continues. "We're fighting this war every day. You know this better than most, being part of our super-soldier, special-ops division. Enemies abroad, enemies within. There is a tight deadline to get the project back on track, and the President himself will be watching. Based on the latest reports from the Terrorism Threat Work Group, he wants the focus increased on the entire Jew-Christian community, not just designated terrorists and persons of interest. All."

"What about Muslims?"

"Not your concern. Besides, we can say joyfully that the Muslims seem to be more focused, at least for the moment, on killing each other, as we see with this destruction of Palestine Israel by the Caliphate. The American government is the best multi-tasking apparatus in the world. Your focus will be the Jew-Christians, dealing with that threat. We have actionable intel about planned future attacks and ongoing plots against the Homeland. We need to start whittling down the domestic chess board of threats. Why fight ten bad guys at a time when you can make it so that you have to fight only one? Jew-Christians have killed and injured many government law enforcement, security, and intel personnel. The President wants direct action, and direct action has been sanctioned to neutralize these threats. He views this essential to his anti- and counter-terrorism domestic agenda. There will be many law enforcement and intel personnel involved at the state and national levels. However, you and your team will report directly to the executive branch through us."

"Sir, I've been in the business long enough to know that things don't just happen out of nowhere when it comes to government. The Terrorism Threat Work Group says everyone and everything is a threat. That's what they do. What's the story behind the story here?"

The President's man smiles. "You know why presidents age so rapidly when they're in office? They know things, things most people on the planet will never, ever be aware of in their lifetimes. We're already fighting a world war of sorts, each and every day, on so many different fronts. He not only wants to maintain our global superpower standing, but to elevate us to a status of the only global superpower. To that end, we cannot have any distracting factors domestically.

"The Jew-Christian terrorists may live far away from our tek-cities, but the security threat remains. Local and state forces utterly failed to manage this problem and they had more than twenty years to get it done. This Office, through you, will take over. Target those where we still have undercover operatives in place, then move out from that center of work to neutralize the rest. These factions are all connected. America will not make the same mistake Old Western Europe made with its religious. Now they're citizen-slaves—those not killed—of the Caliphate that rose from within their own population. The President wants—no—demands a *solution of finality* to the Jew-Christian situation."

"I have full sanction to use whatever means necessary?"

"Yes, and you and your team have already been transferred to Special Services. Have you chosen a code name?"

"Yes. Lycan."

"Agent Lycan, will there be any challenges to you faithfully executing your new job duties in defending America and its people?"

"None."

The Abortion: A Horror Story

"If statistics are right, the Jews constitute but one percent of the human race. It suggests a nebulous dim puff of stardust lost in the blaze of the Milky Way. Properly, the Jew ought hardly to be heard of, but he is heard of, has always been heard of. He is as prominent on the planet as any other people, and his commercial importance is extravagantly out of proportion to the smallness of his bulk. His contributions to the world's list of great names in literature, science, art, music, finance, medicine, and abstruse learning are also away out of proportion to the weakness of his numbers. He has made a marvelous fight in this world, in all the ages; and had done it with his hands tied behind him. He could be vain of himself, and be excused for it." – Mark Twain, "Concerning the Jews," Harper's Magazine, 1899

Net-Dictionary: A·bor·tion (noun) [Medical]

- (Obsolete) to terminate the pregnancy of before term
- (Obsolete) the removal of an embryo or fetus from the uterus in order to end a pregnancy
- (Obsolete) any of various surgical methods for terminating a natural child-birth pregnancy, before or at fetal viability
- (Obsolete) the products of abortion or the aborted fetus
- (Rare) a person or thing that is deformed

Jew-Christian Center Office, Mount Vernon, Virginia
10:55 a.m., 3 July 2080

A globe drone on standard surveillance whizzes by twenty feet in the air.

Gone are the days when Americans visited this town to see the place that the nation's first President and Commander-in-Chief called home for forty years. The area is half commercial offices and half historically preserved residential homes. Thank God for the British who fled to America in droves after the Fall of Western Europe in 2065 to the Supreme Islamic Caliphate. It is these new Americans who have been preserving Washington's Estate and the entire town, not "native" Americans. What irony: George Washington led a people to create the great world nation of America, and the descendants of those people he liberated know nothing of him, while the descendants of the British Empire he defeated are the ones who want to ensure his immortality.

In the entire District, the only designated worship center for any Jew-Christian—the scarce few left—is here, eighteen miles away. The Washington District of Columbia Metro Jew-Christian Center is in a nondescript, two-story gray building two miles from the George Washington Mount Vernon Estate, Museum, and Gardens. Most of the building houses various artists, and the largest tenant is some pornography company.

Rabbi Susan drives up, arriving on time. The hours of the Center are Mondays and Wednesdays from eleven a.m. to one p.m. Though she is a division-level director, in no less than the executive branch of government, she is also the designated, and only, registered Jewish Chaplain for the entire District.

Religious activities, whether private or public, are illegal on government property, which in practical terms means the entire tek-city of ten million. Only authorized zones, such as the Center, are exempt. Any *registered* Jew could come here for any religious matter or counseling. Any *unregistered* Jew could also come here to register and get in compliance with the law by identifying their specific religion and certifying full acceptance of all government anti-hate crime legislation.

She shares the office with her Christian colleague, but Bishop Joe hasn't been here in several months. He told her that he was too busy with his official government duties, his two husbands, and some boyfriend on the side to do his normal chaplain duties, but he would find a replacement. Guess he never got around to it.

Rabbi Susan uses the hours to catch up on work, have uninterrupted, quiet lunches, or take a nap, all away from the bustle of Capitol Hill. It's been more than eighteen months since anyone has come to the Center.

She walks inside to the first floor offices and stops. A woman sits on a bench in the hallway. Rabbi Susan smiles at the unexpected visitor.

"Good afternoon. Are you here for the Jewish Center or the Christian Center?" she asks.

"Jewish," the woman says.

She seems to be of average height, though she is sitting down, with jet black straight hair and blue eyes. She's dressed in a short-sleeved silky black dress that reaches her ankles, and sandals.

"Let's go inside. What is your name?" Susan touches the doorknob. Its bio-recog instantly recognizes her and unlocks.

"Klara Heidel." The woman speaks with a strange accent, but Susan cannot place it.

"You're pregnant. When's it due?"

Klara stands with her huge pregnant belly and follows Susan into the office. "As soon as I can terminate the monster."

Susan stops and stares at her.

Medical Offices of Doctor McLane, Bethesda, Maryland 11:00 a.m., 26 June 2080 (One Week Earlier)

Like much of the District, residents and workers in Bethesda are very rich, highly educated, and very connected. If they aren't directly part of the political elite, they are related to someone, living with someone, or sleeping with someone who is.

"Klara Heidel," the nurse calls out.

The woman stands revealing her pregnancy. There are a few other well-dressed people sitting in the waiting room too, and they all look at her. The nurse stares at her for a moment before leading her through the door to the back offices. She motions her into the third office.

Klara sits in the plush chair in front of the doctor's desk and says, "I'm not a Jew-Christian or some poor person, if that's what you're thinking."

The nurse ignores her. "The doctor will be in right away." She walks out.

Three minutes later a man enters. "Hello, I'm Doctor Ben McLane."

Klara nods and smiles. "Well, of course you are. I'm Klara Heidel."

The doctor looks more like a movie star or stereotypical good-looking politician—perfect hair, perfect skin, perfect teeth. He sits down and touches the screen of his table computer. Her file appears and he reviews it. He looks up. "How many months pregnant are you?"

"Seven months."

"Is there a reason why you're having a natural childbirth?"

"It was the instructions of my doctors. Using a host was not possible in my case."

"Is there a reason you're not consulting with them now?"

"They would not carry out my wishes."

"What might those be?"

"It must be aborted."

Doctor McLane sits back in his chair and studies her. "Ms. Heidel, no one does abortions anymore. In fact, no one has natural childbirths in this town anymore, except for the poor, which if you're sitting in my office is not you; those with some kind of rare medical condition, wherein a host procedure is not possible or advisable; or Jew-Christians."

"I'm here for an abortion. Just cut me open and rip it out. How hard can that be? You're a high-priced, highly skilled doctor."

"Ms. Heidel, I am a doctor, but I have never done a fetal abortion. No one does them anymore, especially the clientele I medically serve. The people who live in the District are wealthy, busy, and obsessively body-conscious. They don't have the time or desire to deal with eight months of childbirth when they can do a simple fetal extraction-implantation into a host female. The *bio-switch* has been on the market for decades and has made that all obsolete, including the need for, what they called back in the past, birth control. No one has unwanted pregnancies anymore, rich or poor, because you have to be 'switched on' to conceive. We can even screen out genetic abnormalities at conception. The rare cases, and I do mean rare, ten billion to one, you can do a seventy-two-hour flush of the embryo. Also, from my recollection of medical history, even back in the 'stone ages' when they did do them, an abortion in the seventh month was an extreme rarity."

"We can do the procedure off the books, if that's what you're worried about."

"Ms. Heidel, what I'm worried about is why a healthy woman walks into my office asking to terminate her almost full-term fetus when the simple reproductive science of the day would have prevented this situation from occurring in the first place."

"Doctor, this procedure needs to be done. I am not mentally unbalanced."

"What I need, Ms. Heidel, is for you to give me the entire, accurate account of this pregnancy."

"I'm a birther."

He looks at her file again on the screen. "You're not listed on the host-mother registry."

"My clients are the less religious of Jew-Christians, unable to have natural childbirths themselves, so I wouldn't be on the registry. Those people loathe anything to do with the government, so I'm not listed anywhere. I would have no clients if I did."

"How many times have you been a host-mother then?"

"Many, many times. Never any complications. Fetal material goes into the womb and I birth their children for them. They get a healthy baby and I get a healthy cash deposit. In this instance, we had to supplement the process with a natural childbirth, as the baby itself was not created naturally."

The doctor's eyebrow rises. "Excuse me?"

"The fetus was implanted surgically."

"Surgically? You mean in vitro?"

"No, through artificial gestation. The fetus was developed in a *hatchery*."

He holds up his hand. "Ms. Heidel, this all is far, far above my pay grade. I'm a doctor, not a bio-geneticist or bio-engineer. Right now, bio-ectogenesis is the standard; extract fetal material and then implant into a human female host. A hatchery? That would be true ectogenesis. Extracting a fetus and implanting—no—that would be growing the entire human, in an artificial womb. We're supposed to be decades away from that…at least, if it's ever attainable, but here you sit, telling me that is what has been done. That would be the complete elimination of host-motherhood. No, the eradication of natural childbirth as a needed biological process for the entire human race, period. That bio-tek knowledge is not supposed to exist. What happened to your original doctors?"

"Doctor, study whatever manuals you need to and let us do this procedure as soon as possible. I want it aborted and I don't want to have an infinite discussion about it. You are my doctor now. My previous doctors are irrelevant."

"Assuming that I believe anything you've told me, I'm not confident in doing what you want."

Klara smiles. "Come on now, doctor. Confidence is something you have an overabundance of. It pays for all your mansions, cars, and lovers. I've done my research on you. You have all the necessary deficiencies in terms of morals, which means with the proper amount of monetary compensation, you'd kill your own mother."

He is not amused. "I think you need to leave, Ms. Heidel."

Klara takes out her e-pad and touches an on-screen button. "What day shall we schedule the murder?"

"Please leave."

"Those of us who make up the filthy-rich class of society pay for services in advance. How much should I transfer to your account…for us to get started? Would this be a sufficient co-pay?" She turns the e-pad screen around so he can see. "Or is the term 'deductible'? I can never remember which is which."

He looks at her and then his eyes focus on her e-pad screen. After a moment, he looks at his table screen, then touches the button interface to open the calendar. "How's next week? My nurses can ensure Thursday morning will be completely free of any other patients."

She smiles. "A wonderful day for an extermination."

Jew-Christian Center Office (One Week Later)

Rabbi Susan continues, annoyed. "Why did you come here? Are you Jewish?"

Klara smirks. "Why is that relevant? You're not Jewish."

"I am the official Jewish Chaplain for the District."

Klara laughs. "Wearing a stupid Star of David on your tie makes you Jewish. My pet tarantula is more Jewish than you are. Stop making me laugh. You'll wake up my evil baby. I'm not here to debate you on your religious delusions. I'm here to hire you."

"Excuse me. I am a division-level director of an entire government agency. I'm not your personal slave."

"Yes, yes, very impressive. You're the closest thing to a Jew and that's what I need."

"Are you some kind of crazy person?"

"Tomorrow I'm going to have my evil baby aborted."

"Aborted?"

She can't really blame her ignorance. The term hasn't been in common usage in ages. "The baby will be terminated."

Rabbi Susan is shocked.

Klara continues. "I don't expect my friends to find me, but just in case, I need someone to help me. I need someone who'd be sufficiently motivated in this matter against my friends. They're Nazis, you see."

"You're either crazy or a comedian, or both. I'm Jewish, so naturally I'd be against Nazis. There aren't any Nazis anymore. They've been gone for over a century, even if people dress up as them every Halloween or for some costume party. The Nazis were an actual political party in Old Germany. The political party no longer exists and the country is part of the Islamic Caliphate. Why are you bothering me? The Nazis killed as many Christians as Jews. Go bother them."

"No, I need a Jew. Jews have a special loathing for Nazis. It's not as personal for anyone else."

"Get out of my office."

"You have a lot in common with my friends."

"How's that?"

"You hate Jews and will do anything for money."

Rabbi Susan glares at her and jumps up from her chair. "Get out of my office!"

Klara stands and her whole demeanor changes from mocking contempt to menace. "I don't have time for this, *Rabbi* Susan. I wish I could do this all myself, rip this evil baby from my womb and throw it into the fire, but I can't. I need the doctor to do it, and I need you to drive me to the doctor, and afterwards, when it's done. I have detailed instructions. Here!" She throws her e-pad on the desk. "You will follow them to the letter. I don't expect you to do any of this just because I tell you to. You will be generously compensated for two hours of your time. Also, belief in one delusion, your fake deity in the sky, is bad enough, but your delusion that you'll ever be a member of my class is offensive. You will *never* be one of us, the power elite. They will never let your inferior Jew-Christian self into the inner circle. One day they'll discard you like the trash you are. Grab all the money and connections you can, while you can. So do you want some extra money today or not? A girl can always use another pair of nice shoes or an exotic massage."

Different Locations, 4 July 2080 (Morning)

Doctor McLane looks at himself in the mirror, shaving with an electric wand.

Nurse Brownell looks at herself in the mirror, brushing her hair.

Nurse Higgins looks at herself in the mirror, putting on her lipstick.

The Medical Assistant looks at herself in the mirror, brushing her teeth.

The Security Guard looks at himself in the mirror, applying lotion to his face.

Klara Heidel looks at herself in the mirror, contorting her face with a skull-like grin.

Rabbi Susan looks at herself in the mirror, straightening her Star of David tie.

Medical Offices of Doctor McLane, Bethesda, Maryland 10:59 a.m., 4 July 2080

Klara Heidel walks in and sees the lone medical assistant behind the counter. The waiting room is empty except for a waiting Nurse Brownell.

"I'll take you directly to the doctor's office," the nurse says.

"You mean the operating room?"

"The doctor's office first."

She is led into Doctor McLane's office. He sits behind his desk; another nurse is seated in a chair to the side. They rise, coldly staring at her.

Klara smiles. "Good morning, doctor. So how did you get my DNA to do your background check on me? Very sneaky. I like sneaky."

"What is your real name?" Doctor McLane asks.

"I'm paying you in full, so my name is not relevant."

"It is relevant."

"Nothing is illegal about this."

"Aside from the fact that no one does them anymore, abortions are illegal because you have to get 'switched on' to get pregnant. Birthing simply to terminate *is* illegal. Moreover, you already disclosed that you are a host, so legally you don't have ownership of the fetus since contract law would also apply here."

"Doctor, you worry too much. I want this evil baby out of me, now."

"And that's another thing," the doctor says. "You keep referring to the baby as evil."

"'Good' and 'evil' are Jew-Christian, religious words. There's no such thing," Nurse Brownell says.

"If you're a psych patient, we can't proceed no matter how much you pay us," Nurse Higgins adds.

"I doubt that." Klara hands the doctor her e-pad. "I want you to read all the instructions carefully. Once the evil baby, and it is evil, becomes aware of what we are doing, it will attack. You are to use whatever means necessary to kill it. I repeat. You are to kill it any way you can."

The medical staff stares at her for a long time.

Nurse Brownell says, "She's a mental."

Klara turns to her. "I will not survive the procedure, so my words are for *your* benefit."

"You are a mental," the doctor says and then turns to his nurse. "Call security." Nurse Brownell runs out of the office.

Klara says, "Doctor, if you actually read what I'm giving you, it will answer all your questions: who I am, who my doctors were, the modified clone that was implanted into me, the genetic and pre-psych conditioning that occurred that justifies me calling it evil, and why you must perform the abortion immediately to kill it."

The doctor takes the e-pad from her hand and reads.

Nurse Brownell returns to the office. "Security's coming."

Klara says, "Please read fast. Do I assume correctly that you made inquiries in the medical community to find out who I am?"

Doctor McLane answers, "Yes."

"Then you've probably unwittingly revealed my location to my 'friends' and they may find us soon. They are very determined people. Read fast please. When we do the procedure, you must not view it as a baby. You must get in the proper frame of mind to destroy it; stab it, cut it, shoot it, I don't care. Drill into its skull and suck out its brains if need be. You must kill it. Again, I will not survive. I'll be dead so don't think about me."

He looks up from the e-pad, his face pale. "What did you all do?!"

Klara smiles. "I knew you would recognize the names of my original doctors. We created an evil baby, doctor."

The nurses read the doctor's expression and are now scared.

Klara adds, "You understand the seriousness of the situation now. This evil baby must *never* get into the general population."

Nurse Higgins says, "Doctor, let's get out of here."

He yells, "Prep the operating room, now!"

Outside the building, Rabbi Susan sits in the black mini-car with a frazzled look on her face. *How can I be doing this?* This crazy woman wants her corpse—she expects to be dead after the procedure—taken to a shed and incinerated. "I don't want my 'friends' to be able to use my genetic material. Leave it to scientists to come up with another way to rape a woman," she said.

Susan sees a security guard appear from around the corner and run into the medical offices. What's happening? Susan continues to sit quietly in the car. Almost a half hour later, she hears a pop. *Was that a gunshot?*

Inside, Doctor McLane appears from one of the rooms with a large axe. "You killed my people! You killed my people!"

The security guard is kneeling near the main entrance, crying. "I shot the wrong person." He looks up and sees a small shadow moving. "Doctor, there it is!"

Doctor McLane runs down the hall. Something trips him. He yells out as he falls and crashes to the ground on the axe.

All is quiet now, too quiet. Susan opens the front door of the medical offices slowly. She sticks her head in and immediately notices the body of the security guard, with blood pooled around him. Her body trembles, but she enters anyway. She points her e-pad all around. The sensors show no motion and only yellowish-blue heat signatures—dead bodies. She swallows hard, walks into the hallway, and sees another woman lying face down with the back of her head blown out. She sees the body of the doctor with the handle of an axe sticking up from his neck at a high angle. Blood is everywhere. Susan freezes for a moment. *Why am I doing this?!* She looks at her pathetic stun-stick in her other hand.

The next room is an operating room, and she fights her fear to peek in; a nurse dead on the floor. And there is Klara Heidel, eyes open, lying strapped to the operating table, also dead, her lower half drenched in red. Susan hears something and peeks out of the room slowly. Nothing. She steps into the hallway, walks slowly to the farthest end, and looks around the corner.

Then she sees him—a naked baby boy, standing there. He is covered in slimy residue and his umbilical cord, almost three feet of it, is still attached to his navel. Why wasn't it removed? Natural childbirth is such a disgusting thing, she thinks to herself. But children are so…godly. This sweet angel must be protected.

She runs over and instinctively picks him up. She puts her collapsible stun-weapon and e-pad in her pocket and uses her jacket to quickly wipe his face and body. "We have to go now. The killer could still be here."

Susan steps into the hall and stops. Nurse Brownell lies on her back on the floor. Why didn't I see her before? The nurse is dead. She doesn't see any wounds, but blood is flowing out of her, too.

She holds the baby tight and runs.

She opens the front door and almost runs smack into a large man, well over six feet tall, muscular, and dressed in a three-piece suit and wide-brimmed hat.

"Where are you off to so fast, *Fräulein*?" he asks.

"We have to get out of here now! And get the baby to safety! There's a killer somewhere!"

"That is why we are here."

Another person appears, a petite woman dressed immaculately in a sparkling black blouse and skirt, with white gloves and a white, wide-brimmed hat. Her lipstick is the reddest Susan has ever seen. "My baby!" She reaches out to take the baby, but Susan refuses.

"Who are you? I don't know who you are," Susan says.

"We don't know who you are," the woman says. "But we know you have saved our baby."

The man commands, "Give her the baby."

Susan notices about a dozen other men in suits approaching. She hesitates, but hands the baby over. As she does, she notices a chain around the petite woman's neck: a swastika. These are Klara's 'friends.'

The woman, in turn, notices the Star of David tie around Susan's neck. The woman takes the baby in her hands and looks into his eyes. "My precious baby. Bad Klara tried to harm you, but we always win in the end. You are going home with the people who love and worship you." The woman looks at Susan and starts to laugh. She says something to the others in another language. All the men start laughing.

One of the men, laughing, says, "*Ballestexistenzen.*"

She doesn't understand their words, but she knows they are laughing at her. She glances at the baby. He stares back. His eyes are locked on hers; the expression is stone-cold.

The woman leads the men to three waiting black cars. One of the men opens the back door of the lead car. The petite woman steps in with the baby and says something to the man. All the other men get into the cars. He closes her door and walks back to Susan.

Susan just stares at him. He looks at her as he reaches into his jacket. Susan doesn't move, doesn't blink, doesn't show any fear. The man reconsiders.

"Ah, you don't know anything, *Fräulein*. And even if you did, no one would ever believe you." He takes his hand from his jacket and smiles. He walks back to the lead car and gets in the front passenger seat. All three cars drive off and she watches them disappear into the distance.

She runs to her car as fast as she can and gets in. She pauses. "If you can't get my body out of the building for any reason, plant these incendiary devices on me, activate them, and all will happen as it should," Klara had told her. Susan slowly gets out and opens the trunk.

She doesn't set foot back in the offices, but manages to work up the courage to instead activate all the devices, toss them into the building, slam the doors shut, and run back to her car.

That night at home, she monitors the newsfeed and sees it: "The luxurious medical offices of Doctor Benjamin McLane burnt down to the ground, with six confirmed deaths."

She expects to see her face on the vid-screen too. In this town, Eyes (the government's ever-watching, ever-recording vid-cam surveillance network throughout all tek-cities in the nation) or drone fly-bys are everywhere. Didn't the police review all external vid-files of the incident? Susan doesn't know how it's possible, but the police never come for her. The following Monday, the guards at the Center never say a thing. It's like she was never involved. It's like the incident never happened.

Susan was so ignorant of childbirth that she didn't even know that babies can't walk when they're first born. "Silly Susan, babies don't start walking until they're a year old or more," a friend told her.

Later, Susan feels sick to her stomach. She will spend almost a decade quietly gathering information about that unnatural day. But she doesn't need an investigation to know what she realizes. She wondered why she was so brave that day and not afraid of running right into the killer. It was because she intuitively already knew, though it seems impossible. *The baby was the killer!*

The Fall of Rabbi Susan and Bishop Joe

"You are the only people who refuse to recognize my divinity!" (said of the Jews) — Emperor Caligula, 30 AD

"I got a call from 'God.'" (nickname for the President of the United States) — Director of Homeland Defense & Intelligence Agency Anita McDunn, 2080

Resistance is Futile: The New Religious Paradigm in America, Prime Time Netzine, 2070. Featured are Rabbi Susan, wearing a white suit and a white tie, with a Star of David, and carrying a large *Good Bible*; and Bishop Joe, wearing his black robe, with a white clerical collar and large gold cross hanging from his neck and holding up his right hand with two gold wedding bands on his ring finger.

There was not a Jew more hated among all the Jewish Orders in America than Rabbi Susan. As America's first Director of Religious Affairs, she had been at the forefront, along with her colleague Bishop Joe, of the nation's compulsory Registration Initiatives. The events that flowed from these actions solidified the Separatist Movement and, more violently, led to the civil wars within American Judaism and the Registrant-Resister wars. The result was the collapse of Reform Judaism and the near-collapse of Conservative Judaism.

Manhattan, New York City
12 noon, 12 March 2074

Crowds of angry, yelling people march in the streets with signs depicting Rabbi Susan crossed out in red; other signs have her with a black, painted-on mustache and swastika armband. The signs say: "Rabbi Susan is Evil," "Destroy Susan the Destroyer," "We Will Never Accept the New Herod," and "Susan is No Jew." Some of the men are wearing *kippot*, some have no headgear at all, and some are dressed in all black with black hats. Most of the men and women wear Star of David necklaces around their necks.

Mobile, Alabama
11:45 a.m., 4 March 2089

Mobile is the second-largest city in Alabama—an amazing tek-city of lights, sounds, automation, and towering skyscrapers.

That prime-time netzine cover was almost a quarter of a century ago. Rabbi Susan back then was an extremely attractive woman with shoulder-length blonde hair and green eyes. She was always professionally dressed in her trademark white suit and Star of David tie. She led the crusade to put a Good Bible in every synagogue and church in the country. She and her "partner in crime," Bishop Joe, were the dynamic duo in politics, the new generals in the culture wars, and they won that war. So what happened?

Rabbi Susan sits at a table inside a busy café with its background neo-ska music playing. She is middle-aged now but looks much older, with no makeup and her hair tied back into a messy pony tail. Her trademark white suit is long gone; she wears a simple, one-piece dark grey dress, almost looking like a homeless person. Though she's a registered Jew, she doesn't dare wear a Star of David in public.

A large cup of coffee sits in front of her, but she has not taken even a sip. She glances around, nervously waiting. People are talking, buying drink or food, looking for other people, looking for seats. She hates to be in public nowadays. She could stay inside her studio home for months on end without coming out, and actually did so once for six months straight.

Susan sees her. The Goth Christian Lila walks into the café, dressed in typical Goth style: all black leather, black makeup, spiky black hair, and tattoos. Lila has three piercings in each earlobe, black eyeliner, and three ring necklaces.

Lila sees Susan and stops for a second before continuing to the table.

Susan smiles faintly and stands. "Hi. Thank you for coming." She instinctively starts to extend her arm but stops herself, remembering that only religious people shake hands anymore, and it's not advisable to be public. "Please have a seat," she says.

Lila takes the seat across from her and Susan sits down again.

"Are you who I think you are?" Lila asks directly.

Susan looks down for a moment. "Please just give me five minutes."

"I can't be here with you," Lila says, upset. "It's forbidden."

"But you're not a Jew, so it doesn't apply."

"Stop being sneaky. All Goth Faithers have reciprocity with all Christian *and* Jewish Orders. You've been excommunicated by all Jewish Orders and we fully honor that punishment. But you know that, which is why you lied as to who you really are."

"Five minutes, please. All I want is for you to give them something for me. Don't even tell them it's from me."

Lila shakes her head. "I don't know how you found me to set this meeting up, but I can't be here. If you want to give something to them, then you have to do so yourself."

"I can't," Susan pleads. "They'll kill me on sight."

Lila stands from the table. "That isn't my problem. You and that Judas, fake Christian sidekick of yours collaborated with the Pagans to destroy all of us. What did you think would happen?"

"I'm trying to atone for that. Give me just one minute."

Lila shakes her head. "I can't get involved."

"You have to forgive me."

Goth Lila stops. "Why? Because I'm Christian? Because we're going into our Christmas this weekend? Have you asked God for forgiveness?"

Susan looks at her, unable to answer.

Lila shakes her head. "Imagine you, of all people, were the designated Jewish chaplain, registered rabbi, for the entire Capitol, before the position was found unconstitutional and abolished. You never honored your Torah. It's just a 'nice story.' You don't even believe in God, do you? Probably never did. Pathetic."

"Please help me," Susan pleads.

"Why? You're already dead to all Faithers. Even your memories won't be acknowledged."

Lila says nothing more. She stands and walks out of the café, the main doors automatically opening and closing behind her. Susan stares after her and then sadly at her cup of coffee. The place is filled with people, but for her, she's the only person in the world.

Key West, Florida
10:05 a.m., 5 March 2089

Susan doesn't really sleep anymore. The depression is sometimes so powerful that she can hardly breathe, let alone sleep. She drove all night to get here. Her beat-up car is parked outside a small shack of a house. She has waited long enough. It's an appropriate time to call now. She exits the car.

The front doorbell automatically rings. An old Robbie the Robot model opens the main door. The outer mesh screen door is still closed. "State your name and purpose. Be aware that if you are a door-to-door salesperson, media, or government person you will be vaporized immediately."

Susan smiles. The robot doesn't even know that it's been programmed to tell a joke. "Tell Joe that his old friend Susan is here to see him."

The robot walks back into the house. Susan can make out a man sitting on a single couch, looking at her. She slowly opens the screen door and walks inside.

"What do you want?" he says. It's Bishop Joe, from those many years ago. He was a clean-cut clergyman who always had a big smile and a twinkle in his eyes. The Joe sitting in front of her is a scraggly looking man with graying dark hair, a beard almost to his knees, a mustache so bushy it covers much of his nose and mouth, and hair so high it looks like an afro.

"Joe, it's me. Susan."

"I know that. What do you want?"

"I was in the area and wanted to visit with you. It's been such a long time."

"Ha, you finally ran out of friends to talk to?"

"No, I came to visit you."

"Sure, why not. Have a seat, Rabbi Susan," he says in a contemptuous way.

Susan ignores the tone and looks for somewhere to sit. Empty boxes and cartons, discarded wrappers, plastic bags, cloth bags, strings, wires, metal pieces, empty tubes; the garbage is everywhere. She moves a stack off a chair and to the floor, then sits.

"What do you want to talk about, Rabbi Susan?"

"Joe, call me Susan."

"No, you're Rabbi Susan and I'm Bishop Joe. We have to stay in character even when we're alone."

"How have you been?"

"I'm a hermit and a hoarder. Don't you see all the crap everywhere? I don't leave my house. I don't bathe or cut my hair. How do you think I've been? I've turned into a crazy old man who hates people. You've turned into a pathetic human being who needs to be with people. But no one wants to be near you." Joe laughs. "How have *you* been, Rabbi Susan?"

Susan thought she'd be able to have a friendly conversation with her former colleague, but even this will be denied her. "I…I just wanted someone to talk to."

Joe smiles and shakes his head. "Why?" He turns his head away from her. "You're a self-hating Jew who wishes she were born anything else. I'm a self-hating homo who wishes he were born hetero with the proverbial wife and two kids. You wanted to hurt the faith community because you wanted to be loved by all the 'beautiful people,' the ones who taunted and bullied you as a child. I wanted to hurt God for creating me by embarrassing the faith community. I was the stupid little child lashing out at the adults. But you—you were an adult. You knew what you were doing, but you didn't care. I was stupid. You were evil."

Susan looks away. There will be only viciousness from him. "I'm sorry I bothered you, Joe. I'll leave now."

"Yes, Rabbi Susan. You do that, and don't come back again. I wasn't your friend even when we were the closest of friends. Now I hate all people, especially people like you."

Susan stands. "Good seeing you again, Joe. Bye now."

"Yes, God bless the disciples, Rabbi Susan and Bishop Joe. Almighty

God is going to grant us the righteous gifts in life we deserve."

She walks out of the house, closing the door slowly and quietly. She gets back to her car, gets in, and stares up at the house. Joe stares back at her with a disgusted look from one of the windows, then moves away, disappearing.

She angrily grips the steering wheel. She yells out, buries her face in her hands, and breaks down crying.

New York City (Eight Years Ago)
10:00 a.m., 23 January 2081

Susan arrives at the apartment complex and a crowd is already waiting for her. They attack her, pushing her back, and one punches her in the mouth.

"In Judaism, you have to forgive me!" she yells. "You must forgive me and let me see my family!" Susan defiantly picks herself up from the ground.

"Shut your mouth! You pagan witch!" a man yells. He tries to punch her again, but is restrained.

Susan's mother appears from the main entrance. She is an older and shorter version of Susan. Her mother has a look of such psychotic rage that several men immediately hold her back as she yells at Susan. "Go away, you witch! You are no Jew. You are not my blood. I will kill you if I ever see you again! Kill you! I wish upon all of God's power that I could go back to when I gave birth to you! I wish I would have ripped you out of my womb and thrown you into a fire!"

Susan's mother glares at her with such hatred that even Susan steps back in fear. Police sirens sound in the distance and the men rush her away, back into the building. Police cars arrive, but so do many more Jewish residents, equally enraged at the sight of a now-fleeing Susan.

Jewish Israel had fallen weeks before.

Key West, Florida
10:37 a.m., 5 March 2089

Susan sits in her car. She never did see her mother again after that day. She tried many more times, but was never able to get anywhere near her. The words haunt her to this day. *I wish I would have ripped you out of my womb and thrown you into a fire!*

Joe has also rejected her, so now there is no one, just the crushing emotions of loneliness and despair. There is only one thing for her to do. She drives away.

Inside the house, Joe leads his robot to the den. It is the only room in the tiny house that is actually clean. All the garbage has been thrown into the outside yard, a massive pile of junk. Science fiction movies were the absolute worst thing for the residential robotics industry. People expected a robot out of the movie *I, Robot*, or Data from the old *Star Trek, The Next Generation* television series, but the fact is that even the most sophisticated domestic robots were not even at the level of Robbie the Robot from the 1950s movie *The Forbidden Planet*. Unfortunately, the public was not interested in that. The robotics industry tried to launch with much fanfare, but crashed as soon as it started.

They wanted "real" robots. They wanted Data or similar androids. They wanted fem-bots and sex-bots. They wanted robotic butlers, maids, and babysitters. They wanted robotic *people*. Anything else was of no interest. The robotics industry abandoned the residential robot market completely and poured all resources into the commercial and military markets.

Joe, however, was one of the first to buy his very own residential robot back then, the line aptly named the Robbie series. He hates people, so his robot Hal is the perfect companion.

"Okay Hal, no more vegetating. We are men, not plants, and we have important work to do. You better not slack off," Joe yells. "Or you know the godless words I'll call you."

"Master Joe, I'm working at peak performance levels. All internal systems are normal and there are no external impediments. You will have no cause for any godless words against me." The robot blurts out a series of curse words.

Joe, after all these years, loves to hear his robot curse. It always puts a smile on his face. Faithers universally condemn cursing of any kind. They call it pagan-speak, but he can't help it. It's the only thing left in life that can make him smile, and smiling is his last remaining pleasure.

"Okay." He walks over to face Hal as if he were posing for a photograph and sits on the stool. "You remember the phrase, Hal?"

"Yes, Master Joe."

"Good, here we go." Joe raises both hands in the air and tilts up his chin. "God, I'm ready for my close-up!"

Hal blows out Joe's brains with the shotgun blast.

Gadsden, Alabama
11:45 p.m., 5 March 2089

Pagans and Faithers live very differently. Pagans live in their tek-cities and tek-towns, ever-connected, even as individuals, to the Net, the Grid, and to tek itself—the word "technology" has been obsolete for decades. Ever since the Separatist Movement, most Faithers live in enclaves, off-Grid, walled communities, secluded and far away from the Pagan tek-metropolises.

All is quiet at the western wall of the enclave. Three men watch the perimeter from their guard tower two stories above the wall. The rectangular tower sits on a column of solid concrete. It is wrapped in large one-way-view, bulletproof, black glass windows. They can see everything from vid-screen monitors, on all optics: visual, infrared, motion, and, when needed, night vision. The men are dressed business-casual, wearing kippot, and are armed with handguns in double waist holsters. The wall is some ten feet tall with thick razor wire at the top.

They hear barking. One of the men walks to one of the large windows and peers out to see the dog barking toward the east. "Got something on the screen," another man says in Hebrew. A third man walks to the monitor bank.

The men watch intently as a figure approaches slowly and then stops. "Tracking." A voice in Hebrew comes in from the console speaker and echoes in their individual ear-sets.

The man touches the screen and the image gets larger. Whoever the intruder is, his face is well-covered, wrapped up in a head scarf.

Suddenly, the figure sprints toward the wall.

An intercept team of four men with machine guns is already waiting at the adjacent watchtower. The Jewish men are dressed in black and wear kippot.

The intruder is about ten feet away and continues running to the wall. From wall speakers near the gate, in English: "Stop! Stop now! This is a restricted, private community. If you do not stop, guards are authorized to shoot with deadly force. This is your final warning!"

The laws on the use of deadly force are very different nowadays. These laws were not changed for the benefit of religious communities, but rather wealthy Pagan ones. Gated communities with their own private security—and, often, their own private police force—are allowed to use whatever means necessary to put down unauthorized intruders.

Still, Jews in the past would have given multiple warnings to an intruder and used non-lethal bullets. These are not those Jews. Those kind of Jews don't exist anymore.

The intercept team aims their guns at the running intruder, who closes in on the main gated entrance. They open fire. A voice over the speaker yells in Hebrew, "There's something in the right hand!" The intruder is stopped as bullets rip through his chest. His body convulses and drops to the ground.

The gate opens and a spider robot runs to the intruder. It looks more like a four-legged silver spider, the size of a large dog, with red lights at various spots on its body. The team covers the robot from flanking positions on either side to watch for any other intruders.

The robot scans the fallen intruder. A yellow beam shoots down from its head. "All clear," the robot announces in a deep Hebrew voice. It picks up something from the ground.

The team runs to the intruder. The robot holds the object that was in the intruder's hand. The lead man grabs the simple black plastic box, scans it again, and opens it. Inside is a data crystal.

Another member of the team takes the headscarf from the intruder's head—it is a woman. They instantly recognize her.

Rabbi Susan is still alive and smiles up at them. She struggles to talk. "Thank you."

The team is disgusted. Suicide by proxy, but it couldn't happen to a more deserving person.

The lead man leans down to her body and says in English, "We're going to get you to a Pagan hospital right away, and they'll save your pathetic life."

Rabbi Susan touches his boot. "No…let me die…I want it, too." The team just looks at her. She stares up at them, her head shaking slightly. "Tell my mother I love her…use the crystal…to…help my people…my last act on Earth."

Susan Ben, known as Rabbi Susan to the world and hated by all Jewish Orders, dies.

There will be no *shomer* to watch over her dead body, no Jewish burial; not even her mother will claim her.

They were once the highest-ranking Jew-Christians in the anti-religious President T. Wilson's administration. They were the center of the violent Registration-Resister wars that nearly destroyed all of Judaism and Christianity in America. But today, Rabbi Susan and Bishop Joe commit suicide on the same day, twenty-four years after their rise to power.

Shoshana, the Iron Rose

"Good guys do wear black. But this ain't the Jewish part of town."
— *Tova Ben-Hurin, the Conservative Jewish Order.*

Rabbi Susan got the blame, but it was President T. Wilson who instigated the series of events that led to the first American Jewish Civil War. There were Jews who supported government registration and its compulsory use of the government's Good Bible (to replace the Bible and the Torah, the Koran exempt) for all religious people; and there were Jews who adamantly opposed both.

On 13 February 2074, members of the Orthodox Jewish Order stormed a High Council meeting of the Reform Jewish Order with charges of Reformer collaboration with the government against all Jews. The heated argument became a violent brawl, a key Reform rabbinic leader was killed, and the four Orthodox rabbis were nearly beaten to death. Intra-Judaic violence erupted across the country, leading to the split and near-collapse of the Conservative Jewish Order, and the complete collapse of the Reform Jewish Order. Fifty-four people were killed over the course of the civil war.

The Second American Jewish Civil War occurred after the Fall of Jewish Israel. Hasidic Jews battled each other on the streets of New York, Zionist Hasidim (namely the Chabad-Lubavitch) against anti-Zionist Hasidim. Anti-Israel Pagans and Muslims came to the aid of the anti-Zionist Hasidim, and the Orthodox Jewish Order came to the aid of the Chabad. Four months of violence ended with dozens dead, many more dozens injured, and thousands arrested, convicted, and imprisoned. The entire Hasidim community was utterly devastated and they mass-exited the tek-cities of New York for their own enclaves in the South. No Jewish communities of significance existed anywhere in Tek World by the late 2070s.

Department of Homeland Defense & Intelligence Agency Threat Memo / 1 March 2081

In the aftermath of the fall of the nation of Jewish Israel, and the resulting explosion of Jewish emigration to the United States, it is the recommendation of the Threat and Terrorist Assessment Workgroup to closely monitor all Jewish males, ages thirteen to sixty-five, and that all Jews in general should be viewed as "persons of interest" by domestic local, state, and federal law enforcement and intelligence services.

Federal Penitentiary Super-Maximum Security Facility, Florence, Colorado
7:59 a.m., 3 June 2089

Rabbi Hendel stares at himself in the mirror with a look of emptiness. His beard and mustache seem to become grayer with every passing day. He's been in prison seven years and expects to die here. He grabs his side locks, called *pe'ot*, hanging from each of his temples, pulls them back behind his head, and wraps a black rubber band around them to form a ponytail. He touches his kippah on the top of his head.

He walks to the door of his tiny solitary cell and stands there.

The bells sound and the doors automatically slide open. He steps into the hall. Prisoners are allowed fifteen minutes outside of their cells in the morning, once before the noon lunch hour and once more in the late afternoon. He looks to his left and right; all men, his men, fellow Chabadniks, look at him. They are all dressed the same way, with their hair tied back in ponytails.

Rabbi Hendel stares at the ground. He is still their *tzadikim*, "righteous man" in Hebrew, or spiritual leader, but he's asked them many times to designate another. He is capable of no other emotion than extreme sadness, away from his wife and children, caged like an animal, and haunted by recurring nightmares of when uncontrollable rage caused him to kill other Hasidim with his bare hands.

Eight years ago, he ran through the streets of New York with his men, enraged and bloodied. Hasidim were running and fighting everywhere in unrestrained mobs.

Location Unknown
6:02 p.m. 3 June 2089

A man in dark clothes and a bright yellow jacket comes out of his third-story apartment and closes the door. He starts walking down the stairs as another man, the square-jawed man dressed in black leather, climbs the stairs.

The square-jawed man asks, "Hello, is your name Louvel?"

The man says, "Yes, who are—?"

Lycan kicks him directly in the stomach, sending the man falling back up the stairs. Immediately, a black-body-armor-clad assault team of several men appear from all the other doors with stun-sticks. They pin the man to the floor, bind his hands and feet, gag his mouth, pick him up, and carry him away like a suitcase. Lycan follows.

Streets of Boulder, Colorado
8:05 p.m., 3 June 2089

Boulder, Colorado is the fifteenth largest tek-city in America, located at the base of the foothills of the Rocky Mountains. As one of the most statist and secular tek-cities in the country, it led the way in anti-Jew-Christian laws. One commentator remarked that Boulder is so anti-religious that it won't even allow any of the new religions—Vampires, Witches, Vulcans, Jedi. Today, not a single Jew-Christian lives in the entire state except for those in prison.

Shoshana walks down the busy street in a knee-length red dress with her head covered by a flowing red-hooded cape. She is tall, five-eight normally, but well over six feet with her heels. She's thirty-four years old, Jewish, and designated by the US government as a terrorist. But tonight she's here for her blind date.

The square-jawed "Louvel" smiles as she approaches him. He wears a simple long-sleeved black tee shirt and silver-gray jeans. "You must be Shoshana," he says.

"You must be Louvel." Pagans don't shake hands; that's a Jew-Christian custom.

"Shall we go in?" He motions her to go in first.

A very cozy restaurant off the main boulevard—dim lights, soft music plays in the background, and a very long waiting list, if you don't get your RSVP in early. Louvel gives the maître d' his name, and a waitress appears to take them to a small round table. People pay no attention to him, but many notice her, with her flowing cape.

Shoshana removes the hood from her head as they sit—her head is shaved bald.

"I must say you have a very unique look about you. My style of dress is so underwhelming when compared to yours," he says.

"Don't feel bad. Most men can't compete with me, so don't

worry yourself. Where are you from? Your name, sounds Old French? I hate Old French."

He laughs. "It may be, but I don't think so. I never really investigated it. What about yours?"

"It's from Canaan."

"Not familiar with that locale."

"One of the old countries overseas. Not important now."

He notices the numbers "14051948" tattooed on her left forearm. "What do those numbers mean?"

He knows exactly what they are: the date the state of Jewish Israel was formed. After the Fall of Jewish Israel, many Jews, especially the youth, shaved their heads and got the tattoo on one or both forearms. The *Solidarity*, as the practice is called, also included making a blood oath that Jewish Israel would be rebuilt again by any means necessary. He knows quite a lot about Shoshana from a thorough study of her surveillance and intelligence files, along with all her known compatriots.

"I hope it's not the phone number of some ex-lover," he continues, smiling. "Nothing political, is it?"

Shoshana says, "I never talk politics or ideology on the first date."

"I was taught that those are the things you must talk about first," Louvel counters.

Shoshana shakes her head. "No, the first date is to take care of the trivialities. Do I like the way you sit? How you smile? How you laugh? Can I even stand looking at your ugly face for more than five minutes? If you can't pass that basic test, it doesn't matter how compatible we are on politics and ideology. It's all about the physical. You were lied to if you were taught otherwise."

"Physicality works for me fine."

Outside the restaurant, a blue car with pitch-black tinted windows is parked half a block away. Two men sit inside and listen to the couple from the dashboard speaker.

Shoshana gives him a playful look and touches his face from across the table. "My, what big eyes you have." She touches his mouth and opens his lips to reveal his teeth. "My, what big teeth you have." Louvel smiles again and enjoys the playfulness, but wonders for a moment if her words have a double meaning. "Can I ask you something?" she asks.

"Of course, anything you like. This is starting out as the best blind date I ever had."

"Are you spontaneous?"

"All the time." Almost as soon as he finishes his sentence, he seems to drift off into a waking unconsciousness.

Shoshana gets up from her chair and sits in his lap as she embraces him. To those watching, it looks like the date is going very well. The truth is that she is keeping him from falling head-first into the table, unconscious. She wipes her hands thoroughly with a table napkin; the drug she rubbed into his face has worked as quickly as it is supposed to. She keeps the napkin as she leans Louvel back into his chair so that it looks like he is simply a bit tipsy from too much drink. She places a black disk on the table and suddenly her pre-recorded voice sounds: 'Why don't I tell you more about myself.' As the disk plays her voice, Shoshana gets up from the table and walks toward the restrooms in the back.

10:15 p.m.

Louvel wakes up slowly and groggily looks around at the table. Two empty plates on the table, two half-empty glasses, and an empty bottle of wine. He doesn't remember eating or drinking anything, though. He touches his forehead and closes his eyes for a bit.

He realizes that he is at the table alone and looks around the restaurant for his date. The place is still packed, but he doesn't see her. His e-pad rings. The number displaying on his wristband isn't familiar.

He touches the wristband display. "Hello?" He answers it anyway.

"Pay the bill and follow me. I'm waiting outside." It's Shoshana's voice. The line disconnects.

Moments later, he walks out of the restaurant, looking around. The red-hooded, red-caped Shoshana stands in the distance at the other end of the street. She motions to him, turns, and starts walking away.

Louvel looks up the street to the parked blue car. He runs after her, disappearing around the corner. The blue car slowly moves forward and then does a complete 180-degree turn to follow in the same direction. It turns the corner and stops. Crowds of people are gathering around something.

The driver says, "Go find out what's happening."

The other man gets out of the passenger side. He bolts from the car and runs to the center of the commotion. Louvel lies motionless on the ground. The passenger immediately runs back to the car.

The driver asks, "What's happening?"

"Our man is lying flat on the ground."

"What happened to him? Is he dead?"

"I don't know."

"Go find out. I'll get backup."

The passenger runs back to Louvel as the crowd grows. People are dressed in a wide variety of styles, from grungy to Goth to sophisticated suits, casual colors of the rainbow to psychedelic flashing glow clothes, shiny silver to virtually no clothes at all.

A voice comes through the car dash speakers. "We've spotted the target. She's running south, two blocks away from your location."

The driver directs, "Chase and apprehend."

The voice asks, "Stun or lethal force?"

"We need her captured alive."

"Acknowledged. We're in pursuit."

The figure of Shoshana runs at a breakneck speed through the streets with her red hood hiding her face and the red cape flapping wildly. Two SUVs race up and follow her. She suddenly makes a hard right, leaps onto a parked car, and runs down a one-way street with the traffic coming the other way. The SUVs swerve right and stop, unable to pass. The doors open and government agents, all in black, exit the vehicles to give chase.

Federal Penitentiary Super-Maximum Facility, Florence, Colorado
10:15 p.m., 3 June 2089

Supermax Florence is a massive structure in the desert, a steel monolith in the middle of nowhere. It holds the "worst of the worst" of criminals, including the highest risks to national security. It is also the oldest continuously running one in the country, but has state-of-the-art security and its protocols are second to none. Prison dignitaries from across the nation and around the world visit the facility to see best practices in the prison industry. Boulder is only two hours away.

East Gate: A semi-truck with a trailer stops. The rear door opens and men jump out. They are oddly dressed in black military uniforms with strange dome helmets and black mesh masks obscuring all the features of their faces. The men, each carrying a rifle, assemble into two lines and run toward the gate in formation.

Inside the facility, intruder alarms are blaring as the warden runs from his office into the Command Center filled with dark-blue-uniformed guards watching the vid-screen monitor bank, showing the approaching dome-helmeted intruders.

"How did their vehicles get past the tek-jammers? Any facial identification?" the warden asks.

"Nothing, they're wearing masks," one guard answers.

"Once they get to the gates, take them down," the warden says. "Hard."

Another guard says, "These clowns can't honestly think they're going to breach the gate."

The warden says, "The world is full of crazies. That's what bullets are for."

North Gate: Several SUVs approach with a convoy of smaller cars. They stop and more of the dome-helmeted soldiers exit. From the lead vehicle, a person exits dressed differently than all the others; wearing a military hat with a large metallic rose on the rim and a long flowing leather coat. Her face is covered by a black mask and her eyes are covered by goggles. The Iron Rose leads the men to the gate.

"*Angriffsmuster* Delta! The *Gauleiter* will have their *ketternhund* here in fifteen minutes!" the Iron Rose yells.

One of the dome soldiers confirms, yelling to the others. "*Angriffsmuster* Delta! *Snell, snell!*"

The Iron Rose lifts her wrist and talks into the wristband: "Wolf Pack Drei Angriffsmuster Alpha! Wolf Pack *Vier Angriffsmuster* Beta!" She lowers her arm and stares at the prison facility. "Blitzkrieg commences. *Plotzensee* burns tonight!"

The warden and prison security watch the monitor bank and listen to the audio feed from the external listening systems that capture all sounds outside the walls of the prison.

"What language is that?" the warden asks. "They're speaking English and something else."

"I think it's Old German, sir," one of the guards says.

"Where are we with the search?" the warden yells.

Another guard is tapping wildly on his tablet. "I found it now, sir."

"Put it up then," the warden says.

The guard hits a button and his vid-screen is shared on a few other monitors. The warden and the guards view the text as it scrolls slowly down the screen.

"It has to be them, the Jewish Wolf Pack," the guard says.

"What's a Jewish Wolf Pack?" the warden asks.

The guard flips to another screen on his tablet, reading. "Sir, they're listed as a domestic terrorist group."

The warden continues, "We picked up a sentence: '*Blitzkrieg* commences.' '*Plotzensee* burns tonight!' What does that mean?"

The guard at the research computer reads. "Plotzensee was a prison where opponents of Adolf Hitler and the Nazis were sent to be killed."

The warden asks, "What does blitzkrieg mean?"

"Blitzkrieg was a term used to describe lightning-fast army attacks with tanks and planes."

The warden and the armed guards watch the intruders running to the North Gate on the vid-cam monitors. He is worried now.

A guard says, "Sir, none of them will breach perimeter."

The warden says, "No warnings. When they're in range, kill 'em."

Boulder, Colorado
10:26 p.m., 3 June 2089

Masked government agents chase the figure of Shoshana down the streets. She suddenly stops and throws something at them. *An explosion!* Two agents are thrown forcibly back into a car and another three are knocked off their feet. Others duck behind vehicles and avoid the blast of the stun grenade.

The assault team gives chase again. One of them takes a shot and misses. The figure of Shoshana darts around another corner.

Supermax Florence
10:26 p.m., 3 June 2089

The prison is on full lock-down and all guards are in riot gear: glass shields and armed with shotguns or tear gas guns.

The warden yells to a guard in the Command Center. "Tell them we need the birds here now!"

He knows there is no way that the state police helicopters will be here in time.

"Warden!" one of the guards yells. The warden snaps his head to his direction. "What's that?"

On the vid-screens they see a massive object floating through the air toward them. The warden bolts out the door, followed by armed guards. They run up the stairs to the top level, get to the bay windows, and look out.

The warden says, "Where is it? I don't see it now."

The wall explodes! Most of the prison guards are blown from the second-floor level and fall, some yelling, to the ground level. The warden and a few of the guards pick themselves up off the second-level floor.

The warden yells, "The south inside wall is breached!" He and three guards run back down the stairs. Other armed guards are running to them, but the warden waves them back. "Back! Back! Secure those doors!"

Projectiles fly into the facility from the breached wall. Multiple explosions! Gas instantly envelops the area. The warden and his men fall to the ground, unconscious.

Outside the prison outer wall, robotic machine guns fire in all directions. One by one they are destroyed by cannon attacks from the air.

Another explosion. A massive section of the north wall is gone. Dome-helmeted soldiers enter the breach with the Iron Rose.

Boulder, Colorado
10:36 p.m., 3 June 2089

"We don't know how, but the suspect is now in a red sports vehicle!" a voice says over the secure channel.

The figure of Shoshana races through the streets. The assault team on foot was literally left behind in the dust. In the air, two helicopters give chase.

"Suspect heading west at speeds in excess of ninety miles per hour."

"Ground forces intercepting now."

"Why isn't the Grid slowing that vehicle down?"

"The city doesn't have mandatory auto-drive on local streets; they allow manual drive."

Four new black SUVs rapidly turn onto the same street behind the fleeing red car.

"Be advised that street has been barricaded. Block off the path behind suspect."

The red car speeds unwittingly toward their barricade. It isn't just a barricade of vehicles with policemen pointing weapons; before them is a solid metal barrier laser-welded to the ground, able to withstand the impact of even a fully loaded super-truck.

One of the barricade policemen yells, "She's not stopping!"

They red car speeds to them without any indication that she will break or try to turn. There is no place to go; it's a one-way street with cars and buildings on either side. The four following SUVs pull back and take positions to block off the street behind her. The chase will end here.

The red car hits the metal barrier at 100 miles an hour!

It is destroyed, crushed like a pancake with pieces of metal and plastic everywhere. Policemen run to the wreckage, aiming their guns—she must be dead. The vehicle's air-bag tek worked and begins to deflate. The red-hooded figure leans back and coughs up blood. *It is not her, but a man!* He smiles, all his teeth gone, smashed into a bloody mess.

"That was better than drugs, man! Can we do it again?"

Supermax Florence
11:47 p.m., 3 June 2089

An army of prison police stand pointing their weapons at the bulletproof glass. The Iron Rose and her soldiers watch them from the other side. She holds up an e-pad and touches the screen. A badge appears; she holds the image to the door interface.

"Access granted," a computer voice says and the photo of the square-jawed Agent Lycan appears on the door's tiny screen. The doors start to open automatically.

The prison guards are shocked. "They have the access codes!" They run away as fast they can and disappear through other inner access doors.

Her soldiers enter the inside facility.

"Secure the warden and prison personnel," the Iron Rose directs.

It doesn't take her soldiers long to assemble all the fallen prison personnel. The warden and all the prison policemen are on their knees in a line with their arms bound behind their backs with plastic handcuffs.

Iron Rose walks to the warden.

"What do you want?" he asks.

She crouches down to him and says, "*Herr Obenführer*, it is a pleasure to make your acquaintance. I am *Eisen Stieg*, or, for you, the Iron Rose. Ah, I see you are true *alte hasen*. You are scared not in the least of our *feldzug*. We came to liberate the Jews."

The warden just looks at her. "You can't break into a federal Supermax prison and get away with it. The full force of the American government will find you and stick you in a little prison box for life, and there won't be anyone to break you out."

She laughs as she stands back up. "Let's test your words, Herr Obenführer." To her men, "*Wir gehen.*" She leads her men away. A contingent of her dome-soldiers remains behind to watch their prison personnel captives.

Outside, a dome-helmeted soldier watches a massive convoy race to the prison in the distance. Into his ear-set he says, "*Eisen Stieg*, the *Ketternhund* from the *Gauleiter* have arrived." Wolf Pack-speak for "state law enforcement and state troopers are here."

All prisons today are multi-gender, but male and female populations are kept separate. Dual-gender, transgender, and asexual are kept in a smaller third area. The dome-soldiers enter the male prison section, knowing the prison guards are somewhere hiding.

Prisoners watch from cell windows on both levels as the dome-soldiers casually stroll down the walk. They are definitely *not* policemen or any other kind of legal law enforcement personnel.

Rabbi Hendel is curled up in a small cot in his cell. The blue nightlight is on and his eyes are wide open. Who knows what is happening outside the walls of his cell? It can't possibly have anything to do with him.

The door of his cell opens.

The Iron Rose stands in front of the jail cells as her soldiers open the doors and bring the male prisoners out, one after another—all Jewish Hasidim. The prisoners are calm. Rabbi Hendel is brought out and immediately walks to the front of his men.

The Iron Rose asks, "Which one of you is Rabbi Hendel?"

None of the men answer.

She removes her mask and hat disguise—Shoshana! She repeats in Hebrew, "Which one of you is Rabbi Hendel?"

The men are surprised. "You are Jewish?" Rabbi Hendel asks.

"Of course."

"Why are you dressed that way?"

"We thought today was Halloween," she says jokingly. "We're breaking you out of here, Rabbi, with all your men."

He shakes his head. "Return us to our cells and go. You can speak Hebrew, Yiddish, Russian, or any other language, but none of us will be going anywhere with you."

Shoshana walks right up to him and lifts her e-pad to his face. "Let me be clear, Rabbi. We did not break into a federal Supermax prison to leave empty-handed. Your eldest son made me promise at his bar-mitzvah to have you home by his next birthday. What should I tell him?"

Rabbi Hendel's eyes well up in tears as he sees the picture of his almost-fourteen-year-old son on her e-pad. When he last saw him, he was just a child.

She says, "What do you want me to do? If we're going, I need you to organize all your men quickly. We must leave the prison now. We have transport waiting outside. I also need you to send three of your men with mine to go into the female section and positively identify your female members."

"What? How many of our women do they have here?"

"Almost a hundred."

Rabbi Hendel's face turns red with anger and he motions to three of his men. "They will go where you want them to."

She turns to one of her soldiers. "Get the women."

The night sky lights up with flash explosions and gunfire erupts everywhere. State troopers are pinned down by a barrage of gunfire and cannon-fire. They fire back, but can't see a thing, and as soon as they use their night goggles, the flash explosions blind them.

Shoshana and the soldiers exit the prison facility with hundreds of Hasidic prisoners. Several massive zeppelins descend to the ground and Shoshana's soldiers race them onto the balloon airships.

The zeppelins, with their mini jet engines, rise into the air, higher and higher into the night sky. Suddenly, all the external lights go out, putting the entire area in blinding darkness.

Shoshana watches them with her high-powered night goggles in the lead zeppelin. She smiles wide. "*Amichai.* My people live!"

Elizabeth Center, Anacostia, Washington DC
4:46 a.m., 4 June 2089

The chaos in the building is everywhere. Homeland Director Dunn arrives, with a string of aides following her closely.

"Ma'am, the entire area has been cordoned off by Homeland and state police. No prison personnel were killed or seriously injured, but none of them can give any descriptions of the perpetrators other than that they are positive they were members of one of the domestic terrorist groups on the watch list," says one aide.

"Ma'am, the Governor of Colorado is demanding an immediate debrief," says another aide.

"Set it up within the next thirty minutes," Homeland says.

"Yes, ma'am."

They arrive at her offices, and standing right at the door is her chief of staff. "Ma'am, the attorney general is waiting for you inside."

The homeland director stops and motions to her staff. They understand, and each walks to their respective offices. She notices a tiny man standing against the wall nearby, watching her. She looks away and enters her office alone.

Inside her spacious office, the A.G. sits quietly in the chair in front of her desk. He sits in a dark blue suit and his long black hair touches his shoulders.

She sits down quietly.

He coldly stares back at her. "I work long hours every day, but when I go home and get to sleep, I expect to sleep. A few hours ago, I was abruptly awoken by my frantic staffers, who told me something that, if I wasn't convinced I was awake, I would have sworn was in a dream. They told me that not one or a handful, but all—more than one thousand designated terrorists whom my office spent years and tens of thousands of man-hours capturing, preparing cases against, going before juries for, convicting, and locking away in prison—were busted out, all of them. The President wanted all unregistered Jew-Christians targeted. And Justice followed his mandate. If you recall, I was the one who strenuously pled with the President to just throw the whole lot in prison, under indefinite detention statutes, under executive authority. But he said, 'No. We want public trials. Send a message.' How did all these designated Jew-Christian terrorists get out of prison? Here's the funny part. They accessed the prison, my prison, using the security ID of some black ops agent whose file is classified so high that not even I can read it, and I'm only the top law enforcer for the nation."

He leans forward. "I am not scared of you or your office. You may fool Congress and the Supreme Senate, but not me. You and I both know that I've seen you naked, and I was as unimpressed by you then as I am with you now, even if you are the President's pet. You better pray to Darwin that not one of those designated terrorists harms or kills any government person, not a one. I am finished with this case and so is my department. You will apprehend them, since you lost them. My office is finished with this case. We did our jobs and you, your division, jumped in. Understand that if anyone takes the fall for this, it will be you. That's what I'll tell the President. You, not me. If you ever do a black operation in my jurisdiction again without informing me, I will end you. I throw terrorists in jail, and you let them escape. My grandparents were killed by a terrorist who should never have been breathing air, and you let a thousand of them out in one night. If you survive this scandal and ever do this again, I will end you."

He stands slowly, never taking his glare off her. With that, he turns and leaves the office.

The door opens and one of her aides walks in. "Ma'am, there's someone here—"

"Stop." The aide freezes. "Get the President's strategic dom-sec advisor in here, now!"

The Crystal Apple

"Once you know something, you can never 'un-know' it ever again." – Adam and Eve

Café American, Miami, Florida
6:24 p.m., 3 March 2090

Miami is one of the most flamboyant tek-cities in America; it pulsates with every color of the rainbow, and trendy standards like hot pink, neon blue, and flaming red. It is a curious place to have a private meeting of Faithers, but the restaurant is out of the way, with more than enough blind spots for those "in the know" to avoid being captured by any Eyes. The real reason for the choice of location is that though Jews have long since left the main city, they still own all of this area, including this restaurant.

There are not many customers, as it's before the dinner rush. Zev waits quietly just outside the entrance to the private dining room of the restaurant. He is a tan man in his thirties, with a well-groomed mustache and a short beard. His boyhood friend enters—Gideon. Zev smiles as they notice each other. He walks to Zev and the men give each strong hugs with firm pats on the back.

Zev says, "You made good time."

"I got here early." Gideon is about Zev's same age, but with dark blond hair. He is clean shaven all around. He is well dressed in a dark suit.

"How have you been? It's been too long."

"Too long. But doing well and keeping out of trouble. At least as far as anyone could find out." Gideon smiles.

He pushes the door open and leads Gideon in. While the large outer area is well-lit and has a vibrant atmosphere with large tables, the private dining area, a quarter of the square space, is dimly lit and sedate. Booth seating areas line either side of the room with oval tables. Gideon notices that there are only a few men at the very last booth in the back, multi-colored smoke hovering above them. The men are talking amongst themselves quietly. Zev leads him to the table.

"This is my good friend, Gideon." He turns to Gideon. "Meet the Wise Men. Mr. B, Mr. C, and Mr. X."

They do not rise as Zev introduces him, uncharacteristic manners for Faithers. They remain seated as each takes his turn shaking Gideon's hand. All three men radiate a conceit of self-importance and are blessed with full, natural heads of hair, though they probably have been gray-white for many years now. In the center is Mr. C, who is the largest of the men, wearing a black shirt unbuttoned to the middle of his torso with chest hairs billowing out. A cigar hangs in his mouth and a wisp of blue smoke rises from the tip. Mr. B, on his left, is dressed in a black sports jacket and a white shirt. He holds a cigar with green smoke rising from it. Mr. X, on his left, is also dressed business casual in a black shirt with a shiny gray silver sports jacket, probably his way of being "Miami flamboyant." He holds a cigar with pink smoke.

Gideon says, "Mr. Benjamin, Mr. Cowen, Mr. Eckstein, nice to meet you."

"Have a seat." Mr. C inhales and savors the smoke before blowing out a puff of blue.

The Wise Men were obviously born in the Mother Country

(Jewish Israel), as American Jews don't smoke products at all. Muslims smoke their nasty traditional raw cigarettes, but so do Arab Jews and Arab Christians for that matter. Israeli Jews smoke cigars, as do Italian Catholics, though no one has seen an Italian Catholic since the Fall of Western Europe. Amish are probably the only ones who still smoke pipes. Goth Faithers, Jewish or Christian, smoke very short cigarettes called blunts, with all variety of exotic colored smoke. The Pagan populace, however, does not smoke naturals; the plain, non-drug ones like Faithers. Pagans smoke psychogenic, hallucinogenic, and stimulagenic ones only.

Gideon scoots into the booth on one side and Zev gets in after him. It is very close quarters and Gideon almost feels as if he's about to be initiated into something illegal or dangerous—if it weren't for Zev.

The Wise Men are among the oldest leaders of America's Jewish community. The joke is that the Wise Men existed from the time of Abraham, Moses, and David. Religiously, they are senior elders in the Conservative Jewish Order, and universally respected among all the Orders due to decades of work and activism on behalf of Jews. If asked about their profession, they always say "businessmen," but they really are professional advocates for the Jewish community. Their "elder" title within the Conservatives is more honorary, as they never do anything related to religion, just business. Their status in the community is also directly a result of their enormous collective wealth. The multi-billionaire businessmen would often say, "We own Miami, the Pagans just rent."

Mr. X summons a waitress. "Another round for us and a simple cocktail for our friend."

"What do you know of Susan the Destroyer?" Mr. C asks as he sips whatever alcohol he has in his glowing yellow glass.

"Who?" Gideon asks.

"Rabbi Susan."

"Oh. Nothing recently. She was excommunicated and all the Orders agreed not to touch her so she couldn't become a martyr for the government. That's all I know."

"She's dead," Mr. C says.

"I heard nothing on the newsfeed."

"And there won't be. She came to an enclave in disguise. Rushed the gate and she was gunned down. Her body was buried off-site. No one will find it. No sense allowing her to be resurrected as a martyr. This was a year ago."

"A year ago?" Gideon has a thought. "Her Christian sidekick committed suicide, too. I think it was a year ago, too."

"Who?"

"That Bishop Joe."

"We didn't know that," Mr. C says.

"It was such a small mention in the obituaries. The only reason I picked it up was that he programmed his domestic robot to shoot him point-blank in the face with a shotgun."

"I thought they made it so that those robots couldn't do that anymore," Mr. C says.

"He had one of the first models before the safeties were made foolproof. If there is even such a thing when it comes to machines. Interesting. Both dead around the same time."

Mr. C says, "The main issue here is she was carrying something. A small box with a data crystal."

"What's on it?" Gideon asks.

Mr. C takes another sip. "You have to understand that emotions are very heated when it comes to this woman. Even the sanest, calmest Jew can get irrational. Many wanted to destroy it, not even look at it. It's encrypted. None of the files are accessible by conventional means, but we think it must be investigated further.

She said before she died that she wanted to help her people as her last act on Earth.”

“You believe that?” Gideon asks.

Mr. C pauses a moment. “Maybe, maybe not. But we’d like you to investigate on our behalf. Zev vouches for you. He trusts you. So we trust you…for the time being.” He lets his last phrase hang in the air for a moment. “You have the connections and resources. Use them. We cannot directly pursue the matter.”

Gideon says, “You said this happened a year ago. Why investigate now?”

Mr. C says, “There’s a time and a place for everything. We believe this is the time to pursue this. Zev says you have a senior position within the government itself.”

Gideon is not entirely satisfied with the answer to his “why now” question, but decides to let it go. “I’ve been a law enforcement agent for almost fifteen years now,” Gideon says. The waitress returns with the drinks and sets them on the table. “Thank you.”

Mr. B asks, “How is it possible that an unregistered Jew gets to be a fifteen-year law enforcement veteran within the government? Reach your level?”

Gideon sips his drink. He puts the glass down and smiles. “I’m a secret agent. So naturally, I have secrets. Even from my government bosses.”

“He’s our own Jewish James Bond,” Zev adds, grinning.

Mr. B says, “Yes. He even has his own real license to kill.”

Mr. C asks, “But who is your ultimate loyalty to? One cannot serve two masters.”

Gideon chooses not to be offended. “Serving and receiving a paycheck are two different things. I serve my people. I work for the government. Hunting organized crime lords, cyber-pirates, murderers, and terrorists helps, not hurts, my people.”

Zev interjects, "Gideon is one of us. He has good resources."

Mr. B smiled slightly. "This is the perfect project for you, then."

Gideon asks, "How quickly do you want me to work?"

Mr. C replies, "This is very important to us. We want you to follow wherever the investigation takes you. If there is even a remote chance that it has information that can help our people, then it will be worth it. The Holocaust may be over 145 years ago, but conspiracies against the Jewish people remain to this day."

"I'll see where it goes."

"What about your compensation?" Mr. X asks.

"My compensation is usual expenses. That's how I always work when I'm doing freelance for the community. Besides, I'll be retiring in the near future. If I get in good with you now, after I retire, I can work for you."

The men laugh.

Mr. C looks at Zev and nods. Zev takes the data crystal from his pocket and hands it to Gideon. "We're anxious to see what you find," Zev says. "I'll be your contact and the liaison with the Wise Men."

Mr. X says, "Mr. Gideon, this is a confidential investigation. Communicate only with Zev. And do not bring any outsiders into our business. Let's keep this 'in-house.' It's bad enough the dirty Pagans call us all Jew-Christians. No need to give credence to their slurs. Keep your investigation strictly a Jewish matter. Let's not bring any of our Christian friends, or anyone else, in on this one. And the data crystal's origin is not to be shared with anyone."

Gideon says, "Understood. Zev can tell you how strictly I guard the confidentiality of my clients."

Mr. X says, "Thank you."

Mr. C asks, "Will your normal law enforcement duties interfere with this investigation?"

Gideon says. "I have a few weeks of extra vacation days that I've been hounded to take. Now I have an excuse."

The Wise Men are satisfied.

Mr. C says, "Keep us updated daily through Zev." He blows out more smoke. "That's all, Mr. Gideon."

Gideon nods. "Good. Gentlemen, sorry I can't stay for dinner, but I'll be heading back. I never like being out of my own community for too long." He looks at Zev again. "How's the family?"

Zev says, "Ruth and the children are just fine. My oldest is eight. My youngest is three."

"You had another child since we last saw each other?" Gideon asks.

"Yes, Ruth was pregnant at the time. When are you going to find a nice Jewish girl and settle down, Gideon?"

"Soon."

"That's what you said last time we saw each other. You should come to the community and spend a few days there. I swear, in a week you'll find a wife."

Gideon laughs. "Is it so easy these days?"

"You think I'm joking, but I swear. We have all the beautiful Jewish women—blond, brunette, redheaded. But you have to move fast."

"Oh my gosh, I'm talking to the reincarnated spirit of my mother."

Zev laughs. "I'll walk you out." He gets up from the booth.

Gideon slides out and shakes hands with the Wise Men again. "Have a good night."

The Wise Men closely watch Zev lead Gideon out of the private room.

Zev says, "Call me soon and do come to visit us."

"I will. Promise," Gideon says.

The men hug each other.

Zev is civilian private security for the Gadsden, Alabama Jewish enclave of the Conservative Order, but Gideon is the real deal: Homeland Defense and Intelligence Agency, United States of America, Florida field office.

Gideon's Apartment Home, Miami, Florida
8:37 p.m., 3 March 2090

Gideon walks to his front door. The sensors on the doorknob are set to require biometric finger contact, a rarity for modern homes of any kind. Doors normally are programmed to open when authorized persons approach. Most don't even have doorknobs anymore.

The Wise Men didn't press the issue, but they were concerned about him being both a government agent and an unregistered Faither. Technically, the penalty for falsifying a government employment application is imprisonment. Religious self-identification, along with sexual orientation, is mandatory. How he managed this was, as he told them, his secret.

His vacation officially started before he had even gotten back into his car after the meeting. He sent the email from his e-pad and the approval came instantly. The data crystal is his sole focus now.

It is a very spacious loft apartment. The room of his home office is covered with digital maps all over the walls of different sections of the city, Florida, and neighboring states. At a large desk are two thirty-six-inch vid-screens on the left, and another two on the right. Suspended by wires above the work desk are six seventeen-inch vid-screens.

Virtually all data today is stored on the Net, but there are still many people—and not just Faithers—who don't trust keeping their files on the government-maintained (and monitored) system. Data can also be stored externally via a data stick, data disc, or a data crystal—the latter being the most secure. Gideon puts the crystal on the computer interface to access the files. A directory automatically pops up on his center left screen, but all the names of the files are blank. There is definitely data on the crystal, but even his software can't access it. If his Homeland security program cannot open the files, the person is either very good at encryption, or the file was created by a government program of a higher security classification than he holds.

When the Religious Registration Initiatives began, defenders said, "Americans have been registering with the government for one thing or another forever," from the Selective Service System to paying taxes to universal healthcare to national ID cards and the Registry. The Initiatives were enacted to require registration of all religious institutions and all their congregants as a condition of receiving tax-exempt status to ensure compliance. It also included adoption of Rabbi Susan's government-sanctioned Good Bible; all other holy books—except for the Koran—were prohibited.

He remembers the special field enforcement units set up to visit religious institutions directly, and require compliance in person or risk forfeiture of tax-exempt status, fines, and possible incarceration. The government actions against Jews and Christians especially made him want to become a "jack-booted government thug," as his late mother called them. He wanted to be a "spy" for his people within their ranks.

The data files are encryption-locked, but he is able to access the vid-files, which she must have added fairly recently. It is Rabbi Susan in a long vid-mail addressed to her mother. It is painful to watch. A woman with the world in her hands early in life, then discarded by her "masters," and finally desperate to reconcile with her people, her family, and her mother.

The Religious Registration Division was disbanded after the Separatist Movement. Jews, Christians, and others simply and completely opted out of general tek-society. Though all the registration laws are still on the books.

He needs to access these data files. "Let's go visit the tek-lord," Gideon says to himself.

Miami Expressway, Florida
9:02 p.m., 3 March 2090

Gideon coasts down the freeway in his two-door black cruiser as he does some simple Net research on the vehicle's dashboard computer; the car is driving itself. In all major tek-cities manual control of one's own vehicle is prohibited. Only in the outskirts of the city (Outland) or even farther beyond the tek-cities (Trog-land) could you escape using auto-drive. The future may not be flying cars and robot drivers, but with GPS-Net interface in the modern smart-car, tek doesn't need you to drive a car. Human error is what caused the road fatalities of the past and with artificial intelligence (AI), accidents of any kind have been reduced to less than a few hundred per year; car deaths have been completely eliminated. Not bad for a nation of six hundred million.

He arrives at one of the smaller Miami Jewish communities, a massive but secure apartment complex. Though one of the top sin city centrals of America, they had no desire to leave, despite the Pagan majority. The residents are descendants of Jews who have lived in the city for generations. Historically, Florida had been one of the three states with the largest American Jewish populations until the Fall of Jewish Israel. Most Jews live in the South.

He drives to the main gate and a robot eye, a bulb-shaped device on a wire-like arm, peers into his car and scans him from head to toe. Other robot eyes scan the entire car: top, bottom, inside, and outside.

"Please state your name, who you are visiting, and the code," the robot says to him.

"Gideon. I'm here to see Goli King-David. Code 2-3-1-9."

"Confirmed. Proceed inside, park in visitor parking only, and enter the closest elevator. It will open at the correct floor."

The gate opens and Gideon drives into the visitor parking. All the non-visitor sections are gated off so he couldn't drive into them even if he wanted to. He pulls into an empty visitor spot and exits his car. He notices cameras on the wall watching his every move as he walks into the nearby elevator. The doors close. There are no numbers at all, so you don't know how many total floors are in the building, and you don't know what floor you're going to. They know and that's all that matters.

The elevator doors open and he walks to the apartment—number seven. The door is already ajar and he enters.

"Goli, it's the police! Put away all your illegal stuff!" he says playfully.

Goli appears with a smile. "You got here fast. It's not pay-off day until next week."

The men greet each other with bear hugs. He's known Goli all his life. A mountain of a man, Goli was ten pounds at birth. By elementary school he was already taller than everyone in his school, and by middle school he was taller than his parents, teachers, and everyone in his community. He's seven feet tall and all muscles. He is the modern-day Goliath (his full first name), but Jewish by religion, with the last name of King-David, of all things. He didn't make up his surname. His father's name really was King, and his mother's maiden name really was David, and both of them were on the more nontraditional side in their youth, so they hyphenated for him and his siblings.

"Thanks for seeing me right away. I know how busy you are," Gideon says.

"Always working, but then my home is my work."

Goli runs his own Net-tek business—everything that had to do with the Net and Grid, both hardware and software. He is a genius when it comes to tek and is Gideon's "secret," remaining an unregistered Jew-Christian in, of all places, the government's super agency of Homeland. Goli hacked into Gideon's secure law enforcement files at the start of his career sixteen years ago, and gave him the appropriate religion to allow him to rise in the ranks. Pagan.

"Here's the data crystal."

Goli takes it and leads him to his "command center," one of the rooms in the massive five-story apartment converted to a high-tek workplace. There is a large, plush leather chair in front of a two-story desk with four vid-screens and two different keyboards on the first desk level, ten smaller screens on the second level, a mini refrigerator and water dispenser under the desk to the left, and file cabinets on the right. The room has eight-foot-tall metal towers everywhere. Most of the interior walls are holo-walls with digital pictures of family, friends, and places, changing every five seconds.

"Who's the source?" Goli asks.

"It's confidential."

Goli stops as he sits down and looks at him. "Gideon."

"I promised."

"Gideon."

"Okay, but you have to promise me."

"Gideon."

"Rabbi Susan."

Goli stops. "She's dead." He studies the crystal.

"How do you know she's dead?"

"I have sources too." Goli is technically of the Israeli Jewish Order, his parents immigrating to America when he was an infant, though this entire complex houses members and families of the Conservative Jewish Order.

Gideon continues. "She had the crystal on her when she was killed. She said something about wanting to help her people as her last act on Earth."

Goli loads the crystal into the interface. "What do you need me for? You undoubtedly viewed the files."

"I'm not able to access the files. Also, I need to verify the authenticity and source."

"Okay, I can have that for you—no!" Goli quickly hits one of the keys on the keyboard.

"What happened?" Gideon asks.

"These are US government confidential data files. They have traces all over them. Tell me you didn't view this from your house."

"My system has trace detection software."

"Gideon, I keep telling you that just because you work in government law enforcement doesn't mean they give you the best tek. They keep the best stuff for themselves."

"Do you think they traced me?"

"If you have to ask, then the answer is yes. Give me a few minutes to debug this thing." Goli starts tapping away on the keyboard; he prefers old-school rather than voice-interface.

Goli is also a contradiction of sorts. He is a wildly successful tek-head, being in the business since before either's bar mitzvah, but despite his genius with tek, he has always had an almost loathing of it. His day job aside, he has all the sensibilities of a Trog (slang for an off-Grider). He doesn't trust tek and avoids it whenever possible, almost viewing it as a type of disease. All tek is connected to the Net, and off-Griders will do anything not to be connected to the Grid— the government's mainframe to maintain the public Net; maintain constant surveillance on all tek-cities for crime or terrorism; and run all communication, transportation, and infrastructure services. Despite the propaganda, it isn't just Faithers who were mostly off-Grid. Large numbers of the Pagan subpopulations—Nihilists, Hedonists, Anarchists, et cetera—also live their entire lives off-Grid, equally paranoid about the Grid government.

"Anything new and exciting?" Goli says.

"Police work is not as exciting as the movies."

"Nothing exciting at all?" Goli taps away a mile a minute. All four vid-screens are flashing code.

"They've had me on wrap-up detail mostly, compiling reports and pushing them through the system. No big cases lately."

Goli takes out the crystal and hands it to him. "There are three hundred thirty-three files. With another three hundred thirty-three hidden files, which are authentication path files for the originals."

Gideon is intrigued. "Really? Like a joke."

"Yeah, I get it. Six-six-six, but this I don't think they meant it as a joke. The files are authentic. She probably did a complete database copy, and probably didn't know the files were omega-encrypted and rotating password locked."

"Can you break open the files?"

"Already done. All the files are open now. I segregated the hidden files in their own file folder and disabled all the traces. Most of the files are classified. Gideon, you need to be very careful."

"I always am."

"You mean you always say that you are. I'm serious."

"Seriously, I will be careful."

"I took this job from a Pagan guy last year. I normally don't, but he wasn't the standard anti-religious bigot. He was doing a strange investigation that was of mutual interest. I gave the Christians a copy. He called me one day to help with another Net search project. I never had a chance to contact him back. They found him dead the next day. Something exploded in his stomach."

Gideon stares at him. "Something exploded in his stomach? What does that mean?"

"Gideon, just be careful. I did a quick source search of the hidden files." He looks at the screen. "Homeland, Congress, Cabinet departments, Special Services. She stole these files and even though she's dead, the government has arrested, prosecuted, and jailed people for simple possession of classified government files. Being a policeman in good standing isn't a defense in an espionage trial. There are far more spy trials here in America than in Saudi Arabia or CHIN territory. Don't buy into the 'land of the free' myth."

"Thanks for the legal advice. I'll be sure not to eat any strange foods either. Goli, the government doesn't run around assassinating people. That's only in make-believe land."

"All they have to do is keep the seventy percent of the population who don't care, tek-addicted, drug-addicted, and sex-addicted. And keep the thirty percent of the population who do care on self-segregated reservations. Incidentally, how do you know they don't assassinate people?"

"You really are one of those conspiracy people. It's like you telling me the reason they want to make all keyboards obsolete is so the government can listen to your voice-interface and that they secretly own all the listening device companies in the country."

"It's not conspiracies. I call it healthy, existential Darwinism. The naïve are killed by predators and the paranoid survive. What concerns me is that you tried to access these files from your physical home with all the traces on them." Goli looks at him, thinking. "Maybe you should stay someplace else until you finish your investigation."

Gideon laughs. "Thanks Goli, but that isn't necessary. Besides, we're partnering up on this investigation. You'll be my cyber-deputy. I know you already have all the best weapons."

"Yes, Sheriff. Just don't get gunned down in the street in the middle of the night."

Gideon's Home, Miami, Florida
6:12 a.m., 10 March 2090

Gideon stares at his vid-screen with a half-incredulous, half-pensive look. Countless hours and cups of coffee he has spent over the past week reviewing the Susan data files. Much of the documents are written in typical "shop" talk: the bureaucratic, almost code-language of a government office. In one sense, even though everything is in English, they might as well be speaking an ancient foreign language. Project this, Project that, Operation this, Operation that.

Susan's division was disbanded and she was fired many years ago, but somehow she still had access to an old portal. Susan wasn't keeping track of the department she used to run out of idle curiosity. She was slowly conducting her own investigation over a period of ten years. The data crystal was the completion of that investigation.

Gideon transfers the list of names to his e-pad from the screen. *Her conclusions can't possibly be true.* He tidies up the work area to prepare to leave. The doorbell rings and he jumps. Goli has made even him a paranoid fool.

He touches a button on the screen and instantly the live vid-feed appears. A lone man stands outside his door, wearing a brown suit and hat. Gideon watches the man quietly. The stranger rings the bell again, waits a few more minutes before ringing it a final time. He waits even longer and then walks away to the elevators.

Gideon is surprised by how unnerved he is. He sits in his apartment for a bit before leaving. He avoids the front or back entrances, and uses the more secluded side exit of the ten-story building. It takes him to the underground parking lot, where he hops into his official government car, different from his private car.

He drives to his Homeland offices and catches the first air shuttle into Virginia. He arrives and takes a taxi to the Virginia Homeland Offices, signs out another government vehicle from the department motor pool, and drives to his first stop: the first name on Susan's list.

Twenty-Two Tower, Langley, Virginia
9:03 a.m., 10 March 2090

It is a very luxurious smart-building in the business section. Gideon doesn't have to wait long as the receptionist takes him to a large, private conference room with multiple clusters of plush chairs around tables. His person comes right out and they sit; the only ones in the room.

"How did you get my name, Mr. Gideon?" he asks. Webb is a thin man with dark black hair, slim mustache, and goatee. His suit includes an old-style bow tie and suspenders.

"I can't divulge that," Gideon answers, "but it is part of my investigation into her disappearance. We're following all leads."

"Of course, you must. The last time I worked with Rabbi Susan was…it must have been well over ten years ago. The Religious Registration Division doesn't even exist on paper anymore."

"Tell me about the division. It doesn't exist anymore, but what work did you both do back then?"

"Mr. Gideon, you work in government, even if it's the mindless muscle for the government—law enforcement. You must pay more careful attention to language; every word, every intonation. I said the division doesn't exist on paper. This is the first and last time I will offer my help for free again."

Gideon smirks a bit. He knows the personality type: intellectual, but a loner. Life revolves around the job, big ego that needs to be stroked often, loves to talk, show off the brainy superiority.

"So the division doesn't exist on paper. Does it exist in reality in its full former capacity?"

"No, its original mission is long since moot."

"Just so I'm clear, what was that mission, officially on paper and in reality?"

Webb smiles. "Very simply, the division was in charge of ensuring that all religious groups registered with the government and complied with an endless litany of anti-discrimination and anti-hate crime laws. Very bureaucratic and useless. Very indicative of a division reporting to the Tax Bureau."

"That's the stated mission. What was the real one?"

"Transform America—from religious to secular. Just like the cradle of modern civilization, Western Europe."

"Yeah, that worked out so well. The secularists fled to America and the Muslims now run Western Europe."

"I never said that secularists can't be stupid too."

"Did your old division achieve its objectives?"

Webb smiles. "Oh yes, splendidly, in fact."

"How so? The religious still aren't complying."

"Yes officer, they have, by doing something even better. They simply opted out of the public society all together. Same difference. Muslims aside, religious America is gone."

"Doesn't sound very conspiratorial and everyone knows this already, so why bother? They were already decreasing in power on their own. I'm not into grandiose conspiracy theories. The simplest answer is almost always the correct one in these things."

"*That* is exactly right, Mr. Gideon."

"What?"

"Conspiracies. Most people, when they hear that word, believe the person to be crazy, off their drugs, or taking too many. No one takes you seriously. In the last one hundred years, how many conspiracies have actually been true? This is the US government. You can't keep big secrets. Why do you think they have constant presidential executive orders in place? People in government are constantly leaking to the press. But Mr. Gideon, the fact is, in the last one hundred years, there have been tens of thousands of conspiracies. A secret plan, not necessarily unlawful or evil, by two or more persons. There is the visible government, the elected officials, and their aides, but that is only the tip of the iceberg. The full government, in all its glory of never-ending tentacles, is actually so much more vast and hidden, below, out of sight. The unknown career bureaucrats are the ones who *really* run everything. Of course, they can keep a secret from the public. It's been done since the founding of the nation. Conspiracy is the word we use when the public learns of the plot or the public suspects something. When they don't, it's called…the work of the day."

Gideon nods slightly.

"Your real problem, Mr. Gideon, besides your personal bias against believing in conspiracies—which is the exact position of the majority of people, so it's totally understandable—is that you are a government bureaucrat yourself. Your bias is not wanting to think ill of your species."

"The division, it accomplished its mission?"

"Of course. The country is no longer a majority Jew-Christian nation, Mr. Gideon." He smiles a big smile. "Utopia has been achieved."

"There have been many non-religious societies in history. I don't know if I would call any of them utopia. People are people; religious or not, they're the same."

"Oh no, Mr. Gideon, the American Utopia, to paraphrase our President, can be achieved only with the absence of any and all religion from the public square, and it will be unlike anything we've seen on Earth before."

"You see value in this mission? Seems like all we've done is stir up a hornet's nest."

"The American government has been social engineering its people for centuries. You don't honestly believe otherwise, do you? This is just the latest chapter."

"But there are still Jew-Christians."

"And?"

"And Muslims."

"And?"

"They're not going anywhere."

"Utopia will not be denied. The government will always find a way. The Jew-Christians are in their ghettoes. At some point, their descendants will tire, join the greater society, and conform. Muslims are easy. Wait for another Nine-Eleven-style attack and then wipe them out. Utopia achieved."

"Government will find a way."

"Government will find a way."

Gideon says, "I thought there might be something more sinister to it all."

"Why did you think there was something sinister involved?"

"I read too many conspiracy books as a child."

Webb laughs. "Well, at least you became a government police officer to catch bad guys; all is forgiven."

"Can you think of possible enemies who might have wanted to harm Rabbi Susan?"

"I imagine that would be the entire Jew-Christian population."

"True, but we believe other parties may be involved. Was there anything strange you can remember from when you worked with her?"

"Nothing I can recall."

"Anything off at all, in something she said or did? Anything you heard about her?"

"No, but I do remember the time she was fixated on these baby pictures."

"Baby pictures?"

"It was a little strange because Susan loathed babies. But there was this time she had these baby pictures all over the place." Webb starts to laugh to himself. "I remember her astonishment at learning that babies don't walk when they're first born. She was so silly when it came to those things. I wish there was something more I could recall that could help with your investigation."

"Too bad we don't have those baby pictures."

Webb looks at him. "Well, Mr. Gideon, actually we do."

11:33 a.m.

Gideon drives along the freeway. "Nothing to report," he says into his dash speaker.

"Are you still in Florida?" The voice is Zev's.

"No, I'm in Virginia. I'll let you know if I find out something."

"I hope something comes of this, but I wouldn't be surprised if you find out that even to the end she was just a bunch of show. The Wise Men really believe there's something here, though. They want you to use whatever in-house confidential resources you need. After all this is over, they've already told me that they want to hire you away from the government to head up a new unified Jewish private intelligence organization for our people."

"I'm flattered. I'll let you know if anything turns up."

"Thanks, Gideon. And remember to come out to the community so I can set you up with a nice Jewish girl. Just give me dimensions and hair color."

Gideon laughs. "Well, if you put it that way. Bye Zev." He disconnects the line.

He has to deliver a good result to this investigation; the Wise Men want to hire him. This is the career move he's been waiting for, but what an impressive start. All he has now are…baby pictures.

1:12 p.m.

Sitting in his car, Gideon eats a bit of his lunch. He's parked in the covered lot of an office building. He can see a small park a block away. The fast-track speeds by on its way to the Capitol. Also in his line of sight are digital billboards with their advids (vid advertisements), an occasional drone, and the bustle of people with their devices, portfolios, and lunches in hand.

There are five names on Susan's list. Webb is one. Two retired and have since passed away. One lives in Australia. The other lives in Virginia, too. Another name has an entire separate file, but it is of a deceased woman, Klara Heidel. He can't find anything on her; it's as if she never existed.

He voice-dials the number via his ear-set. It connects. "Hello, Mr. Hall. This is Mr. Gideon calling on time. Thank you for responding to my request yesterday. Again, I would like to ask you a few questions about the time you worked with a Rabbi Susan."

Gideon set up the phone appointment with the man's home secretary earlier, but he seems surprised at the call. "Mr. Gideon, I'm sorry to hear about this disappearance, but there seems to be a mistake."

"What mistake?" Gideon asks.

"I never worked with her."

"Didn't you work in the same building?"

"Mr. Gideon, working in District, in the same building, means nothing. I worked on the same floor for twenty years and knew only about a dozen of the hundreds of people I passed every day. That's just the way it is. I don't remember even seeing her in person."

"I was told you knew her."

"I don't know why anyone would say that. We didn't even work in the same division."

"What division did you work in when she was in Religious Registration?"

There is a long pause. "I'm sorry Mr. Gideon, but I think you have gotten all the information you need. I never worked with her."

"That was not the question I asked you."

"I have nothing else to add, and I'm not going to have this sort of conversation on an open line."

"It is a secure line, Mr. Hall."

"There is no such thing."

"We can't talk unless I fly to Australia?"

"That's it. Call my secretary if you ever do. Have a good night or morning or whatever time of day it is there. Bye." He disconnects.

Curious for him to say that his secure-encrypted police line isn't secure, but Goli always tells him the same thing. If it flies through the air, someone can "catch" the transmission. Only the President has a true secure-line.

Five minutes later, his ear-set rings while he eats more of his now-cold lunch. He looks at the dashboard interface, but the number is private. The only time a phone number comes in as private on his police line is if the person calling is from a government agency of a higher security clearance. He decides to answer it anyway.

"Yes."

"Mr. Gideon."

"Mr. Webb. How did you get my private number?"

"What is this investigation really about? You're talking to people who never worked with her?"

"This is not an official investigation yet. It is a simple inquiry at this time."

"Mr. Gideon, I've been in government all my life. If a policeman of any kind is asking questions, then it's an investigation."

"Is there something you didn't tell me?"

"Everything I said was absolutely the truth."

"Then what truth did you *not* tell me?"

"Mr. Gideon, we're not stupid. We've been at this game a lot longer than you have. You have an agenda that is separate from an inquiry into the disappearance of a former division director. If you don't end your investigation, I will have to inform your superiors."

"Feel free to do so. I'm sure you can illegally obtain their private phone numbers too."

"Mr. Gideon, I have to protect myself in case you run afoul of the wrong people. I can't jeopardize my retirement. I'm short, you know. Just three months. I've given forty years of my life to country and I don't need any complications."

"I'm not some kind of amateur, Mr. Webb. I know how to do a discreet inquiry. If you're overly paranoid, that's not my fault."

"Just because one is paranoid doesn't mean nothing is wrong. And you, Mr. Gideon, are wrong. We know you aren't authorized by any of your superiors to conduct this inquiry."

Gideon is tense now.

Webb's voice continues. "Are you doing this for yourself, or other individuals? Are you working for the Jew-Christians? We know you're an unregistered Jew-Christian yourself."

Gideon is caught off-guard. "Why would you want to libel me with such a lie?"

"Slander."

"What?"

"Slander is spoken. Libel is written. Spoken is a warning. Written is when it's official and your Homeland police career comes to a crashing end."

"You just made me angry, Mr. Webb. I'm not going to stop my investigation. And I'm not a Jew-Christian. Just because she was one doesn't make me one. This is purely about the disappearance of former government personnel, but you can slander me with whatever you want, with whomever you want. I got friends too."

"Yes, but my friends have bigger teeth and claws than yours do, Mr. Gideon. I imagine you've got only a day or two before Special Services gets to you." The line disconnects.

Gideon stares off into space. The bastard has truly threatened his career.

6:02 p.m.

The car drives while he works. He dials Goli first.

The line picks up. "Yo, Gideon!"

"Goli, I need some work done fast. I'm on a time crunch. First, I emailed you some baby pictures earlier today. I need them identified. Second, I need you to securely get in touch with a colleague of mine, federal police in Australia…"

6:31 p.m.

Gideon arrives at the man's house—the final name on Susan's list. He walks up the long walkway to the front door. A man opens the door.

"Good evening, Mr. Gideon."

Gideon smirks. "So they called you already."

"The intelligence community is a small one. We all stay in close contact with each other," Smith says.

"I don't know why everyone is so paranoid. I'm just doing an investigation and everyone is treating me like a leper. We're on the same team. I'm actually working on your behalf."

"Why couldn't this wait until tomorrow then?"

"Can I come in so we can talk like normal people?"

Smith lets him enter and closes the door. He directs Gideon to sit down with him at the dining room table. He is a tall but slender and effeminate man with thinning gray hair. He is wrapped in a velvet robe and wearing casual, white pajama pants and velvet slippers.

Gideon decides to embellish his cover story a bit. "It is a critical issue because I'm not only investigating the disappearance of a former division director, but the fact that highly classified information may have been leaked into public channels. It has to be investigated now. You did work with Rabbi Susan?"

Smith looks at him. "I'm curious as to what prompted your investigation. Are you suggesting that she leaked information, even though she was fired over a decade ago?"

"I can't divulge any of that. But I do need your help."

Smith stands from his chair. "Who are you really working for?"

Gideon stands and points at him. "If you don't answer my questions, I won't report you; I'll have you taken into custody!"

Smith sits back down slowly.

Gideon sits down and says quietly in a nonthreatening manner, "I'm simply trying to find out what happened to her. I was told you worked with her. We can't have anything happening to government personnel—active and former. I need help putting all the pieces together."

Smith says, "I don't know anything."

"You're not cooperating with me."

"Call your superiors and have me arrested then."

Gideon shakes his head. "Why call anyone?" Gideon stands

again. He pulls his gun from his inside jacket holster and aims it at him. "Stand up!" Smith does so with a look of astonishment. "Turn around and clasp your hands together."

"What are you doing?"

"I'm placing you under arrest. I'll take you down to headquarters and we'll keep you in indefinite detention for failure to cooperate with a federal investigation." His cover story may be fake, but his power to arrest is very real. Cold handcuffs around one's wrists do have a very tangible quality to them, unlike words.

"Okay, I'll talk!" Gideon sits him back down. "It was so long ago. How can it possibly have anything to do with anything now?"

"What are you talking about?"

Smith just stares at him.

"Mr. Smith, what did you do for the government when Rabbi Susan was the division director?"

"I was a chief forensic psychologist at Langley."

"How did you two come into contact then? She was in the District, you in Virginia."

"Simple. She came to see me."

Gideon is intrigued. "Why?"

"She was interested in a research paper I had written for the sciences division."

"What was it about?"

"She wanted to know, hypothetically, how sophisticated our psychological conditioning for human beings was. I told her it was promising."

"Not the Manchurian candidate thing."

Smith laughs. "That's all science fiction. The only practical purpose for such a thing would be to create a Manchurian *soldier*. Mentally and psychologically increase the killing potential and eliminate any post-traumatic stress syndrome potential without the subject's knowledge. Take our military super-soldier programs to the next level. We're not there yet, though."

"But you said promising."

"Promising and possible are two different things."

"What else did she say or ask you?"

"She asked me, hypothetically, would it be harder or easier to condition…a human clone."

Gideon pauses. "A clone?"

"I told her that if such a thing were ever to become possible, meaning our genetic engineering capabilities had so advanced, that a human clone could potentially be far, far easier to condition, especially if it were possible to accelerate maturation. She asked if said clone could be made to believe itself to be whatever we wanted. I said, theoretically, yes. I knew it wasn't hypothetical, but I never did learn what she was directly talking about."

Gideon looks at him for a moment. "You're lying. You did find out."

Smith smiles. "Yes, I'm lying, Mr. Gideon. But then a liar like yourself has a natural ability to identify your own kind."

"Should I take out my handcuffs again? What is the meaning of that conversation you had with her?"

"You already know, Mr. Gideon. The fact that you're here tells me that. You're just trying to confirm what you suspect. Do you want to see them?"

Gideon looks at him for a moment as Smith smiles at him. Gideon now has a feeling that something is not quite right.

"Susan saved this baby on the day of its rebirth, as it had originally been created in a lab. A very unique baby. A group of people took the baby from her. Everybody in that medical office died except for that baby. The entire building burned down. The birth mother—no, the host surrogate—was part of a cult. She was actually a gifted scientist. It was all very amazing. Susan undoubtedly learned that the baby wasn't really a normal baby after all."

"You know quite a lot."

"I should," Smith says. "I was a member of the cult. Aren't you going to ask me more questions? Ask me more questions," Smith snaps. "You still don't realize how far out of your depth you are. A miniscule little ant on the sidewalk, about to be stepped on."

"I came here to be civil and conduct a professional investigation, but you want to be obstructive."

"You'll get what's coming to you."

Gideon stands again. "Did you just threaten me?" Gideon holds his face inches from Smith. "Did you just threaten me?"

"No."

"Threatening an officer of the United States Government is a felony."

"Or it could be an exercise of free speech."

"The only freedoms you have are those the government gives you." Gideon pauses. "See what?"

Smith is confused. "What?"

"What did you want me to see? You asked me if I wanted to see them before."

"Mr. Gideon, we're not stupid."

"Are you going to answer the question?"

"Did *you* make Rabbi Susan disappear, Mr. Gideon?"

Gideon ignores him. "Answer me!"

"As we speak, we're reviewing your full Registry file: family, associations, education, criminal background, work background, political ideology, spending history, debts, assets, sexual partners, secrets you don't want anyone to know. By tomorrow, it'll be over for you. You're dealing with seasoned national security men here. A very serious situation you stepped in. Your own people won't be able to save you."

"What do you want me to see? What do you mean?"

"Do you want to see the New People?"

"What are you talking about? What are the *New People?*"

Smith seems almost giddy, smiling.

"Are you helping me now?"

"Yes."

"Why?"

"I'll give you the address. When the tour is over, make sure to insist on being taken to the morgue. That will be the best part."

"Why are you helping me now all of a sudden?"

"I've always been a natural contrarian, predisposed to do the exact opposite of what I'm supposed to. Let's see how it works out for both of us."

Gideon realizes what's going on.

The front door is opened instantly from the inside by Gideon.

Standing there with his right hand reaching for the door, frozen, is the same stranger in the brown suit who had visited Gideon's place earlier that day. But Gideon's place is in Florida. This is Virginia. Why is this guy holding a large gun with a silencer in his other hand? And look at the stupid, surprised look on his face.

Gideon stares at the stranger, who smiles as if to relieve the tension.

"Are you the government assassin?" Gideon asks.

The stranger wants to laugh, but can't get over the awkwardness of his predicament. "Why would you say that? I would never work for the government."

"You're not here to kill me?" Gideon asks.

"Why would you think that?"

"You're holding a gun with a silencer."

"No, I came to kill the guy who lives here."

"But you came to my house in Florida."

"Oh, so you saw me?"

"Yes."

"That's very unfortunate."

Gideon aims his gun at the man. "Drop the gun and get down on your knees. Raise your hands above your head and clasp your fingers together."

"I'm wearing a bulletproof vest."

"Are you wearing an invisible bulletproof vest over your head?"

"No."

"Then do what I said."

"Is the other guy inside dead?"

"No, I knocked him unconscious so I could come to the door to see you."

"A purple, prickly, putrid pickle crawled up my pecker."

Gideon ducks instantly and dives at the stranger. The men fall backward down the three outside steps and crash to the ground. The men wrestle to get each other's gun.

Gideon trained with the best Faithers around, most notably the Shogun, and learned every kind of fighting technique: Karate, Aikido, Jiu-jitsu, Krav Maga, Taekwondo, et cetera. He preferred the wild, effective, and vicious close-combat, hybrid version of Spanish Keysi for multiple attackers and Brazilian Jiu-jitsu for ground fighting.

He lets the man take his gun away, but then suddenly and repeatedly smashes the man's Adam's apple with the incredible force of hammer fist punches. The stranger tries to yell out, but Gideon begins to beat the man's face not into unconsciousness, but into a coma. Gideon grabs the man and, using him as a shield, facing outward, moves back to the open door of Smith's house. He dives back in, ducks down, throws the man to the ground, and kicks the door closed.

Bullets rip through the door, into the back of the Stranger. His "purple pickle" word routine was the trigger-phrase for his unseen sniper accomplice.

Alliance of the Chosen

"When the American spirit was in its youth, the language of America was different: Liberty, sir, was the primary object." – Patrick Henry, attorney, politician, American Founding Father

"Whenever I hear the government say, 'I'm here to help you,' I immediately release the safety latch on my gun." – Shoshana, the Jewish Wolf Pack

Homeland Director's Office, Elizabeth Center, Anacostia, Washington DC
10:00 a.m., 4 June 2089

The tiny man sits in a chair, legs crossed. Homeland stands with her arms folded, angry. The President's advisor sits on the edge of the main desk.

"Why didn't you tell us this before?" she asks.

"Why didn't you tell us that you reassigned the Werewolf SS to Special Services?" the man answers with attitude.

"Why did you want to see us?" the President's advisor asks.

The tiny man opens up his portfolio with his tab and looks at the screen. "A concern. Agent Lycan was not only drugged, but he may have been probed. We found a microscopic puncture on his right arm. The puncture was deep enough to go to the bone. It is possible they only collected a blood sample—the hurried, incompetent technique of an amateur—for their own DNA database on our agents or…"

"Or what?" Homeland asks.

"They were collecting a deep-gene sample."

"Why is that a concern?" the President's advisor asks.

"If they had the know-how and the equipment, they could reverse-engineer the sample and discover that that our agent is a *modified* human. With that knowledge they could do many things."

"They do not have that kind of tek," Homeland says.

The tiny man stands. "I'm happy that you are so sure. I was on the debrief team for the Kansas Event. Do you remember that one, back in '76? I believe the Jew-Christians sucked up an entire air attack force into a…tornado."

"That's not what happened," the President's Advisor says emphatically.

The man smiles again. "Well, I will let you all continue with your op and I'll just return to my basement office. I see everything is in control."

The President's advisor adds, "Tiny, I'm instructing you not to share what you told us with Agent Lycan, his team, or anyone else."

"I hope, sir, that you both are clearly cognizant of the bigger picture here. We're not talking about the compromising of a single agent or a team of agents, but rather that unauthorized persons may have access to information of the highest level of classification and knowledge directly related to this nation's Two-War strategic readiness plans. I must insist, sir, that we bring the President into this conversation, as I believe Project New People has been compromised."

Key West Command, Key West, Florida
7:31 a.m., 5 June 2089

Lycan's eyes burn with rage as he sits in his chair. He sits at the head of the rectangular conference table with his entire team of black-clad mercenaries; the only outsider is a civilian to his right in a suit. Except for this civilian, all of them are not only abnormally muscular, but some have unnaturally elongated limbs and unnaturally large hands and feet.

Homeland's face is on the main vid-screen at the front of the room. "Why was this initial switch made with this Louvel person?" she asks, casting a displeased gaze at them.

"We had them under surveillance for several months," the civilian answers. "Of all things, he had a blind date with our terrorist, one of those random opportunities out of nowhere. A perfect chance to infiltrate by substituting Agent Lycan."

"Obviously, it wasn't as random as you thought. They seem to be much smarter than we are. Smarter than you." She looks back down at her report. "They used Agent Lycan's access to breach the Supermax Florence facility."

"Yes, all perimeter barriers, gates, and doors."

"They broke out…more than one thousand prisoners."

"All Jew-Christians."

Homeland continues. "The man who was impersonating the female terrorist target?"

"An insignificant local drug addict. They hired him for the job. Paid him in drugs to lead us on a wild-goose chase. We're convinced he knew nothing more.

Homeland says, "Traces on the weapons, cars, explosives, ammo?"

"Nothing as of yet, but the investigation is moving rapidly."

"Surveillance? Satellite?"

"They were all wearing masks that blocked any facial recognition."

"What happened with Agent Lycan?"

Lycan is angry that she's talking as if he's not even in the room, but he remains quiet.

"He was definitely drugged so that she could slip away, and they had the druggie stand in."

"Was this Iron Rose actually our primary target of this…Jewish Wolf Pack?"

"Not conclusively confirmed, but we do believe so."

"Do we know their whereabouts?"

"They eluded all tails and surveillance. But we have solid leads: Colorado, Texas, Idaho, the Dakotas."

"So this operation, which was supposed to round up the entire Jewish Wolf Pack organization—a designated domestic terrorist group—in one night, has instead become one in which we've lost all of them completely, lost some one thousand federal prisoners, and a major federal prison facility, one of the best in the nation, has been rendered unusable for the present time.

Homeland shakes her head slowly. "We had heard so many great things about you, Agent Lycan. We brought you into the circle. Are the vaunted Werewolf super soldiers no better than pathetic Vampires?"

Lycan smirks. "Maybe if you keep all your alphabet soup people away from me and let me run my op, we'll make this right, and the Jew-Christian slag and all the targets will be taken down." Even though the Homeland Defense and Intelligence Agency was the merging of the old CIA, FBI, NSA, and a dozen other separate federal law enforcement agencies of the past. They were now specialized departments within the super organization.

Homeland says, "You mean *capture* the targets."

Lycan responds, "I obviously meant that."

Homeland continues. "Then let's find them."

Lycan says, "No, *I'll* find them."

Kibbutzim, Idaho
7:45 a.m., 5 January 2090

In former Jewish Israel there were many kibbutzim, collective communities that were traditionally centered on agriculture and were self-sustaining. After the Fall of Jewish Israel, millions of Jews re-settled all across America, mostly in the South and West. However, some of the more radical elements settled in the Northwest. Kibbutzim here are totally self-sufficient enclaves arranged in a network of compounds, each with a specific purpose: living, agriculture, livestock, water, defense, schools, vehicles, etcetera.

This entire kibbutzim is under large anti-satellite camouflage nets. Near the main gate, Tova Ben-Hurin sits in one of the communal waiting areas. She is middle-aged and a senior elder in the Conservative Jewish Order. Three of the skinhead Wolf Pack members stand across from her; one of them holds a vicious German shepherd on a leash. Tova is uncomfortable, but she smiles at the watching dog.

Shoshana enters the waiting room, sipping from her metal Klingon cup. "Shalom, Fraulein. What can we do for you on God's fine day today?"

Tova stands. "Shalom. Rabbi Oren is expecting me."

"You're of the Conservative Jewish Order."

"Yes, Tova Ben-Hurin. And you must be Shoshana, a member of the Jewish Wolf Pack."

She smiles. "No. I *run* the Jewish Wolf Pack."

"You all used to wear those wolf-head masks."

Shoshana laughs. "That was years ago. We wore wolf-head masks with a big Star of David in the center of the chest, and claw attachments for the hands. I used to dress like Red Riding Hood. I loved that long flowing red cape. I still sometimes wear it for special, casual occasions. We had to stop that, though. Once flagged by the government, with their surveillance Eyes and drones and satellite scans, they could zero in on us in seconds if we appeared in public. So we changed uniforms."

"Red Riding Hood and the Seven Wolves," Tova says. "I've notice your group speaks a lot of German, or English mixed with German words. Why do you do that?"

"We find it amusing. As we find the Gestapo amusing."

"Gestapo? Who's that? Your nickname for what?"

"Government storm troopers, of course, in the employ of the Fuhrer."

Tova takes a deep breath. The current President T. Wilson is indeed hated by all Faithers. The Christians called him Galerius, after the ancient Roman Emperor who was the most vicious murderer of Christians. Mormons called him President Boggs, after the Missouri Governor who issued an extermination order of all Mormons in 1838 America and forcibly expelled thousands from the state. Jewish Orders called him Haman after Haman the Evil, who was a fifth century BC noble of the Persian Empire who instigated a plot to kill all of the Jews of ancient Persia, but was foiled by Queen Esther.

"Please tell me that you don't talk like this in public with outsiders."

"We are in public now."

"Please don't call him Fuhrer, Hitler, or any derivation of that."

"Everyone else calls him President Haman."

"That's different."

"We're different."

"Such language makes us look like extremists."

Shoshana smiles. "I am an extremist. What about you?"

"Jews should not be fixated on World War Two Nazis."

"We're not, the world is. They won't let them die. Before the Islamic Caliphate assimilated Western Europe, do you know what their most popular books were? Nazis, history of Nazis, all about Hitler, justification for the Holocaust, Nazi Vampire Bitches from Planet Nine. The Caliphate takes over Germany and what do they do? Rename it Germania just as Hitler planned to do. I hear they still make movie comedies about Nazis in Arabic."

Tova thinks for a moment. "But the Audition for Springtime for Hitler was one of the funniest things I ever did see, though."

"What?"

"Never mind. My father used to tell me as child, 'Get your mind out of the concentration camp, Jewish princess of God.'"

"I used to tell my father as a child, 'Never forget they burned us in ovens and used our ashes as fertilizer.'"

Tova stares at her for a moment, wondering if Shoshana is just toying with her.

"You're far too pessimistic for your age," Tova says.

"You're far too optimistic for your age," Shoshana says. She smiles. "The makings of a great friendship. Why are you such a long way from your nice, cushy enclave in Alabama?"

The people wait in a sunny, cozy communal home. Rabbi Hendel sits on a couch with his wife holding his hand on one side, and his children on the other, his eldest son closest. His wife wears a long black skirt and a long-sleeved shirt with a high neckline. Her head is covered with a white scarf.

Around them on either side are other Hasidic men, some seated in chairs, others standing. All the men, including Rabbi Hendel, are wearing dark suits with white shirts and black fedoras. They have continued their custom of tying their side-locks into ponytails rather than the standard tradition of having them dangle down the sides of their face. Across the room, waiting, are members of the Orthodox Jewish Order.

At the door stand several skin-head members of the Jewish Wolf Pack clad in black tops with a Star of David in the center, black military fatigue pants with fully armed holstered belts, combat boots, and leather jackets. One of them stands by himself on one side of the window. Another stands closest to the door with a German shepherd on a leash, crouched down to the floor, staring at everyone.

Hasidic, Orthodox, and the Jewish Wolf Pack all wait in the room; no one says a word.

The door opens and Rabbi Oren, the leader of the Orthodox, enters with Tova.

Tova notices. "Another big dog I could almost ride like a horse."

Another rabbi enters, followed by Shoshana. He walks over to Rabbi Hendel with a smile and extends his hand as he greets him in Hebrew. "*Yom tov, Rebbe.*"

Rabbi Hendel rises with his wife and shakes his hand. "Yom tov," he says. "I can no longer, in clear conscience, hold to the title of Rebbe. Rabbi is fine."

"I understand. I'm Rabbi Kanter, the leader of the religious order at this enclave." He turns to Shoshana. "Please have the dog wait outside."

Shoshana motions to her man, who exits the room with the large German shepherd.

"I apologize. The dogs are part of our community's overall security."

Rabbi Hendel says, "We will happily adjust to life here. You need not make any special considerations for us."

"In Old Italy the Christian Catholics have a special security force to protect the Vatican, the Swiss Guard," Rabbi Kanter informs him. "The Wolf Pack is our special security force and, as you've learned first-hand, they are quite capable in other, more provocative operations. However, you really have Rabbi Oren to thank for making the case and convincing us to rescue all of you. It was a massive operation."

Rabbi Hendel says to both men, "Thank you for giving me back to my family, giving us all back to our families. God bless you both."

Mrs. Hendel asks, teary-eyed, "Why would the Orthodox do this for us?"

Rabbi Oren answers, "We felt that circumstances were so grave that it required the Orthodox to do something we don't normally do—get involved on behalf of another Order. We couldn't allow you to sit in prison when you helped so many of our members escape the government those horrible days."

Rabbi Hendel asks in a quavering voice, "Rabbi did we…do the right thing?"

Rabbi Oren doesn't hesitate. "God said, 'Cursed are those who curse Israel.' Doubly so for those traitors who dare called themselves Jews. What has the world come to when you had Muslims in Israel helping Jews escape, and Jews here in America cheering at the Fall of Israel? Give no thought to what happened. They are not worthy of your attention or your remorse."

He turns to Tova. "I do want to introduce you to Tova Ben-Hurin. She is here not in her capacity as an elder in the Conservative Order, but in her professional role as a psychologist and counselor for almost twenty-five years. You, your family, your people need help. She can help you and bring others here who can help you. That's what we need to do. Help each other."

Rabbi Kanter says, "Rabbinic authorities in the late eighteenth century said of the Hasidim, 'They conduct themselves like madmen; in their behavior, every day is for them a holiday. When they pray, they raise such a din that the walls quake.'" He smiles. "We want those Jews back, the transmitters of unconditional joy."

Rabbi Hendel smiles. "Yes, we will accept the help."

Tova adds, "Besides, among Jews you are the only ones who can really dance."

Rabbi Hendel smiles as his family and people laugh.

Rabbi Kanter says, "Your people can stay here as long as you need or want. Don't worry about anything but rebuilding your community."

Rabbi Hendel and the other Chabadniks profusely thank them all again. The Hasidim are led out of the room by the Orthodox. Wolf Pack security follows.

Kanter, Oren, Tova, and Shoshana remain behind. They close the door again.

Rabbi Oren says to Kanter, "We thank you again for housing them and their families. We will provide any assistance you need."

"Thank you."

Rabbi Oren says, "I never imagined that this operation would be so successful. But how are we going to do this? You can hide a few people or even a couple of dozen, but how can we possibly shelter thousands of people from the government? All of us will be at risk. The government still has all Jews aged thirteen and older designated as *persons of interest*."

Tova says, "They did the same with the Christians. Now they're focused on us."

Rabbi Oren says, "To their bigoted eyes we're all the same."

Shoshana adds, "*Wehrkraftzersetzung*."

Tova asks, "What does that mean?"

Shoshana continues. "The Nazis used to create crimes out of thin air to charge people with. *Wehrkraftzersetzung*: the crime of negatively affecting the state. Anyone they wanted to destroy, for whatever reason. Now the new Gestapo has their new phrases."

Rabbi Kanter says, "They'll be safe here. We can protect them and we've made all the arrangements. Our entire community is ready and prepared."

Shoshana says, "Everything we do is well-planned in every detail. If it reassures you, all Wolf Pack members come from military, intelligence, and law enforcement families. I'm third-generation Mossad myself. I was the only surviving child to carry on my father's service tradition."

Rabbi Oren nods.

Tova says, "The operation was very impressive, but…"

Shoshana says, "Thank you, Tova. Sounds like a 'but' with a big butt is coming."

Tova smiles slightly. "They've increased your ranking on the Terror Watch List."

Shoshana laughs loudly. "I don't care what the Gestapo does. My name moves up the Terrorist Watch List. I'll get non-stop marriage proposals now."

Tova says, "We've been through the Fall of Israel and three civil wars in less than a decade. We have to be honest. It has weakened all the Orders."

Shoshana declares, "Israel will be reborn one day. Have no doubt about it."

Rabbi Oren asks, "What do you have in mind?

Tova answers, "We have to do more than survive."

Rabbi Oren says, "Persecution is an old story for us and we always survive and advance, even despite ourselves."

Tova says, "I want to ensure that is the case. I view this coming together to help the Hasidim as a sign of something greater. Why not formalize a new alliance?"

Rabbi Oren shakes his head. "Politics? Politics has been the most disastrous thing to Jews since the Fall, Pagans, and Muslims. Not interested."

"Oren, this isn't politics. It's all about mutual survival. If we aren't unified, our decline will continue," Tova says.

Rabbi Oren asks, "Is this your idea or the Wise Men's?"

Tova looks at him with confusion. "What do they have to do with this?"

"They're part of your Order. They're your best friends. They're the godfathers to your children," Oren answers.

Tova says, "I know you have always had problems with them, but this is my idea. We haven't even spoken to them in months."

Rabbi Kanter asks Oren, "Why do you have a problem with the Wise Men? We are still feeling our way through all the players in the community."

Oren says, "Don't let me influence you."

Kanter presses. "No, seriously, I respect your opinions."

Tova says, "You can speak freely. I know how you feel about them."

Oren says, "There are two kinds of Jews: those who believe being a Jew is about God, the Torah, and our faith. And those who believe being a Jew is *only* about looking for the next Big Anti-Semite or the next Hitler, and if they are not there to be seen, they imagine them and manufacture their existence. I am old enough to remember the time before President Haman and his ilk seized power. The Wise Men were the biggest offenders. I called them out when they called Rabbi Susan a Hitler. And you know how much I despised that woman. They called everybody they didn't like a Hitler. It may seem counterintuitive for me to say these things now, with the state of the country against us today, but my father told me when I was a very young child: 'Do not cry wolf, ever, Oren. Because if you do, when the real wolves come, you will have no language to use to rally the people against them.' My father was right. The real wolves came and we weren't ready. Language matters. But let's end this part of the conversation here. As you said, you know how I feel."

Shoshana says, "It's better if we are not unified. They won't be able to hit all of us if we're not one big target."

Tova says, "Shoshana, the Jewish people have survived only because we were united. 'United we stand, divided we fall.'"

Shoshana smirks. "Yes, Abraham Lincoln."

Tova says, "A good Christian with a Jewish name."

Oren says, "I appreciate what you want to do, Tova, but…"

Tova adds, "Yes, I believe you tried to do so in the past."

"Yes, and it went no place. I believe your own Conservative Order was very hostile to the idea."

"Don't blame me for that. My husband and I weren't on the Council yet. That has all changed."

Oren says, "We have to chart our own path. Besides, let's be honest. Most of the Orders are weak, slow to act, paralyzed by fear, and some have government informants."

"Informants? Are you referring to the Conservatives, Oren?" Tova asks.

"You don't honestly believe the excommunication of Rabbi Susan and her disciples solved the problem of government collaboration?"

"Yes, I do."

Shoshana says, "Tova, ultimately our groups have different philosophies. Ours is *Frieden durch Angst*, Peace through Fear. Our enemies will respect us only when they fear us. Are Jews feared? Back when we were called Israelites, we were feared throughout the known world as fierce warriors. We bested the ancient Greeks, could have even defeated the ancient Romans if not for their numerical superiority. Then we devolved to the lowest of lows when five pathetic Nazis could tell five hundred Jews to get on an empty train bound for the concentration camp, and we'd voluntarily do so. No, Tova, for too many of the Orders, the philosophy is still Peace through Hiding, Peace through Negotiating, Peace through Concessions for Nothing. Even after all we've been through. Israel followed that path and look what it led to. And still people cling to that path. We never will."

Tova says, "I couldn't agree more, which is why I want us to create our own Continuum, a unity of all the Jewish Orders. Our faith allies have already done so and it's to all our benefit if we do too."

Shoshana says, "You mean the Christians."

"Yes, the Christians mostly, but others."

Rabbi Oren says, "You spend a lot of time with them."

"I do."

Rabbi Oren says, "Now we come to your real inspiration. Are you doing this to copy the Christians?"

Tova says, "I'm doing this to fulfill my father's dream, just as you tried to do so yourself to fulfill your father's dream. You knew my father."

"Yes."

"He was convinced that the *only* thing that could destroy Jews was not the Muslims or the Pagans, but our own lack of unity."

"Tova, I believe you are setting yourself up for heartbreak again," Oren says.

Tova asks, "If we organize the meeting, will all of you at least come, hear us out, help us get everyone there?"

They are silent.

She says, "It must end, all this doing separate things. Look what we can accomplish together. We can make this Jewish Continuum a reality."

"For what purpose?" Oren asks. "We have escaped their wicked tek-cities for the sanctuary of our own communities. And now we have liberated our brothers and sisters."

Tova says, "The one thing all of us have in common in this room is instinct. We perceive things happening long before others do. That's why we're leaders. The persecution is increasing. Their lies against us are increasing. The surveillance is increasing. We don't have to live in their tek-cities to see what is happening. Our enemies have an alliance. Why in God's name would we not create our own alliance? It doesn't matter if we tried and failed in the past. We keep trying until we make it stick. Something is coming and we all know it. And this isn't me or the Conservatives 'crying wolf.'" Tova looks at her. "Shoshana, you have an extensive intelligence network out there, and though you pretend to be this over-emotional extremist, I know you are a disciplined, pragmatic, level-headed person who never lets her feelings cloud her decisions. What are your Mossad-family, Wolf Pack instincts telling you?"

Shoshana smiles. Guess she really has been peering into people's souls for decades. "For the last tribes of Abraham, Moses, and Jacob, the wolves are coming."

The Last Tribes of Abraham, Moses, and Jacob

"God, I know we are your Chosen People, but couldn't you choose somebody else for a change?" – Sholom Aleichem, Yiddish writer and playwright

"The identity of Jews cannot be defined by tragedy, persecution, and permanent victimhood. Otherwise Misery becomes our God and not God Himself. I'm not speaking of ignoring our full history or real threats. I'm speaking about recognizing our full significance as a People and that to be a Jew is so much more. If we allow only the bad to be our reality, then forget our children and our children's children, I wouldn't want to be a Jew." – Rabbi Kanter, the Shamar (Jewish) Order

Department of Homeland Defense and Intelligence Agency Security Dispatch / 7 January 2090

Informant has learned that key leaders of Jew-Christians will be meeting in secret at an off-Grid Alabama settlement. Exact time, date, and location to be determined. Strong possibility that federal prison fugitives from Florence Supermax prison break will be in attendance. Notify LYCAN.

Little Israel Jewish Enclave, Gadsden, Alabama
7:52 a.m., 2 April 2090

Tova's day is here! It's rare to gather representatives from all the American Jewish Orders in one place. The walled city of Little Israel controls the region and is surrounded by open land, so any and all possible intruders can be seen for miles away. There are also large Christian enclaves nearby, providing further safety from Pagans and the government.

The site chosen is a large, two-level barn, converted by one of the community families to an open town hall space. As with any real Faither meeting, two things must be present before any business takes place: God and food. Plenty of good food and giving thanks to God.

An army of volunteers has been working on the setup for the last three days. Security has been working on the event for the last few months. The adults are done with the major work, so the children are allowed into the space.

Tova walks in to survey the setup. The food is on the main tables, with Jewish children standing ready to serve. All the entrances are guarded by armed men. The meeting table itself is a large round table. One of the dogs, a golden-haired terrier, gets in for a moment, but before he can get at the food, he is chased out by some of the children.

Tova is plainly but sharply dressed in black and white, a nice one-piece dress with a band-belt. The belt has a gun holster that is never empty.

One of the men walks in. "They're here."

The first to arrive is Rabbi Oren of the Orthodox Jewish Order with his five-person delegation. In the pre-modern era, the Orthodox constituted less than 10 percent of Jews in America; now they are more than 30 percent, making them the second-largest

Jewish Order. All the men wear black: long buttoned coats, shoes, pants, kippot on their heads. All have full beards and mustaches.

Tova greets him with a simple nod, her hands held together, as the Orthodox don't touch women—not their wives or family, as is their religious custom. She directs them to the food table.

The Arab-Persian Jewish Order is the second group to arrive. The traditional term for them is the Mizrahi, Jews of the Arab world. Rabbi Haza of the Arabic Jews looks very similar to the Orthodox in dress, though with a much fuller and larger beard and darker skin. Haza's family roots are in Egypt, but his ancestors fled the country over a century ago.

Rabbi Nahai of the Persian Jews wears a black kippah too, but is dressed in a black suit with vest, a white shirt with a brown tie, and brown leather shoes. Most of the Persian Jews are from Iran, a small percentage from Iraq.

Both Orders had been in the United States for centuries, but the number of Persian Jews rose dramatically after the fall of secular Iran to Islamists in the 1970s. The next major wave was after the formation of the Islamic Caliphate with the fall of Western Europe. The last major waves of Arabic Jews fleeing to America, along with Arab Christians and Coptic Christians, started in the 2020s.

Everyone is greeting each other and eating when the Goth Jews arrive. Tova knows this will be the first significant tension within the group for the day. The Goth Jews are viewed by some Jewish Orders as nothing but Pagans in black clothes and black makeup. They don't wear religious head cover and the men have no facial hair of any kind. Their leader, Mikel, arrives with two other Goths. Tova greets them with handshakes.

Shoshana of the Jewish Wolf Pack arrives next with six other skinheads—the second tension of the day—in their customary military fatigue pants and jackets, black combat boots, and black t-shirts with a Star of David in the center. Shoshana has a necklace with a Star of David. All of them wear waist holsters: gun on the right, knife on the left. Tova greets them.

Rabbi Henriques arrives next with one other member. He is dressed in a nice but simple brown suit and brown kippah on his head. He seems to be an almost meek man, which is in direct contrast to the thunderous sermons he gives at his main synagogue in the Florida Panhandle. The Judeo-Spanish Order can best be described as traditional Jews whose worship is greatly influenced by their native cultures of the Spanish Americas: Mexico, Central America, and South America.

Rabbi Hendel of the Hasidic Order and his group arrive next. They look very similar to the Orthodox in dress, but wear black fedoras instead. Their now-customary side-locks are tied back into ponytails.

The Israeli Jewish Order arrives next, the third major tension for the day. Almost a dozen men are led by their leader, Yisrael. Only a few wear kippot and all are dressed business casual, suits with no ties. Tova suspects that they waited in their cars so that they would be the last group to arrive. With the fall of Jewish Israel, Israelis fled by the millions, mostly to America, though most harbored a deep hatred for the country that abandoned them to the Caliphate.

What should have been a natural union between Israeli and American Jews was anything but. Israeli Jews are disliked because of their perceived hyper-aggressiveness and desire to "take over" all Jewish power centers in America. At least that was the claim. A common saying of sympathy is: "We can't blame them. The Fall of Jewish-Israel made us all lose our minds, but they lost even more." The dislike is mutual, as Israeli Jews felt that most American Jews were "spoiled," "weak," "over-privileged," and "never truly connected to the Motherland." Israeli Jews are now the largest Jewish Order in America.

Finally, there is Tova's Conservative Jewish Order, the hosts of this national meeting. Everyone is seated at the Round Table. "*Shalom and Yom Tov*! Rabbi Oren will lead us in prayer," Tova says to start the meeting.

Everyone stands and Rabbi Oren says, "Are there any objections to my saying it in Hebrew?"

No one objects, though Mikel feels that he is referring to the Goth Jews.

Rabbi Oren gives a short but uplifting prayer in Hebrew, praising God, the day, the group, and the meeting they are about to convene.

Shoshana interjects in Hebrew, "And all the Jewish people say together: Amen!" Rabbi Oren gives a slight smile. Tova continues. "I also want us to keep in our hearts, minds, and prayers all the Jews trapped within Islamic Caliphate territory. One day we will all be united."

The group acknowledges her words with yeses and nods.

"Please be seated," Tova says. As everyone sits, she motions to the children standing quietly in the background. Tova starts again. "There was this great planetary spaceship built, called the USS Exodus, because a series of disasters came upon the Earth. Godzilla was rampaging, burning buildings and vehicles and people to a crisp. Aliens from Planet Star Wars were invading, snatching up humans to be slaves. Zombies were attacking all over the world, devouring humans. People were panicking like crazy, trying to get on the spaceship to escape. In one of the many lines of people to get on the spaceship, some of the panicking people noticed a little man standing patiently, waiting his turn to board. Another man asked him, 'Why aren't you panicking like everyone else?' The little man turned to him and said, 'I'm a Jew. We've been dealing with disasters for over five thousand years. This is nothing.'"

The group smiles and laughs. Children start placing pitchers of ice water in front of each delegation.

Tova continues, "I think that's a good joke to start our meeting. Despite the trials we've faced, we must retain our determination in dealing with them. I'd like to go around the table and introduce everyone. I don't believe everyone knows everyone else."

Yisrael interrupts, "Before we do that, Tova, I'd like to ask about some of your guests. Why do you have these Pagan Jews and Nazi Jews here? What kind of new Jewish Council is this going to be? Some kind of United Nations of Jews?"

Tova responds quickly. "That is deeply offensive. This will not be a United Nations of anything." Few things got under the skin of Jews more than the mention of the organization that became defunct after the Fall of Western Europe to the Muslims. Many felt the UN paved the way for the formation of the Islamic Caliphate, and later the Fall of Jewish Israel. "Maybe you'd prefer a version of the Old Knesset?"

"No, I wouldn't," Yisrael answers. "No one in our Order is missing all that useless yelling with very little ever getting done."

Goth Mikel's face is still red at Yisrael calling him a "Pagan Jew" and is about to say something, but Tova motions him not to. "Yisrael, everyone here is essential to the success of this new council. Years ago, Rabbi Oren tried to do this very same thing, but as we all know, we were sidetracked nine years ago. You don't want certain groups here? Good, let's talk about it."

"Maybe the Israeli Jews shouldn't be here," says Rabbi Hendel.

Yisrael glares at him. Rabbi Hendel keeps his gaze down into his folded hands.

Tova says, "Our goal here is to create a strong alliance of all the Jewish Orders. Our enemies are unified against us. We must be equally unified. First, the Goth Jews are here because we must have Lot Jews on the Council. They live in the Tek World, while most of us don't. We need the edge, the intelligence they can bring to the table. As for the Wolf Pack—"

Shoshana stares at Yisrael. "I am a *devout* Jew and I will not tolerate anyone suggesting otherwise."

Yisrael says, "By dressing up as Nazis?"

Shoshana snaps, "We don't and have never dressed as Nazis. We dress to intimidate non-Jews. It's our way. The Wolf Pack's sole purpose is to defend Jews."

Yisrael says, "We know how to defend ourselves and we don't need you."

Shoshana says, "You are doing such a wonderful job of it with half your ranks sitting in jail as a result of the government's jihad against us. None of my people are in jail or dead in the ground."

Just in time! The children are placing food in front of each person at the table. Tova smiles as she looks at them. The children's presence seems to momentarily calm the conversation.

Rabbi Oren asks, "May we skip this line of discussion for more important concerns?"

Tova asks, "Such as?"

Rabbi Oren looks at her. "You?"

Tova asks, "Meaning?"

Rabbi Oren answers, "The Conservatives took in all those Reform traitors and your Conservative traitors were allowed to stay. Honestly, we view your whole Order as illegitimate." Tova is taken aback. "Oren, you never pull any punches, do you? I thought this was resolved years ago. I can assure you that it is not a legitimate concern. There was great turmoil within the Conservatives over this matter. The Reformers who did come to us and begged us to accept them were given a full hearing. We examined what they did—"

Rabbi Oren says, "You mean their crimes."

Tova says, "Okay, their crimes. And we decided to forgive many and allow them back, but with conditions."

Rabbi Oren is upset. "Why? They wanted to collaborate with the Pagans against all of us. They should have been excommunicated for life!"

Tova says, "Oren, it was a painful thing for us. You know that. We had Conservatives who were so angry and against it, like you, that they left our communities. We don't know where they are, or if they're safe. The Reformers who joined us, and the Conservatives who had aligned themselves with Pagans, live in a separate part of the enclave. For forty years is the agreement. They live by our laws and our rules. They are not allowed to hold any leadership in the community. That is fair, Oren. What would you have us do? A fellow Jew comes to you crying their eyes out, begging for forgiveness, yelling they were wrong and they will do anything to be united with their people, that we can't cast them back out into Pagan-land. That they would rather die. There were families that said to us that if we didn't take them back they wanted to die, but that we should take and raise their children. They were deadly serious! Oren, this damn thing nearly destroyed the entire Conservative Order, but I stand by our solution."

Shoshana says, "I agree with Rabbi Oren. This is the same kind of mindset that led to the Fall of Israel. Jews so wanting the world to like them, wanting to be compassionate, accepting standards no one else would accept, sticking their heads in the sand at any transgression against them, ignoring blood libels against them, forgiving and coddling their enemies. Being nice. Look what it got us: the end of our Homeland. No, Tova, I can't agree with you. Actions must have consequences. If you want to create a true union of all the Jewish Orders, we have to be ruthless. Bad people don't respect niceness. All of them should have been cast out. Otherwise, we are mocked. 'I almost helped destroy all the Jews in the nation, but if I give a good performance with fake tears, my fellow Jews will take me back.' No! Throw them out. Throw them in a ditch where they belong."

Tova shakes her head. "We didn't take everyone back. Some were excommunicated for life."

Shoshana asks, "How many?"

Tova says, "What does it matter?" She shakes her head again. "You all were not there! You don't know what the deliberations were like! We had violent fistfights among the council. You have no idea what our Order had to go through!"

No one speaks for a moment.

Rabbi Henriques speaks, "Tova, you did the right thing for your Order. We had similar issues that we had to deal with. What does a community do with its collaborators? Kill them, expel them, forgive them?"

Tova says, "What did you do?"

Rabbi Henriques says, "We expelled all of them. But unlike your Order, we were less sure about our decision. There is never a day that has passed that we wonder if we did the right thing. All you can do is make the decision you believe is right."

Rabbi Haza says, "I must say that I also agree with Rabbi Oren, but not for the same reasoning. My concern is ongoing security threats, ongoing collaboration with the Pagans. It's not my place to second guess your Order's decision, but for the sake of this new alliance that we are trying to create, there must be a constant consideration as to information we want to remain secret, away from the Pagans, Muslims, or any other outsider. And this isn't an attack on your Order. It goes for all of us."

Shoshana says, "Yes, quislings among us."

Rabbi Nahai says, "Well, that's not a good start to this. Be afraid of our own communities, our own people because there may be spies, though we have no proof of it."

Yisrael says, "That's what being a leader entails, making the hard decisions. And I take great offense as to why Jewish Israel fell." He stares directly at Shoshana. "It was not because we were weak."

Shoshana says, "Yes it was. Be an adult and take responsibility."

Yisrael stands up and slaps the table with his hand. "What do you know?"

Shoshana smirks. "I know that the reason for the creation of Israel was to give Jews a Homeland to be free of anti-Semitic persecution. We get a Homeland and then we give it away piece by piece to be free of anti-Semitic persecution. Including, my personal favorite, the outrageous and unforgivable offense of taking terrorists, murderers of our innocent people, who should have been executed, but whom you instead put in prison for life, supposedly, only to habitually release scot-free to murder more innocent Jews. Pathetic! If the Wolf Pack were running Israel, we wouldn't have allowed the Muslims or Pagan Western Europe roll over us like we were a fat whore lying prostrate on the ground."

Yisrael yells, "Shut up!"

Shoshana stands. "Come here and shut my mouth for me!"

Yisrael kicks his chair to the ground and walks to the main entrance to leave.

"Yisrael! Get back to the table!" Tova yells.

Yisrael stops. "Not until she leaves!"

"Everyone is allowed to speak their mind. If I can take it, then you can. Sit back down. But maybe women are tougher than men."

Yisrael stops angrily for a moment at the entrance. Some of his men pick up his chair.

Tova says, "We don't have to solve all our issues in one sitting, but we have to have that dialog. And none of you have to roll your eyes. I know how negative that word *dialog* is to us. I don't mean endless talk with never a solution in sight. I do mean solving the small stuff first and then the harder things. We must be willing, to use another dirty word, to *compromise* in some way. If we were all the same, then we'd all be the same Order. Can we continue, or do we need a break?"

"A break," Yisrael utters. He promptly walks out. His men get up and follow.

Others rise slowly and walk to the food or outside for air.

Mikel stands and says, "Everyone yelling at each other. Well, at least we know this is an *authentic* Jewish meeting." Tova smiles. He walks out with his fellow Goth Jews.

Rabbi Henriques says, "My goodness, there is a lot of anger in this room."

Tova says, "Yes, there is."

Henriques says, "I really admire what you are trying to do."

Tova asks, "Ever had to deal with this?"

Henriques smiles. "There aren't enough Hispanic Jews in this country, or the world, to be blessed with having to deal with real crises."

Tova says, "You may be a relatively small community, but you are a very tight-knit community, so you are blessed in that way."

Henriques says, "Hopefully, we survive. We have the same problem that Jews have had historically—losing our youth to Paganism. For us, it used to be Catholicism. Now it's Paganism."

Tova says, "Let's get some air too." She looks to the remaining members and they all walk outside together.

Thirty minutes later everyone is back at the table.

Tova, still standing behind her chair, says, "Ladies and gentleman, the man in the back is my current husband, Mister Tova."

They all look and notice the man. He is in his fifties and balding, but very muscular, strong, confident. His skin is tan and he is dressed business casual.

Rabbi Nahai asks, perplexed, "What do you mean your current husband? How long have you been married?"

Tova says, "Thirty-two years, six children and ten grandchildren. But he knows that he has to always behave himself or I'll throw him to the curb and get me one of those twenty-something Jewish male studs."

The group laughs.

Mr. Tova says humorously, "This is what I have to contend with! She's always threatening me." He eats his plate of food standing up.

Tova says, "I would like to go back to what we didn't do at the beginning: have everyone introduce themselves. So you at least know who you're yelling at or being yelled at by."

They go around the table and introduce themselves and their Orders.

Yisrael says to Rabbi Hendel, "What was that crack you made about Israelis before? We shouldn't be here? I'd expect that kind of comment from the Arabs."

Rabbi Haza snaps, "Why would you say that? That is hitting lower than below the belt and is uncalled for, Yisrael." All the Jewish Orders had long ago removed the term "Arab" as a pejorative from the common language in respect to the Arab Jewish and Arab Christian Orders.

Yisrael half-apologizes, "You know what I mean."

Rabbi Hendel focuses on Yisrael and says, "You know why."

Tova interjects. "Please, gentlemen, let's not fight again."

Yisrael ignores her. "I wouldn't ask if I did."

Rabbi Haza says, "I see you haven't lost your ability to alienate all the Jews around you."

Rabbi Hendel says, "My people told me what you did while we

were in prison. You all took land from us that we had been waiting years to acquire. You came in and intimidated the local city council and got them to give you the area that was supposed to be for us."

Yisrael angrily says, "So we stole land? We're going to have the entire Palestinian Lie—"

The group objects. "No." "Not that word!"

He continues. "The Muslim Lie then, of land stealing."

Rabbi Hendel says, "That's not what I said or even implied. You purposely took land we were going to purchase and used underhanded, back-room politics to do so. I should add, against other Jews."

Yisrael turns. "We survived a war and had millions of people to settle. How many people does your Order have? A handful. Of course, we had to take priority."

Rabbi Hendel stands. "I would remind you that every member of the Chabad Hasidim in Israel fought in the war to save it. We have the graves to prove it. You Israelis seem to have a genetic inability to distinguish us from those anti-Israel Hasidim who actively supported the end of our Homeland. We were the first to excommunicate them."

Tova says softly, "He knows that. He didn't mean that."

Rabbi Hendel says, "Just remember this: We never forget a slight against us. I'll deal with the skinhead Jews with their vicious demon dogs before I deal with you."

Tova jumps in. "Gentlemen, let's not say things our pride will prevent us from backing away from in the future."

Yisrael says, "No, this exactly what we need to know. I can see that we will not be a part of this new alliance."

Mr. Tova says, "Yisrael, stop being so hypersensitive. You should have had this attitude *before* Israel fell."

Yisrael says, "Maybe if we didn't have so many Jews abandon us when it mattered most, our Homeland would not have been lost."

"And who might you be referring to? Because my wife and I both were in the IDF and lived right in Jerusalem," Mr. Tova counters.

The two men stare at each other.

Rabbi Oren stands up too. "Tova, thank you for this, but we must be getting back home."

Tova says, "What? Why?"

Tova's husband walks up to him. "My wife told me what you said, Oren. You had no right to belittle us like that. We're not like you. The Orthodox. Everything *you* do is right. The Super Jews. Well, we human Jews did the best we could. You have no right to condemn us. We made decisions. We voted. One of them was a lifelong friend, the best man at our wedding. When we threw him out, I spat in his face for what he did to us, all of us. Then he came back to us crawling on the floor like an animal, begging for forgiveness, begging for us to let him and his family back in. What should we have done? Not even listen? We had people who said they wanted to come back to the community and that they'd do anything to come back, anything. Then we had others so angry that they yelled at us that if we let any of them back in, they'd leave. What were we supposed to do?"

Rabbi Oren says, "I am always amused by Jewish Orders that find involvement in the outside world more important than involvement in their own Jewish community. And then are shocked when those entanglements damage their own communities. Yes, Mr. Tova, you did the right thing for your community, but was it the right decision for Jews? You all say you understand, but you don't. You should have expelled all your traitors to protect the community. If they wanted to redeem themselves, then the burden should have been put on them to do so. Not with you. And the Orthodox are not the only ones who believe your Order has traitors within it.

There are many more Rabbi Susans out there and most of us believe they are in your Order."

Mr. Tova yells, "That is crap! There are no spies in our Order."

Rabbi Oren says, "We don't believe that, and the only way for me to ensure there are no threats to my Order, and especially my community, is to not formally involve ours with yours. I also don't believe in your heart that you really believe that the Conservative Order, which absorbed the Reformers, has not been compromised."

Mr. Tova says, "Actually, that is exactly what we believe. We are not compromised."

Tova says, "We need this alliance. Let's not abandon the concept before we even try to put it together. Can we not even try, Oren?"

Rabbi Oren said, "Tova, I came to your meeting as a favor to you. However, the differences we have here seem to be insurmountable. A unity of all the Orders must be based on not just respect, but trust. We must have that trust to move forward. You said yourself that we are under greater government scrutiny, and even greater danger."

Tova says, "The Christians have done it and they had far more Orders than we do. They've turned their wing of the Resistance into something so much greater. If they can do it, why can't we?"

Rabbi Oren says, "They spent many years building their alliances and have *decisively* dealt with their traitors. Yes, they have done so, Tova. Bless them."

Tova says, "So what are you really saying? We're going to quit before we even try."

Rabbi Henriques speaks, "I don't think it's important that we agree on everything. That should not be the goal because if it is, we'll be here for forty days and forty nights and we'll still be at square one. What we need to focus on is this: What is our purpose, what are we trying to accomplish? The purpose is, for us, to unify, to work together against threats to all of us. Then that is a very doable thing. There is a threat, we all pick up the line, we call each other, we come out, and we all fight back in our own way. Then as we work together more and more, that in itself will establish unity. Fighting together. Look at the last great world war for America; you had all these men from all over the country—different nations and cultures, different creeds, and so on. But when they were all in the same military uniform and all in the same foxhole, they didn't care who was a Jew or Gentile, who was light-skinned or dark-skinned. It was just 'kill Nazis.' That created the unity."

Rabbi Oren says, "I hear you. However, desire and reality are two different things. They must never be confused. For this to work we have to respect and trust each other, or at the first occurrence of a crisis we'll crumble like a house of cards. More importantly, our enemies will sense this and use us against each other, as has been done to us many, many times in the past. It doesn't matter what foxhole we're in." Rabbi Oren looks directly at Tova. "When you figure out a way to make this motley bunch an alliance, then you will have created an amazing thing, but sadly you never will, as you are not even honest about the state of your own Order."

Tova says, "Then why not help?"

"We have no desire to start this alliance of Jewish Orders. If it's created, we will join if it makes sense to us, but our focus must always be our own Order, our communities, our families. Sorry." Rabbi Oren leaves with his men.

Tova is crushed. Rabbi Oren did try to do this very thing a decade ago, but the Fall of Jewish Israel and violent Jewish civil wars had so soured him on the notion that he now felt that true Jewish unity was impossible.

Shoshana watches Tova fight back tears. Tova wants this alliance so much and she will never quit, but she will never succeed. The

Conservatives cannot lead this alliance. It has to be another Order. Shoshana knows that there is an ulterior motive for Tova wanting all the Jewish Orders to be unified, separate from unifying against their mutual enemies. There is something being planned by the Christians and maybe even the African Collective. She must know what the secret plan is. Where Rabbi Oren and Tova failed, she will make a Jewish Continuum a reality.

Body Farm

"This is normal." – Doctor Godwin, chief scientist, Project [redacted: classified Top Secret-SCI]

Private Home, Simi Valley, California
2:00 p.m., 20 May 2075 (15 Years Ago), Eve of Jerusalem Day

Rabbi Kanter stands at a podium addressing the five-dozen-plus gathering. Men sit around tables. Some have beards, some are clean-shaven, most are wearing kippot.

"I feel it to be divinely inspired, the work all of us do in this room in earnest, in secret, on the Antiquities Project—a project of such singular importance to all our people. It will ensure the preservation of both our past and our future. But I've felt a very heavy hand on my shoulder. The project could never be about mere things, no matter how holy; it had to be, even more so, about our people.

"Slavery to the Ancient Egyptians, slaughter and exile by the Ancient Romans, centuries of the Diaspora, scattered across the world without a Homeland, the evil Holocaust, the Caliphate, and now an America that hates all religion, but especially us. Today, we are not defined by a distinct identity, but for far too many, we are the people who are always the victim. That is not who we are. We are God's people, but we don't act like we believe anymore.

"I have deep respect for all our Jewish Orders. The Orthodox and Hasidim, but they are isolationists. Outside of their communities they have no concerns even when it comes to other Jews. The Israelis are consumed with fighting for dear life in the face of a growing Islamic Caliphate now that Western Europe has fallen. A religious civil war between the Conservatives and the Reformers rages. One or both of those Orders will be lost to us. The Ethiopians are fixated on what many of us predict is an inevitable war in Africa. There are other Orders. But none of them are focused enough, or large enough in numbers, to make their mark.

"I propose that it's time for a new Jewish Order, one that will not fixate on our tragedies, but consume itself with this question of identity and the future. We have plenty of Orders to worry about the body of Jews. We need an Order to focus on the soul of Jews. We need an anchor…a way to see through any despair or hopelessness. Our identity must be preserved, watched, nurtured, guarded, because the horrors will come. They always do. God runs the universe and time, but here on Earth, the devil is running the show, so don't be shocked by the bad stuff. And the bad stuff can come in sizes and shapes you could never imagine in your wildest dreams, or darkest nightmares."

Miami, Florida
4:06 p.m., 11 March 2090

Inside the underground parking, Gideon sits in his car, gripping the steering wheel with an anguished look on his face. *They tried to kill him.* The Stranger was killed by the sniper bullets ripping through the door. Smith awoke and was hysterical; the man starting crying and telling him everything.

"What have I gotten myself into?" Gideon says aloud, rubbing the back of his neck.

He notices Goli walking to the car from the elevator. They are at

Goli's apartment complex. Goli immediately notices the wild look in Gideon's eyes. He has never seen his best friend like this.

Gideon pleads, "I do need it today, now."

Goli stands, leaning into the car. "You will cross a line and you will never be able to turn back," he says.

"Will you help me or not?"

"A forged government security badge with a top secret clearance. We're not talking about just felonies. We're talking life imprisonment and they will throw away the key. It will effectively end your government career and your public life—prison or fugitive forever."

"They will never catch me. Millions of people successfully live off-Grid their entire lives. Goli, if you can't do it, I understand. Just get me someone who can."

Goli hands him a card. Gideon stares at it: Special Services. "Does this mean you've done this before?"

Goli walks away, back to the elevator. "Sorry, I didn't hear what you said. Gideon, you are able to keep your life right up to the moment you use the card. Once you do, that's it. You become classified an enemy of the state for life. I'll be on lifeline though 'sheriff.'" Goli disappears into the elevator and its door closes.

Gideon drives out of the underground parking lot. Gideon didn't tell him about the kill team. If he had, he would never have been able to simply walk in and out with Goli's forged security card. The sheriff *did* almost get gunned down in the middle of the street, but his deputy did warn him.

Arlington, Virginia
6:00 p.m., 11 March 2090

He made his private flight from Miami to Washington DC, but really, despite the perception, there is no such thing as a private flight. Passengers are monitored as much, if not more, than they are on public flights, but he wanted to at least avoid the main airport. He takes a taxi rather than a shuttle to the underground parking lots. It doesn't take long for him to get to his car.

Gideon looks at his fake identification card one more time. He exits his car and walks to the building, putting the card in his pocket. In his entire law enforcement career, he has never done anything even remotely illegal or inappropriate.

The building is a nondescript twelve-story structure. The glass tower has no visible security, camera, or guards, and besides the street number, there is no identification. He walks up to the main entrance; there is a red buzzer. He pushes the button, but there is no sound.

A guard inside appears from around a corner and approaches the glass doors. He is wearing an ear-set. "May I help you?" His voice comes through the door speaker.

Gideon puts the badge on the glass. "Special Services."

The guard gets closer and examines the badge. He then focuses on Gideon's face. He looks into his eyes. "Are you armed?"

"Yes."

"Take out the weapon and any backup weapon and show me."

Gideon takes his gun from his inside jacket holster and holds up the weapon in the other hand. "No backup weapon."

The guard opens the glass door and lets Gideon enter. "Follow me, sir."

He is led around the corner to a guard counter with five more guards. One takes his weapon and passes a wand over him from head to toe. The wand beeps when it passes over his left ankle.

"My spare ammo," Gideon says and he reaches for it to pull it from his ankle holster.

"Who are you here to see, sir?"

"Whoever is in charge."

The guards call ahead. The elevator opens and two guards lead Gideon to a man and woman waiting in white lab coats. The guards return to the elevator as it closes.

The man says, "Good evening, sir. We didn't know Special Services would be visiting us. How can we help you?" The man is about six feet tall, lanky with black hair, and wearing unusually thick, clear glasses, which is very strange since no one has 'bad eyesight' anymore. People wear clear glasses only for fashion, to clip on their ear-sets, or to use visual interface features with their mobile device.

"My name is Mr. Gideon."

The man says, "I'm Dr. Godwin and this is Dr. Mary."

Dr. Mary looks like Godwin's twin, only female and five inches shorter. Her glasses are very fashionable, though.

"I'll try not to keep you too long. I'm here to investigate an incident," Gideon says.

The doctors look at each other. Dr. Godwin asks, "Which incident are you referring to?"

Gideon is curious. "Is there more than one?"

Dr. Godwin says, "I don't know how to answer that. Tell me what you are here for."

"What are you keeping here now?"

Dr. Godwin says, "Standard units. We can service up to ten thousand currently."

"Let's go see them."

"See them?"

"Yes, the units. We can talk while we walk."

Gideon has never been inside a body farm facility, even though they have existed for decades. Colleagues who had visited them simply told him: "It's the freakiest thing you'll ever see."

The doctors lead him back into the elevator.

Gideon says, "How many incidents has this facility had?"

Dr. Godwin says, "There is only one."

"What happened?"

"This was all investigated."

"Indulge me. What happened?"

"One of our scientists had a mental breakdown."

Dr. Mary continues. "She destroyed some of the subjects. Nothing has ever happened like this before in the entire history of the facility."

"What happened to her?"

Dr. Godwin says, "She escaped and is still at large. That's all we know. The case is being handled by the authorities. Maybe even your branch. What incident were you referring to then?"

"We have a security leak. Information about the facility, classified material, got in the hands of people who shouldn't even know this place exists. The information is just too specific."

The scientists look at each other. Dr. Godwin says, "A leak? Impossible."

"That's why I'm here."

The elevator opens. Dr. Godwin asks, "Sir, have you ever been to a body farm?"

"Not in person."

Dr. Mary stops. "Maybe we need to talk about what you will see in detail, just a quick briefing."

"I'll be okay." Gideon exits the elevator and steps into a massive open area. He sees what appear to be large above-ground pools, orderly arranged and spaced ten feet apart. He walks to one and looks inside, then jumps back. *Inside are dozens and dozens of human arms, grabbing and flailing around; a variety of different skin pigmentations.*

Gideon walks to the other "pool" and sees that it's filled with disembodied legs jerking around. He peers in another, much smaller pool and can't make out what is in it, but the whole floor is moving. He stares at it and focuses and now realizes what he is seeing: hundreds of moving fingers.

Gideon is slightly unnerved. He quickly walks away from all the pools and to rows of eight-foot tanks. He stops in front of one. It looks like silver kelp moving back and forth in a thicker-than-water fluid, *only at the top of each is a human eye.*

Dr. Godwin says with a smile, "Think of all the millions of people maimed or injured each year. In the past, all they could do is wait around like ghoulish, living Frankensteins for someone to die so that we could harvest their body parts. That practice has been permanently made ancient history. Patients now have the choice of a primitive prosthesis or an advanced cybernetic implant. But as good as all that is, as good as the bio-tek has gotten in the merging of metal and flesh, it ultimately is a merging of two incompatible mediums. A bio-replacement is the perfect solution. The arms and legs you saw, for instance—moving, contracting, and extending. That's due to constant electrical stimuli to ensure that the muscle systems don't atrophy."

"Are they really grown?"

"Yes, a fantastic process. Millions of Americans altered by accidents can have normal lives again. We can replace any limb, external body part, or major internal organ except for the heart and liver. For those, the cybernetic replacements are still superior. But give us time."

"Brains?"

He laughs. "No, no. Neural reproduction is forbidden by law and all you end up with is a blob of organic matter. Unfortunately, we're still decades or centuries away from being able to do that...the complex electrical impulses and brain cells that create the essence of who we are. We can't do that yet. There is quite a heated debate about it in the scientific community. Some believe we never will be able to. The brain-mind is just too complex. However, we don't believe there is anything we can't do. It's all a matter of time."

Gideon asks, "Why aren't you more public? Use of body farms is so commonplace now."

Dr. Godwin answers. "We'll always have to be fearful of religious-based terrorism. That's why all facilities are secret. Jew-Christians are quite dangerous."

"You mean Muslims."

"We don't really make those distinctions, but you're right, Muslims. The other ones just protest a lot."

Dr. Mary says, "It's a shame that their religious close-mindedness keeps them from appreciating this process."

Dr. Godwin adds, "We also have to be very careful of Vampires and witches, too. And various mentally deranged people."

"What is that?!" Gideon points to super large, rectangular glass tanks. *Inside there seem to be people!* He runs to the tanks, but they aren't people; they are skins of full bodies!

Dr. Godwin says, "We grow skin here too. We're able to save all burn victims no matter what degree of the burns. We're very proud of it. Strangely, we were able to master limb growing before full skin growing. It's a trickier process."

"So the term for all of these is 'bio-units?'" Gideon asks.

"Or just units."

Gideon looks at the doctors. "What's the difference between units and clones?"

Dr. Godwin is suspicious now. "Well, units are real. Clones are science fiction."

Gideon looks at him. "You mean one is unclassified and the other is top secret."

The doctors look at him; neither says anything.

Gideon says, "I have the proper clearance and I've been read into the program. Where are they? The 'you-know-whats' that exist only in science fiction…and here at this facility. You already slipped up before by using the word *subjects*."

Dr. Godwin answers, "Unfortunately, after the incident we had to remove all subjects from this facility."

"None are here?"

"None."

"What about the *dead* ones?"

The doctors are caught off guard. "Dead ones?" Mary asks.

"Yes, dead ones."

"None of our subjects are dead."

"What about the ones your mental breakdown scientist destroyed?"

Caught! The scientists hesitate. "I'm not sure—" Godwin starts.

"How many did she destroy?"

"I'm not sure if—"

"How many?"

Dr. Godwin answers, "Three."

"Then take me to the bodies."

"We cannot do that. It's not allowed."

"Take me to the morgue now."

The doctors are nervous.

They exit the elevator a few levels down. Everything looks familiar. As a law enforcement agent, Gideon has been to many of them in his career. They enter a large room where the body-lockers are. An orderly stands waiting, obviously alerted that they'd be coming down.

"Show me the first one," Gideon commands.

Dr. Godwin says, "I think we need to talk first."

Gideon says to the orderly, "Open up the first locker." To Dr. Godwin, "I'm not a morgue virgin. I've seen plenty of dead bodies. Open all of them up."

The orderly opens the first locker and slides out the first body, covered from head to toe with a sheet. He moves on and opens the second and then the third.

Gideon touches the sheet at the head of the first corpse and hesitates. He pulls it down and stares at the face. He is stunned! He covers the corpse back up. He walks around to the second body and looks at the face, then covers it up again, then the last one. He stares at it for what seems to be ages. He covers it back up and glares at the doctors.

Dr. Godwin says, "These are just simple experimental trials. There is no other significance."

Gideon says, "Testing a new vaccine for the flu is an experimental trial. *Human clones of mass murderers?*"

"Actually, these aren't clones," Godwin says. "There would be no genetic material surviving from that time to ours to make such a thing possible. This is actually advanced plastic surgery."

Gideon looks at him as Godwin smiles. Both scientists now seem very satisfied with themselves. The explanation seems so plausible, so logical.

Gideon says, "That makes sense."

Godwin smiles. "Yes."

"Except for one thing," Gideon says.

Godwin hesitates. "What would that be?"

"You're scientists, not plastic surgeons. This is a body farm, not a face factory. You wouldn't know how to give someone a new face any more than a common doctor would know how to grow someone a new arm or new skin."

The doctors watch him silently.

"Why would you do this?" Gideon asks.

Dr. Mary says, "Please turn off your imagination. This is just a project."

"Why would you do this?" Gideon asks, shaking his head.

Dr. Mary says, "The project is just an experiment of our scientific capabilities."

"Because you can? That's the answer? Is this supposed to be normal?"

Dr. Goodwin says, "Normality is an imaginary construct of Jew-Christians. In science, there are only possibilities. No preconceptions. No morality. *This is normal.*"

"Mr. Gideon, I thought you were read into this program," Goodwin says.

Ignoring them, Gideon's eyes spot larger body-lockers on the opposite end of the room. "Are these the only subjects here?"

The orderly answers, "Yes."

Gideon points. "What are those?"

He looks at them and by the expressions on their faces he can tell that something is wrong. He walks to the large locker; an elephant on its side could fit in one of these lockers. Gideon looks back at them. The three look like criminals who did something bad, but are nervously pretending they did nothing.

The orderly says, "There isn't anything in them."

Gideon opens the first one, empty. The second one, empty. He moves down the row…

"Stop!" Dr. Godwin yells. "You do not have clearance to look in there."

Gideon looks at him. "I am from Special Services and I do have clearance!"

The orderly reveals and points a gun at him. "No you don't. You open that door and I'll shoot you. If you look in there, then you will not be able to leave this facility, as the contents are well above your current secret clearance. That knowledge is the property of the US government and *you* become the property of the US government."

Gideon stares at him. "You aren't an orderly, are you?"

Gideon walks away from the lockers and to them. The orderly lowers his gun. Gideon reaches Dr. Mary and grabs her e-pad from her chest pocket. He touches the screen and activates the camera function. He walks back to the locker and while staring at them, opens the door. The orderly points his gun back at him. Gideon aims the e-pad camera inside the open locker, without looking inside or taking his eyes off of them, and flashes away, taking pictures. He stops and closes the door.

"I'm taking this with me."

The orderly says, "No, you're not."

"You say I don't have clearance. Fair enough. You're right. But my boss or someone in my division will and they'll read me into this, too. I think you all are up to unauthorized activities here."

Dr. Godwin says, "All of this is legal and authorized by the highest levels."

"You all don't act like it, but we'll find out for sure." Gideon walks to the main exit. The orderly looks at the doctors; none of them knows what to do.

Gideon continues out of the room and heads back to the elevator. He pushes the button and turns. No one has followed him. Suddenly the doctors appear at the door, staring at him.

"Who authorized your visit this facility, Mr. Gideon?" Dr. Godwin asks.

"My division, of course."

"Surely you have a name. Some specific person we can call to verify."

"I don't have time to play games. You had one incident here

already. Then another with this security leak. And now I suspect that you are doing things here that you shouldn't be. I will talk to my superiors first. If they say it's okay, I'll come back here, get on my knees, and apologize. If not, you're in trouble."

The doctors watch him. Dr. Godwin says, "I don't think you can leave."

"Excuse me. Watch me."

Dr. Godwin approaches. Gideon clenches his fist to punch him. The doctor touches the button and the elevator door opens. "Only facility personnel can activate the elevators."

"Well, thank you for the tour."

They stare at each other as the elevator closes. Gideon rides the elevator back up alone.

The doors open and three guards are waiting. He walks out and to the main guard station. The three guards follow closely. "My gun and ammo, please," he says.

One of the two guards behind the station reaches down and puts both on the counter. "Have a good night, sir."

"Thank you." He grabs them and walks around the corner to the main glass doors. He pulls it and then pushes it; locked. He turns around. "The door is still locked."

A guard appears. "Sir, the doctors said you should come back down to talk with them. They don't want there to be any hard feelings."

"There are none. But I do need to go now."

A second guard appears. The other guard continues. "They were very insistent."

"Open the door now," Gideon says angrily. The guards are not friendly anymore. Two more guards appear. "Are we really going to play games? They can see from the street."

"Who are you referring to, sir?"

"My partners."

"There's no one else outside, sir. We have full sensors everywhere."

Gideon smiles. "Just because your sensors don't see them doesn't mean they're not there."

The guards pause for a moment. "There's no one else out there," one guard says.

Gideon turns back to face the street and waves his arms around. The guards look out and then back at him. *Suddenly something hits the glass.* The four guards jump.

Gideon turns back. "Open the damn door! Or they'll shoot it out!"

One of the guards runs to the entrance. Once he touches the door, it unlocks and he pushes it open. Gideon bolts out.

Gideon runs to his car and gets in. Goli's voice comes through the dash speaker. "What was the rock trick for? Were they really not going to let you leave?"

Gideon ignores everything. He races out of the parking lot. A moment later, he slams on the brakes. He grabs the e-pad he took from Dr. Mary. "Get all the files off this now!"

"Okay."

"Do it now in case they have an e-link back to it and try to erase the files."

"Finally, you're starting to think like a healthy, paranoid off-Gridder."

Gideon speeds off. His brain races at what he's seen—and not seen. They are all real!

The Dark Wolves Are Here

"With the benefit of more than fifty years since the end of direct American involvement in the pre-Caliphate Middle East, we can see in stark detail that despite the miraculous advancements in medical tek and forever-changing gear, the human soldier has remained virtually the same after several thousands of years. I fear we may have already arrived at the 'NHA Battlefield'—no humans allowed—as future wars will showcase such an array of biologically destructive machines and weapon systems that no normal human soldier will be able to survive, for even a moment. Any future 'manned' wars will be with surrogate robots and cybernetically advanced or genetically engineered super soldiers." – Colonel "Tiny" Garrison, MD, PhD, M.I.T Military Academy, 2079

San Fernando Valley, California
10:12 a.m., 5 May, 2080

Shoshana remembers it like it was yesterday. It was her twenty-first birthday, but instead of celebrating at a party with friends or driving the town in her new car, she is huddled in the living room with her family watching the vid-screen. The Islamic-Christian War rages in Africa.

"You said this would happen," her mother says to her father.

"It was inevitable," he says. "The Muslims take over all of Western Europe, but they still are not satisfied. They never will until they get all the world, or they're stopped."

"I'm glad you retired from Mossad," she says.

"But if they ever recall me, I will go."

Shoshana turns to him, "Next it will be Israel."

Her two brothers and her three sisters sit around her. Her oldest brother, Amir, says, "They would never be so reckless, Father. They know we'll use our nukes."

"You need allies in the world, not nukes. Alliances are what will stop the final conflict. Remember, they believe that if they die they go to heaven and get seventy-two female slaves from their god. If we ever have to launch the nukes, we've already lost."

Shoshana says, "No, Father, I don't believe they love death as much as they'd like us to believe. Fire the nuke first and hit the right target. Kill them before they kill you."

"We can't kill them all," her father says.

"Yes, we can, Father. We just don't have *real* men running the government there."

"Shoshana, don't talk that way about their government. They know what they're doing. They live with the conflict every day," her mother chastises.

Her father shakes his head slightly. "You're young, Shoshana. At twenty-one, the world is such a big place and anything is possible. When you get older, have a family, you realize how small the world really is and possibilities are not as plentiful as you would like. For Israel, the options are ever dwindling."

Shoshana says, "If I were in charge, all this would end."

Her mother says, "Shoshana, you are talking nonsense again. Leave the politics to the men."

Shoshana declares, "I will be the next Golda Meier and Margaret Thatcher. They called Thatcher the 'Iron Lady.' I will be the 'Iron Star!'"

Her siblings laugh.

Her mother says, "Oh, a Jewish superhero, huh?"

"*Mishegas*!" her eldest sister yells. ("She's crazy!")

Her father looks at her. "Did you do what I told you to do last week?"

Shoshana looks back at him with a vacant expression.

"Shoshana, don't pretend with me. Did you?"

"I need the books for my studies."

Her mother looks at her father and then back at her. "Shoshana, you still have those Nazi books?!"

"They are World War Two books, mother."

"Nazi books! We told you to throw them out!"

Amir looks at her with disgust. "She wants to be a Jewish Nazi."

Shoshana glares at him, "Shut up!" She looks back at her parents. "Mother, I'm studying history. I want to know everything about the evil Holocaust murders people are so fixated upon."

Amir says, "I think you admire them."

Shoshana jumps to her feet. "Shut up! Or I'll beat you up!"

"Sit down! Both of you!" their father yells. They both sit on the ground. "Shoshana, you will throw out all those Nazi books right now. No discussion. No debate. Now. Since you have so much free time for those type of studies, I'll have your mother sign you up for more religious study classes. I wish you had the same passion for the Torah and Talmud that you do for World War Two Germans."

"I do, Father. I can do both my religious studies and my personal studies."

Her mother says, "Shoshana, you say people are fixated on these evil murders. But you are one of those people."

"No mother, I'm not. I just want to study the evil thoroughly so that when it comes again, I won't be weak and allow myself to be marched into the gas chambers."

Her siblings laugh. Her older sister, Hannah, says, "She's crazy, Mother. Listen to her talk. The Holocaust could never happen again. Stop your crazy talk."

Shoshana looks at her sister coldly. "It could happen again! The Muslims now completely surround Israel. Mass murders are everywhere. Millions and millions of people have been slaughtered since the Holocaust ended in 1945—all over the world; the genocides never stop."

Her siblings watch her walk away, shaking their heads at the overwrought emotional intensity of the youngest of the family. Her parents watch her too.

Her mother touches her temple. "How did we end up with such an angry child?"

Her father shakes his head. "Shoshana must get her own place. I will not wait until she gets married."

In 1000 BC, Jews founded the nation of Israel, then called Judea—1,000 years before Jesus Christ, 1,600 years before Mohammed, 2,776 years before the United States of America, 2,945 years before the now-defunct organization of the United Nations.

Shoshana and her family, as with the world, had no idea what was coming. Jewish Israel fell the next year, in 2081. Shoshana lost her father, her oldest sister, and both her brothers in the battle and subsequent evacuations.

Same house – 2090 (Ten years later)

Her frail mother sits in her favorite chair. Shoshana stands in front her. "Mother, this is not a debate. I want you to live with me so that I can keep an eye on you and take care of you."

"I'm not leaving my house! This is your father's house! And I'm never leaving!"

"Father will be with you no matter where you are, Mother, whether here or with me."

"No, I'm not leaving!"

Shoshana looks at her with sadness. What can she do? Severe depression, not age, has turned her mother into a hollow shell of a person who never leaves the house. They are the only two remaining in the family. Both her surviving sisters committed suicide years ago, after the Event that took their father, brothers, and Homeland.

"I see you have cut off all your beautiful hair. Are you supposed to be a Nazi soldier or a Jewish concentration camp prisoner? I can never tell with you."

"Mother, you can try your best, but I will not fight with you. I'm not dropping the issue. I need to make sure you are safe. This place is not safe. The entire neighborhood is controlled by Pagans."

"They don't bother me."

"But you bother them."

"One little old Jewish woman in a house. They don't care."

"Mother! You are making me mad."

"Leave then! I didn't ask you here. Go do whatever Nazis do nowadays."

"I chose not to be insulted by you today, mother. Are you going to force me to do it?"

"Do what?"

"I will drag you from this house."

"No! You will not take me from your father's house! This is my house and I will die here! I am an adult and you can't make me go! Don't take me from my home! You can't hate me that much!"

"Mother, I have never hated you." She calms herself. "Can we compromise?"

"What do you mean?"

"What if I were to move the entire house?"

"What are you talking about?"

"Mother, we don't live in the caveman days. They have house movers. They will lift up the entire house and we can truck it to anywhere we want in the country."

"No, they'll break up the house!"

"No they won't."

"No, just leave me alone. Go away and leave me alone."

"There's two of us left and we need to stick together now."

"Well, that wouldn't be the case if you got married and had children like a normal Jewish girl."

"If you move, I'll get married and you'll have your grandchildren."

Her mother gives her a look. "What? What craziness are you talking about now?"

"You heard me. That's the deal: You move with me to my community and I'll promise to get married and have kids."

"You can't be serious. That's not why you get married and have children."

"Saving my mother from death? That seems to me to be a better reason than most. Mother, what's it going to be? Grandchildren or loneliness?"

"You are a crazy person. The things you say and do." Shoshana stares at her. Her mother looks all around, then back at her daughter. "This is a joke."

"Mother, you're stalling." Shoshana walks toward the door. "Okay, you don't want grandchildren. I tried. Have a good day, Mother. I'll try to visit next year some time."

Shoshana leaves the room and her mother can hear the door open and close.

"Okay!" Her mother yells so loud Shoshana is sure the entire block heard her.

Shoshana's head pops back in through the crack of the open door with a smile.

"Don't smile at me. You are very crafty. You were always crafty, even as a toddler. Okay, you win. You'll be goose-stepping all the way home with joy now." Her mother points her bony finger at Shoshana. "But if your house movers damage your father's house in any way, you'll see why even grown men are scared of little old Jewish mothers."

Orthodox Main Synagogue, Georgetown, South Carolina 11:01 a.m., 5 April 2090

The synagogue is much more than a place of worship; it is the nerve center of the community. Rabbi Oren doesn't even recognize her. One of his men entered his office and said, "There's a Shoshana Israela here for you, Rabbi." He walked out expecting to see the same young woman with a shaved head and wearing some type of military fatigues and black combat boots. Instead, in the main congregation space he sees a new Shoshana, her bald head covered with a long white headscarf, wearing an off-white dress that reaches her ankles and a Star of David emblem necklace. She also wears tan flats —no combat boots.

"Plain, dignified, respectable. Why don't you dress like this always, Miss Shoshana?"

"I do," she answers. "When I'm not on duty."

"So what allows me to see you in your true form today?"

"I am here on behalf of my Order. The New Shamar Jewish Order wants to move forward with the creation of a formal alliance, starting with yours."

Rabbi Oren smiles. "So this notion of the Conservatives has captivated you too. My Order still believes it is unworkable."

"Will you allow our chief rabbi to make our case?"

"Of course, but I always believe in giving a quick 'no' rather than a long, drawn-out one when 'yes' is not possible."

"We believe it is possible and will convince you."

Rabbi Oren directs her to his church office. He motions her to take a seat and he sits behind a desk. Another young Jewish woman enters the room with empty glasses and a pitcher of water. "This is my youngest daughter. She takes care of me here at the offices."

"Nice to meet you," Shoshana says. The Rabbi's daughter nods and exits, leaving the door open.

"Tell me more about your Wolf Pack organization."

"We're the military wing of the Shamar Jewish Order. We are what the Old Mossad was in our Homeland." Oren nods approvingly. "In that way, our Order divides our religious and security duties and shares in the governance of the community."

Rabbi Oren says, "Names are very important to me. I remember years ago, when I was around your age, I got into heated debates with two Jewish Orders that existed back then: Messianic Jews and the Jews for Jesus movement. I gave them hell. I yelled at them, 'Either be a Jew or be a Christian; stop straddling the religious fence and being grossly offensive to both. We need strong Jews and strong Christians, not some foolish hybrid.'"

"What did they do?"

"Most joined Christian denominations as they should have. Others rejoined Jewish Orders. I did say names are important to me. Shamar? To keep, guard, watch, preserve."

"Yes. Keep from harm, damage, danger, or evil."

"I heard rumors of this Order. Where has the Shamar Order been hiding all these years?"

"In plain sight."

"I take it you are the ones working with the African Collective?"

"Yes."

"When do you want me to meet your chief rabbi?"

"We would like you to come to our kibbutzim as a guest."

"Why me? I'm just one man."

"I appreciate your modesty, rabbi, but you are a lot more than one man. Your words have clout in all Orthodox enclaves in the nation."

"You overemphasize my importance, but so be it. You are continuing with Tova's work? You were of the opposite mind at her meeting."

"Yes, but other considerations have changed my mind."

"When you look at all of Jewish history, and I do mean all, you see a people who have been divided more than they have ever been unified. The joke that goes, 'you have two Jews in a room and five different opinions' is not far from the truth. We had bloody religious civil wars. We had Jewish rulers succeeding another by assassination. For me, the issue is not unity among us, but the continuity of our people. That we survive is what is important. Not that we do it as one, holding hands, Chabad-dancing under the rainbow."

"We're not expecting a united kingdom of Israel under Kings Saul, David, or Solomon, but we can come close."

"You're making my point. There was far less real division of ideology back then, and Jews still couldn't unify. After King David, after King Solomon, their sons and grandsons made an utter mess of Israel. Split our great kingdom in two. Much like former Israel with its near-perpetual schizophrenic governments: embrace our enemies like friends one day or treat them as the enemies they truly are the next. This whole unity thing has to do with the Conservatives' fixation on what the Christians are doing."

"Not a fixation. An instinctive sense of something they are planning."

"What do you mean planning? Everyone plans. Nothing is unique about that."

"Tova may be blind to how compromised her own Order is, but she is exceptionally perceptive in other matters. I suspect there is much more behind her fairly recent zeal to create this unity of all of the Jewish Orders."

"What would that be?"

"They no longer call themselves the Resistance. The Christians call their alliance the Continuum. It's far more than a name change, and it also involves the African Collective."

"Why haven't they engaged us, then? Jews have been part of the Resistance from the very beginning with them. We also have connections with the Ethiopian Jews within the African Collective."

"Ironically, they don't trust us fully for the same reason we don't trust the Conservatives. They believe we're compromised. Our religious leader, Rabbi Kanter, believes that a greater Faither Alliance must exist."

"Rabbi Kanter is the Chief Rabbi of the Shamar Order?"

"Yes."

"Why didn't he say so? Why didn't you?"

"We are very cautious people, like the Orthodox."

Rabbi Oren says, "I accept the invitation, but I will not promise anything."

"That's fair. Thank you."

"Have you spoken with Tova?"

"Not yet."

"You better do so, because at the very least her feelings will be hurt. The biggest project of her life has been taken from her."

"I will speak with her."

Secret location, Nevada
6:30 a.m., 3 July 2089

Inside the large conference room, men and women in fatigues are seated in chairs or on the table, or are leaning against the wall or standing. All the talking and joking can be heard from down the hall. Shoshana enters in her normal paramilitary dress and the Wolf Pack members quiet. Everyone takes their seats.

All of them automatically activate the tabs in front of them to begin the presentation.

"What are the final conclusions from the deep-gene samples?" she asks.

The man to her left answers. "The target is confirmed to be a modified human."

"Modified how?"

He touches a button on his screen and now all of them can view the files.

Shoshana shakes her head.

"The Pagans have been modifying their bodies for physical appearance, childbirth, sex…why not killing? 'Captain America' was written back in 1941 and now it's real. It always seems to go back to the Nazis. What's the threat?"

"Conventional close-combat methods or normal bullets would not be effective," another man answers.

"Not even our bone-shredders?" Shoshana asks.

"Not likely."

"What's the intel we have on my new boyfriend?"

The soldiers around the table smile.

A female soldier answers, "We haven't IDed him yet. Hacks, bots, moles—all zero so far." The best tek-lords could hack into the government's systems or they used bots—the Net equivalent of drones to do the hack for them, and they even had their own network of confidential informants in all levels of government. "They keep their top black ops agent files off the Grid on private detachable servers in secret data banks, but we'll get the information. One of our overseas contacts says that they may be a black ops team called the…Werewolf SS."

There are smiles, chuckles, and laughter from the group.

"Vampires before, now werewolves, what next? Trolls and zombies? Find out for sure," Shoshana directs. "Action items?"

"Enhance all our body armor-tek and firepower. We were doing it already," says the first man.

"Others?"

"Contact the Christians to see if the target is in their database," the woman says.

Shoshana nods. "We conducted a flawless op in Colorado. All of you should be proud of yourselves and this team. But let's not fool ourselves. The Gestapo *will* respond. Let's make sure we have the appropriate welcoming party for them for when they do arrive."

The Wolf Pack growls in unison.

Main Synagogue, Kibbutzim, Idaho
9:00 a.m., 8 April 2090

"Today we give honor and praise to Yahweh."

Rabbi Oren is the guest rabbi for the Saturday prayer and worship services for the Shamar Order. The congregation is divided into thirds: unmarried men in the first third, families in the center, and unmarried women in the last third.

The inside of the synagogue is stunning architecturally, with high vaulted ceilings and white and gold marble. One would never know this from looking at the plain wood exterior of the building.

Rabbi Oren has been with them for a few days now, spending about half his time in rabbinical studies at their synagogue with their rabbis and sitting in on Torah study classes of children, young adults, and adults. He spends the rest of his time visiting with various families throughout the enclave.

With services over, people walk back to their homes for lunch and family time. Rabbi Oren and Rabbi Kanter decide to take the long way to Rabbi Kanter's home.

"Thank you for an inspiring service, Rabbi Oren," Kanter says.

"Please, call me Yitzak. You call me Rabbi, I call you Rabbi. Soon we'll forget who we're talking about."

Rabbi Kanter laughs. "Yes. Call me Jonah."

Rabbi Oren says, "How long have you been the head of the religious life of the community?"

"For the last three years."

"And what of Shoshana and the *Adat Z'evim?*"

"The Wolf Pack runs all security and intelligence services and, when needed, other operations. She has a natural aptitude for it and she has grown considerably after learning to control her anger after the Fall."

"Even those of us who didn't lose anyone, lost everything. Since your Order is new, what were you before?"

"Actually, I was born and raised in a pseudo-secular Reform home. I can remember as a youth viewing faith as nothing more than behavior of an out-of-date, out-of-touch people living in modern Tek-World. I didn't even have a bar mitzvah. As I left home and became my own man, venturing into the world as secular as I was at the time, it was clear how anti-religious, anti-Jewish, anti-'me' the world was. It hit me when I was at university: death threats for praying for the people of Israel, the Holocaust couldn't be taught because Muslims said that it didn't happen and Pagans said that it was illegal religious indoctrination. I heard more than a few times that we needed a new Holocaust for Jews and all religions in America. I was quite shaken by university life. Not only did I become more religious as I grew older, I had my own epiphany when I first came to know God in my life. I came to embrace the Separatist Movement. We couldn't defeat or reverse the bigotry, only avoid it by establishing our own separate world. Maybe this new anti-religiosity could have been defeated before, but we were long past that time."

"You are the real Theodore Herzl story. The Orthodox have done everything possible not to be swept up with politics. The Separatist Movement was that for us with the walled enclaves, but now we all have walled enclaves."

"A counter-Tek-World was inevitable."

"How do you like our enclave now that you've had a chance to spend some time with us?"

"Very impressive. Nice balance of the community, your machines, and nature. How many affiliate communities do you have?"

"We have dozens throughout the country."

"I heard a rumor, Jonah, that you were the Jews involved with the Antiquities Project." Rabbi Kanter looks at him directly. "Don't worry. The Orthodox know how to keep secrets."

"I'm not worried about that, but how you found out to begin with."

"We have a fair amount of contacts ourselves. In this world, it's very hard to keep a secret when you're doing good works. Actually, the Orthodox in Jerusalem had a plan in place in case the unthinkable happened. It did happen and we moved into action only to find out that another group had already acted. Was everything saved?"

"Yes."

Oren takes a deep breath and smiles. "Knowing that all of Israel's holy artifacts were rescued from the Fall would be such a powerful and uplifting revelation, an instant renewal of excitement and hope, which all the Orders desperately need."

"We will make it all known when appropriate. But how did you find out?"

"The day of the Fall. You remember the panic, the chaos. Jews all over the world desperately trying to get to Israel to help in whatever way possible. Once we realized that we were well past any military solutions to stop the outcome unfolding before our eyes, our focus shifted to how to get people and, if possible, our holy items out. The entire American Orthodox purchased an airline."

"You bought an airline?" Kanter asks incredulously.

"Fifty planes. We were going to fly there ourselves all the way to Israel. Not caring if we were shot out of the sky by the White House, more concerned with being supposedly neutral, or the Muslims, or whoever. We were getting ready to fly out of Georgia when I received the message from my brother, a chief rabbi in Jerusalem. It said: 'I know what you are going to do, but stay in America. The Antiquities Project with other Faithers is successful. Use all your energies to pray and settle as many people of Israel who can escape to America.'"

"I didn't know he was your brother. He was a valuable member of the Project. We miss him."

"We all do. And you were the architect of the Project."

"Yes. What a very small world."

"The world is big. The world of Jews is small."

"So, Yitzak, what are you thinking?"

"What is your Order planning with the Christians? The Antiquities Project was the largest historical artifact rescue operation in human history, and one of the largest human evacuation operations in modern history. Tens of thousands, hundreds of thousands of our people saved. We have always wondered who was involved, since every world government, including America, rendered no assistance and no one has ever come forward to publicly acknowledge it. It was your new Shamar Order."

"Yes."

"What is being planned, then? If the Antiquities Project is any indication, it must be massive. Even this *little* thing of rescuing the Hasidim, you all broke out more than a thousand people from a super maximum security, state-of-the-art prison like it was nothing."

Rabbi Kanter smiles.

Rabbi Oren smiles too. "You will not tell me?"

"Not yet. We have to do the work that needs to be done."

"This New Jewish Continuum?"

"Yes."

Location Unknown
4:05 a.m., 13 April 2090

The shadow helicopters land in a secluded airfield. The doors open on the lead ship and Lycan exits with his men. They are dressed in full black body armor and accessorized with a full weapons pack: pistols, knives, grenades, ammo, collapsible rifles. They walk to their awaiting armored attack vehicles.

Galicia Enclave, Georgetown, South Carolina
5:34 p.m., 13 April 2090

When Shoshana told Tova that the Shamar, Orthodox, and Hasidic Jewish Orders had formally allied, and that they would jointly create the New Jewish Continuum as the Conservatives had envisioned, she was less than pleased. However, Tova put her emotion and pride aside and said she would support the effort wholeheartedly.

Galicia is a large Hasidic community some fifteen miles from the Orthodox enclave of Rabbi Oren. It was founded after the mass exodus out of New York after the Second American Jewish Civil War.

The meeting is being held in the large town hall building

attached to the main synagogue. Just as Tova had started, there is a large round table for all the attendees. Already present are Rabbi Oren and his Orthodox delegation, Rabbi Hendel and the Hasidic delegation, and Rabbi Kanter and the new Shamar delegation.

Tova arrives with her husband and the Conservative Jewish Order delegation.

She is somewhat offended by the Shamar Order. For her meeting, they sent Shoshana and her people dressed in full paramilitary gear. For this meeting, they send their chief rabbi in dignified attire.

There is plenty of food and drink on the tables closest to the main entrance. Just as Tova had done, children are the main helpers at the event. This time, cute Hasidic boys and girls eagerly help everyone who enters with food, directions to restrooms, and information about the seating arrangements.

The Israeli Jewish Order arrives next, with Yisrael leading. Tova notices that they have foregone their need to arrive last.

The Mizrahi arrive next: the Arab and Persian Jewish Orders. Rabbi Haza leads in his Arabic Jews and Rabbi Nahai, his Persian Jewish delegation. Rabbi Henriques arrives next with a larger Judeo-Spanish delegation this time. There are no Goth Jews, but there is a new group that arrives, led by a young, casually dressed woman whom Tova has never seen before. She imagines they must be teks.

Tova and her husband hover around the food table. One of the little girls runs up to Tova. "Are you Mrs. Tova?"

"Yes, I am. What is your name?"

"My name is Bina, of the Hasidic Jewish Order."

"Well, I'm Tova, of the Conservative Jewish Order."

"Mrs. Tova, can you accompany me? Someone wants to talk to you outside."

"Can I bring my husband?"

"Oh yes."

They follow the little girl outside. Tova now glances at her husband's face. He isn't upset like she is; he's downright furious. They stole the Continuum idea from them.

Once outside, the girl takes them around the corner to an office. Shoshana appears from an open door in all her paramilitary glory.

"Thank you, Bina," she says.

"You're welcome, Ms. Shoshana." The little girl runs back to the main hall.

"Please have a seat."

Tova says, "I must hand it to you, Shoshana. You've so completely taken my idea from us that no one will ever know it came from the Conservatives."

"No Tova, everyone will know the idea originated from you. You gave birth to the idea, but others will make sure that it will move from idea to reality. But that's not why I've called you here."

Mr. Tova asks gruffly, "Why then?"

Shoshana hands a tablet to Tova. She touches the screen and, with Tova's husband looking on, opens the single file in the center of the screen. "I know this has been a source of great annoyance and anger for you. The charge by others that your Order is compromised. The file is a detailed list of all the spies within your Order."

Tova takes the tablet, walks to the table, and sits down with it to read. Her husband follows.

Mr. Tova yells, "This is crap! You can't prove any of this. You all won't let this alone. We know exactly who collaborated with the government before. We're sorry we didn't round all of them up and execute them as you all wanted. We've been through this already."

"The file lists prior collaboration with the government before they were taken in or taken back by the Conservative Order after individual trials were conducted by your high council. The file also lists those who have continued to collaborate with the Gestapo."

"Gestapo?" Mr. Tova asks.

"Her pet name for the Capitol," Tova says and looks at Shoshana. "I don't believe it, any of it."

"Their highest-level informants are on the next screen."

Tova swipes to the next screen on the tab. She and her husband look up. They read and the expressions on their faces change to astonishment.

Shoshana continues, "These collaborators have also informed their handlers about the exact details of *this* meeting. All the proof is attached for your own in-house teks to verify."

Rabbi Hendel of the Hasidim stands with his glass in the air, toasting to the beginning of the meeting. "As our first act of this new alliance, the Hasidic Order will eliminate an issue of contention between us and the Israeli Order. We will formally recognize all the holidays of Old Israel: Yom Yerushalayim, Yom Ha'Shoah, Yom Hazikaron, and Yom Ha'atzmaut. This will be our act of solidarity to our former Homeland."

Yisrael is speechless for a moment, but takes his glass and returns the toast. "I don't know what to say."

Rabbi Haza starts clapping. "Bravo! *Yafe meod! Kol hakavod!*" ("I like it! Congratulations!"). Everyone at the table starts to applaud too. "This is how we start a meeting!"

It was an issue of contention for quite some time between the Hasidim and the Israelis; the Hasidim refusal to recognize four Old Israel holidays. Yom Yerushalayim, or Jerusalem Day, was the holiday that marked the 1967 reunification of Jerusalem and the Temple Mount under Jewish rule during the Six-Day War, almost nineteen hundred years after the destruction of the Second Temple in Jerusalem. Yom Ha'Shoah, or Holocaust Remembrance Day, was inaugurated in 1953 to commemorate the six million Jews and five million others who perished in the Holocaust at the hands of the Nazis. Yom Hazikaron, Israeli Memorial Day or Israeli Fallen Soldiers and Victims of Terrorism Remembrance Day, commemorated the memory of soldiers killed in the line of duty, and civilian casualties, too. The day also now recognized those who had died in the Fall of Jewish Israel. Yom Ha'atzmaut, or Israel Independence Day, included the lighting of twelve beacons, one for each of the Tribes of Israel.

Hasidim had resisted the formal recognition of these Israeli holidays, not out of malice, but on the grounds that they were secular. But Rabbi Hendel leads all the Chabadniks now, and exceptions can be made for the sake of this new alliance.

Tova and her husband return and take their places with their delegation at the table. They have very stern looks on their faces.

Rabbi Kanter says, "I am glad the Tovas are here, as we have them to thank for the initial courage and foresight in relaunching this attempt to create this esteemed council of all our Jewish Orders, the New Jewish Continuum."

Everyone starts to clap. The Tovas manage smiles.

Kanter continues. "Also, the group known as the Goth Jews will not serve on the council, as we mutually agreed that their group is not a specific religious Order, per se. They are our chief intel gatherers in the outside world. We also must connect with those Hidden Jews and Lot Jews, those living in secret communities in the tek-cities, and those hiding in plain sight, in Pagan tek-cities throughout the country. Overseeing that effort will be Ms. Rachel Glick." He acknowledges the young woman with her delegation, whom none of them have met before. "In time, our hope is that all join, or at least become affiliated with, one of our Orders. Let us begin with our agenda."

A storm seems to be rolling in, making the outside look much darker than normal.

The Jewish Wolf Pack is ready for them. The Hasidic Order may not be involved with the outside, secular world at all, but all their communities have excellent tek-security. The enclave is surrounded by nine-foot walls with razor wire, trip lights, stun cannons, and the latest in surveillance and defense tek. Armed men patrol the perimeter and guard the entrances.

Lycan and his team crouch low to the ground a quarter of a mile from the enclave wall, waiting. He watches the main gate through his scope goggles; only two armed men.

He whispers into his ear-set. "Move."

The seasoned mercenaries lie flat on their stomachs and one after another, single file, they roll forward on the ground to the wall. No real tek is involved; with the strength of their pectorals, abs, and legs, coupled with the rolling mechanism of the chest of their body armor, they quickly slither like snakes.

The last man stands erect a foot away from the main wall, squats completely, and jumps. He lands outside the pack of crouching mercenaries clustered close together inside the wall. Lycan scans left and right; nothing outside, but he can see heat signatures inside the buildings. The team moves low to the ground, farther into the enclave.

Twenty yards away from the backyard of one of the community houses, the Wolf Pack waits. Shoshana crouches low to one side behind a two-seater car. All around her are other skinhead Wolf Packers also crouching close to the ground behind cars, trees, and each other.

Loud noises erupt nearby, outside the enclave wall: explosions, voices over bull-horn speakers, helicopters in the air with bright search lights beaming all over.

"This is the federal police! Prepare to receive police personnel with warrants. Do not move and keep your hands in the air! Deadly force is authorized if you do not comply!"

All that follows is gunfire: shots from Jewish residents at the helicopters and police, who return fire.

Lycan effortlessly leaps into the air to land on top of a two-story building. His mercenaries also jump onto buildings and trees to do their final recon. The main police force outside the wall is the distraction, visible and loud, while the true attack force is already inside.

The gun battle grows in intensity as more residents join the fight against the police forces.

Lycan and his mercenaries leap through the air from building to building, tree to comm (communications) pole, as if they can fly. They reach the main town hall entrance with guns drawn. Half remain on top of the building, while the rest leap to the ground without a sound. Two of the men grab the main doors and swing them open.

Shoshana whispers into her ear-set, "*Panzerfaust Angriff!*"

The Wolf Pack attack begins. Several mercenaries are suddenly struck by projectiles so hard that they yell out as they are knocked into the building or several feet into the empty town hall building. Others run for cover as they are hit by direct gunfire.

Lycan lies on his chest and notices that the large projectiles being fired at them are metallic-looking replicas of human fists from the hand to the elbow. The optics of his goggles adjusts from night to infrared sight. He sees a few of the attackers twenty yards away. He aims his machine-gun pistol. Suddenly there is an explosion.

The blast throws him back a few feet and rattles his teeth. He shakes it off quickly, but tastes the blood in his mouth. He focuses again through his goggles to reacquire his targets. He sees them and hops to his feet, crouching low to fire again.

This time he's hit in the neck by something. He is now unable to hold his gun; it slips from his right hand and falls to the ground. He feels light-headed and it seems like time itself is slowing down. He touches the object that is now embedded in his neck and yanks it out to look at it. It is a metal Star of David. He looks up and there is Shoshana.

"Hi lover. We meet again," she says with a wicked smile.

She walks to him slowly with her gun aimed at the ready and circles him. Lycan realizes that he's having great difficulty standing.

"When did you think you were smarter than us? You think of yourself as *ubermensch,* but you're nothing but the lowest of *untermensch*! This is the second time you and your *mischling* quislings fell right into our trap! My trap!" Shoshana yells. "And you are too good for there to be a third. You didn't even get a chance to show off your super-soldier powers." She leans forward.

"Your Jew-killing days are over, Mr. 'Man Pretending to be Louvel' Agent Lycan. There will only be *nacht und nebel* for you."

How did she know my code name?

The death poison on the Star of David throwing star is starting to take its full effect. Fighting with all his might not to slur his speech, he finally says, "Let me blow you a kiss before I go…you Jew-Christian slag."

The trigger from his other hand releases and the bombs in his vest start to explode. Shoshana instinctively releases her own trigger. The "lobster's claw" instantly pops out from the upper back portion of her body armor and wraps around the front of her. The high-tek collapsible shield protects her from the full blast as she is blown back and crashes to the ground.

A Wolf Packer fires his missile launcher. The projectile hits the blades of one of the helicopters and electrical explosions erupt. The pilot tries to fly away, but it's too late; the helicopter spins violently and crashes to the ground. The air vehicle's passenger pods, with its occupants, are automatically jettisoned away from the main body of the craft as it explodes in a ball of yellow and orange fire.

It is complete chaos. Small groups of residents have become hundreds—men and women firing guns, shotguns, and mortars at the invading police force. The police respond with heavy fire.

Shoshana appears at the town hall building, unscathed and armed with a machine pistol in each hand, with her squad. A door opens; the Jewish Continuum members exit the hidden panic room and assemble around her.

Shoshana announces, "Their main assault team is almost here, but my people will lead all of you out of here to safety and back to your enclaves." She looks at Rabbi Hendel. "We'll take you and your people out first. They're here specifically to capture you."

He shakes his head. "No, we won't leave our Hasidic brothers. We'll be okay. Besides, to the Pagans, all Hasidim look alike."

Another Hasidic man says, "We already put calls out to every Jewish enclave within one hundred miles. In thirty minutes, there will be more Jews here with guns than former Israel. And we called the Christians. They'll be here in *fifteen* minutes."

Shoshana smiles. "Now that's the old Resistance at work!"

"What is that?" another Hasidic man asks. They all turn to see.

Two Hasidic walk with him, but all eyes are on the mountain of a man as he marches to them in full body armor from his neck to his toes, a large Star of David on his chest plate. He carries a machine gun so large it seems impossible for any human to pick it up, let alone carry it.

"You must be Goli," Shoshana says.

"Goli." Tova is surprised. "Why are you here? You're a tek-head…"

Goli has a look of disgust. "Not tonight I'm not. Get everyone out of here."

"But the enclave will be destroyed if the community doesn't stand down," Oren says.

"This isn't Galicia Enclave," one of the Hasidic men says.

"What?" Tova asks.

"We'll explain later," the Hasidic man says.

"It's a replica town," Goli says. "Now go! I have an army to destroy."

Shoshana looks at everyone. "Ladies and gentlemen, our departure has been requested immediately."

Goli says nothing more. He touches a button near the neck part of his body armor and a spiked, titanium helmet encloses his head. His face is completely obscured, but the eyes glow red.

The Continuum members follow the lead Wolf Packers. Tova and her husband move to the front of the group. Tova whispers to Shoshana, "We need you to drop us off somewhere."

Shoshana nods.

Goli, in his mechanized body armor, watches them leave. He turns his focus back to the main wall in readiness. The gunfire between enclave resistance and police forces is everywhere. Goli slowly rises in the air.

The Wolf Pack gets the Continuum members and their delegations into black SUVs and speeds away on the dirt road out of the enclave. They pass a caravan of other SUVs, cars, and trucks racing by in the opposite direction, filled with armed men. It must be the Christians. In ten minutes, they pass another caravan speeding past them. The cars, trucks, and SUVs are filled with armed Jews.

Miami, Florida
11:25 p.m., 13 April 2090

Tova remembers when Christian Orders killed Master Pastor. Among his many sins, he had been a top government informant. Orders do not interfere in the internal business of another. It was not her place to criticize the action, but here she was about to do the same thing.

Mr. C, the head of the Wise Men, opens the door. A smiling Tova and Mr. Tova greet him.

"Godfather, my boy!" Mr. Tova gives him a bear hug, for which he was quite known.

Tova shakes his hand. "Oy vey, husband, don't crush the life out of him." To C: "Where is Jana?"

Mr. C says, "It's girls' night out for the wife."

Mr. Tova looks at him. "Sad for you."

Mr. C smiles. "No, good for me. I can't get a thing done without her constant interruptions. This is my cherished alone time. Oh, let me show you something." Mr. C runs to his living room desk and opens the drawer.

The first bullet from Mr. C's gun misses Mr. Tova by inches, but the second one hits him in the shoulder. Mr. Tova falls back. Grabbing at anything, he pulls a large mirror from the wall. The frame crashes to the ground with a thunderous boom before the glass itself smashes into millions of pieces.

Tova's first bullet hits Mr. C in the center of his chest. He cries out in an almost high-pitched squeal. Tova's second bullet hits him in the forearm. Tova can't fight her impulse; she looks to her fallen husband.

Mr. Tova's first bullet hits just above Mr. C's head, shattering the window. His second and third bullets hit the wall, missing Mr. C, who throws his body to the ground as he shoots his third bullet, hitting Tova in the center of her chest; she collapses to the floor.

Mr. C lies on the ground, staring down at the hardwood floor. "You're both pretty pathetic in your old age. I'm still alive!" He touches his chest. His flesh-colored bulletproof vest—complete with fake chest hairs—has saved his life. He reaches with one hand to pull his e-pad from his pocket and starts to dial a number.

Mr. Tova lies on the ground, staring up at the ceiling. His eyes are tearing up, not because of his wounds and the pain, but because he's wondering if the bastard just killed his wife. He and Tova had met in Israel. Two young Jewish Americans leaving their birth country to join the Israeli Defense Force, which had become almost a rite of passage among a large segment of American Jews. They were at the top of their class in marksmanship, and through their frequent contests to best each other had fallen in love and married. But that was over thirty years ago, and even then they never shot a live person, only realistic robot targets.

Mr. Tova yells, "Forty years we've known you! You're the godfather to our eldest children. And you sell out your people to the enemy! You Herod bastard!"

Mr. C says, "Look at us. We're talkers, not fighters. Look at us on the ground. We can't even last through one gunfire exchange."

"You're a dead man, C! And so you know, your government masters didn't get us."

"I gathered that, you fat monkey, when you and your dumb wife stood at my door with your stupid fake smiles."

"I'm going to kill you, you Philistine monkey, and then stuff you in the toilet for your masters to find!"

"Go fornicate yourself! You had your chance! You're no Cowboy Rabbi! You're nothing!"

"Why would you do this?! Decades of publicly fighting for our people while in your black heart selling us all out in the end to our blood enemies. To that evil President T. Wilson, who wants to purge every religious person from the country by any means necessary—except for the Muslims, of course. Millions of our people mean nothing to you. So President Haman found something to buy even the billionaire Wise Men with."

Mr. C calls out, "Is this where I'm supposed to confess all my sins and tell you the whole story? Sorry, wrong religion. That's the Catholics. Figure it out yourself."

Mr. C crawls forward a bit and opens the bottom drawer of the desk. He's about to grab the two grenades inside. *I'll blow them to pieces!* He senses something and turns his head.

Tova is standing there, aiming her gun at his head.

Mr. C says, "Do it, but if you kill me, you won't learn a thing."

Mr. Tova stands next to her, pointing his gun. "We're Jews. We're accustomed to a little disappointment in life."

They fire their guns in unison, killing Mr. C with multiple shots.

I Prefer the Lawyer, You Keep the Sword

"Even in a nation where the Constitution has been found to be unconstitutional, a good lawyer is still the damn scariest thing to have, second only to a terrorist bomb." – Elliot Finegold

"As your attorney, it is my duty to inform you that it is not important that you understand what I'm doing or why you're paying me so much money. What's important is that you continue to do so." – Hunter S. Thompson, gonzo journalist

Georgetown, South Carolina
11:45 p.m., 13 April 2090

High above the sky, in the clouds, a drone hovers. Its surveillance mode targets a large group massing. The image gets larger and larger to reveal more federal police in attack vehicles rapidly racing toward the enclave. Suddenly, the dozens of vehicles simply coast to a stop. All of their lights go out. The drone turns and flies out of region. Was it told to do so by the Grid, or was it—?

Goli switches his optics from regular to thermal as he continues to watch them.

"What do we do, sir?" one of the policemen asks. "There's

nothing. No power. No comms. No Net."

"I never heard of tek-jammers working so far away from the source," the commander says. "I thought these people were backward Trogs. Okay, everyone get out of the vehicles. Grab as many weapons as you can carry."

"What are we doing, chief?"

"We're going to walk. We're only two miles away."

The policemen look at each other.

"Walk? Sir, people don't walk. That's something only animals do."

"Sir, I'm not allowed to do any physical activity below the waist, except for sex. This is totally unacceptable. Can't we call a taxi or something?"

"Everyone shut up! Grab your weapons and start walking. That's an order!" the chief yells.

"Sir, the ear-sets are not working either. We can't hear you. Use the bullhorn."

11:52 p.m.

Hundreds of federal police march through empty, flat prairie with their old-style squeeze flashlights and weapons swinging. They stop, noticing first two glowing red dots approaching, representing the eight-foot frame of a man—it can't be a robot; no tek is working. They notice the enormous machine gun in his hands. The police immediately begin firing at him.

Red dots appear on the chest of all the men. Goli squeezes the trigger and projectiles pour out of the weapon, guided toward the bodies of the attacking police force. Screams are everywhere. In an instant, they all lie flat and motionless on the ground.

Washington Park, Washington DC
10:32 a.m., 14 April 2090

The Christians came to the "New World" in the seventeenth century, fleeing the persecution of the Christian theocracies of Western Europe. In 1776 America, 98 percent of the people were Protestant, less than two percent were Catholic, and 0.2 percent were Jewish. The public square everywhere reflected that religious, and specifically Christian, majority.

One would never know that American history now. The Capitol is devoid of any religiosity—a triumphant epitome of American religious-free zones. All religious images and engravings had been expunged from every government building. "Holiness to the Lord" engraved on the Washington Monument was sand-blasted away decades ago. The murals from the Rotunda Wall of the Capitol building are gone: the Pilgrim's prayer, the Baptism of Pocahontas, De Soto's planting a cross on the banks of the Mississippi, George Washington passing into Heaven. America's religious history had been cut out and shipped to the farthest, darkest corners of the Smithsonian Institution.

The Ten Commandments had been removed from the US Supreme Court building, as had happened in every courthouse in the nation so many years ago, along with the sculpture of Moses holding the Commandments over the east portico. The "fascists," as Elliott calls them, tried to have even the Martin Luther King Jr. Monument condemned. "Such a display of the government, this statue of a Jew-Christian leader is an explicit endorsement of religion and is therefore illegal" was what had been said, but fortunately the anti-skin-color bigotry work of the historic civil rights leader had saved it—at least for now. Even the Abraham Lincoln Memorial was under assault; they wanted it destroyed. They had already succeeded in getting the inscriptions from his Second Inaugural Address and

Gettysburg Address removed from the north and south side chambers because of references to God.

Elliott Finegold sits in the park across from the Abraham Memorial, eating his lunch. The park is relatively quiet by rush-hour standards. There were only about a few hundred people milling about. When lunchtime officially starts in an hour, there will be many thousands of people around.

Elliott is forty-something, with short black hair and flecks of gray throughout, a full beard and mustache, and a two-piece black office-suit with a solid white shirt and a black tie. It is all he wears. He is one of the highest-paid lawyers in the District and a registered Jew. In fact, he has been the only religious person among the Top Fifty Power Lawyers of the District for the last eight years.

He loves his quiet time, relaxing before and after a case. He notices two fellow lawyers walk past. They glance at him but continue walking, not saying a word. He's been in the same courtroom with them for years, but they have never once said a simple "hello." He could care less; he hates lawyers.

There was a time when being a lawyer was admired among Faithers. Not anymore. Pagans had so artfully used the law as a weapon against all Faithers that lawyers were reviled. Unfortunately, there was such an overrepresentation of Jews among their ranks that it was religious Jews who helped eradicate the phrase "secular Jew" from common language. All Jews were religious and any secular person was a Pagan.

Elliott went into the legal profession not to be a lawyer, but to use the law against the Pagans. They used the law to hurt his people. He was going to use the law to hurt them back tenfold, and that's exactly what he had done over his two-decade career. He had often said, "The law is war—war without bloodshed…barely."

There is one notable exception to the religious-free zone—

Muslims. They are eager to register and walk around with their armbands adorned with crescent symbols. Two of them boldly walk down the sidewalk. He recognizes them as lobbyists for the Islamic Caliphate. Elliott laughs to himself. It was like Joseph Stalin and Franklin Roosevelt. Yes, they were allies against the Nazis in World War Two, but everyone knew that once that was done, their guns would be pointed at each other. The détente between President T. Wilson and the Islamic Emperor Al-Siddiq would inevitably evaporate one day.

Muslims registered with the government because they saw it as a religious calling, not a despicable invasion of privacy and religious liberty, as all other Faithers did. For him, he didn't view his own registration as hypocrisy, but a necessary evil that allowed him to legally protect his people from the government.

Elliott's e-pad rings in his jacket pocket. He grabs his ear-set from his pocket. "Hello." Elliott listens for a few moments. He jumps up. "What?! I'll be on the next plane!"

Georgetown, South Carolina
12:02 p.m., 14 April 2090

The shootout at the Jewish enclave is on the newsfeed everywhere. It is referred to as "a communal habitat in Trog-land." Reports mention the hundreds of wounded policemen who were incapacitated by an "unknown army of assailants" two miles from the main site. Law enforcement has the entire area encircled.

Elliott stands staring at the burning, charred remains of what was once the Jewish enclave of Galicia. Firemen—biped robots with hose cannons snaking from their backs and arching over their heads—walk among the ruins and extinguish the last remnants of fire by spraying white-water. Human firemen ceased being used decades ago in America.

Simón Bolívar International Airport, Venezuela
9:07 a.m., 11 April 2090

A large crowd watches the plane land from inside the airport. The Vice President of Venezuela smiles as he watches the special passengers disembark. Rabbi Hendel and the entire prison fugitive Hasidic Jews.

The Jews are received by a female aide who greets them with a nod and leads them to the restrooms. "You and your families can freshen up. We are not like America; we have separate restrooms for man and woman. Afterwards, the Vice President will meet with you all."

She nods again and walks away as the men and women march into the restrooms.

It has been over twenty minutes and no one has come out yet. She walks into the female area. "Hello. Are you ready?" She sees no one. She opens each stall and every one of them is empty! *Where did all the women and children go?* She starts to panic and runs for the door, but stops. She slowly walks to the garbage receptacle and pulls out something. It is a mask of a woman, with lifelike hair and a headscarf attached.

She runs to the men's area and into the main restroom. It is empty. She frantically walks in circles and starts to breathe heavily.

Two security men run in. "Where are the people? Where are they? What's happening?"

Washington DC
11:11 a.m., 14 April 2090

The Florence Supermax warden faces the Attorney General. Other elected officials, aides, and agents stand for the impromptu meeting.

"It's confirmed. The prison break fugitives are in Venezuela.

They flew into the country two days ago. We still don't know which airline. Their President himself called us to gloat," says one of the agents.

"That damn country," mutters one of the aides.

The warden shakes his head. "Excuse me. If the escapees were in Venezuela two days ago, why did Homeland attack some Trog-land ghetto town last night? I was told the intel was rock-solid. The arrest warrant was one hundred fifteen pages! How could we be so wrong? How many agent casualties?"

"Hundreds," an aide answers. "No fatalities that we know of, though."

"I have to meet with the lawyers for the Trog-town at 4:30," the Attorney General says. "Apparently, they want to sue the government."

"Are we going to pursue the escapees?" the warden asks.

The Attorney General says emphatically, "Yes. This office will pursue them wherever, and we don't care what country doesn't like it."

The warden shakes his head. "They break out of prison, get out of the country. This is not good. They want to close my prison permanently. My job is on the line."

"Let me get ready for the stupid lawyers and we can talk afterwards and figure it out," the Attorney General says. He points at one of the aides in the room and motions for him to follow him to the opposite corner of the room. "Were there any fatalities in the raid?"

The man hesitates, but answers, "We lost the entire special ops team and their bodies were burned in the airstrike fire."

The AG looks at him angrily.

"We had to call in an airstrike," the man says. "We couldn't do a normal drone strike because of their tek-jammers. We couldn't get in close, and the gun battle was so intense. But it was a very localized strike."

"The entire town is a burnt-out mess. That's not localized." He notices the President's advisor standing just outside the door. To the man: "Get the President to classify the entire thing to shut down the media."

The man nods and the AG walks into the hallway to the President's man.

"I'm on my way to talk to their stupid lawyers," the AG says.

The President's man leans forward and says softly, "We are two years out, but we are officially in election mode. 'God' wants there to be no issues with this incident, these Outlanders, or especially the Jew-Christians. Review the vid-file I sent, and if any of the lawyers are on that list, you are to settle the case *immediately* and make it all go away."

4:30 p.m., 14 April 2090

The conference room is overflowing with lawyers yelling at the justice department aide. They are the legal representatives of the Trog population: Anarchists, Hedonists, Nihilists, Pagan Goths, Nudists, Space Cadets, and common Trogs.

"The Attorney General will be here shortly," the aide says loudly.

"We are going to sue all of you for a billion, no, a septillion dollars!" Skanky Sally yells. The Anarchist lawyer stands proudly in her reflecting black body suit, a skull and bones tattoo on her forehead.

A District policeman enters and holds up his hand. "Everyone, please listen. The Attorney General will be entering the room. Please remain standing where you are and do not approach him; he will approach you. Do not shout over him. Do not make any threatening moves. Any other behavior is unacceptable and will be punished by immediate detention and incarceration, revocation of any legal license, and forfeiture of any legal standing you have before the court."

The group quiets down just as Elliot Finegold enters and quietly moves to the back of the room. The policeman sees his Star of David armband.

"Sir, as an officer of the court, I hope you're in compliance with the Rule of Law, which includes all Body Integrity laws."

Elliott stops and looks at him. "Oh, the circumcision thing again. Too bad 'body integrity' doesn't apply to children being sent for gender change operations or toddlers having breast augmentations. Pass a law to supposedly protect Muslim women and against child abuse, but use it against Jewish men. Should I pull it out now for your inspection, or should we go to your office? I do need to urinate, and it might as well be on you."

The policeman's face turns red. Most of the lawyers are smiling or chuckling. Elliott turns away from the policeman and takes a seat near the back of the conference room.

The AG enters the room with two bodyguards. The lawyers see him and surround him. All of them are yelling at the same time.

"Shut up!" he yells and the lawyers quiet down. Immediately, Bloke raises his hand. The lawyer's entire face is covered in piercings and he is wearing dark black eyeliner. A sharp contrast to his white suit. "May I?"

The AG nods.

"Thank you, Mr. Attorney General. Thank you for meeting us directly. Unlike your predecessors, we see you at least pretend to take us seriously. Our rights have been violently trampled on."

"Average Americans never talk about rights," the AG says. "The only people who talk about rights all the time are criminals. Honest people don't worry about that because the government looks out for them."

The lawyers stare at him, some incredulous, others contemptuously.

"You all can bring whatever lawsuit you want against the United States of America, its fifty-three states and commonwealths, but this office will vigorously defend this case. And I hope you realize that with loser-pays statues, you will be liable for any costs borne by the government in this frivolous case."

"I hope you know," Bloke continues, "that off-Grid populations are Americans too, and those of us who chose not to live in your dictatorial tek-cities are not lesser humans."

"Save your speeches for the opening remarks of your case." The AG suddenly notices. He walks slowly to the only person now sitting down. Elliott looks back at him with a slight smirk.

The AG continues to watch him. "Miss Flo."

"Yes, sir?" The justice department aide moves closer to him.

"Prepare all the paperwork and settle this case for all damages."

"Excuse me, sir?" She is shocked, and so are all the lawyers in the room. The AG turns and exits the room with his two bodyguards.

The room erupts in talk again. Elliott quietly stands and leaves the room, too. He walks past the elevators to the stairs.

"Mr. Elliott," a voice says behind him. Bloke stands there with Skanky Sally and two other lawyers: a Goth wearing white man-panty hose and another man who is so grungy it looks like he hasn't washed in years. Elliott waits as Bloke moves closer. "Mr. Elliott, I don't know what game you Jew-Christians and the government are playing, but please leave us out of it. The tek-city dwellers think you Jew-Christians live in Trog-land, but we both know you live beyond Trog-land. We have our space and you have yours. You and I both know that the Jew-Christian town the government destroyed in that airstrike wasn't there three days ago. Leave us out of your dangerous games. You Jew-Christians believe in your afterlife nirvana, but we want to enjoy our nirvana here on Earth, as long as our bodies and minds can take or last. Don't use our people as pawns again."

"I'll see you all at the settlement hearing to see how much money we get." Elliott gives a fake smile and walks toward the stair exit.

Location Unknown
9:11 a.m., 15 April 2090

Elliott Finegold is led, blindfolded, down a flight of stairs by two skinhead Wolf Pack members. They remove the thick blindfold from his face. He looks up at the dozen people sitting at a long conference table, facing him.

"So is this the new vaunted Jewish Continuum I've been hearing about?" he asks.

"Maybe," a man's voice says.

"You all hurt my feelings by blindfolding me." His eyes adjust to the dimmer light and he immediately notices the Tovas. "What happened to you?"

Tova says, "We're okay, Elliott."

"What happened? You look wounded."

"Yes, but you should see the other guy," Mr. Tova says.

"Was it the government?"

Mr. Tova says, "Not directly, but yes."

"What do you mean?"

Shoshana says, "Pagans use the slang term mole. We prefer *quisling*, a traitor or collaborator. My favorite is *nacktschnecke*, a slug or an organism lower than a crawling, filthy rat."

"Spy? Who?" he asks them.

"You knew Mr. C," Tova says.

Elliott is taken aback. "Knew? The Wise Men? You're joking."

Tova shakes her head. "No joke here."

"I've known him as long as you and your husband have. Where is he?"

Tova says, "Dead. Which happens when my husband and I shoot you multiple times."

Elliott is stunned. "What proof do you have?"

Mr. Tova answers, "The bullets he tried to kill us with."

"But they were the ones who had me working with Gideon and Goli."

Tova asks, "What about Goli? Working on what?"

"Who's Gideon?" Mr. Tova asks.

Elliott looks at them again. "You mean you don't know? Goli and Gideon are working on an investigation. And Gideon is in hiding now because of the investigation."

Tova and her husband look at each other, then back at Elliott. "What are you talking about? The Conservative Elders authorized no investigation."

"What about the other two Wise Men?"

Shoshana answers him. "They've managed to disappear with their families."

Elliott shakes his head again. "I can't believe I'm hearing this. Mr. C a spy? The Wise Men?" He looks at the group. "What's the motive?"

"Who cares?" Mr. Tova says.

"Motives matter."

"A Muslim wakes up one day, leaves his wife and four kids, straps a bomb to his body, and blows up innocent people. Who cares what the motive is? All we care about is the action," Shoshana says.

Elliott realizes. "That explains how they had terrorist arrest warrants against all of you, by name, even though you're all supposed to be off-Grid."

Tova says, "Warrants made up with manufactured evidence."

Elliott says angrily, "The government can indict a kosher bagel, and they can arrest anyone they want for being a terrorist. President T. Wilson even had a previous president classified as a terrorist. Don't be naïve. I suggest, as your attorney, that number one: you keep a very, very low profile for the next eighteen months at least. If you want to do anything, contract out the work. I can assure you that you have no idea what real government surveillance is, but you're going to find out. Number two: Talk to Gideon and Goli about the investigation they're working on. You must follow up on it. I don't know all the details, but what I do know is that they've uncovered disturbing information. Number three: Find the damn motive for why Mr. C and the Wise Men would betray us."

Mr. Tova says, "They wanted to be the Head-Jews-In-Charge."

"That's ridiculous. They wouldn't betray for that, something so petty."

"Wouldn't they? Power is not petty to a lot of people. It's how President Haman got so many to betray us over his Project Purify, grand ghetto in the desert, plan for all of us."

Elliott says, "I know none of you really believe that is the motive." He shakes his head again. "I really came to tell all of you to please keep a low profile. No more prison breakouts, airstrike tricks, wiping out hundreds of federal agents at one time, nothing. Not all the Pagans are stupid. Some of them may actually figure out things if we're not careful.

"Listen to me, all of you. We all live under a secular government and secular laws. I don't care how much we want to wall ourselves up in our own religious communities. The law matters. Everything can't be a violent, physical battle. It's not possible, but more importantly, it's not necessary. Let's make the law work for us."

Shoshana makes a disapproving sound. "Before the Nazis started shipping us off to the gas chambers, they started with the law. Four hundred separate pieces of legislation that defined, isolated, excluded, segregated, and impoverished all Jews. The law today simply tells us what force they will use against us tomorrow."

Elliott says, "All I'm saying is, we must use the law to our benefit where we can. Use me to your benefit. Always remember, this country is run by its elite, like every other. Everybody else either doesn't care, is too addicted to whatever vice they have, is too crazy, or is too stupid. They're followers, sheep. The elite run everything from behind the curtains. And no matter how hateful the public is toward religious people, what they hate more is government authority messing with innocent citizens. How do you think I've become so rich defending religious people in an anti-religious, secular country? You remember that and you become bulletproof. If we're going to return to our ancient violence, please be sure to follow the path of the Maccabees, and not the Zealots. The former introduced fighting for religious freedom. The latter introduced religious terrorism. The former liberated Ancient Israel for centuries from the Greeks. The latter led to the destruction of Ancient Israel at the hands of the Romans. Let's not help President T. Wilson hurt us."

"That is what the Continuum is for," Tova says.

Elliott gives a laugh. "With this group after them, the last two Wise Men are going to wake up in the middle of the night with an unkosher horse's head next to them in the bed."

Tova says, smiling, "Sounds like a great idea."

Elliott says, "So we're back to the days of ruthless Jews in America."

Shoshana says, "That's what has always been needed. The days when we weren't known for our religiosity, intellectualism, and piety, but as ruthless, ferocious fighters."

"Fair point, but let's not lose ourselves in the role, shall we? Remember, I'm paid a lot of money to legally defend Faithers against the government and bypass the raw confrontations. I win my cases."

A young woman, also at the table, speaks up for the first time. "Mr. Finegold?"

He looks at her. "Yes?"

"My name is Rachel Glick. You are a wealthy man, and the one thing I learned from my former boss—who is a very wealthy man—is that birds of a feather flock together. I agree with you that we need to find the other two Wise Men. You've traveled in their circles. They set in motion an attack that was designed to obliterate us. I believe I know the motive, but we need to find these men. Do you understand?"

Elliott pauses. "I do. But do you realize that they would have already fled the country? Gone to where we wouldn't have any contacts, and their billions can buy them new identities and anonymity for life. If you didn't catch them by now, they're gone."

Tova leans forward. "How much would it cost for us to find them, then?"

Elliott shakes his head. "Let it go. We have too many major issues to deal with. Remember, you're the vaunted New Jewish Continuum. You have to ignore the little things and focus on the big things. If they are the traitors you claim, they'll get what's coming to them. You have to have faith in that eventuality."

Shoshana says, "We believe in tying up loose ends."

"They will be tied, just not now." He smiles. "It'll be an Eichmann operation."

She smiles too and nods. "Yes, it took us a decade and a half, but we hunted down our prey."

Tova announces, "Well, Elliott, welcome to New Jewish Continuum. You passed your interview. Now tell us about this one working with Goli, this Gideon."

The League of Artifacts, Curios, Curiosities, Mementos, Relics and Antiquities

"Moses is our greatest prophet. He led the Jews out of slavery, unleashed the Ten Plagues upon our enemy of Egypt, guided us for forty years in the wilderness, carried down the Torah from Mount Sinai, and prepared the Jews to enter the Promised Land. Moses was the last human being on Earth to see the very face of God." – Rabbi Oren, Orthodox Jewish Order

"Let me tell you something that we Israelis have against Moses. He took us forty years through the desert in order to bring us to the one spot in the Middle East that has no oil." – Golda Meir, 4th Prime Minister of Israel (Jewish Israel)

Washington DC Center Mall
10:05 a.m., 2 January 2080

Mr. Haggard is an imposing man, both physically and politically. When he was a young man in his twenties, he distinguished himself in the boxing world. Even now, forty years later, he looks like he could still beat anyone into a sloppy pile of poo.

He walks into a retro analog bookstore. In Tek World,

bookstores all but vanished many, many years ago. What's the point when you can download any book ever published in the world, in any language, to whatever device you want? However, they were making a comeback of sorts and it wasn't just Jew-Christians who were shunning untouchable *digitality*. Growing numbers of people wanted things you could touch and pick up, and that, more importantly, weren't connected to the Net.

"Can I help you?" the small man behind the counter asks.

"I'm looking for a real Jew. Not a fake, registered one."

"Excuse me? We sell books, not Jews. Also, what is a Jew anyway?"

Haggard smirks. "You sell these analog books. So you know your customers. You know the Pagans from the Jew-Christians. And don't be coy. You know what Jews, Christians, and the religious lot of them are. I'm looking for a Jew, not older than thirty-five, extremely well-educated, specializing in history preferred, great work ethic, and looking for work. I want to hire him or her. But it has to be a Jew. I want to finish all my interviews by week's end."

"Is this a joke?"

"Do you know who I am?"

The small man pauses. "Yes."

"Then you know I don't make jokes and I have lots of money. How many analog books do I need to buy for you and me to establish some goodwill?"

"Start buying and I'll tell you when my nether parts start tingling."

"The Castle," Washington DC
10:00 a.m., 18 January 2080

It is the official headquarters of the Smithsonian Global Institution, and like many of its building complexes, it is also a historical and architectural landmark, established on 10 August 1846.

Mr. Haggard knows that the first half-dozen or so people inquiring about his job opportunity will be "decoys." Jew-Christians are truly paranoid people. But he can't blame them with the current occupant of the White House and the disposition of the government for the last half century. Being an unregistered Jew-Christian is still punishable by fine, and noncompliance, or lying about religious affiliation, could even put a person in jail. As usual, Muslims are exempt, but everyone knows that it's just a matter of time before that will change.

He has a good feeling. He thinks he has a real one waiting in his office.

Rachel Glick sits quietly and admires the museum-like quality of the spacious office: paintings, statues, figurines, busts, and a seeming endless array of curios.

Mr. Haggard enters and sits behind his spacious antique desk. "How are you?"

Rachel is twenty-six years old, petite in form, with very fair skin and shoulder-length brown hair. "I'm fine, sir."

"You're a Jew? Prove it."

She stares at him. The *chutzpa* of these Pagans. "Why?"

"You're here for the job, right?"

"Yes."

"Then prove it."

"I repeat my question: why?"

"Good. You have a semblance of a backbone. To answer your question, only a real Jew will have the innate grasp of Judeo-Christian history that I need. I don't have time to train the person. They must know it already. And Jews, as a people, have a longer history of historical preservation than even the Christians, so I need a Jew. So prove to me you're a Jew."

"What does religious affiliation, or lack thereof, have to do with working for a museum?"

"Are you offended by my request?"

"Extremely."

"Good. Now suck it up and get over it. And the Smithsonian is not a museum. So prove to me you're a Jew. I don't have all day."

"As a Jew, a member of the oldest monotheistic religion on the planet, and a people who have existed for over five thousand years, I will not be demeaned. Maybe your logic makes sense for a Pagan, but you are not going to find any Jew, or any other religion for that matter, who will sit here and answer such a ridiculous question. The only entity I have to prove myself to is God, and you are certainly not Him. We've dealt with far scarier villains than you, Mr. Job Interviewer, persecuted by the best of them, various subspecies of Pagans, Europeans, and Muslims. I shall not be continuing with your job interview, so take my Torah and shove it."

"Christians."

"What?"

"You and the Christians seem to be like conjoined twins nowadays, but they persecuted you too. Some two thousand years of Christian…anti-Semitism, I believe is the word."

"Yes, persecuted and killed us. Persecuted and killed Christians, too. Both Jews and Christians today call them dark Christians, but they no longer exist. Christians remain our strongest allies in the world, even more so now than when they first appeared over two thousand years ago. I would add, Jews survived sixteen hundred years of anti-Semitism, but we almost didn't survive four years of Pagan Nazism."

"I can't argue with that. Which side of the Wiesenthal-Wiesel debate do you take?"

"*Oy vey*, am I still being interviewed? I didn't get such intellectual questions even when I was at religious university. Both men had value in their positions, but I side with the Simon Wiesenthal position. The Holocaust shouldn't be viewed as just a Jewish thing. It, along with all the world's genocides, should be known by all people. Though I totally respect Elie Wiesel's position that the Holocaust was uniquely Jewish."

"Why aren't you registered?"

"Why should I? I'm a human being, not a slave, and I will not be registering now or ever for some fascist database, no matter what laws they pass."

"How do you feel about working for not only a Pagan, but for the government, in a sense?"

"I'm not sure. What's the job?"

Mr. Haggard is satisfied. "Do you know what the Smithsonian is?"

"I would say the largest museum in America, but you'd get offended again."

Haggard smiles. "A British scientist by the name of James Smithson bequeathed his vast fortune to America. This was pre-Muslim Britain and he gave it to the fledgling nation of the United States of America; a country that he never set foot in. Some say he was a prophet himself, who saw the rise of this nation and the decline of his own. His estate gave ten million dollars to the US government and that was back in 1829, so that was serious money. That's still serious money to ninety-nine percent of the people today. What was Smithson's goal? Bestow upon the government of America the ability to create the 'establishment for the increase and diffusion of knowledge among men.' That statement still gives me the shudders today, the premier patron for the preservation of history.

"The Smithsonian is the largest collective of libraries, museums, and research centers on the planet. We are open every day of the year, no holidays. Because of our research centers, we are one hundred percent privately funded, either through direct commerce or private donors, with a total budget of two billion dollars annually. The US government owns most of our national treasures, but we retain them. We have an inventory of over two hundred fifty million objects."

Rachel is impressed. He points to a plaque on the wall behind her. She turns around and sees:

"I marvel at the resilience of the Jewish people. Their best characteristic is their desire to remember. No other people has such an obsession with memory." - Elie Wiesel.

Mr. Haggard continues. "That quote inspired me to go into the career that I've spent most of my adult life in after I got bored in my twenties, beating up people for money as a boxer on the national circuit. People are meaningless to me. They grow old, wither, die, and disappear. But the things we create, build with our own hands, can last forever and, in my mind, can be more real than we ever were. History is what I'm obsessed with—studying it, collecting it, maintaining it, protecting it. Sadly, my fellow Pagans don't share my reverence for history. Instead, their hatred for the religious and the ancient has made its way to even these hallowed doors. I'm the sole gatekeeper, keeping the barbarians from permanently destroying the very history of America. They're insane. They're like the Muslims. Mohammed had no problem with the Buddha statues in Afghanistan, but his descendants had to destroy them in the name of Mohammed at the beginning of the millennium. Likewise, the Pagans of early America had no problem at all with the fact that America was founded by Christians, and that was reflected in all our founding documents, but their descendants are on their own jihad to erase that historical fact." He looks at her. "When can you start?"

"What do you want to hire me to do specifically?"

"You will be my first hire of my League of Artifacts, Curios, Curiosities, Mementos, Relics, and Antiquities. A mouthful, but that's what I like about it. You will hire everyone else in the League. You will be my secret society within our Smithsonian Society. Those of us who have given our lives to protecting the history housed in all the Smithsonian facilities. The League will be charged with one specific mission: to protect all American artifacts, documents, and antiquities of a religious nature. The Mayflower Compact, the Federalist Papers, the Constitution and the Bill of Rights, the Inaugural Addresses of our American Presidents for the first two hundred years of the nation, especially George Washington and Abraham Lincoln, copies of all State Constitutions, the Declaration of Independence, the Gettysburg Address, and the Emancipation Proclamation. You will never allow any of these items to be given to the government for any reason, even if you have a signed order from the President of the United States himself. If necessary, you and the League will *liberate* these items to a secret location that we will establish."

Rachel looks at him. "Is this job…dangerous?"

"Life can be dangerous."

"Do you honestly believe that the nation's historical items are in danger of being destroyed by the government? That could never happen. Even a Pagan population wouldn't stand for it."

"Have you converted to atheism?"

"Excuse me?"

"Have you converted to atheism?"

"No."

"Well, I've been a Pagan all my life, and I've personally raised some ten billion dollars for the many political residents of the

District, both on Capitol Street and Pennsylvania Avenue. You know your people. I know mine. The League is essential. The Muslims took over Western Europe and they immediately started destroying the museums, libraries, and monuments. Pagans, Muslims, same difference."

It takes Rachel some time to trust Haggard. After all, why would a Pagan do this thing? What was his motive? She soon got her answer: Haggard, as a twenty-seven-year-old man, did a work internship overseas at Jewish Israel's Yad Vashem, the revered living memorial to the Holocaust. He was the only Pagan on staff. It was there where he became obsessed with the preservation of history and imparting its meaning for future generations. When he returned to America, his life's mission was set in stone.

Smithsonian, Washington DC
9:01 a.m., 6 February 2080

Rachel leads Mr. Haggard down in the basement offices of the museum. "Everyone, I'd like you to meet our boss, Mr. Haggard."

It takes her just two weeks to hire her team: seven college kids, four male and three female, all in their early twenties.

Mr. Haggard carries two large, long tubes. "Gather around, everyone. I want to show you the historical symbols of the League." He walks to the large, main work table and unwraps the paintings. "These are two versions of what the Great Seal of America could have been. Both of these paintings are by Benson John Lossing, born 12 February 1813, died 3 June 1891. He was a prolific and popular American historian, known best for his illustrated books on the American Revolution and American Civil War.

"When the United States of America was founded, three men were tasked with coming up with what would be the Great Seal of the country: John Adams, Thomas Jefferson, and Benjamin Franklin.

The first two men would become our second and third US Presidents. Two of the three men came before Congress with similar designs for what they wanted the Great Seal of the USA to be. We know the Seal today as the bald eagle on one side and the pyramid with the eye at the top on the other, but what two of our Founders wanted to depict was the scene from the Israelite exodus from Egypt."

Haggard takes out his e-pad and touches the screen. "These are Benjamin Franklin's notes in his own handwriting. 'Moses standing on the shore, and extending his hand over the sea; thereby causing the same to overwhelm Pharaoh, who is sitting in an open chariot, a crown on his head and a sword in his hand. Rays from a pillar of fire in the clouds reaching to Moses, to express that he acts by command of the Deity.' His suggested motto: 'Rebellion to Tyrants is Obedience to God.'"

"I never met a Pagan who can quote religion like you, Mr. Haggard," one of them says.

"It's religion for you; it's history for me." He continues, "Thomas Jefferson's suggestion for the front of the seal was the children of Israel in the wilderness, led by a cloud by day and a pillar of fire by night. Congress ultimately rejected their choices for the new Seal and chose the eagle, but they kept the words for our country's motto: E Pluribus Unum, From Many One.

"Make sure to take full advantage of your opportunity of working in the Smithsonian. Explore it every chance you get." To Rachel he says, "How did you find everyone?"

Rachel says, "I put out the word and interviewed applicants from different Hillels, local and in other states."

"What's a Hillel?" Haggard asks.

"A Jewish religious college," Rachel answers.

"That's right. Jews and Christians don't send their kids to public schools."

There is an eruption of laughter. "No!" "Never!"

"What do you call your elementary, middle, and high schools?"

"Day schools. If it's solely religious, yeshiva, or for post bar-mitzvah ages, a mesivta."

Mr. Haggard nods. "Well, good. You got your team from Jewish colleges. So everyone on your team is Jewish?"

"Well, Sam isn't. He's our token Christian."

"Interesting. Why would a Christian go to a Jewish college?"

Sam says, "For biblical studies."

Mr. Haggard seems intrigued. "Is that common?"

Rachel says, "Oh, yes. Lots of Christians study Torah with Jews. For us it's the Torah, for them it's their Old Testament."

Mr. Haggard says, "Like I said before, your two religions are like conjoined twins. Well, get the League to work. Lots and lots to do when it comes to artifacts, curios, curiosities, mementos, relics, and antiquities."

The Fall of Jewish Israel – Jerusalem Proper, 2081 (11 Months Later)

Explosions, mortar fire, and gunfire are heard in the distance. Helicopters fill the sky, evacuating residents, and military gunships flying into the battle.

Rachel runs through the streets leading four very young League members. They are terrified by the chaos. People are running frantically everywhere, carrying what they can; an occasional car madly drives by filled with people, furniture, supplies, or all of the above. Mortar shells are still dropping nearby.

That noise! What is that noise? The haunting sounds echo through the air, sounds of millions of crying people, children, not human though. Cats! Rachel and her team see them: cats everywhere making sounds that could only be described as…crying. The cats of

Jerusalem abandoned; their masters dead or left them behind. They see the hastily written graffiti in English on the wall: "*G-d has turned His back on Israel!*"

One of the kids yells at her, "We have to get out of here! We're going to die!"

Rachel yells back, "We must find our contact!"

Another kid yells, "We have to leave now! We're Americans! The Muslims will kill us for sure!"

Rachel leads them quickly into an empty synagogue. "Mr. Tendlar! Are you here?!"

There is no answer. The building is empty and looks as though every religious item was stripped from it some time ago.

One of the kids says, "They're gone already!"

Suddenly, an explosion makes them all dive for the ground. It was outside the building.

"We're going to die!" a kid yells.

Rachel huddles them all together. "Listen to me. We'll get out of here. We're not going back to the truck, it's too dangerous. We're going to run as fast as we can to the evacuation point."

"What if they've already left us or been killed?!" The kid is almost hysterical.

"No, we'll make it home."

"Rachel Glick?" a voice says.

They are startled. A man stands at the edge of the entrance, holding a machine gun. Rachel stands in front of her people, shielding them. She trembles, fearing the worst.

"Yes," she says.

The man says, "Follow me very close. They've overrun the country. We have to make it out of here now or we'll never get out. Follow me!"

The soldier doesn't even wait to make sure they understand, but hurries out of the synagogue and, staying close to the outermost edges of the street and to the buildings, runs. Rachel and her people follow. Explosions start destroying buildings nearby. Then, another in their line of sight explodes.

They arrive at the makeshift evacuation point. Several helicopters are waiting with rotor blades already spinning. The soldier points them to one of the helicopters; a group of armed men in military fatigues notices them. One of them—Rabbi Kanter—runs to them.

"Are you with the League?" he asks.

"Yes, we were supposed to meet our contact, Mr. Tendlar, at that synagogue," Rachel says. "It was all prearranged with our Haredi and Dati contacts."

In Israel, they didn't divide themselves like they did in America. There were no Orthodox, Conservatives, or Reformers. In Israel, you were religious or secular. The term "secular" had long since disappeared in America, but in Israel the non-religious were Chiloni. Half of Jewish Israelis were Chiloni or secular; the other half were religious Dati, very religious Haredi, or traditional Masorti.

"He's dead," Rabbi Kanter says.

Rachel is shaken. "I spoke with him on the e-pad just ten minutes ago."

"He was helping draw fire while the people evacuated." Rabbi Kanter continues, "Get on the helicopter. We're leaving. It's our final evacuation airlift." He leads them to the bay of the closest military helicopter and men onboard pull them on one by one. "How could your Mr. Haggard have sent you into an active war zone?!"

Rachel says, "It was our decision. We insisted. We thought the IDF would hold them back and repel them. He sent us to provide whatever help you needed. How long will it take for the Americans to get here?"

Rabbi Kanter looks at her. "Israel has fallen. It's over."

Rachel says, "What are you talking about? What about the Americans?"

Rabbi Kanter touches her hand. "It's only us. It's always been only us. The country has fallen."

Rachel and the League kids are stunned

One kid says, "That's not possible. Israel has always escaped destruction."

"Israel is invincible. We've always defeated them," Rachel says.

One of the kids is crying. "No one came to help us?"

Rabbi Kanter answers, "The Christians came, the Mormons came, the Armenians, African Catholics, Ethiopians, and other religious Orders. People, not countries. No countries came."

Rachel says, "Then we failed. All the history of Israel is gone. We failed, then." Rachel starts crying, as do the other League members.

"We didn't fail. The Antiquities Project was accomplished. Now we must pray for as many people to escape this dark day as possible."

A man runs up to him. "Are you Kanter?"

"Yes, Rabbi Kanter."

"So you are the one who has our Israeli holy artifacts, texts, and treasures?"

"Yes, the Project Antiques. We've been airlifting everything out."

"Why did you do this? You have no authority to do this."

"Who are you?"

"I am the Israeli representative for the Wise Men. They had their own fail-safe operation in place, and we get here and find your people. How could you have Christians and other outsiders handling our holy Jewish artifacts and treasures?"

"Israel is holy land for Jews and Christians. Project Antiquities is liberating *all* artifacts. And I have all the authority in the world. It's called the Prime Minister of Israel, so get out of my face. This is a war zone, we have people dying, and you are not helping."

"This is outrageous. The Prime Minister has no authority to give away our treasures to outsiders. The Wise Men will not stand for this." The man runs away in a huff.

"Who was that idiot?" a soldier asks.

"Did you notice it too, boss?" another asks.

"Yes," Kanter replies. "He used the word 'treasure' three times. Are they the ones you mentioned?"

"Yes, they had an army of air transports and they got to all the sites after we did."

"Did they have any transports to rescue, evacuate the people?" Kanter asks.

The soldier shakes his head. "No."

Kanter looks at Rachel and her team. The explosions are getting closer. "See you in America."

The League members are strapped into their seats as the helicopter rises in the air, flanked by two gunships already hovering. The air caravan flies away. Kanter waves to the League members and they sadly wave back.

The Fall of Jewish Israel occurred in 2081. The celebration in the Muslim World went on for endless months. The Palestinians renamed the entire country Palestine, including both Gaza and the West Bank.

The victory was relatively short-lived. Eight years later, Palestine was wiped off the face of the planet by Supreme Islamic Caliphate military forces. The Caliphate had decided that the very existence of the new Palestine Israel was a threat. "These animals of the Muslim world" would not be tolerated anymore after "frequent insults to the Supreme Rule of the Islamic Caliphate and Almighty Allah," said the Islamic Emperor. The Fall of Palestinian Israel occurred in 2089.

Something Wicked

"Religion is an opiate of the masses and needs to be removed in order to construct the ideal society." – attributed to Josef Stalin, Premier of former Soviet Union, 20ᵗʰ century (killed at least 20 million people)

"Many have tried to destroy the Chosen People: the Egyptians, the Romans, the Dark Christians of Western Europe, the Nazis, the Communists, the Pagans. They have failed and have always failed. We will always be here until the end of time and time has no end." – Rachel Glick, Director of the Holy Land Antiquities League (future President of New Israel)

Facility Unknown, Location Unknown
9:42 a.m., 6 March 2090

Idle hands are the playthings of the devil.

She doesn't know why the phrase popped into her mind. It wasn't the first time.

"I know they aren't human clones," she says. The Keeper sits quietly in her chair, watching him as he views samples on the microscope vid-screen, both in white medical scrubs and lab coats. She has short, light brown hair, and her skin is very pale. Her internal struggle is making her physically sick.

He looks up briefly from his work. "Why do you say that?" The Chief is a bald man of average height and weight. No one would know from his unremarkable appearance that he is one of the greatest scientific minds in the world.

"There was no genetic material surviving from those originals."

"As far as you know. Hardly the basis of such certitude on your part."

"Why do you want to convince so many people that you're cloning people who have been dead for so long, when that is not what you're doing? They are not bio-copies, but biological transfigurations of some kind."

The Chief smiles. "So much unsubstantiated speculation for a gifted scientist."

"Who is funding the program?"

"Why is that important?"

"Because it will tell me who is running the program."

He ignores her. "Be careful with your mental meanderings. We have an aggressive schedule to maintain."

"How can I, when my bosses are busy creating evil things rather than pursuing legitimate science?"

"*Evil?*" He almost laughs. "That's an outmoded, manufactured concept of religion. Anti-science. Inferior."

"No, I have seen evil. I've seen it all around me and it is real."

"Am I to assume you plan to do something about your new personal discovery?"

"You owe me those reassurances at least. I am your biological daughter."

"I am your boss. That is the only thing of relevance here."

"You always told me that a true scientist always questions."

"We are here to protect America. Give it all the weapons needed to protect itself from all foreign enemies. Science has always been the tip of this war effort. The Project is that and more. What is offensive to me is that my own offspring is now developing misgivings about work she's done without any trepidation her entire life. I am ashamed of you. You are a walking disgrace to the scientific community. You know how many scientists in the world would kill to be part of this project if they knew of it, and you were handed the opportunity on a silver plate; the chance to be immortal, to have all speak your name. Scientists will be at the forefront of war, not passing afterthoughts as in the past."

"This is freakishness and not anything noble you would pretend it to be."

"Nobility? I have no opinion on that concept. We are ensuring the peace."

"Yes, Father dearest."

"Please stop using that bigoted, backwards term. Mother, father…I am your *guardian*, but that has zero relevance here." He glares at her. "You will do your work as I direct, or there will be consequences."

"Yes, you would probably need to kill me since I know too much."

"I would, without hesitation, without emotion. Any defective or inferior biological should be terminated."

"I have decided. I'm going to kill all three of them."

"I'll kill all of your children in the Zoo if you ever say that again."

"Come, Zasthrust." She's not talking to him and he realizes it.

He turns as an inner chamber door opens at the opposite corner of the room. His eyes widen in terror. One of her "children" prances in—a massive porcupine-like creature, the size of a horse, with the claws of an armadillo.

She is already at the door and stares into the eyes of her child. She sings with perfect melody, "Eat, eat, eat! Flesh, bones, meat!"

The Chief runs around the lab table to get away from the creature. The Keeper steps out of the room and locks the door behind her. She glances through the door window to see the creature rise on its hind feet and pounce on the man. "Bye, guardian." The anti-acoustical material composing the door and walls prevents anyone from hearing the violence inside.

She puts it all out of her mind and walks down the hall, passing an occasional scientist, lab assistant, or inspector. She doesn't have much time. The alarms could only be delayed, not disabled.

She arrives at the subject lunchroom. She ignores everyone else in the large room and focuses on them. Adolf Hitler playfully competes with Joseph Stalin to be the center of attention by instigating a heated debate. The crowd of scientists all around them watch, take notes, smile, and talk amongst themselves.

Mao Zedong sits quietly at another table, though he, too, is surrounded by scientists to observe and interact with him. He can't stand his two *brothers*. He notices the Keeper watching them from the main entrance door. Their eyes lock. It's as if he knows what she is planning.

Arlington, Virginia
12:01 a.m., 12 March 2090

Gideon's car burns with raging orange and blue flames.

A mile away, a lone Gideon crouches on one knee, naked, on the cold ground behind bushes. After he got off the dashboard-phone speaking with Goli, he stopped the car and jumped out. He threw all his electronics and the doctor's e-pad into the nearby lake. Then he stripped off all his clothes and threw them in, too. At the time he couldn't explain it: he just had a sudden premonition that he needed to run from the car.

He watched it burn in the distance. The glow lights up the sky. The missile that blew up his car, he saw for only a split second. It was only visible because of a small light on its tip.

Gideon looks up and sees an aircraft fly through the air without any sound and no lights—super stealth tek. The helicopter is a large, shadowy thing flying to the wreck that used to be his car.

Everything now is like a waking dream. Gideon is mesmerized by the machines sent to kill him. Twenty years in government fighting terrorists and crime lords, but he never came close to being in real danger, let alone so many real kill attempts in one long day.

Two cars speed down the road. They too are using stealth-tek, and they glide just above the road at ninety miles an hour toward the site of his exploded car.

Everything is quiet now. He stays motionless for a moment. He knows he has to get out of the area quickly. They will still be hunting him and the night is young; he can still be murdered today.

In the post-modern era, they used to have something called pay phones. He saw pictures of them at a museum when he was a child: booths that were tall and wide enough for a person to enter, and one could call someone manually using an old analog stand-alone phone device. They disappeared a long, long time ago. What he'd give to have a simple phone booth now on every public corner.

Gideon has been walking two hours, naked, back into the city. He is cold and his feet are raw. Luckily, he has been able to stay just inside the field of trees lining the side of the road, only stopping to hide when a car appears. The closer he gets to the main tek-city, the fewer places he'll have to conceal himself.

He reaches the outskirts of the tek-city. He could boldly walk down the street and most people wouldn't even notice his nakedness. After all, this is Tek World, and all standards are equal, even no standards.

Gideon walks to the first business he sees: a food truck on the corner. He has managed to make a kilt from an old cloth he found in the nearby garbage; he wrapped the cloth around his waist so that at least the lower half of his body is covered. Inside the food truck are three men, two on the grill and one at the order window.

Gideon says, "Sir, can I borrow your e-pad to make a call? I've been robbed. Or can you make the call for me?"

The counter man looks at him. The two other men look up, too.

The man asks, "Is this a scam?"

"No, they took everything. If you call my friend, I can get them to come get me."

One of the grill men says, "You're not naked under there, are you? Haven't you ever seen that movie? You don't want parasites to bite it all off." The food truck men laugh.

The man asks, "Are you going to ask me for food or money?"

Gideon smiles. "If I did that, then it would be a scam. No, the call."

"Okay, what's the number to dial?"

Gideon hides in a dark alley near the main street. The car he waits for arrives almost an hour later. It stops and Goth Lila gets out, looking all around.

Gideon stands and walks cautiously to the car. She sees him.

Location Unknown
2:00 a.m., 12 March 2090

Gideon finishes dressing himself, pulling on a long-sleeved top, and walks out of the bedroom into the main room. Four Goths are playing poker, sitting at the dining room table.

Lila stands up from the living room couch. "Are you hungry?"

Gideon answers, "No, I just need some sleep."

"You can use the bedroom."

"Is this house safe?"

"It's off-Grid. No one knows about it. You're safe."

"I'd rather sleep out here. I'll use the couch. I can't sleep in quiet.

The noise will help me sleep."

"They get rowdy when they're playing poker."

"I'll get to sleep faster, then."

"I'll get you a small blanket. And I'll be back later tonight with your friend."

"Thank you. Can I ask one more thing?"

"Yes."

"Are you all armed?"

Lila looks at him and laughs. "Are you serious, Mr. Policeman? We're Goths. We have plenty of weapons. Don't worry. No one will interfere with you, with us here."

Lila gets him the blanket and says goodbye to her colleagues. One of them stands up, so as she leaves, he firmly locks the door.

Gideon, now wrapped in the blanket, tries to sleep. He closes his eyes. The noise of the Goths playing poker, laughing, talking, is helpful, but his mind just won't stop racing...too much to think about.

It is just thirty minutes later when there is a knock at the door. The Goths immediately draw handguns. One of them stands up from the poker table and walks to the side of the door. He touches the screen and the vid shows that there are three other Goths outside.

The door is opened and the Goth leader, Mikel, walks in with his two men. Gideon is still lying flat on the couch and looks right into Mikel's eyes. Something is wrong.

Gideon suddenly feels intense panic. Was it wise to go to the Goths? Most Jewish Orders don't like the Goths. They aren't an Order, but a collective made up of different groups, some friendly to each other, some hostile to each other, and others completely indifferent to each other. The Goth Jewish Order is so diverse it really can't even be called an Order, as some members are barely practicing Jews, while others are extremely orthodox and everything in between.

Mikel walks over to him. Gideon immediately sits up and braces his body back against the chair. He clenches his fists beneath the blanket, ready to fight. All the Goths are watching him.

Mikel asks, "Who exactly are you, policeman?"

"What do you mean? You know who I am?"

"What did you do?"

"I didn't do anything."

"You did something because I've never seen this kind of heat on the street before."

One of the other Goths asks, "What's going on?"

Mikel says, "They've locked down the entire city."

"What!" All the Goths at the table stand up and stare at Gideon.

Mikel continues, "They have his picture everywhere. They say he escaped from a military hospital, and has an extremely infectious disease that can kill anyone who comes into contact with him if not treated."

"That's a lie. It's a cover story to capture me," Gideon says

Mikel says, "We know that, but this is the first time I've seen them actually shut down an entire tek-city. So I ask again, what did you do?"

"Just get me to my friend and I'll be out of your way."

"It's too dangerous for your friend to come here now, so we're going to have to get you out of the city." Mikel turns to one of the Goths. "Did you scan him thoroughly?"

The other Goth answers, "He's clean."

Mikel says, "His friend told me something, so let's check it out." He walks to Gideon. "Give me your hands and feet. I need to check something." Mikel takes a pen-sized object from his pocket and grabs Gideon's right hand. Mikel pushes the button and shines a light slowly over every inch of his hand. He does the same with his left. He kneels down and does the same to the sole of his left foot and then his right foot. He looks up at Gideon.

Gideon breaks the silence. "I'm clean."

Mikel says, "You're not."

"What?"

"You're infested with trackers."

"What are you talking about?"

Mikel stands up and says to his men, "This whole thing is a ruse. They know exactly where he is, so this whole city quarantine thing must be a trick to capture all of us too."

Gideon stands up, angry. "There are no trackers on me."

Mikel walks back to him. "Mr. Gideon, your body has dozens of trackers imbedded in your palms, and under your feet too."

Gideon shakes his head. "I already removed my government tracker when I ditched my car and my clothes. I know exactly where it was, but I removed it. There aren't any others."

"Your friend Goli told us how to do it. We're going to irradiate your entire body and kill all the trackers."

"Irradiate me? No."

"We either do the procedure or you stay here by yourself."

"Show me the trackers, then."

Mikel hands the light-pen to Gideon. He shines the light on his left palm. He sees under his skin a blue dot, then another and another. "What are those?!" He sits back down on the couch and shines the light under his feet. There are blue dots underneath the skin of the entire foot, both feet. Gideon angrily throws the light-pen across the room.

Mikel says, "You need to control that temper, Mr. Policeman. We need that pen scanner."

"I'm not a policeman. I doubt I'll ever be law enforcement of any kind ever again."

"Are we doing the procedure?"

Gideon angrily looks around before he blurts out, "Do it."

"Also, I hope you're not planning on having any children."

"What?" He punches the couch with his fist. "What's next? Maybe I'll change my name to Job after all this."

Mikel puts his hand on his shoulder. "Mr. Policeman, on days like this you always have to look on the bright side. At least you're not dead."

Minutes later, they sneak out of the safe-house using hidden passages to a nearby building. He is led down so far into the ground that it seems to Gideon they are walking to the center of the Earth.

After almost an hour, they arrive at a makeshift clinic where they place Gideon inside some type of bio-bed that looks very similar to an MRI scanner. The irradiation procedure to destroy the bio-trackers in his body takes almost a full hour.

Bio-tracking has a very limited range, but like most tek is improving exponentially. It is rumored that every man, woman, and child in CHIN territory is "tagged." Conspiracy theorists said that mandatory flu shots under universal healthcare is the government's cover story to tag everyone in America. Faithers and off-Gridders, of course, did not participate.

Gideon is secretly smuggled out of the tek-city. In the SUV with blackened windows, he doesn't know where they are driving him, but he doesn't care. He is so tired and weak that all he wants to do is sleep. He lies on his side in the backseat and does so.

Secret Safe-House, Outland of Pittsburgh, Pennsylvania 12:47 p.m., 15 April 2090

Gideon sits in his chair, incredulous. "The Wise Men were informants? But they hired me. What about Zev?" His empty lunch plate sits on the side table, a half-empty glass nearby.

Goli says, "He's cleared. But C is dead, and Mr. X and Mr. B have disappeared with their families, belongings, money, everything. They have real estate all over the world, besides owning most of South Florida, which will continue to generate massive income without them ever having to show their faces. It's all under their corporations."

"Why would they hire me, then? It doesn't make sense."

"It does. They were using you on a real investigation to try to identify all our internal resources in the community that they were unaware of, but forget about that now. How are you feeling? You're looking better."

"Almost one month of rest in a plush safe-house will do that. I didn't know Goth Jews could play poker for so long. I'm almost back to my normal self. But I don't know how many knock-down, drag-out fistfights I'll be winning in the future."

"You'll be back to your normal self and more."

"Well, deputy, you did warn me. I'll never laugh off your conspiracy theories again."

"I expect you to change not a bit. We need to focus on the briefing. This is our time to get all our facts together to present."

"The New Jewish Continuum. I feel honored. So the Christians have a Continuum. And now we have one. All we need now is a new Holy Temple, a new Jewish homeland, and life on Earth will be perfect again; except for one thing. I wonder if they grow *that* in the body farm." He laughs, but there is sadness behind it.

"Gideon, you'll have fifty kids if you want to. The scan's side effects are temporary."

Gideon is quiet for a moment; his eyes start to tear up. "I never knew this Resistance thing was so exciting."

"Let's take a walk. You haven't been outside in the sun in a month, and there's little real fresh air there in the tek-city. We have to put together a solid briefing and then get on the road. I suspect everything will explode after we get done telling them what we're going to tell them."

Theodore Hertzl Jewish Enclave, North Carolina
9:16 a.m., 15 May 2090

The city-enclave is much more metropolitan. It is definitely, not Orthodox or Hasidic, who prefer more simple and plain communities. It is the joint community of the Mizrahi, the Arab-Persian Jewish Orders.

Everyone is preparing for the meeting. Goli and Gideon arrive and the security is formidable: the Wolf Pack, all men with shaved heads, in black, and heavily armed; and burly Persian and Arab Jewish security men. The two men are led to the general conference hall. They are happy to see the familiar face of Tova, who greets them.

"We'll get started soon," Tova says. "Gideon, did your best friend tell you how he single-handedly destroyed an army of one hundred storm troopers?"

"No, he didn't," Gideon smiles at Goli. "But I've always known Goli can be a Goliath."

Shoshana appears. "Hi Tova. Who are our new keynote speakers today?"

Tova says, "This is Gideon. His unaffiliated Miami community has joined the Conservatives. Everyone calls him the Jewish James Bond."

Shoshana says, "Ah, nice." She looks at Goli. "That was quite an impressive assault on the Gestapo at our Continuum meeting. Two hundred men!"

They laugh.

Gideon says, "By the end of the week it will be seven hundred men. I'm now starting to wonder if Moses really did lead our people forty days and forty nights through the wilderness. Maybe, it was just forty minutes, but Moses thought it was so long because of all the Israelites complaining nonstop."

Shoshana says, "That is an interesting last name, King-David. I bet your nickname was Goliath, even as a toddler."

"Yes it was," Goli answers.

Shoshana says, "You'll do nicely."

"What do you mean?" Goli asks.

"You're not very quick though, for a man, but I'll overlook it." Shoshana walks back to her post.

Goli glances at Gideon. "Did I just get married without my consent?"

The meeting starts within the hour and the two men are led into the inner conference room. Inside are the members of the New Jewish Continuum, sitting around the circular table: Rabbi Oren (Orthodox Order), Rabbi Kanter (new Shamar Order), Rabbi Hendel (Hasidic Order), Tova (Conservative Order), Yisrael (Israeli Order), Rabbi Haza (Arabic Jewish Order), Rabbi Nahai (Persian Jewish Order), Rabbi Henriques (Judeo-Spanish Order), and Rachel Glick (liaison to Jewish Hidden and Unaffiliated communities).

Shoshana stands at the closed doors with two other Wolf Pack bodyguards.

Rabbis Haza and Nahai make very cursory introductions. With the security concerns, the briefing begins immediately.

Gideon sits at the presentation chair; Goli sits at his side. They face the Continuum members. Gideon opens his tab and touches the screen to view his notes. "*Boker tov*. Thank you, Rabbi. It's especially gratifying to see this unity among our people. It is said that when there is a crisis, God will put the right people in the right place at the right time to see the important things through.

"I have until recently been in the employ, as most know, of the

Homeland Defense and Intelligence Agency as a law enforcement agent, based in Florida. Three months ago, I was contacted by an old friend, Zev Larson, on behalf of the Wise Men, the longtime power brokers in our community, whom I have been informed were actually government informants. A little over a year ago, one Susan Ben, known to all as Rabbi Susan, was shot dead at the Gadsden, Alabama Jewish Community of the Conservatives. She had on her person a data crystal that she was attempting to give to the leadership. She knew that she'd be killed, so it was a suicide by proxy. The data crystal was given to me and I was hired by the Wise Men to conduct a thorough investigation of its contents. I did so, with the aid of Goli and brief assistance by a colleague in Australia. The investigation led me eventually to a regen-facility."

Rabbi Hendel asks, "What is that?"

Gideon continues. "A regenerative bio-facility, or the more common slang is a 'body farm.' Human parts such as limbs, organs, and skin are grown for wounded human victims." Continuum members nod. "However, the matter for this group is what I found in the morgue of this facility. Three dead…clones that were being prepared for transport, destruction, or both."

Rabbi Kanter asks, "Clones?"

Gideon says, "Yes, human."

Rabbi Kanter asks, "Isn't that illegal?"

Yisrael interjects, "The only thing illegal in Tek World is all of us."

"The Pagans were eager to make science fiction into reality," Rabbi Oren adds. "Satan must be so proud of them."

Gideon says, "The clones were killed by a scientist they claimed had a mental breakdown, but I don't believe that."

Rachel Glick says, "I'm still not following. A clone would be creating a twin by non-natural means. It's not duplicating a person's mind, personality, and soul, just the body, even though we have endless science fiction movies that have erroneously told people that. What are you trying to say? Clones? Who did they clone?"

Gideon pauses. "The first clone was of Josef Stalin. The second was of Mao Zedong. The third was of Adolf Hitler."

The group freezes all at once, speechless.

Gideon says, "The young lady is correct. A clone is just that, a copy of a person, but they are not that person. You can't copy a brain or, more precisely, you can't copy the mind or memories. So the clone would look like their original, but that's it. However, these clones were created with invasive psychological conditioning so that they would…*believe* that they were, in fact, their originals…reincarnated, as it were. Apparently, the Hitler clone was also further modified so that it would have certain powers. The other two may also have had powers."

"Powers? What powers?" Tova asks.

Gideon answers, "We're not sure, but it was able to kill several people when it was just an infant."

The group stares at him with mouths wide open, speechless.

Gideon continues. "It is, or was, called Project New People. The Christians were aware of the name, but not the details, some years back. I think we have only scratched the surface in regards to the full details of the project."

Shoshana breaks the silence. She walks straight up to Gideon. "Is it dead? Are they all dead?"

"Yes."

"Are you certain?"

"Yes."

"What else did you see? Just the three of them?"

"There was also some kind of monster. It was dead too, but I couldn't tell what it was. I wasn't able to inspect it, but was able to take a picture."

Shoshana stares at him. "They're making mass murderers *and* monsters! Stop! I don't want to hear anymore." She turns and walks out of the room. Her two Wolf Pack members are clearly unnerved too, but close the door and maintain their posts.

Tova speaks slowly. "Is there more?"

Gideon answers, "There's quite a bit of accompanying data, such as info on the personnel involved and the kill teams sent after me, but you have the main items. It's like putting together a crossword puzzle without knowing what the final picture is."

"You can retire to your rooms," Tova says. "We'll call you when we've had a chance to discuss these revelations you've brought to our attention."

Goli stands and the two men leave the conference room.

2:00 p.m.

Gideon sits at a small table reading and eating a snack. Goli lies on a couch. As usual, he's so tall that most of his legs are hanging over the side. There is a knock at the door.

Continuum members enter, along with the lawyer, Elliott. Both Gideon and Goli rise and join them near the door.

Rabbi Kanter says, "Is there any more?"

Gideon stands. "You have the full overview of the facts."

Rabbi Oren yells, "Why would they do such a thing? What's your theory, Mr. Gideon? You worked in the government. Law enforcement, security, intel."

Gideon thinks for a moment. "Biologics warfare: clone armies, super-soldiers, creating new life for military purposes."

"I thought all military spending was tek-related. Robotic armies, better drones, better attack vehicles for air, land, sea, and space," Kanter says. "If there ever is a World War Three, we better make sure we are nowhere near it."

Gideon adds, "There was a host mother, the one who birthed, or rebirthed, the Hitler clone. The woman was actually some kind of biogeneticist. Her university thesis was on bringing back mass murderers as a means to study overall human behavior."

They look at him incredulously.

Elliott says, "I think we all need to take a breath. They have a phrase in law—extremely prejudicial. Facts are introduced that are so emotionally explosive that they taint the case and are therefore excluded. Let's step back and examine this without the emotion. Everything isn't about us. We all hate President Haman, but it could be they just did this just to do it."

Yisrael says, "Another Holocaust is what they're planning. That's what this is."

Rabbi Kanter says, "As sick as this is, what is the real threat to us? And I agree with Elliott that it may have nothing to do with us. Rabbi Susan stumbled on it. A coincidence."

Gideon answers, "I believe the creation of these clones was not the end goal. It was a beginning step."

Rabbi Oren asks, "What's the next step, then?"

Gideon says, "I don't know. Without knowing what the final picture looks like, I'm having problems putting everything together."

Tova says, "Maybe we can only put these pieces together as a group. All the Orders and our other Faither allies."

Rabbi Oren says, "Let's get to it."

Rabbi Henriques asks, "Who tried to kill you? Some rogue element?"

Gideon shakes his head. "No, it was the Capitol. The teams sent to kill me, twice, the stealth-tek weapons, no, only the highest levels of government could have authorized such operations."

Rabbi Haza says, "I'm sorry, but we can't just assume that all this has nothing to do with us. Maybe it is normal military war-building, as I'm sure the Caliphate and CHINs are doing, but we have to know for sure. None of us will be able to sleep otherwise."

Tova says, "Do you know the Cowboy Rabbi?"

Gideon says, "I've heard of him."

Tova says, "He's with the Underground Railroad."

"What's that?"

"You don't know your American history? It was a secret civilian organization that operated prior to the American Civil War and rescued slaves from the slave-owning states in the South of the country to the anti-slavery states of the North of the country and Canada. These days, it is a secret civilian organization that rescues Jews, Christians, and others from Islamic Caliphate, CHIN, and Russian Bloc countries and move them to here in America or Africa."

"I didn't know this."

"I would hope so. Only those in-the-know know that it exists. We told the Christians about all this, your report. They immediately called a meeting of their Continuum. Were you working off a list of names for this investigation? Five names, to be exact?"

Gideon looks at her, surprised. "Yes."

"Two of them retired and died?"

"Yes, how did you know?"

"Not me, the Christians. The two men didn't retire and die. They were killed by the Magi."

Gideon says, "We need to find out what everyone else knows."

Tova says, "Exactly. We need to get the data crystal to a contact out of the country. The safest way for us to do that is to send it to them via courier. We'll send the Cowboy Rabbi. He'll take it to that contact."

Gideon says, "Where will he take it?"

Tova says, "Mexico, to the Spanish Americas, to the contact."

Yisrael asks, "Why through the Spanish Americas? What are the Faithers there like?"

Tova answers, "As a region, it's wide open for covert ops."

Rabbi Henriques adds, "The Spanish Americas as a territory is controlled totally by organized crime and corrupt governments. There are no strong Faither alliances there of any significance."

Rabbi Kanter says, "We must convene a meeting of the Continuums. Tova can contact the Christians. Rabbi Oren can contact the African Collective. I'll contact others."

Tova says, "Let's get the Cowboy Rabbi to Mexico."

Tova's Home, Gladsden, Alabama Jewish Enclave
7:00 p.m., 15 April 2090

The doorbell rings and Tova walks quickly to the door with her husband right behind her. She opens the door and there stand the man Moses and his wife Emma (known by all as "M"), their decades-long best friends. The couples greet each other with hugs. "General" Moses and M are not only founding elders in the New Protestant Order, but leaders in the Christian Continuum.

"What are you two doing here?" Tova asks. "Don't you have your Easter tomorrow?"

M smiles. "Yes, but it was important to see you."

Mr. Tova says, "Yes, this was quite a day for us."

Moses says, "No, it doesn't have to do with that, but after the High Holy Days, the Continuums will have our first joint meeting."

Mr. Tova says, "Aren't we hosting our annual Passover Seder dinner this year?"

"We and the children are looking forward to it," M says.

Moses gestures to them. "Let's go outside. We know you want to rest after your day today. But we did want to bring you an official welcome gift from the Christian Continuum to the Jewish Continuum."

The Tovas look at each other, intrigued, as they follow them outside. In front of their house is a two-seater car with a large trunk compartment attached. Two enclave security men stand with the car. Moses walks to the trunk and opens it. "I believe these belong to you."

Inside are a bound, gagged, and unconscious Mr. B and Mr. X.

Get Your Ass to Mexico

"I'm gonna take my right foot and hit you on the left side of your face." – Billy Jack

Pecos, Texas
7:01 a.m., 14 June 2090

Pecos still claims it had America's first big rodeo in 1883; Arizona and Wyoming loudly protest and each respectively claim the honor. It is a dusty town with the wind blowing sand, dirt, and dead insects through the air. It may be America, but Mexico took it back a long time ago. The town population is just under twelve thousand and has been the same for one hundred years or more; nothing has changed. The only thing indicative of the late twenty-first century here is the transnational fast-track, and the monorail train will be here soon.

Outside the run-down waiting station sits an elderly man. At the far corner stand two men in their twenties talking Spanish a mile a minute. Inside a lone attendant behind a counter sits on a stool and reads a pornographic netzine on his dirty tablet.

There is never much traffic going into Mexico from this location; most is coming into the States. It is the next-to-last stop, that being Alpine, before crossing the border into the Mexican state of Chihuahua.

The only other person inside is a lone man, all in black, with a long, bushy black beard and a bushy mustache. His piercing blue eyes stare straight ahead. He keeps his hands clasped on his lap as he waits patiently. On his head is a kippah. This man is a Jew.

The gangsters arrive. The lead man, Mr. White, is in a casual white linen jacket and pants set, a flashy white T-shirt, and dark black glasses. He has sandy blond hair and stubble on his face. The second man, the Hawaiian, is about the same height and wears a small white cowboy hat, dark glasses, a bright Hawaiian shirt, and black jeans. He has a clean-shaven face with a goatee. The third bald man, Baldie, wears dark black glasses, a blue jean vest, and blue jeans. The fourth man, Soldier, is taller than all of them. He also wears dark glasses, and has black hair down to his shoulders. His muscles are clearly visible through his tight-fitting black shirt and military fatigue pants.

The four men look all around the virtually empty waiting room. Mr. White motions to the other men. They split up and physically walk through the entire space while Mr. White waits. The Hawaiian and the Soldier check the unisex bathroom, then join Mr. White at the front entrance.

Mr. White looks at the lone man sitting inside. He slowly walks over to him. "Hey."

The man unclasps his hands and looks up at him. "Good morning, sir."

"Have you seen anyone else in here?"

"No, only the three people outside, the man at the counter, and me. I haven't seen anyone else at all, sir."

Mr. White nods. "Can I ask you a question? I hope it doesn't offend you."

"Not at all, sir."

"Are you a Jew-Christian? Because only Jew-Christians say 'sir' and 'ma'am.' The only exception to that is government people, but none of us are wearing suits."

He laughs. "Actually, there is no such thing as Jew-Christian. Though it's a slang term everyone uses. Jews and Christians are separate religions. But yes, I'm a Jew. A believer of and practitioner of Judaism."

"What do you call your religious leaders? Not imams?"

"Rabbi for Jews. Pastor or reverend for Christians. And since we're so close to Mexico, they call their religious leaders priests, bishops, or cardinals."

"I see. We're here to meet a rabbi."

"Really? Maybe he'll be on my train. What's the name of this rabbi?"

"He goes by the name of Cowboy Rabbi."

"What a small world! I know him. He wears a black cowboy hat and a wears a pair of shiny silver guns on a waist holster. You can't miss them. You can see those shiny guns a mile away."

"That's what we were told. Thanks." Mr. White looks at his men and they start to walk back outside.

"You're welcome, sir. Maybe I can help even more." The man stands up and reaches behind his back with his right hand. He firmly places a black flat-top cowboy hat on his head. Part of his clothes is a light black jacket with just the top button done. He reaches near his waist and opens the jacket more, pushing the flaps to his back and revealing a double holster, one on each side of his waist, each holding one of the shiniest silver guns one has ever seen.

The Cowboy Rabbi stares at them. They stare back, frozen.

Mr. White smiles. "You're a tricky one." He starts to laugh. "Are you supposed to be… scary?" He laughs even louder.

Cowboy Rabbi says, "I'm glad you're laughing, because now all kinds of holocaustic things will be happening up in here." He stares at them coldly. "I don't like laughing."

Mr. White stops and his smile disappears.

The Soldier reaches slowly for his gun underneath his shirt, in the back of his pants. "Fancy guns. Do you know how to use them, Jew-Christian?"

Cowboy Rabbi moves literally in the blink of an eye. The Soldier is shot dead and the remaining three men jump, barely perceiving the lightning-fast motion of the rabbi's right arm grabbing his gun, firing, and placing the gun back in the holster. The Soldier's body collapses to the ground with a hole in his forehead the size of a baseball.

They hear a noise to the side; the attendant jumps over his counter, stops, goes back, grabs his dirty tablet, and bolts out of the waiting station.

Mr. White stares back at the Cowboy Rabbi. The Hawaiian and Baldie glare at him. Cowboy Rabbi stares back, but only into the eyes of Mr. White. He is the leader; the other two are just punks.

Mr. White asks, "Were you expecting us?"

"Of course. My name, the mission, was leaked to you…by us. We identified and neutralized all your spies; now we neutralize all your contractors. Thank you for your cooperation."

"I always knew Jew-Christians could be tricky. But I'm still feeling pretty frisky today. I predict you'll never make it into Mexico alive. I predict you'll never make it to your destination in South America. I predict your contact there will just disappear." He smiles.

"Lots of predictions. Are you a prophet?"

"Yes, I can see the future. And I don't even have to believe in your fantasy snowman in the sky, or whatever trash you Jew-Christians worship."

"I see the future too."

"What are your predictions, then?"

"Seven dead little monkeys."

"Seven? Who's a monkey?"

"The first is already on the ground."

"How do you get to that number?" Mr. White suddenly draws his gun, already firing.

The Hawaiian and Baldie jump to either side, firing their guns. Their bodies never get a chance to hit the ground under them. They, like Mr. White, are blown back through the air and crash into the wall.

The Hawaiian lies dead on the ground with a massive hole blown through his chest. Baldie's chest is also blown out, and Mr. White's forehead is blown out with his mouth locked in an expression of shock.

The Cowboy Rabbi's guns literally smoke as he holds them, pointing.

Suddenly, from outside, the two young men burst in, shooting wildly from their guns. The Cowboy Rabbi shoots both dead. That leaves just one more outside.

The Cowboy Rabbi stares at the main entrance, listening for even the slightest sound. The head of the elderly man peeks in. He stares at the Cowboy Rabbi and then at the carnage of the dead bodies.

"*Aye, los hombres muertos!*" he says.

Cowboy Rabbi straightens up. The elderly man jumps in spraying machine gun fire. Cowboy Rabbi shoots him twice, dead, once in the chest and the last in the head.

There is a sound. *A shotgun blast!*

The Cowboy Rabbi is hit, but spins around firing with his other hand. The shooter is the counter attendant, who's traded in his dirty tablet for a sawed-off shotgun. The man is killed instantly.

The Cowboy Rabbi stands straight again. He can feel the wound. No sense standing around waiting for another "innocent bystander" to come in and try to kill him.

The whistle of the approaching train sounds. He keeps his guns drawn, but steps over the dead men and out of the building.

"I better get my ass to Mexico before I pass out."

THE CATHOLIC ORDER

(Prelude to the New Catholic Order)

Mexico

The Last Plane From Durango By Way of El Dorado

"I don't think it's nice of you laughing." — Hollywood icon Clint Eastwood, A Fistful of Dollars

"I'm glad you're laughing, because now all kinds of holocaustic things will be happening up in here." – Cowboy Rabbi

I am going to die here on these streets unless God sends me an angel.

It was known as Imperio Mexican, the Mexican Empire, in the past. The previous Aztec Empire fell in the early 16th century to the Spanish conquerors under the command of Hernán Cortés, not because of superior military might, but by smallpox unknowingly brought to the land, which killed millions of Aztecs. The territory became part of the Spanish Empire and was named New Spain.

The United Mexican States, Mexico, is the largest Spanish-speaking country in the world, with more than one hundred fifty million people. When it won its independence from Spain, it named itself after its capital, Mexico City, which was founded in 1524 and sits on top of the ancient Aztec capital of Mexico-Tenochtitlan. One empire had replaced another.

The Free and Sovereign State of Durango, Mexico
6:51 p.m., 14 June 2090

The little boy frantically runs down the street. He is a "walking store" of trinkets and items hanging all over his body: scorpion necklaces, scorpion wristbands, scorpion rings, scorpion e-pad cases, scorpion caps, and scorpion t-shirts.

"Sir, I have it all!" he says to the Cowboy Rabbi. "You can't leave Durango without buying your own official scorpion keepsake. It's our state symbol. It's tradition. Do you know there are more than two thousand species of scorpions, like the Hairy scorpion, the Imperial scorpion, the Deathstalker scorpion, and the Devil Scorpion? Scary! But only about forty-five of them have venom strong enough to kill a man with their stinger tail. Scorpions are part of the spider family and eat other insects for food. They can be anywhere from half an inch to eight inches in size. They love to hide in dark, snug places, like your empty shoes! Scary! But they have florescent stuff in their exoskeleton shell, so in ultraviolet light, they glow in the dark. That's cool! Most people know they have eight legs and two big front pincers, but did you know they can have up to twelve eyes? But they can't see good at all. They use smell and vibrations to 'see' where to go and move around mostly at night. They can go without water for several months and food for up to a year. Now, the female scorpion is a real bad 'chihuahua.' After mating with a male scorpion, she may kill and eat him. Scary! She gives birth and carries the little scorplings around on her back! She sometimes will even eat them if she's hungry. That's cool!"

The boy is talking a mile a minute, but the Cowboy Rabbi can only think of one thing: I need to sit down, now. He slowly bends and then lowers his body to sit on the paved sidewalk. He touches his side and looks at his hand—blood. The boy stops talking immediately and dashes away at the sight of the bloody hand.

Damn, they got me, he thinks to himself. The wife did tell me to wear a better bulletproof vest to cover my sides. I can hear the mother now: "Listen to your wife, listen to your wife."

A young man walks up to him and stops. "Sir, are you okay?"

The Cowboy Rabbi looks at him. "I'm sorry, but I don't speak Spanish." The boy earlier probably would have wished he'd told him that, too.

The young man says, "It is okay. I speak English."

"You're a priest?"

"Yes, my name is Father Marcos. I'm newly ordained to the Catholic Order. You're a rabbi?"

"Yes. I didn't think it was obvious."

"Oh yes, from your vestments. Rabbi, you're bleeding."

"I got myself shot."

"We need to get you to a doctor right away. You're slowing down, which means you're losing a lot of blood." Father Marcos gets him to his feet and helps him to a nearby car.

"Are you going somewhere?" The Cowboy Rabbi sees the car is filled with boxes.

"Yes, I'm going to my birthplace of Lerdo City. I'm hoping to get my own church there one day soon. Start my destiny."

"Yes, I remember when I started my first synagogue. Will you be a good priest?"

"If God is the great composer, I hope for the duration of the symphony, I can play my instrument at one hundred and ten percent and always be worthy of his orchestra."

"You have the absolute right attitude. You will be a good priest."

Father Marcos drives down the very busy road with trucks, vans, cars, motorbikes, manual bikes, pedestrians, and dogs. The region is so rural that there is no auto-drive.

"Rabbi, I did not ask. Who shot you?"

"Banditos."

Father Marcos smiles. "Ah, you do speak Spanish. Did you see their faces?"

"Yes, when I shot all of them dead."

"You are a real American western cowboy, rabbi."

"Yes, they call me the Cowboy Rabbi, in fact. But this is the first time I've actually been to the Wild West."

"Yes, Mexico can be a violent country, even its clergy sometimes, too. That is Mexico nowadays, even the main cities. I will drive you to the doctor as fast as possible."

The Cowboy Rabbi looks down at his seat. "Oh no, I'm getting blood all over your car."

"Please don't worry, rabbi."

"Father, under no circumstances are they to give me blood. No transfusions at all. It's very important that they don't. I don't care if they say it's safe synthetic blood."

"You're very smart, rabbi. I wouldn't either. Don't worry. He never uses blood products, natural or synthetic. The doctor I'm taking you to I've known for years. He's good, clean, fast, and owes me a favor."

"I need to get to the airport too. My flight is tonight. The last one. I must get that flight."

"Durango Airport?"

"Yes."

"It's okay. You will make your flight."

"I must get to South America tonight."

"My doctor friend is in El Dorado; it's a very small town on the way. He'll get you fixed up, get some food and drink into you, and then I'll get you on the fast-track to Durango. Get some rest, rabbi. I'll get you to El Dorado within the hour. I hope you like Bach, because that's the music I listen to."

"But I wouldn't be a good rabbi if I didn't tell you my jokes to pass the time. There's the one with the Jew, the Christian, and the Mormon in heaven. They see the Messiah and they run to him…" The Cowboy Rabbi finally passes out.

Father Marcos pushes a button so that the passenger side window goes down a bit and the breeze can come in. He focuses his gaze back on the road. He'll play Bach another time. He'll let the rabbi have a nice, quiet rest.

Night of the Chupacabras

"Evil is not something superhuman, it's something less than human." –
Agatha Christie, British (Pre-Islamic England) crime writer

Bram Stoker did not invent the vampire when he penned the iconic novel *Dracula* in 1897, as the belief in some version of these mythological creatures spanned centuries before. What he gave birth to was the "modern" vampire genre, which, after almost two centuries, is still with us. By the twentieth century, the superstition had become a standard recurring fascination of the popular culture. Now it has expanded past even the books and movies that made them immortal by becoming a real-life recognized religion in the United States and elsewhere.

But the vampire myth came from ancient Eastern Europe, Eastern Europa of the Russian Bloc. That's "gringo" stuff. The Spanish Americas needed to have their own bloodsucking creature mythology—chupacabras.

Ciudad Lerdo (Lerdo City), Mexico
11:57 p.m., 15 June 2090

Clack-clack! Clack-clack!
The old street lights barely illuminate the dark, empty streets. It

would be completely quiet if not for the strange sound repeating in the distance. The sound grows louder; it is a woman running in heels. The silhouetted woman continues to run awkwardly down the old paved street, a mix of residential and commercial buildings on either side. There is still no one visible on the streets as the young woman frantically runs away from…something.

She stops. She jumps to one leg and violently rips one shoe off one foot, then hops on the other leg to do the same. She grabs something from her side and bends down to place it on the ground. The object sounds off with the same strange "clack-clack" sound as if she were running down the street. But it is not her anymore. The object must be her e-pad, now cleverly playing the repeating "click-clack" sounds.

Now barefoot, she darts off down the street in another direction, mostly hidden in the shadows. She takes a hard left around a corner. The clack-clack decoy sounds are still heard as she runs farther and farther away. Running barefoot at night is always a dangerous thing in any small village in the Mexican state of Durango, but better to step on a stinging scorpion than to be caught.

Sprinting down the street, she now begins to stop briefly at each building, looking for someone, anyone, to help her. There still is no one around, but she now notices the sprawling church at the end of the street. High up on its bell tower is an eerily glowing blue cross. She runs to the buildings immediately opposite the church; she is still concealed in darkness.

Unlike the rest of the streets, the open space some twenty feet to the church is well lit. If she runs across, she will be visible. She looks around for a moment. Suddenly…

"They always run to the church." A sinister male voice comes from out of the darkness, almost right on top of the woman, then laughs.

She is startled out of her mind and jumps away, into the light, falling down. She looks into the darkness to where the voice came from and now sees two glowing red eyes staring back at her. And then hears the laughter.

She gets up and bolts away down the street.

The chupacabra was a legendary monster of the Spanish Americas, Hispaniola, and Puerto Rico. Its name came from the monster's habit of attacking and drinking the blood of livestock, especially goats ("chupacabra" means "goat sucker"). Its description varied widely: heavy or small, the size of a coyote or bear, a row of spines from its neck to the base of its tail, a hairless dog-like creature, or resembling a mix of hairless dog, rat, or kangaroo, a rodent-like animal with fangs, a long snout, short front legs, and long back legs, a reptile-like animal with leathery or scaly greenish-gray skin and sharp spines or quills running down its back, a dog or panther-like nose and face, a forked tongue, and large fangs, glowing red eyes.

From seemingly nowhere, another figure appears from the darkness, looks back, and then runs after her. It is obviously another man. It is obvious that he is wearing a mask; the "head" is dog-like with glowing red eyes, fangs, a forked tongue hanging out of the mouth, grayish-green, and wearing "gloves." The arms are leathery and gray-green, ending in long, clawed hands.

He starts his chase as another "monster" appears, then a third, a sixth, a thirteenth. The pack runs after her, disappearing into the darkness.

Father Marcos

"My Mama always told me that nowhere was there a better Catholic boy than me, who loved his Mama, his Papa, his sister Angela, his town, and his beloved country of Mexico," — Marcos Agustin de Arango

"I must go down, like Moses into Egypt, to lead them out," — Harriet Tubman, American abolitionist, Union spy, and woman suffragist (1820-1913)

Ciudad Lerdo (Lerdo City), Mexico
11:57 a.m., 16 July 2090

When the Church of Saint John Paul II was built sixty years ago in Lerdo City, it was a majestic structure, perched like a beacon on the hill to give a long-suffering, poor, working-class rural village some sense of relief from what was the all too common "3 Ks" of Mexico—kartels (cartels), killings, and kidnappings.

However, community pride quickly evaporated after an endless series of incompetent parish leadership. The people weren't angry or sad or even disappointed anymore, just collectively tired. In one particular year, their church had fifteen different parish priests, and no priest had ever been elevated to the title of bishop by the Vatican. Why would they? Lerdo was like most of the towns and villages in Durango and Mexico in general, with a consistent net migration to the tek-cities. Lerdo was a dying town.

Today, the church is far from the beautiful building it was over half a century ago; it is dilapidated and empty. Dull gray walls with many of the sections peeling, or covered with multicolored graffiti or blotches of different paints to cover the decay, the graffiti, or both. The center of the building is three stories tall with the domed tower of the church bell. A neon cross sits on top, but the people complain that at night, when it does work, it makes you think of the Day of the Dead or Halloween in America, not God. Two-story living quarters surround the center public area, with one-story common areas on one side and the large open church on the other.

There are a few meagerly paid staff and volunteers to do the barest minimal upkeep. Other priests and nuns come and go. Only Sister Maria, who was born in the church some three decades ago, is the only ever-constant face for the people of Lerdo.

But today the church is not empty. Standing outside the church are hundreds of waiting villagers. The crowd has old and young, men and women, children, and several dogs running about. You could take a digital snapshot of the people and see that the dress really hasn't changed in centuries, in this village at least. Men wear loose-fitting pants and shirts of natural fibers, of different colors. If a hat is worn, it is most likely a sombrero, which rich people always refer to as "poor man's sunscreen." The women wear loose-fitting dresses of natural fibers, of different colors, sometimes two-piece, but most often one-piece, and sometimes a head scarf— "poor woman's sunscreen."

For the children, it was quite another matter. There is the traditional wear, but also "city clothes," the leather jacket or the suit with tie, or the techno-colored psychedelic top or pants, or the shiny silver "futuristic" clothing of some future that existed only in some stupid movie.

The crowd grows louder in anticipation as they see a long line of cars approach. It is the Vatican People!

All the cars are identical black limousines. The procession stops in front of the main church entrance as the crowd moves closer, especially the children, who see them as the closest thing they will ever get to celebrities. The doors of the limousines open in unison and priests exit each car. These priests, dressed in their long black garments (cassocks) and white clerical collars, hold the doors open as others exit from the cars. The cardinal and bishops, dressed in long red garments with white clerical collars and red soft-sided caps (skufias), get out and walk through the crowd to the main church entrance with their entourage of priests and bodyguards. The Vatican People enter the parish. The crowd follows.

Inside, the Vatican guests immediately move to the front of the church between the altar stage and the congregation pews, where tables and chairs are already set up for them. The people take their seats. Some run to the front seats, others prefer to sit strategically in the middle rows, and others simply sit where they find an empty space.

Once everyone settles in, one of the red-robed Vatican People stands. Another priest quickly walks to Cardinal Cassiano and attaches a wireless mic to his collar. Two other priests take positions on either side of the long table with round speaker units hanging around their necks by thick black rope.

Cardinal Cassiano is a well-built man in his fifties. An imposing stature of six feet three, with perfectly tan skin, a clean-shaven face, manicured hands, and sophisticated, styled, graying hair. He seems more suited for the role of an actor or billionaire playboy than a celibate churchman. But the Italian is one of the major movers and shakers within the Catholic universe. He was hand-picked by the Pope for his inner circle and is a lifelong friend. Catholic clergy everywhere call him the "Chairman"— a reference to his insatiable love of the music of the twentieth-century actor and singer Frank Sinatra, but one that really speaks to his status within the Church hierarchy itself.

How did such a tiny town get such a celebrity?

Then there's Bishop Dominguez. The bishop is powerful only because he stuck to real powerful people like a flea to a dog. The sycophantism worked. He has risen to the position of Bishop of Durango City, the largest city in the state of Durango. He is actually a very small man at just over five feet. He's in his sixties, with a pudgy face and a mustache and beard. He was born to an extremely wealthy family in Southern Mexico and did the whole Mexican "elite thing." He went to the finest private schools and university in Mexico City, made all the right contacts, but instead of marrying the next eligible bachelorette from another Mexican elite family, he joined the Church.

Bishop Garza runs the church in nearby Gomez Palacio. He, too, was born to a wealthy Mexican family, but never was full of himself like Bishop Dominguez. He truly has a deep affection for rural people, but has gotten a bad reputation for his efforts to get all villages to move into the cities. He is often quoted as saying, "The only thing there is in the isolated villages is scorpions and the devil." It probably was not the wisest thing to say to villagers who viewed big cities as nothing less than the "devil's playground," despite the fact that the vast majority of the state's population now lives in the cities. He is five feet seven and in his fifties, balding with graying black hair and a bushy white mustache.

Cardinal Cassiano begins to talk. He starts out in a whisper, but with the portable speaker units on his two priests, his voice reverberates forcibly throughout the church. "Let us begin, fine people of Lerdo City. I know Bishop Dominguez was here last month and Bishop Garza has been here several times. For those who don't know me, I am Cardinal Cassiano from the Vatican, and I am extremely gratified to have this opportunity to meet with you. I always treasure the times I am able to travel outside of Rome and visit with fellow Catholics in villages, towns, and cities all over the world. This is your meeting. We want to hear from you, and I've heard that none of you are shy about expressing your feelings."

"Why do you give us a church, but you don't name it after a local patron saint, but some Russian one? Aren't Mexican saints as good as Old European ones for the Vatican?" a man asks defiantly.

"Mexico is Catholicism!" a woman shouts.

"Isn't Saint John Paul Polish?" says the first man, correcting himself.

"Poland is a long way from Mexico," another woman says to everyone.

"We are tired of the disrespect. Respect us with a Mexican saint. This is a Mexican church," another man declares.

"You should be thankful to God that Mexico hasn't become like America. Satan runs that country now and they have Christians living in ghettos!" another says.

A young man stands up quietly. "May I speak?"

The young man is Marcos Agustín de Arango—Father Marcos. He is a clean-cut young man in his late twenties, dressed in a black long-sleeved shirt and black pants—nothing indicative to the public that he is a priest. He is a confident but unassuming, intelligent "city boy."

People look toward him, some realizing that he is a stranger.

"I find it very disturbing to hear talk like this from fellow Catholics. Are we Mexicans or Catholics? Our Lord and Savior, Jesus Christ, wasn't born in Mexico. Should we renounce Our Lord then? We are all descendants of Adam, Noah, Abraham, Moses, and

David. And we are all brothers and sisters in God through Christ. Why do we disrespect ourselves by talking otherwise? Whether our Catholic brother or sister was born in Mexico or Poland or the planet Mars, they are all every bit as equal in God's eyes. If our saint works miracles in Lerdo or Mexico City or Neo-Tokyo or Atlantis colony far below the sea, their providence is no less a testament to the power of God. Let us remember, we are good Catholics first and Mexicans second. When we do that, then that's when we are doing our best for Mexico."

The crowd is quiet. The Vatican People watch him intently and are equally impressed.

Father Marcos continues. "Let us keep our focus on the reason for today's meeting with our honored guests. Why can't the Vatican find a decent priest to lead our local parish?" He smiles adding, "A Mexican one."

The crowd laughs and acknowledges him with claps and cheers.

Cardinal Cassiano booms into his neck-mic. "Why?"

The crowd is put off by his response. People look at each other as if he's joking. Father Marcos stands quietly and doesn't take his eyes off of him.

Another man stands. "All you give us is one corrupt or drunken priest after another. All my life, that is all we see."

"Are all the priests corrupt in the Catholic church?" a woman asks.

Cardinal Cassiano responds. "No, Señora. The Catholic Church is not and has never been corrupt. But we are people too, flesh and blood, just like you. We have the good, the bad, the beautiful, and the ugly, just like you. I will be brutally honest with you, which is why I am speaking and not Bishop Garza who, again, has been before this community many times. God created me without a diplomatic bone anywhere in my body. I only know how to be brutally honest. I note that not one of you has pointed out the real problem. Maybe our verbally gifted young man will."

People look at the still-standing Father Marcos.

Cardinal Cassiano continues. "As both Bishop Garza and Bishop Dominguez can attest, it has always been Church policy to choose clergy leadership indigenous to the native country. In fact, that has been policy for centuries, with very rare and specific exceptions. You speak of Church corruption, but what of Mexican corruption? It is neither my responsibility, nor God's, to reach through the heavens and place a 'good priest' nicely before you to lead your parish. It is your responsibility as Mexicans to identify that leadership for us. The Vatican is a long way from Mexico. Bishop Dominguez has begged and begged for clergy referrals for years. He even put in place a program to pay for such referrals. How many referrals has he gotten from your village, and all surrounding ones, in the last ten years? Zero. You scream you want a priest. If we were to bring in a non-Mexican, you would scream that the Vatican is imposing an outsider on you. We empower you to find good Mexican priests for us to appoint, and you remain silent. Then when we appoint them on our own, you tell us we have another narco-priest, or a drunk. Find me a virtuous man in Mexico and then you will have a virtuous priest."

A woman yells out, "Maybe all the good priests have been killed by the cartels."

Cardinal Cassiano snaps back, "Maybe all the good ones in Mexico would rather work for the cartels while the people sit back and remain silent."

A woman says, "So we can be killed too."

Bishop Garza chimes in. "That's what police are for."

The crowd laughs.

"Yea, the narco-police," one man snaps.

The prefix "narco-" is very common in the language nowadays.

Narco-police work for cartels and do their intimidation, kidnapping. and killing. Narco-priests work for the cartels and take their blood money. Narco-lawyers work for cartels and defend them from prosecution. Narco-judges work for cartels and protect them from prosecution or conviction. Narco-journalists work for cartels and plant false stories in the media to protect the cartels or use the press to destroy or expose witnesses. The list went on ad infinitum.

Bishop Dominguez adds, "We relieved the last priest from duty as you asked. However, your parish will remain without leadership until new referrals are provided."

A man yells out, "No one cares about the villages anymore!"

Cardinal Cassiano announces again, "Find me a virtuous man in Mexico and then you will have a virtuous priest. We give the people the clergy they want. Do not blame us for '*nadie se mete*.'" ("No one gets involved.")

This is how much of Mexico had become and no matter how true, people didn't want to be reminded of their inadequacies to their face. The Vatican People remain quiet, and no one in the crowd speaks either. After several minutes of one side watching the other, the man who yelled out before stands up and gathers his family, a woman and three children. They leave. Almost in unison the crowd begins to stand and walk out of the church. Everyone is disgusted and no one walks up to the Vatican People to talk privately. There would be no help from them.

Everyone has left the church except for Father Marcos, who still stands quietly.

Cardinal Cassiano asks, "Are you stalking us, Father Marcos? You are not from Lerdo."

Father Marcos is surprised that they know him. "I drove two hundred miles to be here. How else would a simple priest like myself be able to privately speak to the elite of the Vatican? And my father was born in Lerdo, and so was I. My parents' house was right next to Victoria Park."

Cardinal Cassiano asks, "So are you a virtuous Mexican man, Father Marcos?"

"I am confident God thinks me so."

Bishop Garza chimes in. "If I could give you some advice, it would be good for you to work on your Mexican nationalism. As you can see, the average Mexican isn't as progressive as you on matters of nationality. If you ever get a church yourself, you might want to keep that in mind, lest your own parishioners cast you out for being too 'open' to different peoples."

Father Marcos replies sarcastically, "Yes, I wouldn't want to act like Jesus."

Bishop Garza is put off. "Yes, 'all cultures are equal,' 'who are we to judge,' worked out so well for the Christians in the non-Spanish Americas."

Father Marcos defends himself. "I have never been a pan-cultural relativist and have never supported that ideology, Bishop."

Cardinal Cassiano says, "You have your private meeting with us. What can we do for you, Father Marcos?"

"If you know who I am, then you know why I'm here."

Cardinal Cassiano walks around their table to him. "Do you know how many times we have met, Father Marcos?"

"I believe this is our first, Cardinal."

"No. The first time I met you was at your ordination in Mexico City, two years ago. I remember all our newly ordained priests. You remember what I said to you?"

Father Marcos now remembers. "One day I'll be the Pope."

"Yes."

Father Marcos smirks. "You say that to every newly ordained priest, Cardinal."

"Yes, which is why I know I'll be right one day."

Bishop Dominguez joins them. "Father Marcos, the Church is not for revolutionaries. We will not go to war with the cartels, here or in any other country. The war in Africa is enough."

Father Marcos asks, "Why not? If not us, then who? Who will save the people from the cartels?"

Bishop Dominguez laughs. "This country has a difficult time finding a priest who isn't addicted to drugs or alcohol, or who isn't chasing the local girls, or boys, but you say it can find some soldier for God to take on cartels. You are beyond delusional."

Father Marcus retorts, "Maybe I'm possessed by God."

Bishop Dominguez says coldly, "Good. Then you'll be able to easily rise from the dead when they kill you."

Father Marcos pauses. "We did it before with Father Morales. The Day of the Demon wiped all the cartels away in a day!"

Bishop Dominguez snatches him angrily. "Never speak of that again! I forbid you! Never!"

Cardinal Cassiano says angrily now, "I was mistaken when I thought you to be an impressive young man, Father Marcos. I see you are actually a little boy who knows nothing of the things he speaks of."

Cardinal Cassiano pulls his e-pad from underneath his robe and puts the screen to Father Marcos's face. "Look!"

Father Marcos stares at him and then looks at the e-pad. He turns away his head in revulsion.

Cardinal Cassiano said, "There is your personal patron saint of Father Morales. That was what was left of his body. He was a close friend of mine, and if you ever mention his name again, I'll knock your head off. We Catholics, never speak of it."

Father Marcos composes himself after seeing the horrific image. "The Church did it once before and all I ask is for you to do it one more time. Mexico was free of the cartels."

Bishop Dominguez says, "And how long did it last? A few years?"

Father Marcos adds quickly, "Because no one was there to fill the void."

The Vatican People shake their heads. Cardinal Cassiano puts his e-pad back under his robe.

Bishop Dominguez says, "Don't bother with him, Cardinal. He knows better than us. He's one of those 'do-gooders' for whom you talk yourself to death to save their lives, but they won't listen." He focuses on Father Marcos. "It's yours."

"What's mine?" Father Marcos asks.

Cardinal Cassiano looks at him with a smirk. "The Church of Saint John Paul II, the church of Lerdo City. Now the people can say they have a virtuous man to lead their church."

Father Marcos quickly asks, "What resources will the Vatican give me?"

Cardinal Cassiano responds, "What resources do you need besides the Word of God?"

Bishop Dominguez adds, "You want to be the great crusader against the cartels rather than do your priestly duties, then you'll have to use your own resources."

Cardinal Cassiano takes his hand. "It was a pleasure meeting you again, Father Marcos, the virtuous man. May it not be the last time we meet."

Cardinal Cassiano turns and walks from the church hall. The entourage of priests and bodyguards hastily follow. Bishop Dominguez follows.

Bishop Garza remains behind for a moment. "We will let Sister Maria know tonight that you are the new priest. However, we will make no official claim of you on the Church Net directory." He turns and leaves too.

In other words, if the cartels kill him, there will not even be a word from the Church, as he was never "official." He knows why they are doing this. He isn't the first, nor will he be the last, to make fighting the cartels a chief part of his community ministry. With the Christian-Muslim war raging in Africa, the Church would not risk having Spanish America erupt in another war. Everyday cartel violence, so common in Mexico, had to remain the status quo, no matter how disgusting. For the Vatican, one country was minor in the grand scheme of things when it had to concern itself with the totality of the global Catholic community. Therefore, the Church had to rein in any do-gooders.

Father Marcos stands in the church, alone.

Dead Girls

"There is no possible way for the average human mind to grasp it; the totality of the evil. It involves everyone; it goes everywhere. The blackness is so black that it becomes a living entity that devours all joy, all happiness, all virtue, all goodness, and all life." – Sister Serena, Leader in the Underground Railroad, South America, 2085

Gomez Palacio, Mexico
11:57 p.m., 10 August 2092 (Twenty-Five Months Later)

Tonight is the night we're going to kill ourselves.

Sitting at the booth, Fernanda and Angelita finish their meals. They sit in the farthest corner of a small, off-the-main-road eatery. It's not known by tourists or outsiders, but it is a frequent stop for locals.

Fernanda is a petite woman with straight, silky black hair hanging down to her waist. She is playing with her food, a large salad, more than she is actually eating it. She sips from her half-empty cup of lemonade.

Angelita is working on her second plate of a carne asada burrito supreme. She is just as petite and beautiful, as Fernanda, probably an inch or two shorter at five feet two, but this night she has the appetite of a sumo wrestler. Two untouched margaritas sit near her plate. Her long, curly brown hair is tied in a ponytail behind her head.

Both women are nineteen, wearing white t-shirts and short denim skirts. Their red lipstick, red-painted fingernails and toenails, and makeup are flawless. Angelita also wears a leather jacket, though Fernanda is the one who is a bit chilly, but it is what they have.

Fernanda says, "How can you eat all that? Your stomach is no bigger than a mouse."

Angelita eats slowly but steadily. "Why does it matter? I want my belly full tonight."

Fernanda looks at her while playing with her food again. "You're not going to back out again, are you?"

Angelita quickly responds. "No. I told you already. Ignore anything I say or do and just do it. Just be quick so I don't feel anything."

"They say suicide is a mortal sin." Fernanda is more thinking aloud than talking to her.

Angelita doesn't look up. "Then I prefer to live in hell. At least this *mierda* life will be over."

Fernanda looks at the time on her e-pad. "We've been gone an hour. We should go now, before they notice."

Angelita looks up, her eyes tearing up. "Okay."

Fernanda touches her arm. "It will be okay."

They both get up from the table booth and walk to the door. They prepaid for their meal, so Fernanda waves to the waitress, who acknowledges them as they leave.

In this non-touristy part of town, there aren't the bright lights of the main cities. Here there are few street lights, so you get whatever light you can from whatever building you happen to be in front of, or your mobile device.

Out of habit, they never park in front of the building they are in, but rather have to walk a bit down the street. They turn the corner and there is their parked pink car. Fernanda pushes a button on her e-pad and the car doors pop open.

The goal for the night is simple: drive all night to the cliffs near Baja, park, take the poison, watch the beautiful view of the sunrise, the blue sky, beach, ocean, boats, and people, fall asleep, then die. Not even two decades on this miserable planet and they're already checking out.

They are about to get into the car. A sporty black car comes out of nowhere and screeches to a stop right next to them, nearly hitting Fernanda.

"Where do you bitches think you're going?!" The burly man hops out of the driver's seat. The car is still moving and there is another man in the passenger seat who has to put the car in park. It is a four-seater and the doors open in the back. Three large men exit.

Fernanda puts on a brave face, but Angelita is terrified.

The man laughs. "Did you think changing your phone would keep me from finding you? I put a tracker on your pink sex-mobile. What do you think about that?"

Fernanda says, "We weren't going anywhere. We just got something to eat and were on our way back."

"Oh, so you want to lie. I'm going to brutalize the two of you tonight, tomorrow morning, tomorrow afternoon, tomorrow evening. It will never stop. What do you think about that?"

Fernanda angrily says, "You better kill me then."

"Oh, I know you don't care about yourself, so that won't happen. But you do care about her." He points his stubby finger at Angelita.

Fernanda stares at him as his three partners laugh like a pack of hyenas. She wants to run or attack him or curse him or do something. But what?

Angelita suddenly runs.

"Run. Run away, little Angelita. I'm going to run you down with my car!"

Then the man just stops. Two seconds later he drops to his knees and falls face first into the dirt.

The other three men stare at him, wondering if he is playing a joke on them. This time they hear something hit the car at the same time that the second man's face explodes and he falls to the ground.

The remaining men draw their guns and take cover. "It's an ambush!" one yells. But they can't see the gunman. The third man is shot dead as he crawls on the ground, trying to get behind their black car. The fourth man is hit in the chest as he stands to run. He falls backward with his head smashing into the pink car.

Fernanda is frozen in fear, standing in the exact same spot all this time.

Angelita is also stopped in her tracks, watching. She looks into the night sky and outstretches her arms, wishing to be shot dead too.

Calm silence. A figure comes out of the darkness. Dressed all in black with a black hoodie, the man walks to Fernanda. She notices the gun with laser-sight and silencer in his hand, held close to his body.

He stops and motions to Angelita to approach. She pauses for a moment, but does so. The women stare at him.

"I want you to go to each man, go through all of their pockets, and take everything, wallet, cards, everything. Gather it all together and put it in this plastic bag." He pulls out a black plastic bag from his clothes. "Then check their bodies for anything else: guns, knives, weapons, electronics. Do it now. I'll take care of their car."

Fernanda and Angelita obey and start searching the first two dead men closest to them. They look up every so often to see the hooded man going through the glove compartment of the black car, then under the front seats. The dead men have all kinds of things on them: digi-cards, phones, knives, guns, food, candy, gum, jewelry, packets of sugar, natural cigarettes and e-cigarettes, nail clippers, mini-toothbrushes, combs, various tubes of lotions, mini shavers, and condoms.

The hooded man is pulling things out of the trunk and dumping everything onto the ground outside of the car. He stops to walk away, back into the darkness.

Fernanda and Angelita are watching him every step of the way. They finish checking the last two dead men.

There is a faint hum and another black car coasts forward. The hooded man gets out of the car and walks to them. "Put everything in the truck of my car. And anything you want to keep from your car. No electronics, though. Leave them in the car."

The two women load everything in the hooded man's car trunk. Fernanda throws her e-pad into the pink car and Angelita does the same.

The hooded man lifts a metal can from the trunk. He walks to the men's black car and douses it with gas thoroughly. He then pours gas on the four dead men and, finally, the pink car. He puts the gas can down and reaches into his pockets. His hand appears and he flicks an already lit match on the men's black car, the first dead man, the second dead man, the third, the fourth, and then flicks one on the pink car. He throws the gas can in the center of the blaze.

He's obviously set fires like this many, many times before, Fernanda thinks to herself. She remembers that this is actually a common "trick" in these rural areas, especially for little boys, pulling out a match and striking it lit at the same time.

Both cars go up in flames. The four bodies, however, not only burn, but burn so brightly. They almost look like they will get up and run away, but then they don't even seem like they were ever once living human beings at all. The women back away from the disgusting fumes of burning flesh.

"Let's go," the hooded man says.

A real "cool customer," Fernanda thinks. He's not afraid in the least bit of being caught after just shooting and burning up four people in the middle of the night. He's either a psychopath, not caring, or a native, knowing that even if the police were around, they wouldn't do anything, as they would just assume it was a routine cartel execution.

"Go where?" Fernanda asks.

"Wherever you want, family, friends, police station, women's shelter." He walks to his car as they follow.

"Why are you doing this?" Fernanda asks.

"You ask a lot of questions. You're free. Accept it. Where do you want me to drop you?"

Fernanda looks at him. "We have no place to go."

"No place?" he asks almost incredulously.

"No place," Fernanda repeats.

"Get in the car, in the back. I'll get you off the street, to a safe place."

Fernanda and Angelita get in the back seat and close the door. The hooded man is already in the driver's seat.

"Put on your seatbelts. I don't want you flying through the windshield if we were to have an accident."

Funny. He just killed four people and set them on fire and he's worrying about seatbelts! However, they obey and put on the seatbelts.

"Why don't you have any place to go?" he asks.

Fernanda is now mad. "We just don't."

She expects him to press further, but he doesn't and drives.

No one talks in the car. The two women know exactly where they are. They have been *chauffeured* through practically every major street and minor dirt road from here to Mexico City. He is not driving to get out of Gomez Palacio, but driving to another out-of-the-way section of the city.

Almost thirty minutes later they arrive. The hooded man coasts the car to a stop right in front of the main arched entrance. He gets out of the car and motions for them to follow. Fernanda and Angelita exit the car. It is a very large, nondescript four-story building, possibly apartments, but no lights are visible except for the street lights outside. The building is either empty or all the windows are shuttered to prevent inside light from being seen.

He leads them through the entrance and both women can now see, though very dimly, a flight of stairs; up the stairs to the second floor, third floor, and finally the fourth. The hooded man leads them down the dark hallway; the hallway lights automatically go on. They follow him to the end of the hall and he opens the door to the room. They notice he hasn't used a key. The lights go on automatically and they follow him inside.

It is a large apartment with hardwood floors, a living room area with a large wall vid-screen, a four-person couch six feet away facing it, and a three-person couch next to it. The dining area has an eight-person rectangular glass dining table and simple, high-back, slim chairs. The kitchen area has a massive refrigerator, the standard stove with an oven above it, a sink with a dishwasher below it, and lots of cupboards. They can see an open door to the right, most likely the bedroom. The wall on the side of the street seems black; it is definitely shuttered.

"Have a seat," the hooded man says.

He walks to the left, opens a door they didn't see before, and disappears inside, closing the door behind him.

Fernanda and Angelita walk into the dining area and sit. They have been through this *routine* before, many times. In a few moments, Father Marcos exits the same door. What they instantly take note of is not his face, but the clerical collar around his neck. Fernanda rolls her eyes. A damn priest!

"I'm Father Marcos." He walks to them. "Your names?"

"Fernanda," she says, annoyed.

"Angelita."

"Have you eaten?" he asks.

Angelita nods yes. Fernanda is not even looking at him.

"Good. This is your safe-house to stay in as long as you need to. Most important is that you can leave at any time."

"How long will you be keeping us here?" Fernanda now looks directly at him.

Father Marcos looks instead at Angelita. "What did I just say?"

Angelita says, "We can leave at any time."

Father Marcos looks at Fernanda.

Fernanda says, "I heard what you said, but men always say one thing and mean or do something else."

He continues, "I'm not going to patronize you with the 'I can't begin to imagine all that you've been through.' I would get you a counselor, but I suspect you're like me and would rather juggle scorpions. So let's take it day by day and see where God takes us."

Fernanda responds, "There is no God."

Father Marcos looks at her. "Why do you say that?"

"Our lives are proof that there isn't a God."

"Who do you think sent me to save you?"

Fernanda smirks.

"Get some sleep. I sleep downstairs. Rules are simple while you stay here: have breakfast ready at seven in the morning and have dinner at seven in the evening. I join you for both breakfast and dinner. Lunch, you are on your own. The entire apartment is yours except for the tiny room you saw me go into; leave that door closed. I use that for simple storage. You can open the balcony doors during the day, but keep the shutters closed at night. Always keep the front door locked. Never leave the apartment unless I'm here, or you plan to leave and not come back. Keep the apartment clean at all times. And always keep an eye out for scorpions. See you in the morning at seven."

Fernanda thinks to herself that he is definitely a native. Only Duranguense, people from Durango, refer to scorpions often in conversation.

Father Marcos walks out the front door, locking it behind him. The women stand there looking at each other.

7:00 a.m.

Father Marcos enters through the front door right on time. Fernanda and Angelita are already sitting on one side of the dining room table. It is filled with sliced fruit, glasses of juice, and quesadillas, all from the fully stocked refrigerator and cupboards.

"Good morning, Fernanda. Good morning, Angelita." He sits down at the head of the table and approvingly looks at the meal.

Fernanda and Angelita start to eat, but he holds up a hand. "Wait. I have to say grace."

Fernanda rolls her eyes again. *Will he say this 'grace' nonsense when we go to shower, use the toilet, and take out the trash?*

"God, thanks for the good meal we're about to receive. Thank you for bringing Fernanda and Angelita into my life as we enjoy our breakfast together. Amen."

He now starts to eat, picking up his fork. The two women watch him a moment and then start eating too.

Fernanda picks at her food with her fork a bit before taking another bite. "Will you say this grace thing at each meal?"

Father Marcos says, "Yes."

Fernanda asks, "Why is it you 'thank God' at the beginning of a meal, and not when you take a bath or brush your teeth?"

"It's religious tradition that is part of the table fellowship dating back to Jesus and the original twelve disciples. Traditions are good. They preserve culture and remind us who we are."

They eat quietly. Angelita is focused on her food, as always. Fernanda notices that Father Marcos is reading the daily news on his tablet.

"What do you two plan to do today?" he asks.

"Sit around," Fernanda says.

"Watch tele," Angelita says.

He adds, "You should have a goal for the week."

Fernanda interrupts. "We're free, aren't we?"

"Yes." Father Marcos answers.

Fernanda continues, "Then let us enjoy our freedom and enjoy watching tele and sitting around."

"How long will you do that?" he asks.

Fernanda says, "We don't know. We've never been free before."

"Makes sense. You'll be ready when you're ready." He smiles. "Within reason, of course."

Fernanda is suspicious. "Ready for what?"

"The way I was raised, when you help someone, you build them up until they are strong. Then they can go off on their own, so you can help the next one, and the ones you helped can also help others. The multiplicity of goodness."

Angelita looks at him. "We're not built up enough."

Father Marcos says, "Of course."

He finishes his breakfast and gets up, putting the plate in the sink. He turns to them. "You two are the boss of this place."

They just look at him. Is there a hidden meaning in that statement?

"See you at seven." Father Marcos leaves through the front door again.

2:44 p.m.

Angelita sits on the couch watching her tele, a four-by-four-foot vid-screen hanging on the main wall. She can literally watch it all day, and her absolute favorite among all shows are telenovelas, "classic" television in the Spanish Americas: raunchy, oversexed, cartoonish soap operas, but millions are addicted to them, including Angelita.

Fernanda sits on the side couch not wanting to watch any, but what else is there to do? The shutters are pulled back now and the large balcony doors are open. She spends her time watching the breeze blow through the sheer curtains, watching Angelita laugh at jokes from the show, and staring around at the apartment.

Earlier, she had gone into that tiny room in which the Father had changed out of his "hooded avenger" clothes—the one he said not to go into. All that was in there were a few sets of black clothes, but mostly tons of canned goods, kitchen supplies, and bath supplies—nothing sinister, as her mind had imagined.

They suddenly hear keys at the door. Both of them are frightened; it is not 7:00 p.m. yet. *Who's at the door?! We knew all this was too good to be true.*

Father Marcos opens the door. He is in his black hoodie again. He reaches to something out of their view and walks into the apartment holding the hand of a little girl.

She must be no older than five years old, dressed in the trademark private Catholic school clothes of a white blouse, dark red pleated skirt, black shoes, and black backpack. She has a truly angelic face with silky black hair and big green eyes.

Father Marcos says, "This is Juanita." To Juanita, "This is Fernanda and Angelita. They will be taking care of you."

He walks her over to them and has her sit down on the couch next to Fernanda.

"I'll be back at 7:00 p.m."

He leaves the apartment, closing the door behind him.

Fernanda and Angelita look at each other and then at little Juanita.

They would learn from Juanita that her entire family was killed right in front of her eyes that day as two warring cartel gangs decided to have a gun battle in the middle of a busy street.

One of the gang members tried to grab her, but Father Marcos appeared from nowhere, killed him, and took her away from the gun battle. If not by the gunman, she probably would have been taken off the street by some spotter, lookouts for the cartels that hang out on the streets looking for young children to snatch for ransom, the sex slave trade, or something else.

Father Marcos walks down the stairs to the main entrance. Standing just outside the entrance is a boy, twelve-year old Rodrigo, in khaki shorts, a black tank top, and brown sneakers. He has dark, tan skin and sandy brown hair. He eagerly waits for Father Marcos.

Father Marcos says, "There are three females upstairs now."

Rodrigo says, "Yes, I saw."

"How many boys do you have on your crew now?"

"I have twelve regulars."

"No one is to ever go up there."

"Okay. Are you expecting trouble?"

"No. No one knows about this building. But I want to be careful."

"If you want, I can make sure you know about anyone who comes within a mile of the building: on foot, by car, anything that flies overhead."

"That sounds like a job for more than a crew of a dozen."

"It is. I need maybe fifty boys to do a good 24-7 surveillance."

Rodrigo always amuses him. Only twelve years old and he talks like a seasoned security agent.

"Is your crew selling drugs?" he asks.

Rodrigo hesitates. "I never do, but they have to eat. I can't tell them not to without being able to give real work and put money in their pockets."

"I don't want anyone on your crew selling drugs or doing any crimes."

"Selling scorpions to the scavenger market doesn't bring in enough money to put food on the table or pay for the roof over the head."

It was a common occupation for children on the street, being an *alacraneros*, or scorpion hunter. Catch and sell them, but the best time is really during the summer. It isn't a year-round thing.

"So if I provide three meals a day and a place to live, that isn't enough?"

"It's great for me and a few of the boys, but not for most. All around them they see the gangs flashing money, driving the news cars with the new music, the new clothes, all that. People want money in the pocket. They're going to work for the criminals and do crimes."

Rodrigo is a "Lost Boy," one of the thousands of homeless and orphaned boys living on the streets of Mexico. They stay alive by begging, stealing, and trading stolen property, selling live scorpions to scavenger markets for souvenirs and hospitals for their venom, and hire out their services to low-level street criminals or the cartels. Some of these boys would become the next generation of street criminals themselves, some would become drug addicts, drunks, or both, and some would be snatched for the sex slave trade. Some would make it out of the street life somehow and live productive lives, while others would simply disappear, never to be seen or heard from again. Others would end up dead in some alley.

Father Marcos says, "No one who works for me can sell drugs or do crimes."

Rodrigo is firm, though. "It's simple: be the one who puts money in the pocket and they'll be loyal to you and not the criminals. You've been on planet Mexico longer than me, so you know this already."

Father Marcos stares at him for a moment. Planet Mexico, funny. One of the many cutesy phrases used on the street. Rodrigo may be technically a child, but he is far more intelligent than the average adult. You can tell he is going to be something big in life. Marcos knew that when he first saw the boy months ago, when he was getting this building ready for his operations. He is a good boy and wants to do right, but he is about the money, doing whatever it takes not to starve and to stay ahead in life.

Rodrigo knows he is being sized up again.

Father Marcos motions to Rodrigo to follow him. They walk around to the side of the building where his black car is parked. He opens the trunk, lifts up a cloth bag, and opens it. It's filled with cash chips. Rodrigo's eyes light up.

When the whole world gave up physical money for digital cash, it actually saved the casinos, which were constantly trying new gimmicks to stay in business since gambling moved from brick-and-mortar establishments to the Net.

But there will always be an underground economy with people who, for whatever reason, want to live off-Grid. Casino chips meant that you didn't need a bank or some authority to give you digital cash. Digi-cards—the digital cash and credit cards that replaced physical money—meant that authority had to know your identity: who you are, where you live, how to contact you, and every other piece of information on you. It isn't only criminals who didn't want to do that.

Authentic and anonymous casino chips had become the money of choice on the street. One could buy a single casino chip that could be of any denomination or state currency, just trade in the equivalent currency.

Father Marcos's bag is filled with larger peso denomination chips. With just one of these chips, one could eat three *big* meals a day for three weeks straight. Father Marcos tosses the bag to Rodrigo, who is almost speechless, happy beyond words at his great fortune.

Father Marcos says, "Hire a crew as large as you need. I want to know anything that walks, drives, flies, or crawls near this building within a five-mile radius. No one in the crew is to sell or use drugs. No thefts, no crimes. No one is to work for the cartels or any *narcomenudista*. They work for us and they follow our rules or get out. Food is to be provided and the first floor of this building is for your crew. And I want an intel briefing every morning after my breakfast. Understood?"

Rodrigo snaps to attention. "Understood, boss. It'll be done before you get back tonight at seven."

"Good. Don't let me down, Rodrigo."

"You won't be disappointed, boss—ever."

Father Marcos closes the trunk, gets in the car, and drives off as Rodrigo takes the bag inside the building.

Rodrigo is elated, smiling from ear to ear. *Now I have money to put in the pocket of everyone! No more working for the cartels or 'rats.' I'm working for God now!*

5:14 p.m.

Rodrigo is now King of the Lost Boys of Lerdo City. He stands in one of the first-floor rooms of the building with dozens and dozens of other boys. Each one of them is holding an e-pad with a map of the city on the screen. He walks to each of them and assigns them a territory.

"Food and shelter is paid up front. Money is given out after only a good day's work the following morning," he announces. "Get to the streets."

The boys start exiting the room. Rodrigo is surrounded by six boys as he walks outside too. Boys fan out in every direction; some walk, some run, some grab bicycles, both manual and motorized, and ride off. Rodrigo and his personal team of six boys will watch the main entrance during daylight hours.

"Get some candy for us," he says to one of the boys.

The boy sprints off down the street.

"It's going to take the rats only a few days to find out that all the boys in this part of the city work for you," one of the other five boys says. "We're going to need weapons, you know."

"Yes," Rodrigo acknowledges. "We'll get what we need."

"Rats" is the slang term for *narcomenudistas*, local street criminals. The powerful cartels controlled most of the crime in the country, dividing up states and regions among themselves, but they focused mostly on the cities nowadays. Most of the cartels had no interest in the seemingly endless small villages of Mexico. That left control of the crime in the villages to the *narcomenudistas*. Most did their own thing and avoided main cartels. For large villages like Lerdo City, they paid money or "tribute" to the cartels to be ignored.

Another boy asks, "Is Church Man solid?"

Lost Boys had already given Father Marcos a nickname, but then again, religious people in general were often informally called "church man" or "church lady" by the public.

Rodrigo answers, "Remember that rat Beak-Nose?"

The boy nods. "That crazy rat killing boys with his car for fun. But someone killed him."

Rodrigo says, "It was Church Man."

The boys are surprised. "Really?"

One boy says, "Beak Nose was, like, eight feet tall."

Another boy adds, "He was a cyborg, too."

Rodrigo nods. "Exactly." The boys are impressed.

6:59 p.m.

Father Marcos enters the apartment right on time. The three females are already seated at the dining table on one side. Father Marcos sits at the head of the table.

"Good evening, ladies."

"Good evening," little Juanita responds. Fernanda and Angelita do not answer.

"Juanita, I will continue to search for any surviving relatives you may have, like I promised," he says and Juanita nods.

He clasps his hands together as they all quietly wait. "Let me say grace." He closes his eyes and bows his head. "God, thank you for the good meal we're about to receive. Thank you again for bringing Fernanda and Angelita into my life, and allowing me to be there to help little Juanita, the newest member of the family, in her time of tragedy. We enjoy dinner together. Amen." He opens his eyes. "Let's eat."

Everyone starts helping themselves to the food.

"So, what did you all do today?"

"Watch tele and talk to Juanita," Angelita says, not missing a beat from eating her food.

"Sit around and talk to Juanita," Fernanda says.

Juanita looks at him, but sheepishly doesn't say anything.

"Did Fernanda and Angelita get you settled in today, Juanita?" Father Marcos asks.

She nods.

Fernanda asks, "So what did you do today, Father?"

"Little of this, little of that. Nothing to get me in any trouble with God, though."

Fernanda pokes her food with her fork. "Oh that's right, you are on a special mission from God. I told you, I don't believe in him. What is your proof of God, Father?"

"Johann Sebastian Bach."

Fernanda looks at him with a perplexed expression. Angelita and Juanita stop, confused.

Angelita asks, "What's that?"

Father Marcos answers. "Music. He's the greatest classical composer ever, gifted by God. When I listen, it takes me right into the Empyrean, the cosmic heavens of God's entire universe."

Fernanda is incredulous. "What kind of priest are you? Your answer for the proof of God is *music*? Not the Bible or Jesus or a miracle, but music? You don't have many people in your church, do you?"

He smiles. "No. That's why God told me to go rescue women and kill bad guys for a while until I learn to give better sermons. I'm very, very bad at the sermons right now."

Angelita and Juanita laugh. Fernanda shakes her head. She still can't figure him out.

He adds, "The problem, Fernanda, isn't that you don't believe in God, because you do. The problem is that you don't see Him as being relevant to your life."

Gomez Palacio, Mexico
12:02 a.m., 30 September 2092

"Do we have a problem?" The fat man, Gordito, is dressed in a flaming lavender and pink long-sleeved shirt, boat slacks, and slip-on tan shoes. He is the "king" of the *narcomenudistas* based in the outskirts of the city. Three of his thugs stand around him.

"We've had seven men disappear from Lerdo City and three more here. And no one can tell me who killed Beak Nose. Is one of the other gangs trying to move in on us or not?"

The men look at each other.

Gordito says, "Am I talking to myself?! I truly wish I could clone myself because you all are useless." He looks at his watch. "Get those girls in here and take care of the party. Go. Get away from me."

The men quickly walk away. Gordito stands and also walks out of the richly decorated office on the second floor. The music is loud. The sounds of many people downstairs are even louder with their talking, laughing, and horseplay.

Gordito walks down the staircase. The mansion is huge. It is party time at Gordito's tonight! One man after another greets him or shakes his hand, and a few even give him hugs. All the guests are men and all of them have a drink in their hands. Gordito continues to make the rounds through the crowd.

Outside the mansion, Gordito's three men lead a line of beautiful women, seventeen in all, down the long driveway, back to the "party." There are men waiting outside, drinking, talking, smoking, and they immediately cheer, clap, and whistle when they see the girls. One man unbuckles his belt and drops his pants around his ankles, gyrating around. The other men laugh and some do the same.

The three men lead the seventeen women up the staircase as all eyes are on them. Gordito looks approvingly as the crowds of men line up behind him, laughing and joking.

One of the men flips off his slip-on shoes and jumps on one of the living room couches. "I say let's toast to our host Gordito! Nobody does sex parties better!"

The crowd goes wild, toasting and clapping.

Gordito acknowledges the praise by raising his glass too.

12:37 a.m.

A convertible races up the driveway to Gordito's mansion and stops. Two men dressed in white suits jump out.

"We're late," one man says.

"It's not late. It's still early. The party won't be done until at least five in the morning. Or it won't be done until we're done." He laughs.

The men walk to the door.

"Why is it so quiet? Are you sure we're at the right place?"

"Gordito has only this one mansion in the city."

They ring the doorbell. No answer. One of them tries the door, but it's locked.

"I think we're at the wrong place."

"No, stupid, everyone's cars are here." He points. There are dozens of parked cars in Gordito's massive driveway. "I recognize most of them." He rings the doorbell again. Nothing.

"Let's walk around to the back."

The silence is eerie. All the lights are on and based on the number of cars, there should be at least sixty men inside. When they reach the side entrance, they see the door is completely open.

"What's going on here? Let's get out of here. Something's not right."

"Wait here. I want to check it out."

He disappears inside. The other man waits nervously. He calls inside, "We shouldn't split up. Haven't you ever seen a horror movie?"

He walks in quickly and he's in the massive living room. It is totally empty, but it's obvious that people were there: glasses with alcohol are everywhere, on the tables, counters, and floor.

"Mr. Cordeno?" a voice says.

He's startled by the voice saying his name. He can't see the person, as the voice is coming from a dark room to the side.

"Who's calling me?"

"Please come here, Mr. Cordeno. Your friend Mr. Tempo and I need your help."

"Help with what?"

Mr. Cordeno hesitates, but enters the dark room.

Ciudad Lerdo (Lerdo City), Mexico
4:15 a.m.

Both Fernanda and Angelita are woken up, but that doesn't take much, as they are very light sleepers. The bed is massive and actually all three of them can sleep there comfortably, with Fernanda and Angelita on either side and Juanita in the middle. They always sleep on top of the covers in their clothes in case they need to get up quickly or run. Juanita, on the other hand, is sleeping in her underwear and under the sheets.

The bedroom door is closed, but the lights outside in the living room are on, and they can hear movement.

What the hell is going on? Why is Father Marcos moving around at four in the morning?

They want to get up, but they don't want to wake up and scare Juanita. They lie there and wait.

5:15 a.m.

They usually get up at 6:00 a.m., but they can't take it anymore. The sun is coming out, so they can see without turning on any lights.

Contrary to her nature, Angelita moves first, hops off the bed, and opens the bedroom door to walk out. She walks back inside and motions to Fernanda to come outside.

Juanita is slowly waking up. Fernanda rolls out of the bed and walks to the bedroom door to join Angelita. She looks out and is stunned. There are young women everywhere: sitting on all the chairs, on the couches, and on the floor. All eyes are on Fernanda and Angelita.

Fernanda swallows hard and feels a bit light-headed. Angelita stays quiet, waiting for her to take the lead.

Fernanda needs time to think. She walks into the center of the kitchen. "We'll make breakfast for everyone. Any objections?" She looks at everyone, listening for a response, but is actually counting them—seventeen girls, average age must be eighteen.

6:00 a.m.

Father Marcos enters the apartment. Everyone is eating. Fernanda and Angelita sit at the heads of the table; all eight seats are taken, with four sitting on one couch, three sitting on another couch, and everyone else sitting on the floor. He notices the shy Juanita, who is peeking out from the bedroom, too nervous to come out and join everyone.

"Good. Everyone is eating. Good morning, everyone. You've already met Fernanda and Angelita, who are the bosses of the apartment. Juanita is the one hiding in the bedroom. I'm Father Marcos. This is your safe-house to stay in as long as you need to. However, most important is that you can leave at any time."

"I don't believe you, churchman. What sick game do you have planned for us?" The woman is sitting on the couch and, in a group of beautiful women, she is the most stunning. Mona Lisa drops her plate to the ground. She curses at him.

"I offered to take you wherever you wanted, remember? And I don't want that kind of language spoken here. No cursing of any kind."

"Your Jedi mind games don't work on me. What cartel boss are you working for, churchman?" She curses again at him.

"His name is God. Do you know him?"

"No, I haven't had the pleasure of bedding him yet, but give it time."

Again, contrary to her nature, Angelita is furious. She obviously wants to get up and punch Mona Lisa in the mouth for being so disrespectful.

"I want to leave now!" Mona Lisa screams so loud that almost all the girls jump. "Now!"

Father Marcos is unmoved by her.

"Now!" Mona Lisa screams again.

"You shout or curse one more time, I'll pick you up and throw you out of the window." Father Marcos has a cold, deadly serious look on his face now.

Mona Lisa stares at him with an angry look. Everyone else holds their breath in silence. Will she scream again? Will Father Marcos really throw her out the window? It's a cat-and-mouse game and Mona Lisa blinks first. "Give me my money that you stole from me. And my e-pad."

"I'll give you the money, but no e-pad."

"Fine. You thief. Give me my money."

Father Marcos marches to the couch on which Mona Lisa sits in the living room area. Everyone is afraid he's going to hit her. "Thief? You forgot killer, too."

Mona Lisa just stares at him. It seems like an eternity of silence. She is relentless. "Give me my money."

Father Marcos walks back to the kitchen as he takes a tiny phone-only from his pocket. He hits a speed-dial button. "Have a taxi here in two minutes." He looks to Mona Lisa. "Which purse is yours?"

Mona Lisa says coldly, "The gold one."

Back into the phone, "And get the gold purse. How much money is in it?" He pauses. "Okay, give it to the woman who will be coming down for the taxi. No. She has enough money to pay the fare herself." He disconnects.

Father Marcos walks to the door and opens it. He looks at Mona Lisa.

Mona Lisa stands. She is already a tall woman, but with seven-inch heels she is towering. She walks defiantly to the door.

Mona Lisa looks him in the eye. "Good luck with your devil work, churchman."

"Why thank you, and God bless."

She walks out and he slams the door.

Father Marcos turns to everyone. "Okay, now that we've finished with the 'internal housekeeping,' I will finish what I was saying: This is your safe-house to stay in as long as you need to. However, most important is that you can leave at any time.

"The rules are simple while you stay here. Fernanda and Angelita are in charge. Have breakfast ready at seven in the morning and have dinner at seven in the evening. I will join you for both breakfast and dinner. Lunch, you are on your own. The entire apartment is yours except for the tiny room to the side, there; leave that door closed. You can open the balcony doors during the day, but close the shutters at night. Always keep the front door locked. Never leave the apartment unless I'm here, or you plan to leave and not come back. Keep the apartment clean at all times. Keep an eye out for scorpions. Now let's finish eating."

Father Marcos begins to sit down, but Fernanda speaks up. "Father, can I talk to you privately, outside?"

"Of course." To everyone, "Angelita, you're in charge."

He walks out the front door with Fernanda following, closing it without locking it behind them.

Fernanda speaks softly. "What are you doing? Are you trying to get everyone killed? You can take a girl or two from the cartels and maybe get away. You can even take homeless, orphan girls who haven't been initiated yet without a problem. But you can't take more than a dozen girls from the cartels. Are you insane? They will cut your head off and dump your body parts in an alley somewhere. They will cut your head off. Their gangs will come after you."

"No, they won't."

"How do you know?"

"Because they're all dead."

Fernanda just looks at him. "You're going to get all of us murdered."

Father Marcos opens the door and peeks in. "Angelita, come here for a moment." To everyone, "Juanita is in charge." Juanita's head pops into view from the bedroom with her mouth wide open.

Angelita joins them in the hallway. "Follow me," Father Marcos says. They follow him down one flight of stairs. *Where is he taking us?*

He leads them down the very dimly lit hall to a door on the right, at the corner. He opens it and leads them inside. The room is similar to the apartment they've been in, but there is not one piece of furniture inside except a single white chair.

Fernanda's eyes now notice the thing of note in the room. On the wall to the left are pictures, dozens, no, hundreds of them. She walks to the wall. They are all pictures of girls!

Suddenly Fernanda gasps at one of the pictures directly in front of her—it is her! A photo of her as a little girl before she was snatched. Fernanda's eyes begin to tear up as she touches the photo on the wall.

She flashes back to that day when a black van drove up to her as she walked home from the market and she heard a voice say, "Are you looking for a new papi, little girl?"

She has completely zoned out, but snaps out of it and almost jumps when an arm comes into her periphery. Angelita points to another picture on the wall. "That's me," she says softly.

Fernanda looks behind her to Father Marcos sitting quietly in the white chair. She looks back to the wall and scans the photos again. She now notices that some of the pictures are circled in thick red. In fact, maybe half the photos are red circled.

"What do the red circles mean?" she asks as she glances back to Father Marcos again.

"You know," he says quietly.

Fernanda looks at the wall and then back at him. She now realizes.

He says it anyway. "Dead girls."

She stares at him. She looks back to the wall. Her eyes return to her own picture. She has nothing left from her normal, innocent life before. Nothing at all.

So Father Marcos has known about them all along. It was not random. The slave-runners snatched girls (and occasionally boys) for their sex slave trade, from anywhere and everywhere. Then would come the rape, drugs, imprisonment, and brainwashing, and then their new "vocation" would begin. The sex slaves would be so isolated that every aspect of their lives was controlled, with no family or friends except for other slaves. There would be no one else but their slave-runners or pimps. Average entrance age into the sex slave trade world was twelve.

"I want my picture." She doesn't even look at him this time.

"Take it from the wall, then."

She looks at him briefly and pulls it carefully from the wall. Angelita takes her picture too.

"I want a tablet also so I can read books and the news during the day," Fernanda says.

It seems like a request clear out of the blue, but Father Marcos has always noticed her watching him read at the table during meals and was planning on getting her one anyway. "Okay."

Angelita touches Fernanda's shoulder and points to the opposite wall.

Fernanda asks herself why she didn't see it. They walk over to the other wall, which is covered with pictures too, but not of girls. All men. No, there are some women, but they are mostly men. While the Wall of Girls is simply one mass of photos, the photos on this wall are arranged in organizational trees.

Fernanda realizes what they are looking at: the criminal organizations in Lerdo, Gomez Palacio, and maybe even the capital city of Durango.

Angelita points. Fernanda's eyes now fix on the photo. Their pig-rapist pimp Hermando. The man Father Marcos killed first when he saved them. He's red circled. Fernanda steps back to get a wider view. Hermando's entire organizational tree is red circled, everyone under him and everyone above him, to the top. She even recognizes the top man, Mr. Gordito. The bottom levels of most of the other organizational trees are also red circled.

Fernanda glances at Father Marcos. He is still sitting quietly in the white chair.

Fernanda looks back at the "Wall of Pigs." She wipes the tears from her face. She now realizes that Father Marcos is not operating at random. It's a carefully coordinated effort, lots of planning. It must have taken him months, years even, to gather the information and execute it.

She now feels calm. She turns to him again. "I still don't believe God sent you to save us. You did this all on your own."

Father Marcos smiles. "There once was a woman who lived in a little house in Veracruz, right in Villa Guerrero. One day the government warned everyone in her town that big rains were on the way and that everyone had to evacuate. The woman refused to go and said, 'God, if you need to save me, just send me a sign.'

"The big rains came and flood waters washed out the roads. A big truck came and stopped in front of her house, and a man rescuing stranded residents yelled for her to come with him, but she refused to go. The big truck drove off.

"The big rains continued. The flood waters rose into her house and flooded the first level. She ran to the second floor. A boat came and stopped in front of her second-floor window, and a man rescuing stranded residents yelled for her to come with him, but she refused to go. The boat drove off.

"The big rains continued. The flood waters rose and flooded her second level. She ran out on the roof. A helicopter came and hovered above the roof, and a man rescuing stranded residents yelled for her to come with him, but she refused to go. The helicopter flew off.

"The flood waters rose and drowned the woman.

"The woman got to heaven and saw God walking. She ran over to him, angry.

"'God, I said if you needed to save me, just send me a sign. You let me drown!'

"God looked at her and said, 'I sent a truck, a boat, and a helicopter to save you. You drowned your own dumb ass.'"

Father Marcos looks at Fernanda directly and says, "Don't be more religious than God. He didn't send an army of angels or a bolt of lightning. He sent me. Don't always be looking for the big miracles. Most times it's the little things, the subtle things, that are the answers you're looking for. That's the sermon for the day. Now let's go back upstairs. I'm hungry."

The Return of Father Marcos

"Give to Caesar what is Caesar's and to God what is God's." And they were amazed at him. — Jesus, New Testament, Mark 12:17

"It will be so when Caesar starts protecting God's children in Mexico from the killers and the slavers." — Father Marcos, from the Grito de Durango (Cry of Durango Sermon)

Gomez Palacio, Mexico
11:57 a.m., 8 December 2092

Inside the apartment, several young women watch a telenovela in the living room. At the table in the dining room area, eight young women play poker. On the balcony patio, six women lounge around, talking. In the bedroom, seven women lie around quietly reading on the bed and on the floor.

In the next apartment is the same scene, but with a different group of women. This room has an even bigger view-screen and a bigger crowd of women. Angelita sits in the center of the crowd, laughing with the others. In room after room are the same activities.

In the rooms on the opposite ends of the hall, women sit at small desks with laptops, typing away. Fernanda walks to one of the girls at a desk to help. Another room is a complete reading room and women, including little Juanita, are lounging everywhere, e-pads in their hands.

The bottom floors are filled with boys. In one room everyone is playing cards; in another, playing video games. In another, everyone is sleeping on separate cots, and in another, everyone is eating at tables.

Outside the building stands Rodrigo, and on either side of him are much bigger boys. He notices something.

Slowly walking down the street toward them is a "scary-skinny" woman. Her short black hair hangs every which way. She wears a one-piece brown dress and carries a very large bag. As she comes closer, Rodrigo tries to guess her age. She looks bad, her very skeleton visible through her skin.

"Can…can you help me?" she asks.

"Who sent you?" Rodrigo asks suspiciously. The apartment building has nearly five hundred people now, but is still supposed to be a "secret."

"I think his name is Paco. He said if I needed help there is a priest here who helps people. Protect you from the cartels, police, and all the other freaks."

"Do have any device in your bag or any electronics?"

"No. The boys at the end of the street already took my e-pad."

"Are you a spy for the cartels or the rats?"

"Look at me. I'm not capable of nothing anymore." Her eyes are sad, her expression desperate.

Rodrigo has seen many drug zombies. She's done so many drugs that her body has not only aged decades, but won't accept any more. She's literally killed parts of her brain.

"Wait here and let my people check your bag again," he tells her.

She hands her bag over to the boys without hesitation as Rodrigo ducks inside.

He heads to the empty second floor. He knocks on a door three times and then enters. Even from out here the music is blaring from inside.

Father Marcos sits at his desk, viewing his laptop. Bach plays from the desk speakers. Classical music is all he listens to, and most of the time the composer is Johann Sebastian Bach. The wall is plastered with photos, diagrams, notes, and numbers. The room is his office command center.

The original "Wall of Pigs" that Fernanda and Angelita saw is now all red-circled. Many more pictures have been added, though. Rescuing slaves has become Father Marcos's primary vocation these years. The slave-runners hunted women; he hunted them. Most of them called people like him *libertadores* (liberators), but some of the more sophisticated cartel-men knew he was much more than that. He didn't just rescue (liberate) slaves; he killed everyone involved. It wasn't like old slavery, in which each slave was viewed as a precious commodity. In modern-day slavery, the slaves were considered cheap, disposable property. If they cause trouble, shoot them dead, and dump them in a mass grave. Rescuing slaves was not enough, because the slave-runners would simply kidnap another woman or "convert" another drug addict. Father Marcos was not just a liberator; he destroyed entire intra-state and transcontinental slaver operations and everyone involved: cartel-men, police, politicians, bankers, judges, civilians, everyone.

Rodrigo has told him many times not to have so many details literally taped to the walls, in case they ever had to leave the building in a hurry and not come back. Father Marcos would respond, "I'll simply blow up the entire building if I need to."

"There's a female drug zombie downstairs needing help. She's not the living dead yet. We're scanning her and her things again now."

"That's five hundred, then, Rodrigo."

"What?"

"She'll make the five hundredth person."

"You've been counting."

"Every last one."

"You're not going to tell me that God told you to save five hundred people. If you do, I'll say that's goofy."

Father Marcos laughs. "Well, I don't want you to think that about me." He stands and opens the top drawer of his desk. He takes a dark blue folder and hands it to Rodrigo. "It's time. Hire a team of movers and I'll call Bishop Garza. It's time to go home."

"Home?" Rodrigo's eyes light up.

"Yes, my church. After two years, it's time to go back home."

Gomez Palacio, Mexico
9:30 a.m., 9 December 2092 (Next Day)

The Church of Gomez Palacio. Bishop Garza administers the Sacrament of Holy Orders, the ceremony of ordination to set a person apart as clergy to perform the religious rites, ceremonies. and duties of the Church. Several of Father Marcos's men are ordained as deacons.

Not customary, but Father Marcos conducts a ceremony to accept their vows: Fernanda becomes Sister Fernanda. Angelita becomes Sister Angelita. Twelve other young women are accepted as nuns. It is all a private but very moving affair at the church.

Bishop Garza walks to him after the ceremony. "I never thought I would see you again, Father Marcos. I am heartened to see that you've been busy with God's work and will have a full staff for your parish. When should I tell Sister Maria to expect you?"

"We'll be there next week."

"That's very good. The people of Lerdo have been without a good pastor for such a long time. Bless you, Father Marcos, for embracing this post. Have Sister Maria set up a time for us to meet at my offices. I will put together a full program that I want you to follow and I will guide you on a daily basis."

"Bishop, I sought you out to ordain my clergy, but know this: I have my own program that I will follow and I will not seek or require your guidance on any matters pertaining to my parish or my city. Two things will happen in the days to follow: you will either grow to admire me and follow my plan, or you will grow to hate me and conspire with your cartel benefactors to try to kill me. Either way, you know where to find me at any time. Please don't forget to call Sister Maria. Good day, Bishop."

Bishop Garza stands incredulous. Father Marcos leads his people out of the Bishop's church.

Ciudad Lerdo (Lerdo City), Mexico
6:46 a.m., 16 December 2092

Inside the church, Sister Maria briskly walks, looking around. She has tried to tidy it up as best she can with her two volunteers. The elderly men are giving the entire parish a final good sweeping.

Bishop Garza called her last night but all he said was, "Father Marcos will be returning in the morning." He didn't even say "hi," "bye," or "good night."

She wonders what Father Marcos has been doing these past couple of years and if he's changed at all. Too bad he wasn't here to do Christmas mass. She remembers he was a very nice young man, but "nice" people don't do very well in leadership of any kind in Mexico. They become "not so nice," leave, or end up dead.

A third elderly man enters the church. "Sister Maria, I think they are here."

Sister Maria answers, "Okay, put away the brooms and make sure nothing is lying around."

There is no denying it, the church is rundown, but that's no reason one can't have pride in the building and maintain it.

Sister Maria runs outside to the main entrance and looks off into the distance. A long line of cars approaches the building, followed by five trucks. The cars are a variety of colors and sizes. The trucks are all identical moving trucks from the same company: Move With Us.

Sister Maria watches as the three elderly male volunteers appear from the building and stand with her. The procession stops at the front church entrance. Father Marcos exits from the passenger seat of the first car.

Sister Maria smiles. "Father Marcos, welcome back." She runs to him and shakes his hand. "We thought we'd never see you again. When Bishop Garza called me last night to say you were returning this morning, I was so excited I couldn't even sleep."

Father Marcos says, "Thanks so much, Sister Maria. I'm glad to be back home. I wanted to be here for Los Posadas." It is the Mexican pre-Christmas celebration commemorating the New Testament story of Mary and Joseph's search for shelter in Bethlehem. It involves candlelight processions and stops at community nativity scenes.

"I can give you a quick walk-around if you'd like, Father."

"A little later. We're anxious to get everything moved in. Let me introduce some of my staff. This is Sister Fernanda. Sister Angelita. Sister Paula. Sister Hermina. This is Deacon Juan Carlos. Deacon Jorge. Deacon Alvarez. Deacon Ruiz. And this is Rodrigo."

Sister Maria is impressed. "An entire staff already."

"Sister, let's talk privately while my staff gets everything moved in and settled."

"When do plan to have your first Sunday services, Father?"

"This Sunday."

"Just four days. That's fast, Father. We can talk in your church office. Let me show you where it is."

Father Marcos nods to his staff to get the work started. Sister Maria leads him inside the parish to an empty office on the side.

Sister Maria says, "Of course, Father, there are so many offices in the parish that you can pick any one you prefer."

"Sister Maria, now that I'm back and I have my entire staff, I was going to have you transferred to another parish. I will write a good recommendation and I'm sure we can move you to Durango, or even Mexico City if you'd like."

Sister Maria is quiet and looks like she is about to cry. "Please Father, don't send me away. I was born in this church. Baptized here. This is my home. Can you tell me why you want to send me away?"

Father Marcos sighs. "I need to have a team that I trust completely and—"

Sister Maria interrupts. "I swear, Father. I won't be a spy for anyone against you."

"Gomez Palacio?"

Sister Maria shakes her head. "Never. Bishop Garza only talks to me if he's told to."

Father Marcos continues. "Durango?"

Sister Maria: "I have no allegiance to Bishop Dominguez. He hates country people."

"Mexico City?"

"They're even worse. We'll never hear or see them."

"Rome?"

"Never."

"Sister Maria, I know you have connections in the Vatican. I just don't know who or what relation."

Sister Maria pauses. "Yes, it is true, but that can be an asset to this church and its people. Why do you think Lerdo has avoided getting even one narco-priest in all these years and problem priests get removed quickly?"

"I always wondered about that. So, Sister Maria, you are our 'secret weapon.'"

"Yes." Sister Maria smiles.

"Never inform on me to Rome."

"Father, that is the wrong approach. Dealing with Rome these days is all politics. Never stop the flow of information, but control the information that they receive. I will never tell them anything that I don't clear with you first."

Father changes his mind. Sister Maria isn't an aimless functionary. She is clearly politically savvy and has more knowledge of the factions in the Vatican than he does.

"Sister Maria, you'll be in charge of protocol and religious liaison."

Sister Maria smiles from ear to ear. "I'm speechless, Father. Thank you, Father!"

"Let's get this place ready for Sunday services."

Church of Lerdo City
7:00 a.m., 25 December 2092

"This is the body of Christ, this is the blood of Christ." Father Marcos conducts the Holy Communion. "Foreshadowing his crucifixion and the beginning of the New Covenant."

Little Juanita is the first in line to receive communion, eating the bread wafer and drinking the tiny cup of wine. A line of parishioners follows. In less than a week, the dusty, dilapidated church has been transformed into a beautiful space.

Sister Fernanda stands on one side and Deacon Juan Carlos on the other. The church hall is packed to more than capacity, with every pew taken and people standing in the back.

Mass has ended and now the community attendees walk up to Father Marcos to shake his hand and have a few words.

"Thank you so much for the kind words, Señora Garcia," Father Marcos says. "I'm glad to be back home too."

Meeting the people is an art form. You must give your undivided attention to each person, but be mindful of the fact that you can spend only a few moments with them before having to move on to the next one. Father Marcos commits to memory the faces of each person he meets, knowing their names will come with time, and truly listens to each of them. Sister Fernanda plays her role: keep the Father moving, no more than a few minutes with any one person. If they need more time, they can set up an appointment with Sister Maria.

Father Marcos knows this is the "honeymoon period" when everyone likes you. Everyone wants to shake your hand and invite you to dinner. Later will come the requests for favors and the commands to do something that is essential, in their eyes, to the parish or the community.

A greasy, lanky weasel of a man with a crooked chin appears before him at the end. It looks like someone stepped on his head and jumped up and down several times. "Father Marcos, a good service," he says.

Father knows there is something familiar about the man. "Thank you, sir."

"Father, now that you are here, it is important that things are set up properly right from the start. Pastors in the past have always gotten off badly, but I can see that you are sophisticated man who understands the way of things in the world."

Father Marcos remembers him. "What can I do for you, Mr. Cabezza?"

The greasy man's eyes narrow. "You know who I am?"

"I made it a point to familiarize myself with the entire criminal element of the city before I accepted the leadership position of this church. So as to know who not to waste my time with."

The greasy man watches him, not knowing if he's supposed to be insulted. "Father, to do business in this city, and the church is a business, you cut ten percent to us as the cost of doing business. That's our discounted religious rate." He smiles.

Sister Fernanda is angry, almost shaking. Deacon Juan Carlos motions to others to approach. Father Marcos puts his hand on Sister Fernanda's shoulder to calm her down, looks at Deacon Juan Carlos, and shakes his head: do nothing.

Father Marcos says to the man, "Wait here."

He walks to the back rooms. The greasy man watches him and glances to the back for a second. A tall, extremely muscular, menacing man walks up the aisle and takes his place right behind Mr. Cabezza, who seems to grow an inch or two, with his henchman backing him up now. *Lo siento chicos.* "Sorry boys and girls." He lifts his jacket to show his gun. "Your Bibles aren't bulletproof."

He now looks directly at Sister Fernanda. "I don't remember nuns looking so good when I went to church as a child. Maybe if they were, I wouldn't have turned out to be the evil bastard I am today." He puckers his lips and then laughs.

Father Marcos returns. Sister Maria appears, noticing what's in the Father's hands. He hands the greasy man a big bag of chips. Mr. Cabezza opens it up and sees the chips inside. "Ten percent," Father Marcos says.

"Very good," Mr. Cabezza says. "I'll return once a week to collect our…tithes and offerings." He smiles and then laughs.

Father Marcos says, "No you won't." He turns and walks away.

Mr. Cabezza stops, an expression of anger on his face. "What do you mean by that, Father?" His henchman glares at him too.

Father Marcos is already on the other side of the church, ignoring him, meeting more people who are waiting to greet him.

Mr. Cabezza wants to go after him, but now Sister Fernanda and Sister Maria stand in front of him. Deacon Juan Carlos returns with ten other men. Cabezza laughs. "We better run away. Before the dangerous church people beat us up." He laughs again as he walks out of the church with the bag and his henchman.

Deacon Juan Carlos isn't taking any chances and sends his ten men after him to make sure he really is leaving.

Sister Fernanda is furious. "Not even back one week and they're here."

Sister Maria turns to her. "This is not a problem at all. Pay them the money and they'll leave us alone."

Sister Fernanda says, "So these pig vultures can bleed us dry? Ten percent today. One hundred percent tomorrow!"

"No, they won't do that. Pay them the money and we can focus on doing God's work in the community. Defiance against these people won't work. This is how things are done. We must not be confrontational."

A smirk appears on Sister Fernanda's face. "Sister Maria, do you know anything about what Father Marcos has been doing these past two years?"

"No, why?"

Sister Fernanda shakes her head. "You really have no clue as to what's coming."

Grito de Durango
(The Cry of Durango)

"Sometimes the most dangerous people in a revolution are not the evil ones that they are destroying, but the good people doing the destroying. Sometimes they don't know when to stop." — Anonymous

Lerdo City, Mexico
11:57 a.m., 9 January 2093 (Two Days Later)

"Santa Muerte," he says proudly. On the wall, prominently displayed, is a skeleton nailed to a cross. Boss Gordo sits at the head of the table, sipping his alcoholic drink in a bluish glass. He is sharply dressed in a long-sleeved white shirt and suspenders to hold up his white pants. "Catholic leaders always fascinate me. They want something that is impossible—the end of evil. Goodness is not the natural state of humanness; that's a myth. Evil is the natural state for humans."

Father Marcos sits quietly at the table next to him. The cartels love their pseudo-Christianity with their fake saints like *Santa Muerte*, Saint Death.

Behind Gordo stand two of his henchmen. Off to the side is the greasy man, Mr. Cabezza, with his henchman.

"And cowardice," Gordo adds, staring right into the eyes of

Cabezza. The greasy man and his henchman are sweating with nervousness. "Thank you, Father, for directly bringing your problem to my attention. I am a fair man. The fact that I am a crime boss is irrelevant. I'm a good Catholic, like you. And to learn that a person in my employ so disrespectfully barged into your church and extorted money from you in front of your congregation like it was a dirty back alley angers me."

Again, Gordo stares directly at Cabezza and his man.

Father Marcos says, "Mr. Gordo, there is no issue with paying money to you. I'm not a tourist. I was born in Lerdo myself, and everyone in the Catholic hierarchy knows paying your fair share is how it has always been done. But when this lowly man comes into my church and takes all our church offerings on no less than our first real Sunday service in a decade, a line has been crossed."

Cabezza is seething with anger. *The priest is lying! He's setting me up!* Cabezza starts to speak, but Gordo darts a cold look at him to shut up. Cabezza knows that Gordo has already made the decision to kill him.

Gordo says, "I agree completely."

Father Marcos continues. "Ten percent is fair, but one hundred percent is—"

Gordo holds up his hand. "Say no more, Father."

Father Marcos nods respectfully.

Gordo says, "Father, tell me something. My men say your church absolutely has the most beautiful nuns they've ever seen. Either they are movie stars or prostitutes. One of my men said that one of your nuns looked familiar to him. He swears he banged her multiple times, maybe a year ago."

Father Marcos asks, "Mr. Gordo, what about this issue of the tribute payments?"

Gordo outstretches his hand to his henchman standing behind him on the right. The henchman removes his gun from underneath his jacket and puts it in Gordo's hand. *Gordo immediately shoots both Cabezza and his henchman in the head.* Gordo hands the gun back to his henchman and ignores the lifeless bodies now on the floor.

"Father, that is, as they say in English, 'a dead issue.' Let's return to the discussion of this nun working for you."

"Oh course," Father Marcos says.

Gordo pauses for a moment. He looks pointedly at Father Marcos. *I just killed two men point-blank in front of this priest and he didn't even flinch. Even my own men jumped a bit, and they've killed lots of people.*

"This nun," Gordo continues, "looks like someone who worked for one of my men running girls in Gomez Palacio. Do you know my man there? He went by the name Gordito, no relation. Always wore these effeminate, flaming silk shirts."

"No, I don't."

"This man of mine was killed in his mansion some months back, last year. Someone killed him and dumped him in his own backyard pool. They also killed every last man in the place, all his lieutenants in his gang, all part of his Gomez Palacio crew, my organization. Dumped all their bodies in the pool, almost one hundred people, and burned down the house. They also took the girls, seventeen of them in all. That nun of yours is one of those girls."

"Mr. Gordo, you must know that we accept everyone in our House of the Lord. I know nothing about the past of anyone working for me. The slate is clean with Jesus and with me."

"That's kind of an irresponsible policy, don't you think? I thought that 'don't ask, don't know' policy was banned from Rome, with all the problems Catholics in the United States got themselves into. All kinds of trouble with that policy."

"Very true, Mr. Gordo. But in a small town like Lerdo, we're more charitable."

Gordo says with a cold expression, "What do you know about who killed my people and stole my 'property,' Father?"

Father Marcos looks back at him.

Gomez Palacio, Mexico
7:02 a.m., 1 October 2092 (Five Months Ago)

The mansion of Gordito is surrounded by police. The building smolders as human firemen try to put out the remaining fires, but there is nothing left.

The greasy man and his henchman arrive and walk through the police as if they are officials rather than killers from a criminal gang, but everyone here is on the cartel payroll.

Mr. Cabezza walks across the massive backyard to the Olympic-sized pool right under the balcony of the master bedroom. He had been in the pool many times before, himself; the water was always crystal clear. Now it is a sickening black color; there are so many bleeding dead bodies floating in the pool that it can no longer be called a pool. It is a mass grave of water rather than dirt.

A policeman walks to him. "There are dozens of dead bodies in there."

There is one body that was not dumped into the pool. Mr. Cabezza stares down at the body of Gordito lying on the ground. He lies there with his eyes and mouth wide open, covered in blood.

Cabezza looks at him briefly. The entire gang has been wiped out. *I hope the boss doesn't kill me when I tell him*, Cabezza thinks to himself.

Lerdo City, Mexico
12:15 p.m., 9 January 2093

Gordo continues to stare at Father Marcos, who is completely calm. This Church Man must have balls of steel.

"Father, you know why we have the Border Wall between Mexico and America. Most don't know this, but it wasn't the Mexican government that had it constructed to keep undesirables out or to keep people in because their government population analysts said that if we didn't, we'd soon have more people living outside Mexico than in it. No, it was us. The cartel families made them do it. Why? Because America is crazy. Nothing is taboo there. Sex-slavery works only if it's against the law. There, you got adults, boys, girls volunteering for it. Vice is legal there, but illegal here. That's why we have the best products, the best services; that's why we run the market. If you have to pay for something, it has value. Free means no value. We go to whatever lengths are necessary to protect our business interests."

Everyone looks up at someone coming down the stairs. Father Marcos recognizes her immediately as Mona Lisa, the woman he saved but who so angrily walked out that night. He wonders if she's the reason Gordo suspects him. His calm is unchanged as he looks back to Gordo.

Mona Lisa makes no eye contact with anyone, but casually walks past the gunmen, Gordo, and Father Marcos, and steps over the two dead bodies on the ground, passing through to another part of the mansion. She walks through an open door and disappears.

Father Marcos rises from the table. "Mr. Gordo, rather than rely on the faulty memories of your men, just attend a service. I'm not going anywhere, and neither is my church staff."

A gunman speaks. "He said your nun was one of his girls."

Father Marcos says without looking at him, "Yes, all Mexicans look alike." To Gordo: "Hopefully, we'll see you this Sunday, Mr. Gordo. I have to get back to the church. I hope this matter will be a 'dead issue' soon, too."

Gordo says, "Yes, Father, I am a man of honor. I run my business fairly with everyone."

Hombres de honor: this phrase was often used by these cartel killers. It was as if they said it often enough, between the drugs, slave-running, killing, kidnapping, violence, and extortion, they would magically become "men of honor."

"See you Sunday, sir," Father Marcos says.

Gordo expects him to shake his hand and do all the pleasantries that are done by civilized people, especially church people, but Father Marcos walks to the main door and opens it. The door closes behind him and the gunmen just look at each other and then at Gordo.

Gordo stares at the closed door in anger. "Get the police chief on the phone."

4:17 p.m.

Father Marcos stands at his desk in his church office. Surrounding him are Sister Maria, Sister Fernanda, Sister Angelita, Rodrigo, Deacon Juan Carlos, and two other deacons.

"I've never seen you do something insane, even when I thought you were being insane. This was insane," Sister Fernanda scolds.

"Father, he could have killed you, made you disappear. You should never have done that," Sister Maria says. "He is an extremely dangerous man and is extremely paranoid, especially now that so many of his men have disappeared or ended up dead."

"I know you all think I did a foolish thing, but I knew what I was doing. If I didn't go there, he would have come here. If I brought bodyguards with me, he would have killed them just for the sake of it. Going alone was the only way."

There is a knock at the door and one of Rodrigo's "men" peeks in. Rodrigo immediately walks outside to the boy and closes the door.

Sister Maria asks, "What do you think will happen?"

Father Marcos looks at her. "He's going to try to kill us."

Sister Maria asks, "Why? There is no reason."

Father Marcos says, "Apparently, some of his thugs have recognized some of the people working here. He's smart. At the very least, he knows I was involved."

Sister Angelita shakes her head. "You mean his people recognized us."

Father Marcos says, "Don't worry about this. A direct confrontation was always inevitable."

Sister Fernanda says, "But Father, this man—"

Rodrigo enters the room. "Father, I need to see you outside for a moment."

Father Marcos follows him to the hallway. Mona Lisa sits in one of the pews in the middle. Father Marcos walks to the same pew and sits next to her.

Mona Lisa says, "I bet you swallowed your own heart when you saw me walk down the stairs."

Father Marcos smiles. "No, I knew you were with him."

Mona Lisa continues. "I had to make sure you were real and the only way I could really investigate you was if I went back to him. When you live in hell, every demon you meet acts like an angel."

"I understand."

"He's going to move against you on Sunday; either his men will do it or he'll have the police make you disappear. I don't know why he's doing this. He doesn't know it was you who wiped out his men."

"It's not important."

"I have names of other girls. Would you help get them out, too?" She pauses. "I don't mean to be rude, but can you do it before Sunday?"

He smiles. "Of course. We can rescue them before then."

"Thank you, Father. I hope you realize that I was testing you that night, with all the things I was saying. It was not personal."

"Yes, I know."

Mona Lisa hands him a folded piece of paper. "Why are you doing this? You see where it leads."

"The Old Testament of the Bible is God rescuing his people from slavery. God hates slavery. God hates evil. First it was the Jews, and then Christians fighting the world war against slavery. Slavers have overrun Mexico like a disease. The church has to be relevant, not just on Sundays, but from Monday to Saturday, too. We'll rescue your friends and make sure they're safe."

"If you survive Gordo," Mona Lisa says. "I'll come back."

"I'm very happy to hear that."

"Good. Thank you again, Father."

They shake hands.

Lerdo City, Mexico
5:45 a.m., 11 January 2093

There is a uniqueness to life within rural areas versus cities. In the city, the early Sunday service would be 11 a.m. In rural towns like Lerdo, by 11 a.m. most churches are already on the third service of the day.

The church bustles with activity, getting ready for the first 7 a.m. Sunday service. The Gray Men, those three elderly male volunteers, the youngest of them not less than seventy years old, are busy sweeping the grounds of the church. Sister Angelita runs the Sunday school for ages three to seven, with another nun handling ages eight to twelve. Sister Fernanda organizes the service team of ushers to direct people to the pews, the media team to makes sure the speaker system is working perfectly, and the tithes and offerings team. She also runs the church's women's counseling sessions three times a week. Deacon Juan Carlos does a final review of songs with the choir team. Sister Maria is in the main office, organizing Father's ever-increasing appointments for the month; she knows that with each service more people ask to meet with him privately. Rodrigo walks through the church, making sure his men station themselves at the proper exits and key public areas of the church. And Father Marcos is in his church office, casually skimming his prepared sermon with his Bach playing in the background.

Rodrigo stops and turns. One of his men runs into the church and yells, "Policia!"

Over a dozen policemen march in line into the church. Rodrigo moves in front of them and the group stops. The last policeman is Police Chief Garcia, a dark-skinned man with a big mustache and wearing dark glasses. Sister Maria appears from her office and walks to them; other church staff follow.

Sister Maria says, "Chief Garcia, may we help you?"

Garcia responds, "We got a tip that guns were being stockpiled in the church. I have a warrant to search."

Sister Maria yells, "This is outrageous! We are getting ready for Sunday services."

Garcia arrogantly says, "Which is why I gave you the courtesy of coming beforehand. The sooner you cooperate, the sooner we will leave."

Garcia directs his men, and they fan out through the church. Father Marcos now appears and walks to them.

Garcia walks to him. "Ah, Father, I was telling Sister Maria that I have a warrant to search this church for guns."

Father Marcos says nothing. Deacon Juan Carlos yells at the policemen. "You are destroying church property!"

Garcia adds, "If anything is broken, Father, you can file a claim with my office. Processing takes six months to a year, though." He smiles.

Father Marcos stands quietly. The church staff is furious. Chief Garcia is surprised by the Father's lack of emotion. "How is Mr. Gordo, Chief Garcia?" he asks.

Garcia answers with suspicion. "I wouldn't know, Father Marcos."

Father Marcos smiles.

Thirty minutes later, the police finish searching the church for weapons and find none. On their way out they even frisk the church staff and, though everyone protests angrily, the Father.

Garcia says, "Thanks for your cooperation, Father. Have a good service." He smirks as he walks out with his policemen.

Father Marcos and Rodrigo look at each other. This was a "dry run." A cartel gang sends their bought-and-paid-for police into a place, either to ensure no one has guns, or to seize all guns. The police leave. Then the cartel's hit men arrive and assault, kidnap, or kill their target or targets.

Sister Maria is still angry. "This is outrageous. Father, we should protest directly to central police authorities in Durango."

Father Marcos looks at Rodrigo and nods. Rodrigo nods and walks quickly out of the church. People start entering the church for service.

"Father, what were all those police here for?" a woman asks, entering with her husband.

"Narco-police, Señora Sanchez, narco-police. They mistook our fine church for their personal playground."

The elderly couple laughs. "Yes, Father, narco-police for sure."

Sunday service begins with Father Marcos at the podium. "The Cry of Independence was shouted from a tiny church, like our very own, in 1810, 282 years ago, in the small town of Dolores, not unlike our own town of Lerdo. This declaration sparked a revolution…the War of Independence in Mexico. It was not started by the rich elite or a powerful army, but by a simple Catholic priest, Miguel Hidalgo y Costilla.

"It was a revolt against the imperialism of the European Spanish colonial government that occupied our land, and Father Hidalgo's army were simple folk, like ourselves. On September 16th, 1810, he ordered the church bells to be rung and gathered his congregation in his church. The war for our independence took a decade, but when it was over, Mexico was free.

"That Cry of Independence marked the beginning of the Mexican War of Independence and is our most important holiday. The September 15th ringing of the bells at eleven p.m. at the National Palace in Mexico City, the President repeating that cry of patriotism with all the names of important heroes of the War, and ending with the three-fold shout of 'Viva Mexico!' from the balcony of the Palace to crowds of hundreds of thousands in the Plaza de la Constitution, Mexicans and others from all over the country and around the world. The bells ring again and the President waves the Flag of Mexico as the masses sing the *Himno Nacional Mexicano*, our national anthem. On September 16th, Independence Day, our national military parade starts in Zócalo, passes Hidalgo Memorial, and ends on the Paseo de la Reforma, Mexico City's main boulevard.

"But I ask, are we really free anymore in our homes, in the countryside, in the cities, in any corner of our beloved country? The imperialist Spanish may have been defeated a long time ago, but have they not been replaced by an even more evil, more imperialist power—the cartels?

"As children of God, we must always be aware of everything, wherever it may be. We must always be vigilant of attacks on the Church and its people. When the Republic of Mexico was created in 1917, it put in place anti-Christian laws—churches couldn't own property, couldn't operate schools, couldn't get involved in politics; religious leaders could not vote, could not criticize the government, even in private. The same kind of laws that exist today in the United States. These laws were lifted in Mexico a hundred years ago, but what was the impact on the churches in Mexico? It weakened them, it destroyed them. It led to the rise of the cartels! That has been our fate ever since.

"The Bible reveals many things to us. It shows a God in love with his Children and deeply concerned with our eternal salvation so we can be with him in the next life, in heaven, but equally concerned with our lives here on Earth. Half the Bible is about how He rescues his Children from slavery—leading the Israelites, through Moses, from slavery out of Egypt to the chosen lands of Canaan. But are we not again under the yoke of the evils of slavery in our homeland of Mexico?

"The exact words of Father Hidalgo during his battle-cry sermon, the most famous of all our Mexican speeches, the Cry of Dolores, are not known exactly, but he said something like this:

"My children, a new dispensation comes to us today. Will you receive it? Will you free yourselves? Will you recover our stolen lands? Will you defend your religion and your rights as true patriots? The time for action for all of us has now come. Will you be slaves of the cartels or will you as patriots defend your families and your children, your towns and your homes, your religion, your rights? We must act at once. We must defend to the utmost! Long live religion! Long live the Americas! Long live our Lady of Guadalupe! And let us not deny what we all know must be: death to the imperialism of evil government! Death to the imperialism of the cartels!"

The church crowd erupts in wild applause. One person stands and then another and then another; the entire congregation is on its feet, cheering.

7:49 a.m.

"I will kill you all!" Chief Garcia yells.

In an open field, Garcia is chained with his hands behind his back to a long metal pole in the ground. All around him are dozens of uniformed men chained in the exact same way—Garcia's entire police force. Next to them is Boss Gordo, also chained to a pole. Next to him are dozens of his thugs; all his men. Rodrigo stands off to the side with an army of men who look to be peasants; they are not from Durango.

In 1531, a simple peasant by the name of Juan Diego saw a vision of a young woman while walking on a hill near Mexico City. She told him to build a church on the exact spot he stood. The church would be built and the Virgin of Guadalupe is still Mexico's most revered religious and cultural icon, often called the "Queen of Mexico" and "Patroness of the Americas." The Lady of Guadalupe was invoked for both the Mexican War of Independence by Father Hidalgo and the Mexican Revolution under General Emiliano Zapata. Juan Diego would himself become a Catholic saint, Saint Juan Diego Cuauhtlatoatzin. The Virgin of Guadalupe would forever be declared Mexico's "protector and advocate of the indigenous peoples"—a powerful religious symbol to be invoked by Father Miguel Hidalgo those many years ago at his Cry of Dolores sermon, and equally powerful to be used in Father Marcos's revolutionary sermon.

Garcia, Gordo, and their men quiet down as they notice a crowd approaching. Father Marcos leads hundreds of people from the church to them. The church crowd is quiet as they take their places around the field in front of the cartel and policemen. Father Marcos walks up to Garcia.

Garcia yells, "I will kill you! Then I will cut off your head and throw it in the toilet!"

Father Marcos calmly responds, "No you won't." Garcia curses at him. Father Marcos steps in front of Gordo.

Gordo glares at him and then yells to the church crowd behind them at the top of his lungs. "I will kill this entire town and everyone in it! All your men will be dead! All your girls will be in my brothels! I will burn down your houses! I will shoot all your animals! The street will flow red with your blood."

Father Marcos says, "No, you won't." He walks away from them. The church crowd grows in size; it seems people are coming from every corner of Lerdo to join. No one is saying a word. A crowd that started out at less than five hundred is now over two thousand and continues to grow.

A small car drives to Father Marcos and stops. Sisters Fernanda and Angelita and Deacon Juan Carlos get out. Father Marcos directs, "Give everyone one."

The church staff opens the trunk. Three more cars drive up and stop behind them. More church staff exit and open the trunks.

Garcia is incredulous as he watches the church staff hand out guns to each person in the crowd: handguns, rifles, even machine guns!

He yells, "This is insane. What's going on here? You can't do this. I'm the police! I got a badge! I got a badge! You can't touch me!"

It takes almost ten minutes for everyone to be armed. The church staff walks back to the cars and waits. Father Marcos stands to the side and makes a quick call on his phone-only. He puts it back into his chest pocket and waits.

The church bells ring! The sound reverberates through all of Lerdo. It rings again and then a final, third time.

Garcia, his policemen, and Gordo's men start yelling direct threats and curses at the crowd again. Gordo looks off to the side where Father Marcos stands. Of all the ways he thought he'd die, he never imagined this.

Gordo calls, "Father Marcos." He says it in an almost sad way. Father Marcos walks to him. "I hope you know that it never was personal."

Father Marcos says, "I know."

Gordo swallows hard. "I want my family to be protected. They have the money they need. I've always had a contingency plan just in case. I want all of them protected."

"No one is going to harm them."

"Get to them before the other cartel families do. That's what happens, you know. Cartel boss dies, and the other families come in and murder every possible member of their family."

"No one is going to harm them."

"You take everything in my main house. Use it to help the city."

"Yes."

"I suppose it's too late for confession and maybe getting God to forgive me."

"If God didn't send you straight to hell, you wouldn't respect him, would you?"

"Yes, that's true. I'd spit in his face if he did." Gordo is crying now. "You can't kill all of us."

"That's something you don't have to worry about."

Father Marcos walks away. He stands off to the side.

Everyone knows what is about to happen. The policemen and cartel-men become even more violent in their yelling.

Señora Mina is the oldest woman in Lerdo, actually in all of Durango, at ninety-nine years old. She has seen it all. Standing all of four feet nine inches, she has always been viewed as the elder of the town. Besides the church priest, the times when they had one, she is the only person in Lerdo whose opinions people ask for.

People are such cowards, she says to herself and hobbles to the front of the crowd with her mini-shotgun. She literally can't lift the weapon.

Her son, at seventy-five years old, holds a cane touching the ground right in front of her.

"Use this as a stand, Mama," he says. She props her hand on top of the cane handle and aims the gun. "Mama, it's too big for you. You'll be blown back like a doll."

"Then catch me! Why on earth did I have children? Hold the cane steady!"

Boom! The first shot hits Gordo in the forehead, killing him instantly. He was the man who had killed eleven of her twelve children.

In an eruption of anger, revenge, and exhilaration, shots ring out from the crowd, cutting down the policemen and cartel-men. Garcia is shot so many times that his body is blown apart. Other men are not so lucky as to die quickly and linger in agony as bullet after bullet hits them.

When shooters in the crowd run out of bullets, they move off to the side for the next group. By now the crowd is more than five thousand in number. Some people in the crowds run back to their homes to return to the site with their own weapons and ammo. All the while, Father Marcos stands quietly to the side.

In his Cry of Dolores sermon, Father Hidalgo didn't say "death to cartels," as there were no crime cartels back then, it was: "death to the Spaniards." It may have rallied the people of Mexico to war, but it was also extremely controversial, and horrified the rich elite of the day.

Father Hidalgo is still known as the Father of Mexico. His cause was noble, a free Mexico; but his army of peasants had other motives. The truth is, the War became a race war. Hidalgo's mixed race and

Indian "army" against the white, oppressive Spaniards.

Father Marcos studied its first battle, the Battle of Guanajuato. It was the first major engagement of the insurgency, four days into the war. But it was no battle at all. It was a massacre by a mob army of eight hundred. People were hacked to death and burned alive in their homes simply because they were rich and light-skinned. There were other atrocities at San Miguel and Celaya. The most dangerous animal in the world is a mob. Father Hidalgo couldn't control his mob army and it lead to his eventual execution.

Either we have a people's war that follows the path of the American Revolution, defeating an imperialist enemy and becoming a civil society, or we will follow the path of pre-Islamic France, defeating an imperialist enemy and degenerating into the horror of the guillotine and killing orgy of indiscriminate citizens. *No Battle of Guanajuato on my watch*, Father Marcos says to himself.

He holds up his hands and walks to the bloody mess that used to be the policemen and cartel-men of Lerdo. Someone notices his movements and yells out to the crowd. The mass shooting stops.

Father Marcos doesn't just stand in front of the dead bodies; he steps into the middle of the carnage sloshing over his shoes. He raises his hands again. "It is done! We have taken back our city! And we must never let go of it again! We rebuild a new civil Mexican society right here, right now!"

He walks to Señora Mina, who is still standing at the front of the crowd, and touches her shoulder. "Thank you, Señora."

She asks, "Why do you remain a Catholic, Father? Rome is corrupt and would never have allowed what needed to be done here. They don't care about us."

Father answers, "I am Catholic because our faith is you and me, it's people. It is Jesus and God, not Rome. We have had corruption in Mexico long before our grandparents were born. Do you want to renounce your citizenship to Mexico? No, because Mexico is us too, not the criminals and the corrupt politicians. Let us not hold Rome to a different standard."

She nods and smiles. "What we've done, today…you know that we've been here before. That freedom didn't last long."

"Then let's make sure it lasts for good this time."

Señora Mina refers to the Day of the Demon. The day rural people hide in their homes on its anniversary and never come out. The day city people laugh and say that it never happened. It was the same day Marcos was born.

Father Marcos says softly, "Go home and relax those feet of yours, Señora Mina."

"Yes, Father." She starts to hand him the mini-shotgun.

"No. Everyone will be keeping theirs."

"Private gun ownership is illegal in Mexico, Father."

"They won't protect us, so we'll do it ourselves from now on."

Señora Mina slowly walks off with her son. Father Marcos moves through the crowd to tell the people the same and to go home.

One of the men in the crowd walks up to him. "Father, can you justify what we did with the Bible? No biblical word games or verbal sleight of hand."

Father Marcos doesn't hesitate. "Unless you can point to a passage where God commands us to be exterminated by cartels and follow cartel-controlled, criminal governments, yes I can."

The man nods. "Okay. I'll join your church then."

Rodrigo and his men have been watching all this time, sitting on the dirt. He hops to his feet and walks to the Father. "I'll have this all cleaned up, boss."

Father Marcos says, "No. I want to make a monument of it."

Rodrigo is perplexed. "Monument?"

Father Marcos says, "Yes, we want everyone to know what we're willing to do to be free from the cartels and criminals. People have very, very short memories. We need a permanent reminder."

Rodrigo counters, "Mexico City will send CSI here to take it all away and then they'll send Federales to kill or arrest you."

Father Marcos smiles. "No, they won't."

Lerdo City, Mexico
10:13 a.m., 19 January 2093 (A Week Later)

The people had had enough of cartels snatching their daughters off the streets; cartels killing their sons, husbands, and fathers; cartels filling mass graves with innocent people; the police and Mexico City doing nothing. Father Marcos was in the right place at the right time.

The killings would be viewed as shocking and barbaric to the tek-city-dwellers, but in the country, similar "events" were not unheard of. After all, no one cares about country people, most of all the government.

Gregorio had finished his masterpiece, his Cry of Lerdo monument. He is known for his rather unique "art of the dead" by turning graves, dead bodies, and scenes of murders into artistic events, "explosions of emotions" as it was called. He would say that he did not glorify or sensationalize death, but in a world where the public had become so numb to commonplace murder in Mexico, he wanted to shock people out of their complacent stupor.

He encased every bullet-ridden, bullet-ripped body, every piece of flesh, every blood spatter, and blood droplet in a luminescent silvery gray resin. He called it *carboniting*. The monument is quite disturbing; every one of the killed men is frozen in time for all eternity.

Rodrigo found him the nearby state of Chihuahua. He is in very high demand during the fall season in preparation for Mexico's Day of the Dead holiday, when family and friends gather to pray and remember loved ones who have died and to celebrate the first and second of November in connection with the Catholic holidays of All Saints Day and All Souls' Day.

Artistically, he had exaggerated the death expressions of their faces, those with faces left. He made the blood everywhere seem to take on a life of its own: shooting out of body parts, splattering, bouncing, spraying, and flowing. A massive neon red circle surrounds the monument with a sign that reads: *"The Cry of Lerdo, The Cry of Durango, 2092. No One Messes With the People of the Scorpions!"*

Many commentators call the sign childish, stupid, and outrageous, but to the people of Lerdo it is a mark of pride.

Father Marcos stares at the monument with Rodrigo. "Amazing, boss, isn't it? I told you he was good."

"Yes, you did." Father Marcos turns to the boy artist and says, "Gregorio, if any church in Mexico needs to create its own modern-day Sistine Chapel, you will be the first one to call."

Gregorio smiles. "Thank you, Father."

Father Marcos notices their looks. "Neither of you know what I'm talking about, do you?"

Rodrigo hesitates. "Actually no, boss."

Father Marcos laughs. "Youth today. You know every movie and music reference in the universe, but don't know one of the greatest architectural achievements in history. It's in the Apostolic Palace, the official residence of the Pope in Vatican City. It's the most magnificent and well-known ceiling painting in the world, done by Renaissance artist Michelangelo and completed in 1512."

Gregorio perks up. "Oh, I heard of him."

Father Marcos says, "What are you waiting for? Both of you look it up now."

The boys take out their e-pads and do a quick Net search. They immediately see the images of the building and the paintings. Father Marcos stares at the monument again.

He will make it an annual ritual for the city, like the Day of the Dead. Instead of visiting graves and cemeteries of loved ones, building private altars to them, buying toys for dead children and alcohol for dead adults, writing *calaveras* (short poems) and hanging skulls everywhere in remembrance. They would proclaim: "No more of our loved ones for the Day of the Dead!"

"My men said a federal helicopter hovered around outside the city last night. The 'dogs of war' will be here soon, boss," Rodrigo says while reading more about the Sistine Chapel on his e-pad without looking up.

Father Marcos says, "Very good Rodrigo, a reference to a classical book. Soon you'll have your first gray hair."

"Ha ha, I was making a movie reference and I'm thirteen. I don't even shave yet, boss."

"Gregorio, see Sister Maria for your payment and stay in touch with us. If you ever need a place here in Lerdo, see Rodrigo and we'll put you up at no charge."

"Thank you, Father. I will do that."

Rodrigo shakes Gregorio's hand. He leads Gregorio back toward the church as Father Marcos follows.

Yes, the dogs of war are gathering and they will be here soon.

Lerdo Church
8:07 a.m. (Next Day)

Father Marcos thanks each of the Indios who helped him arrest the Lerdo policemen and cartel-men. They are so humble, holding their straw sombreros in their hands. When Father Marcos was the same age as Rodrigo, he went on his first mission trip with his church to the southern state of Yucatan. Many of his fellow missionaries didn't like being in the country without all their tek "creature comforts," but Marcos loved it and quickly made long lasting friendships with the locals. These days in Mexico, friendships between the country and the city are rare.

"How bad is it there now?" Father Marcos asks their leader.

"It never ends, Father. The cartels kill our people to take our land for their drugs and slave-running. The government kills our people to take our land for whatever political scheme. They won't leave us alone."

"I know what I suggest is controversial, but I don't think we have any choice. We must unify to protect ourselves. If you agree to my proposal, you will get all the land you need, a base to sell your goods without interference, and protection. Lerdo's population has been shrinking for decades. And so is Yucatan. But if we join forces, we'll instantly double our population and multiply our power."

Señor Rios nods. "We like your plan, Father. If it were anyone else we wouldn't even consider it, but we trust you completely. We've known you since you were a boy and you have always been good to us. But what will your people say about us?"

"Señor Rios, we will all be Duranguense. We will all be Indios."

"We will travel back home and make the preparations."

The men shake hands.

Northwest Durango, John Wayne Ranch
11:07 a.m., 7 April 2093

Father Marcos and Deacon Juan Carlos ride their horses. This part of Durango is heavily mountainous with the Sierra Madre Occidental. There are many John Wayne Ranches in Mexico. The American actor, who has now been dead some 113 years, really did have his own ranch in Mexico, falling in love with the land after filming so many movies here. This ranch belonged to Señor Juan Wayne, no relation.

Señor Wayne stands on the porch of his main house with twenty of his cowboys around him. Father Marcos and Juan Carlos dismount their horses. Juan Carlos hasn't ridden in a while and it shows, but Father Marcos is a pro.

"I was told, Father, that you were a city boy, but you ride as if you were born on the saddle," Señor Wayne calls out.

Father Marcos laughs. "I lived with Indios when I was a boy and they taught me to ride."

"Very good. When you learn riding from Indios, you will always learn the right way." Father Marcos and Juan Carlos walk up to him and shake hands. "What can I do for you, Father? I've been hearing a lot of interesting things about you, almost on a daily basis."

Father Marcos says, "I need your help, sir."

Señor Wayne takes them to a large round table on the corner of the porch and gestures for them to take seats. Two women appear from the front door with glasses and a large pitcher of beer. "We make our own beer here. The real thing, not that synthetic piss they make in the cities."

They drink as they talk. "Señor Wayne, I want to hire you."

Wayne is amused. "Hire me?"

"I want to hire your cowboys to protect my people, all along my town's western front—your eastern front. I also want to pay you for information, any threats from cartels or the government or anything that would impact our region. I also want to pay you for use of your land in smuggling people to and from my area."

"For?"

"Rescuing slaves."

Señor Wayne is intrigued. "You will pay me for all of this?"

"Yes."

"The cartels pay me now to use my land for their drug runs."

"I'll pay you more not to. And I'll get some of those college kids from Nueva Lerdo and Mexico City to come here, train you in marketing, and turn your little John Wayne Ranch into a major Durango tourist attraction: new hotels, new restaurants, new transportation. You'll be making much more money working with God than anything Satan's cartels could pay."

Señor Wayne pauses just a moment, then extends his hand. "Father, let's get started."

Lerdo City, Mexico
2:45 p.m., 10 April 2093

Mr. Blond sits in the chair quietly. He is a Caucasian man with piercing blue eyes, blond hair tied in a ponytail, and a thin but muscular build.

"Thank you for coming down to meet me so quickly, Mr. Blond." Father Marcos also sits.

"I never turn down a free vacation, even if it's across the border." Mr. Blond speaks fluent Spanish with a thick American accent.

"Were you able to review my proposal?"

"On the plane, I did. But I'd like to know more about you."

"Ask me anything. I'm sure you did an exhaustive background on me."

"I'm more interested in your theological philosophy."

"I'm a good Catholic boy like you."

Mr. Blond smiles but presses. "What's a favorite theme in your sermons? Every pastor and priest has a theme they like to revisit."

Father Marcos answers, "The devil. Sadly, our people are so ill-equipped to deal with him. You would think if there was an evil super-angel dedicated to our destruction that we'd know every single thing about him, to defend against him and thwart his schemes against us. The other is relevance in the world. Not becoming one with the world, but being a beacon of light and righteousness within it."

"What's your stance on the Manhattan Doctrine created by the American Christians?"

"Even Catholics can be envious of the renewed focus and authority of their new unified Protestant Order? It's an impressive document laying out religious, political, and cultural positions from a faith perspective: debates, essays, discussions. A Christian version of the Talmud, I'd say. I support it completely, including its many references to 'resisting tyranny' and 'helping the vulnerable' and, I would add, reigniting the war against slavery. And, in the case of the Spanish Americas, criminal super-organizations that have now either become part of the government or have replaced them altogether in some countries."

"That's a lot of people to make war against," Blond says.

"In the Spanish Americas the majority of the slaves are Christians and the majority of those being murdered by the cartels are Christians. We're already fighting the war. I plan to do here in Mexico what Archbishop Masai has done for South Continental Africa."

Father Marcos notices Mr. Blond smile at the mention of the Archbishop.

"What's your plan, Father?"

"Move all of the 'Heaven's Devils' from Texas to here. There's plenty of land and your money will go much farther here in Mexico."

Blond and his people were all descendants of the Hell's Angels. The American gang went through many changes through the decades, with some chapters becoming benevolent community activists, some violent drug-runners, some simply motorcycle aficionados; but it was when their ranks began to be infiltrated and taken over by neo-Satanists and Vampires that the organization splintered and an internal civil war exploded.

Blond's grandfather, a Catholic convert, started a separate group, the Heaven's Devils. Blond's father was framed for a crime he didn't commit by a rival gang. It was Father Marcos's father, a professional lawyer, who successfully defended him in court. They became best friends.

"What about guns? Your government are gun-grabbers. My people won't tolerate that."

"Everyone in this town is required to have a gun."

Blond is surprised. "That is your public position?"

"Yes."

"What about your federal government?"

"Mexico City? Lerdo now has almost one hundred thousand people, all armed, each distrustful of the cities in general, Mexico City in particular. We've dealt with all our narco-police and cartels. Half our people are now Indios, which means we have the support of all Indio people throughout Mexico. A quarter of our people are cowboys, which means we have the support of all the rancheros in Mexico. I'm not concerned about Mexico City."

"But they have the military, tanks, air gunships."

"Mexico isn't China or Russia or the Caliphate or even America. That's not how it's done here. The government won't blow up civilian areas from afar with drones or missiles. It's….un-Mexican. If they come, it will be with a ground army, and our people are its own army."

"Who else will you be adding to your new Mexican *Alliance of the Good?*"

Father Marcos smiles. "Just one more group."

"Who would that be?"

"The rich."

Mr. Blond nods. Father Marcos understands how the world really works. If you don't have some portion of the elite in your corner, you are going nowhere. He's not one of these idiots who runs around waving signs and shouting slogans about "power to the people." He stands up.

"I can speak for my people already. We like your offer. We would like to get out of America anyway. You're a very lucky person, Father. We don't trust easily. If my father hadn't known yours, we wouldn't be having this meeting at all. I know your father is dead now, but I don't know how. The cartels?"

"No, drunk driver, both parents. Mexico doesn't have auto-drive everywhere like America does, and especially not in the countryside."

"I would have liked to have met them. My dad died from a heart attack, of all things. The man did triathlons every year."

"Well, at least their good Catholic sons will be able to do business together."

Father Marcos's Office, Lerdo Church
10:56 a.m., 30 April 2093 (Children's Day)

They sit in comfortable chairs in front of the desk. Ms. Flores and Mr. Santos work for the Durango Times, the leading news netzine for Durango. Mr. Torres is a respected reporter in Mexico City. Being a journalist in the world today is very dangerous. In the Muslim world, which includes all of former Western Europe, there is no free journalism at all, and all media is controlled by the Islamic sharia government. In Chinese-Indian territory, it is hit or miss; you could publish a critical story and be lavishly awarded or you could have government agents burst into your bedroom in the middle of the night bland stick you in a prison cell for twenty years. Canada and the Russian Bloc are dangerous, but doable. Australia and the remaining unaffiliated Asian countries are pretty open. America is open, but the government had the power to classify any story as a matter of national security and render the media subject to fines, imprisonment, or both if they did publicize the story. Latin America is open too, as long as your critical stories are *not* about the cartels or government corruption.

The reporters wait quietly. They've heard all about the New Hidalgo of Lerdo: the Catholic priest who kills narco-police and cartels by day and rescues girls from sex slavery by night. It sounds noble on paper, but is quite insane in real life. He's going to end up the same way the legendary Hidalgo did: his decapitated head on display somewhere.

Father Marcos enters the room and shakes their hands. "Pardon me for the delay." They all sit.

Mr. Torres says, "It's okay, Father. We know you are especially busy these days. You probably have no time to even read the Bible anymore."

"I read the Bible every day without fail. I'm never too busy for that."

Mr. Torres says, "Of course, Father. Sorry for the insult."

Mr. Santos asks, "What can we do for you, Father?"

"I would like you to write a series of stories for me. The theme will be the New Cry of Durango. The focus will be government corruption and its unholy alliance with the cartels. We will name names."

Mr. Torres laughs. "What reporter do you think will be stupid enough to write that story?"

Father says, "I was hoping it to be the three of you. I've read much of your work in the past and you are well respected among the people."

Ms. Torres says, "Yes, but I would like my head to remain on its neck."

"Let me inspire you, then. Please follow me."

The reporters look at each before following him outside the church building. A large SUV waits and they all get in. Deacon Juan Carlos drives. Two other cars follow as they drive thirty minutes outside Lerdo. They stop at what looks to be an archeological excavation site. Father Marcos hops out. "Please follow me."

He leads them to the edge of a massive hole dug into the ground. It is filled with decomposing bodies—including, unknown to any of them, the woman who ran from the pack of "chupacabras" some three years ago.

"What is this?" Ms. Flores asks.

"You've seen and heard of them many times before. A mass grave," Father Marcos answers. "Filled with dead women. This is what Mexican soil is being used for mostly these days. Dead bodies."

"Do you know who did this?" she asks.

Father Marcos leads them to another area, where there are about twenty bodies covered by a tarp. He bends down and uncovers all of them: men in chupacabra masks. "We caught them burying the bodies. We got them to talk and then killed them."

"Cartel-men?" asks Santos.

"Yes." He pulls the chupacabra mask off one of them and stands again. "We have one mass grave of fifty people, another with ten girls, another with thirty, another one between Lerdo and Gomez Palacio with more than a hundred. This is what I want you to write about. We've hired our own CSI team to identify every last corpse. I want you to do profiles on every last murder victim and their cartel killers."

Torres shakes his head. "Everyone knows this is happening. Where's the new news? I'm sorry, but no one cares, Father."

"No one cares that the National Palace is personally involved in murder, kidnapping, and slavery of Mexicans? The Presidential

Guard Corps? The Presidential High Command involved as narco-mercenaries?" Father Marcos challenges.

"There is absolutely no way you could prove any of what you just said," Torres says.

Father Marcos asks, "Are you sure?"

The reporters stare at him as if trying to call his bluff.

Torres is angry. "This is nonsense. You're making it up. And none of my readers will care about dead country people. I can't even get them to care about dead city people." He throws up his hands and walks away, back to the SUV.

Father Marcos looks at the remaining two reporters. "What about the two of you?"

Ms. Flores asks, "What is your motivation for this? Do you have a death wish?"

Father Marcos seems to mentally drift off in the distance as he talks softly. "I'm fully aware of the consequences of this war. I remember when I was twelve years old I confronted a cartel-man on my street. I hated these cartels even as a child. The man had punched an elderly woman in her face because she wasn't able to move fast enough out of his way as he walked into a store. I walked up to him and yelled at him and told him that if I were bigger I'd kill him in front of his own men. The man laughed at me and pulled out a gun. He aimed at me and fired. The bullet passed by my left ear. He said to me, 'Somebody has to die. As long as I live, someone has to die. Not today for you, but someone.' He walked away. I heard a scream from behind me; I knew it was my mother. I ran to the scream. There was my mother screaming hysterically. The bullet missed me but traveled through the air, through the walls of the store behind me, and into the forehead of my little sister, Angela. She died instantly. My parents were never the same. Yes, I know the consequences. The very first dead girl for me was my very own sister."

"We're sorry, Father," Santos says. "We didn't know."

Father Marcos: "Will you write the stories?"

"Yes."

Church Offices, Lerdo City
9:34 a.m., 7 August 2093

Sister Maria leads Father Tezuma and another priest from the main church into the administrative offices to an awaiting Father Marcos. Father Tezuma is ecstatic and shakes his hand aggressively. The other priest, whom Father Tezuma doesn't introduce by name, shakes his hand as well.

"Father Marcos, thank you for meeting with me, brother. Word of your good deeds is spreading fast. Soon you will be more famous than Barco and Selina!" He refers to two top entertainers in Mexico today.

He leads them to the chairs waiting for them. "Please have a seat."

"Yes, brother."

Rather than sit behind his desk, Father Marcos sits close to them in a facing third chair.

Father Tezuma starts. "Again, thank you, brother, for agreeing to meet with us. We brothers have much to accomplish. There are great things happening all throughout Mexico these days. You here and us in Sinaloa."

Father Marcos says, "I was intrigued by your comments on reforming the Catholic Church. Not another Martin Luther in our midst?"

Father Tezuma laughs. "I believe the Reformation was a net benefit for Catholicism. Do you not agree?"

Father Marcos nods. "It absolutely was. Anything that gets at corruption. What were you referring to, though?" It was the racket of the Church selling indulgences, pardons for sins, and eternal salvation for money that led to the disillusionment of Martin Luther and the 16th-century Reformation that split Christendom into separate Catholic and Protestant Orders.

Father Tezuma says, "It's not my main issue, but we should do something about the prohibition against married clergy."

"Haven't you had children since becoming a priest?"

Father Tezuma smiles. "Yes, eight so far."

Father Marcos asks, "Same woman?"

Father Tezuma hesitates. "More than one."

Father Marcos already knows this. "First, I am more than open to a debate as Catholics about clerical marriage prohibition. It is very true that the twelve Apostles were married and our first twelve Popes were married. Jesus, our ultimate life model, wasn't. So there are good arguments on both sides. However, there must be honesty in the debate. I also can't help noticing that this debate comes up only with Catholics. When there were Buddhist monks, it didn't; with Hindu monks, there is no debate, only with Catholicism. Eastern religions do it, it's noble; Catholics do it, it's bad. Second, you can't be a spokesperson for clerical marriage when even if it were allowed, you would have already broken your marriage vows. You must be an honest advocate on these issues."

Tezuma smiles and nods. "You are as wise as Solomon, brother. You are right on the first point and I am definitely hypocritical on the second. I'm curious, brother. What is your stance on 'deunification?'"

Father Marcos hesitates. It is a notion that has become somewhat of a subtle, underground movement with some rank-and-file Catholics. Each continent or country would have its own Pope separate from the Vatican. "I'm strenuously against it," he says. "I question whether the idea came from Catholics in the first place. If we as Catholics have problems with Rome, then let's deal with it privately. This is not the time for Catholics to break apart into continental regions. We have too many enemies who would view it as an opportunity to attack us. We have grievances with Rome. That isn't new. This has been ongoing in Catholicism for centuries.

"But you said there was a main issue you wanted to raise with me."

Tezuma leans forward. "Yes, Father, we believe, based on your great Grito de Lerdo sermon and your alliance with the indigenous people of Mexico, that you can truly relate to the movement we are a part of in Sinaloa and that it will spread. I speak of the Neo-Mayan and Neo-Aztec movements."

"I'm not familiar with those movements." Father Marcos is being less than honest.

Father Tezuma continues. "Mexico, like the rest of the Americas, was conquered and raped and subjugated by European invaders. Our movement wants to return to the great era that existed before these colonial invaders landed. We must re-embrace our original history. Abandon the speaking of racist languages like Spanish."

Father Marcos interrupts. "Spanish is a racist language?"

Father Tezuma nods. "Oh yes, brother."

"What will we speak then?" Father Marcos asks.

Father Tezuma replies, "Our original indigenous languages. The Neo-Mayan and Ne-Aztec movement is about returning us to the real Mexico, a Mesoamerican people."

Father Marcos sits back. The radical, secular, anti-religious movement had swept over America, with religious people living in self-segregated enclaves throughout the country for safety. The Pagans had won the culture war there and had set their sights on "transforming" the Spanish Americas, too. Pagans always seem to find willing, religious "useful idiots" to do their work for them.

Father Marcos asks, "Does that mean we'll start up human sacrifices again?"

It is an odd moment. Father Tezuma just looks at him. Father Marcos wonders why he isn't responding. Father Tezuma finally says, "Neo-Mayans and Neo-Aztecs reject that practice."

Father Marcos challenges. "Why? It was the centerpiece of their culture. Mayans, Aztecs, Incas, and Toltecs were cultures that worshipped death, just like the Ancient Egyptians did. The Aztecs' human barbarism, throwing people into roaring fires, carving out people's hearts while they were alive, cannibalism, human skulls everywhere, adults and children—it shocked even the ultra-violent, Spanish-Inquisition-era Spaniards. Toltecs, Incas, Mayans, and Aztecs were cultures of death; Jews and Christians were cultures of life. Why aren't you embracing the entire Mayan and Aztec cultures, if that's what you want to return to?"

Father Tezuma pauses again. "Father Marcos, the movement is about returning us to a more natural, pre-Spanish society. The gods we will worship will only be one: God through Jesus Christ. So sacrifices will not be necessary. We will remove all the imperialist influences from our society. Elevate our superior, indigenous peoples."

Father Marcos looks at him. "And not speak Spanish."

"Speaking is such a minor thing in this movement and it will take time for people to be reeducated to the true Mexican way that has been kept from them over centuries of colonial brainwashing."

Father Marcos stands up. "Father Tezuma. Thank you so much for coming down to meet with me. Let me reflect on all that you have told me."

Father Tezuma stands slowly with his priest companion doing the same. "Thank you so much, brother." He smiles again widely. "I know you possess the intellect to understand what we are doing.

I look forward to meeting with you again soon. We must stay united."

Father Marcos nods. "Yes." He calls outside the door. "Sister Maria." She appears quickly at the door. "Show our distinguished guests to their cars." Father Tezuma kisses Father Marcos's hand before smiling and following Sister Maria out with his priest.

Father Marcos's smile disappears and he sits down, deep in thought.

Two minutes later Sister Maria appears again. She sees he's deep in thought. "Rodrigo says that Bishop Garza is at one of the grave sites 'causing trouble.' He wants you to go there."

Father Marcos is still deep in thought.

Sister Maria asks, "What's wrong, Father?"

He looks up. "I feel like this is 1933 and I just met with a new young Adolf Hitler."

Sister Maria looks down. "He and his people are very dangerous. There are rumors about them."

"What rumors?"

Sister Maria says, "It's only a rumor. There are no facts."

"Sister, sometimes your unfounded suspicion is better than a fact to me. What rumors?"

Sister Maria relents. "*Brujeria.*"

Witchcraft! He had heard rumors too, animal sacrifices, possible cannibalization, but he dismissed them since they were coming from extreme anti-religious bigots. But if Sister Maria's sources were hearing the same thing, he had to do a serious investigation. Hitler had a fascination with the occult too.

"What independent contacts do we have in Sinaloa?"

Sister Maria says, "I will have a detailed list upon your return, Father, but Bishop Garza—"

Father Marcos sighs. "Yes. He's causing trouble."

11:45 a.m.

Bishop Garza yells at reporters flashing away with their camera e-pads at another uncovered mass grave. He tries to block them, and his entourage of priests and body guards also try to push the media away. In an instant, he is shoved and finds himself at the bottom of the hole. He stands up, removing his body from a barely covered skeleton.

Bishop Garza looks up angrily and sees Father Marcos!

Garza's men reach down to help him out of the open grave. "I'm going to speak to the Holy See directly about you! I will have you removed from your parish! I will have you run out of Mexico! I will do my best to have you excommunicated! Murdering people. Bringing outsiders into our towns. Bringing reporters here who have no other agenda but to make us look bad to the outside world."

Father Marcos slaps him. Bishop Garza looks at him with shock, holding the side of his face. Father Marcos yells, "Shut your mouth or I will throw you in the ditch again! You are the disgrace, Bishop to Lerdo, to Gomez Palacio, to Mexico, and the entire human race. You are the disgusting epitome of the narco-priest. You are not angered at innocent people murdered, lying dead in a mass grave, but you are angered by reporters who dare to tell people about it. Go back to your cartel masters!"

Bishop Garza yells back, "You have no right to talk to me that way! I have been here from the beginning! You come here from nowhere and think you run everything!"

"Yes, Bishop Narco-Priest."

"I am not a narco-priest!"

"Bishop, we know all about you: the eager acceptance of cartel blood money—kidnappings and killings; the money from drugs and slavery, the cartels building your new church offices, the eager trading of *narcolimosna* for cartel donations."

"I have broken no Church policy. It's not my church's responsibility to determine where donations come from. Money is money. Are you going to pay the money we need daily to keep our church doors open? If there is someone willing to support the community church, who cares where the money comes from?"

"Why did you praise Mr. Gordo and other cartel crime lords at your church, in your sermon?!"

"Don't tell me how to run my church!"

"An evil man who would have young girls snatched from our streets, locked in rooms to be raped, addicted to drugs, and run as sex slaves all over the world!"

"That is a lie! He was a businessman!"

Father Marcos is so angry that he has to stop himself. He knows that if he hits the Bishop once he will not stop until he beats him to death. The Bishop can see this in his eyes.

"You have no right to talk to me that way! I do what all of us have to do to survive. What could I do? I'm not a killer. I couldn't even kill a fly if I wanted to. They threaten your families! I have dozens of people in my family! What could I do? You weren't here! I have to survive. I have to keep my family safe!" Bishop Garza is sobbing now. "It's always easy to condemn someone else. Most people are not brave. They just want to live."

Father Marcos points at him. "Go back to your church, Bishop." He turns his back on him and walks to a waiting car.

"I can't be condemned for wanting to live!" The bishop's entourage takes him away after noticing that every reporter has been watching.

Gomez Palacio, Mexico
8:05 p.m., 8 August 2093

It is one of the many nondescript streets of the city. But this night is different, as an army of well-armed Cowboys leads women, children, and men from their homes to waiting SUVs. In less than a minute they are all inside and the SUVs speed off.

Lerdo City, Mexico
7:30 a.m., 1 September 2093

Church staffers watch from the main entrance of the church. Mr. Blond has returned, but not alone. He exits a pickup truck. Behind it is a long line of trucks, vans, SUVs, and cars. The Heaven's Devils—the Texans! They exit their vehicles. Some men have guns in belt holsters on their hips, others have shoulder holsters under their jackets or vests; still others carry rifles, shotguns, or machine guns.

Father Marcos walks out and greets Mr. Blond with a handshake and a firm hug.

Bishop Garza's church, Gomez Palacio, Mexico
8:30 a.m. (Next Day)

This is his third time here. Father Marcos sits across from a now-docile Bishop Garza. "I've had all your sisters and brothers moved into New Lerdo with their families. So was your mother, your uncles, your aunts, all your nieces and nephews. No one will ever be able to get to them, ever again."

"Thank you, Father," the bishop says with tears in his eyes.

"You will continue to run your church here, but will focus solely on ministry and services to the people."

"Yes, Father."

"I have assigned a team to see to your personal safety and you will live in a secure house. Not even your people will know of its location."

"Yes, Father. Thank you."

In real terms, Father Marcos is the Bishop of New Lerdo, as the residents are starting to call it, *and* Gomez Palacio. He is the power in all of northern Durango.

Church Lerdo City, Mexico
3:00 p.m., 4 October 2093

The three services for mass may be over, but the Sunday services are not. Father Marcos conducts baptisms for the church at the indoor pool, which is solely used for these rituals. He starts with baptisms of newborns; however, he is always especially moved by the adults who make their individual choices to accept Jesus and be "reborn." His first adult baptism is Mona Lisa.

"When you believe in God, know that He is not ashamed of your past. When you believe in God, know that He loves you." Father Marcos gently lowers a crying Mona Lisa under the waters. She wears a white robe like all the waiting adults. He lifts her back up and to her feet. "You have been reborn in Christ." A group of women clap.

Lerdo City, Mexico
12:02 p.m., 10 October 2093

Señor Gustavo, one of the richest men in Mexico, arrives. The extreme wealth is on display as the Gustavos also arrive with seemingly more private security than even the President of Mexico.

Church staff members bring dishes and beverages to the table: cabrito con tamales, carnitas, barbacoa, menudo, chilaquiles, beans, a variety of sauces, and drinks. Father Marcos, the Gustavo power couple, and Mona Lisa sit at the cozy table in a nice patio area of the church. It may seem like a casual lunch get-together, but this private meeting is probably the most important one for Father Marcos to date.

Señor Gustavo comments, "The food is excellent, Father. Is this from your staff or catered?"

Father Marcos answers, "The food was prepared by volunteers from the community. We have many new residents from all over Mexico now, so it truly is a blessing for us to have such a variety of dishes on a weekly basis."

"Well, be careful. We may try to hire them away from you."

"New Lerdo is happy to share, Señor Gustavo."

"Father, you must know that you are the center of much discussion across the country. Among very powerful people. And very dangerous people. What are your thoughts about this?"

"We have a saying in New Lerdo: 'Trust in Jesus, but carry a big gun.'"

Señora Gustavo smiles. "Forget the myth of the Mexican Holiday of Independence. It's very dangerous to have Father Hidalgo as your revolutionary role model. The government executed him. And Augustín the First of Mexico, the Mexican Army General who marched into Mexico City in 1821 and ended the Mexican War of Independence, became Emperor for a year, even designed our Mexico flag; he was also executed. The people may sing songs about you, celebrate you on holidays, but only after they kill you."

"I plan to live a long life and die in my sleep at the age of one hundred and twenty."

Gustavo laughs. "So Father, what are your thoughts on the rich? Do you feel we should be rounded up and killed, like a lot of country people feel, or have our hard-earned fortunes and property confiscated, like many of your fellow priests believe? What do you think about Robin Hood's saying: 'Steal from the rich and give to the poor'? Quite frankly, Father, I do not trust your Catholic church. The only reason we are here is because of our daughter." Mona Lisa looks at her parents. "I hear you made a Christian woman out of her and baptized her last week."

Father Marcos replies, "It was a very moving ceremony. Baptizing our newborns is our way, but every rebaptism and adult baptism I conduct so moves me emotionally and spiritually."

Señora Gustavo speaks now. "Father, you found our daughter when all our wealth was useless in finding her. You saved her from hell, and my husband and I owe you a debt for the rest of our lives. But your religious allegiance is very difficult for us. Rome, Italy. What do they know about Mexico? Except for our daughter now, we are not a religious family."

Señor Gustavo adds, "Now, don't get us wrong. We're not those anti-cleric, radical atheists who run America, and we would have no use for the Mexican Presidents of the past like Benito Juarez or Elias Calles. We want a separation of state and church, but that doesn't mean destroying the church or Mexican religious history, or killing or persecuting religious people. But the Liberals and the Socialists were a reaction to the awesome, unrestrained church power in Mexico then."

Mexican President Juarez in 1851 was determined to destroy the power of the Church. President Elias Calles in 1924 was even worse: a mass murderer.

Father Marcos responds, "The Church has both a shining history and a stained one. The Church is perfect, but the men who run it are flawed flesh and blood like any other human being. Whatever bad was done in the past, there is no hesitation to acknowledge or repent for any wrongs or evils. Saint John Paul II publicly apologized to the world and asked for sincere forgiveness during his lifetime no fewer than a hundred times. Despite our shortfalls or lapses, people of faith have always been the main drivers of goodness in the world, and the Church has been an especially positive force in Mexico. If it were not, I wouldn't be a Catholic and I wouldn't be a priest."

Señor Gustavo agrees. "Bad is bad, no matter who does it."

"Señor and Señora Gustavo, I cannot answer for other priests elsewhere or in other times. I can only be a leader in my corner of the universe and be the best beacon of light for my faith that I can be. The fact that you are unbelievers is also irrelevant, as my work as a Catholic to non-believers is as important as my work to Christians. And Catholicism isn't Islam. There will be no forced conversions or theocracies here. Our government did a very disastrous thing for Mexico those centuries ago when it passed all those anti-clerical laws, and we're suffering still for it. Mexico has had corruption for so long, most people don't even know what the absence of it looks like.

"To answer your original question, Señor Gustavo, I am no kind of anti-capitalist. In fact, the Church today calls socialism a moral sin in many Pastoral Announcements. It's in the Bible: 'Thou shalt not covet your neighbor's belongings.' Do not desire what is not yours and certainly do not take it away from them through force."

Gustavo nods. "All my wealth I earned with my own two hands. I started working when I was five, ten- to sixteen-hour days. And I may not be knowledgeable of everything within Catholicism, but I do know that there are as many anti-capitalists in the Vatican as there are in the Mexican government."

"Very true, but those are factions within the Vatican, not the Pope or the Church itself. But both of you know what passions govern my heart. In socialism, the government controls virtually all major aspects of the people's life. Why on earth would we want our corrupt narco-government controlling Mexican life? The people must have the means to provide for themselves and protect themselves. That means, as one of my chief staffers always tells me, it's about money in the pocket. The more money the people have, the more money the Church has to help the poor and the needy, which we are commanded to do by God. And unlike the case with the government, you don't like what I do, you can get up and take your money and voluntarily give it to someone else."

Gustavo says, "You have the people, the Indians, the cowboys, the rancheros, Gomez Palacio, and we hear you brought in your own gringo civilian army from Texas. But what role do rich Mexicans like myself have in this new world of yours in Mexico, Father?"

Father Marcos hands him the large tablet on the table and pushes a button. A diagram appears on the screen. "The population of New Lerdo has tripled in size. We need a new church."

Gustavo takes the tablet. "You can't be serious. We don't even believe in God."

Father Marcos smiles. "But you do believe in financing worthy projects. The large, state-of-the-art church of Nueva Lerdo will be possible thanks to the generous donation of the Gustavo family…and friends. Out here so far from Mexico City, it is the church that provides services to the people. We need a coalition of people that includes country people and the city, working poor and wealthy elite. If we don't make this coalition, it is only a matter of time before the government or the cartels, or both, pit us against each other for their mutual benefit and our mutual destruction."

Gustavo asks, "Are you opposed to meeting with my business colleagues?"

"Not at all."

Gustavo looks at his daughter for a moment. "Rich people can be very egotistical, Father. They require a lot of pampering and special attention. Can you deal with that?

"I already have plenty of practice. Dealing with the Vatican."
They smile.
Gustavo says, "We'll build your church."

Sister Cyclops and the
Betty Boop Twins

"You may choose to look the other way but you can never say again that you did not know." — William Wilberforce, English politician, philanthropist, and leader of the slave trade abolishment movement (1759-1833)

"In any pocket of endless oppression and incredible horror against women, there will arise two species: the doe—innocent, frail, weak, needy of a protector—and the she-wolf—a vicious alpha-predator that men dream about only because they have never met one in real life and would run if they did. Essayist Dame Andromeda postulated that one of our future world wars will be between men and women. I differ only in this: half the women would fight on the side of the men." — Dee Tocqueville, pre-Islamic French expatriate, author, essayist (2079)

The Underground Railroad, circa 1817 to the end of the American Civil War in 1865, was neither underground, nor was it an actual railroad. It got its name because its activities had to be carried out in secret and because of the railway terms or code words that were used by those involved. It was a network of persons who helped slaves in the American South escape to mostly the northern American states and Canada, but sometimes even to Mexico and overseas.

However, even at its height, fewer than one thousand slaves were able to escape per year. The highest number of slaves claimed to have been rescued was one hundred thousand, but the actual number could have been much lower. Regardless, it was still a small percentage of slaves, who numbered four million by 1860. Although the economic impact of the Railroad was tiny, the psychological impact on Southern slaveholders was immense.

Ocosingo, Chiapas, Mexico
5:06 p.m., 6 June 2094

A shapely woman approaches the men, strutting her stuff. She walks to the gate wearing an orange tank top over her busty frame, a very short lavender leather skirt and orange heels. Her flowing black hair comes down to the middle of her back. Serena is beautiful and flawless, except for the black patch over her left eye. She reaches the nine-foot-tall metal gate with two guards armed with machine guns on the inside. They grin as they look her up and down.

"So boys, why are you being so mean to me?" she asks.

"How are we doing that, Señorita?" one of the guards answers.

"I want to see your big, big…house. But you have me standing out here by myself. I'm getting cold."

"We can definitely warm you up," he says. The men laugh.

"Then let me in."

"Who are you, though?"

"I'm the beautiful one-eyed woman with big assets whom you're talking to."

"Where are you from?"

"Just down the street."

"We've never seen you before, Señorita."

She pretends to faint and almost falls to one knee. "I'm so hot outside here. I need to be in a big, big house on a big, big bed."

The men cannot help themselves and open the gate. One of them wraps his arm around her waist and she grabs the other by the hand. "We'll take care of you, Señorita."

"Oh yes. I really need that big, big bed. Do you have other big, big things you can show me?"

The men laugh hysterically. "Oh yes we do!"

The massive mansion is more like a fortress, with vid-cams and lights everywhere. They reach the main door and a third man, Pepe, opens it.

"Are you two crazy? You can't bring some strange woman to the house!" he yells.

"Mind your own damn business," the man yells back at him. "She'll stay in my room."

"You're on duty. Get back to the gate!" Pepe commands. "The crew will be back soon."

"No! I'm taking my break now."

Pepe starts to pull out his concealed gun from his jacket, but the other two men are already aiming their machine guns at him.

"Not a smart thing to do, Pepe."

Pepe is furious. "The boss will feed you to the alligators!"

The two men laugh. "Get the hell out of our way!"

Pepe stands aside. The two men lead her inside, but it is more like she is pulling them. "Wow, this is a big, big house," she says. "Take me to the bedroom and put those machine guns away."

The men laugh as they take her upstairs. Pepe watches them furiously. They disappear, but he can still hear their stupid laughter. He begins to walk to another room but stops. *Did I hear something?* He begins to walk up the stairs but stops again.

He suddenly turns and jumps down to the front door, throws it open, and runs as fast as he can. Bullets fly all around him, but miss. He sprints to the gate, throws it open, and runs.

He tries to pull his gun from his concealed holster, but it drops to the ground. He doesn't dare stop to pick it up.

Serena bolts from the house, firing at him with a machine gun. Pepe is lucky, as the metal gate and large trees shield him from most of the bullets. She runs down the path and out the gate after him.

He hears car doors behind him close; he glances back quickly. Right behind her are two more women, equally provocatively dressed, running after him—the Betty Boop twins.

Pepe runs down a hill to the main streets. Bullets fly past him again, but he's far enough away and still shielded by trees and bushes. He nears the street; cars zoom by in both directions. He either has to stop or run across the traffic. Timing it just right, he jumps the fence onto the street and runs, barely missed by one car, and runs down the middle of the street with cars speeding past him on either side. He runs as fast as he can, but looks back.

Serena is just a few car lengths behind him, running barefoot. The two other women are closing in, too.

How did she catch up to me so fast? And who are those other two bitches?

Pepe sees his opening and darts across the lane of traffic, then takes a hard right, running into a busy shopping area and pushing people out of his way.

A SUV stops right next to him and the men inside yell out. "Pepe, what's going on?"

Pepe notices them. "It's an ambush! Kill those bitches! Take out the one-eyed one first! I'll lead the other two away until you can get to me! Give me a gun!"

Serena dropped back as soon as the SUV stopped in front of Pepe. He runs off again and the SUV does a fast one-hundred-eighty-degree turn. She motions to the Twins to follow Pepe. The SUV races at high speed directly at her.

She runs hard to the right, using other cars to shield herself from the oncoming SUV. The vehicle stops as other cars block them from quickly running her down. She darts away from a car and, now unshielded, sprints across the open street.

The driver of the SUV laughs as he drives around some blocking cars and races toward her again. Serena stops and turns around. She shoots one shot at the windshield.

The bullet bounces right off. The driver laughs. "It's bulletproof, bitch!"

Serena pulls another gun from her back waistband. She aims the strange gun and fires once. The driver is hit through the windshield in his forehead—dead. She fires a second time, killing the man in the passenger seat. The SUV is still barreling toward her; the men in the back seat scream, but can't get to the driver-side controls. Serena steps to the right one pace and the SUV speeds past her and crashes into the solid brick wall of a store. The dead bodies of the driver and passenger are mashed against the windshield. The two gunmen in the back seat are only stunned.

She walks to the SUV, opens the driver-side door, and sprays the backseat with bullets, killing the two remaining men. She pops the trunk and walks to the back. Inside is an arsenal of weapons and ammo.

"Exactly what I was looking for." She grabs two grenades, pulls the pins, and tosses them in the SUV. She casually walks away and looks at her GPS wristband. She runs in the direction of the Twins. The SUV blows up in a massive explosion; people on the street run away in every direction.

Pepe continues to run from the Twins. *I got to lose them!* He runs into a clothing store, pushing people away. He runs to the back, then out the rear door. He runs to the store behind it and does the same, in the front and out the back. He's not even looking back anymore. The crowds are bigger to one side of the street and he runs into the center, pushing people away. The alleyways! As soon as he gets there, he can see an almost endless route. He sprints through, but then slows down halfway. He's completely exhausted. He looks back and there is no one. He smiles. *I lost them!*

He walks into the main street as he pulls his e-pad from his pocket and dials. No one in the crowd notices the gun in his hand.

The Twins appear! Both wield long silver knives and they stab him repeatedly. His gun drops to the ground. He tries to punch them, but when he goes to punch one, the other twin attacks. He screams and kicks randomly, hitting nothing.

The Betty Boop Twins got their street name from their fascination with—and unique slicked-back hairstyles from—the 1930s cartoon character of the same name. The word to describe their knife-attack fighting style is—beautiful. They are not two separate people, but a single entity with four arms, four legs, and four knives that view the target from every angle of the X-Y-Z axis.

Pepe is stabbed dozens of times. One of the twins slices his right forearm from his wrist to his elbow when he tries to hit the other. The other twin stabs him in a rapid machine-gun fashion in the small of his back when he tries—and fails—to kick the other. He tries to run but realizes that he can't move, and he falls to his knees.

He screams out, now enraged, but is helpless to do anything. Death by a million cuts and a million stabs. He falls back to the ground, coughing up blood.

Serena appears and watches him with the Twins. A small crowd of people surrounds the scene to watch or snap pictures. He drowns on his own blood; below his neck, it drips and squirts out of his body. Pepe, the chief slave-runner for the state of Chiapas, is dead.

The gate to the mega-mansion is still open and so is the front door. It all seems deserted. Serena and the Twins run back into the mansion grounds and up to the main house, but don't enter. They stand against the wall outside of the open front door, ready to fire with their weapons. Serena touches her ear with its hidden ear-bud receiver. "How many hostiles left in the house now?"

"It's all clear," the voice says.

"Where are the 'packages?'"

"They're in underground rooms. Looks like a lot more than fifty, though."

"Bring the team in."

Four black vans appear and drive through the open front gates. They stop in front of the main door. Armed women dressed in black army fatigues exit the first two vans. They enter and fan out in pairs, doing a visible check of every room, every closet, and every corner. Two of the women carry what looks to be a mechanical mannequin inside.

Sister Fernanda exits from one of the vans. She enters and joins Serena and the Twins. "That man should never have been able to escape into the streets," she says.

Serena stares at her, annoyed. "How was I to know that the man would do a Speedy Gonzales out of here rather than come upstairs? Anomalies happen. We'll be out of here in fifteen minutes." She turns to the Twins. "Seize all the surveillance logs and destroy every piece of electronics in this place." Back to Fernanda: "Let's get the packages."

Several of the women in army fatigues have cut through the secret door to the basement level of the mansion. Sometimes these passages are booby-trapped, so they are very cautious. One of them drops in the mechanical mannequin. The robot walks down the stairs to another locked door. It shoots out the lock with its built-in hand weapon and pushes the door open. On either side of the basement are closed doors, but none are locked. The robot opens the first door and looks in, then the next door, and so on, until all the doors are open.

Fernanda walks down with a squad of armed women. She goes to the first room. Inside are partially clothed women, bound and gagged, sitting or lying on the dirt ground. It is the same in all of the rooms. Sex slaves bound for other parts of Mexico, America, the Russian Bloc, or Islamic Caliphate Territories.

The women are untied, wrapped in towels, and led to the waiting vans.

Serena listens to the voice of the lookout in her ear-set. "There are six armored SUVs approaching! You have five minutes!"

Serena yells to them. "Get them out of here now! Six armored SUVs are approaching."

Fernanda yells back, "There are far more women here than we were told. There are almost two hundred of them. We don't have enough vehicles."

Serena says, "Pack them in the vans and go. One driver and one guard and that's it."

Fernanda answers back, "We can't jam all these women into four vans."

Serena says, "Yes we can and we will, if that's what we need to do."

Fernanda asks, "And us?"

Serena smiles. "We'll be leaving in one of those armored SUVs coming for us."

Fernanda shakes her head again. "We are off-mission."

Serena ignores her and runs outside as the last of the women are loaded into the vans; there's so many of them. They are so scared. They don't know what's what, who's who, where they are going. She wishes she could stop to explain, but there is no time.

No one thinks of labor slavery, whip-and-chain slavery, ancient slavery anymore, which is less than five percent of the trade. Ninety-five percent is sex slavery.

Serena wildly motions to the drivers to move. The vans race out of the gate and onto the road. Serena closes the gate and runs back to the mansion, closing the door.

"How much longer on the hostiles?" she asks.

"They're here now," the voice says.

Everyone walks to the surveillance room, which has a wall of active monitors; every inch of the mansion grounds is watched by camera.

The six SUVs stop at the main gate as it opens. Someone in the vehicles has the access code.

The female squad leader, Diaz, looks at Serena. "How do you want us to handle this?"

"Let's see what we're dealing with first."

The SUVs enter and well-armed men exit. They instinctively look around, concerned but not panicked.

Serena says, "They're looking for the gate guards." To Diaz: "Take your team and Fernanda upstairs to the last room and hide there. The Twins and I will handle this."

Fernanda is surprised. "How? Three of you will take out…" She looks at the screen. "…more than two dozen gunmen?"

Serena says, "Squad Leader, do it now."

The squad leads Fernanda upstairs as Serena and the Twins put their guns down on a table.

Fernanda and the squad sit in the room so quietly it is as if they are not even there. All the drapes are drawn to make it as dark as possible. The squad leader and her team keep their fingers on the triggers of their guns; they are closest to the door. Fernanda sits farthest away, in a corner.

They hear someone come up the stairs, the sounds of heels

hitting the marble. There is a special knock at the door. "Let's go!" It is Serena's voice.

The squad leader looks to everyone as she slowly opens the door. The entire squad aims their guns at the door, ready to fire. Serena appears. "Come on, let's go."

The squad and Fernanda follow her downstairs. The Twins wait at the front door, playing with their silver blades. Fernanda thinks to herself, *I always play with my food while I eat; these two play with their killing knives.*

"We'll finish up and take all six armored SUVs," Serena says.

Everyone fans out again. Some search the mansion, room by room again. Others rummage through all drawers, shelves, and cupboards for anything of value: money, electronics, weapons, hidden safes, secret compartments. Still others remote into any systems to download databases. Money will be put in a bag, seized weapons in another. Everything is checked for trackers.

Fernanda walks up to the Twins. "Where did all those men go? We didn't hear a shot."

The Twins smile in unison. One of them motions to her with her finger and she follows them to a room in the back. The door is pushed open; Fernanda peeks in. The men are stacked like wood in the corner, all thirty-five of them. She notices the blood pooling at the base of each "stack."

Fernanda glances at them in disgust. The Twins grin.

"You are a very strange chica, Sister Fernanda," one of them says. "You were one of these girls not too long ago, but you always seem mad when these rapist pig slavers get killed."

Fernanda says, "I'm glad they're dead. You all just seem to like the killing way too much."

"Yes, Sister. Will you be our counselor?"

Fernanda walks away, back to the main door in a huff.

Serena raises her hand, touching her ear-set. "Hold on!" They can all see the expression change on her face. "Our four vans are on their way back."

"Why?" Fernanda asks.

Serena says, "There is a military caravan on its way here. All armored attack vehicles."

One of the Twins says, "This was a trap."

Serena says, "We don't know that yet, but let's get everything outside and blow the house."

The other Twin says, "It must be the General."

Fernanda looks at them. "Who's that?"

Serena replies, "A narco-military officer hired by the southern Mexican cartels." To everyone: "Let's move fast!"

Fernanda still has questions. One of the Twins says to her, "He's hunting us."

The four vans with the women return. Everyone exits the house. Serena directs the squad leader. "Get everyone out of the vans and all of the equipment. We're going to walk by foot through the jungle. They won't be able to follow us through there."

The squad leader is concerned. "These girls are half-naked and in no condition to walk barefoot anywhere, let alone through the jungle."

"Okay, let's wait here for the narco-soldiers and get slaughtered." Serena folds her arms and waits.

Squad Leader Diaz concedes. She runs to her people near the vans and shouts instructions. Her people open the doors and lead the women, all one hundred sixty of them, back out of the vans. Everyone gathers together outside and moves back. The last of the squad members runs out the mansion, and in a few moments a ball of fire explodes. The mansion is engulfed.

Other squad members are torching the four black vans.

Serena looks at Fernanda and says, "I know this is off-mission, but we have no choice. This is going to be your toughest operation ever, but all you have to do is take care of the women. We'll take care of everything else. These women are scared out of their minds and they need you."

Fernanda asks, "Can you get us out of here and back to Grand Central?"

Serena nods. "Yes."

"Then I'll do my work." Fernanda walks to the group of women huddled together.

Serena and Squad Leader Diaz look at their tablet. It is a detailed topographical map of the area. Serena says, "We need the best path for us and the worst path for them. Now."

Diaz studies the map for a second or two, touches the screen to enlarge a section. "I got it. I'll take point with three team members. We'll have the flanks covered and two thirds taking up the rear point."

Another woman races up on her electric bicycle, stops, and jumps off to join the squad. She is dressed in casual clothes and wears an ear-set, with a large bag strapped across her body: the Look-Out.

Serena says, "Good, we're all here. Let's do it, then. Diaz, you're running the show."

Diaz runs to the front of the group with three of her people. She raises her hand, motions to them, and they jog forward. In five minutes they will be in the heart of the Lacandon Jungle.

General Lobo stands at the gates of what used to be the mansion. They know they just missed the "liberators." Criminals have many names for the people who freed or tried to free their sex slaves, but "liberators" is the somewhat universal term nowadays. The General is not only a slave catcher; his actual primary job function is to kill liberators for the cartels.

"We just missed the one-eyed woman and her twin accomplices," he announces. "But…" He smiles. "I'm confident we will have them all in the next forty-eight hours."

He is a standing member of the Mexican military with the menial rank of sub-lieutenant, but freelancing for the cartels, he's a General and that's what he demands to be called, outfitted in full green uniform with jet back hair, mustache, and beard.

He turns to his men, his own private army at his command, dozens of highly trained, well-armed men in military uniforms, and a caravan of armored SUVS with gun turrets. One of the men is his chief tracker.

"Where did they go?" General Lobo asks.

The Tracker looks off in the distance and points. "They're headed for the jungle on foot."

"Can we follow them with our vehicles?"

"No, it's too dense and mountainous in there. And we don't have to. We know where they're going, so all we have to do is drive around the jungle and wait for them on the other side."

"This is not a small jungle. We will have to drive all night to get to the other side."

"Yes, but they can't travel at night. If they use lights, we can see them and they won't do that with all the wild animals in there. Drive around the jungle and catch them in the morning."

The General nods. To another man he says, "Have both the rivers and the air monitored. I also want all air communication jammed within the entire jungle. I don't want anyone coming in to rescue them. Tell the Leader that we'll have his 'property' back and the liberators dead by tomorrow."

Lacandon Jungle, Chiapas, Mexico
6:30 p.m.

The trek through the Lacandon Jungle will not be easy. Though the northeastern Chiapas rainforest has decreased in size due to deforestation caused by the population growth of surrounding towns, people, roads, agricultural farm expansion, and cattle-raising, it is still a massive ecosystem of six thousand square miles containing as much as twenty percent of Mexico's total animal- and plant-life diversity. The vegetation consists of tropical forest, savanna trees, pine-oak forest, gallery forest, and dozens of varieties of orchids with occasional open wetlands.

Father Marcos was very influenced by the history of the Underground Railroad of the United States some two centuries ago, adopting not only the same name for their considerably modern— and more dangerous—slave rescuing operations, but also its code names.

The Squad Leader, Corporal Diaz, is the "Engineer." A specific operation to rescue slaves is the "train" and the "engineer" makes sure the train gets in and out of the target area. She commands the soldiers to protect everyone on the operation and plans the entire route from assault on a "plantation" (where the slaves were kept) to the arrival at a "station" (any secure stopping or hiding place, a safe-house) or "Grand Central" (New Lerdo City), the final destination. The rank of corporal is just a designation.

New Lerdo, under Father Marcos's control, had now also become a haven for honest police all over the country and those tired of working for the cartels. Diaz, at the age of twenty-five, was the chief of police of her small town after all her predecessors were murdered by cartels. She escaped before they could do the same to her, as she, too, refused to work for them or accept their bribe money. When she escaped, she took all the remaining police force with her.

Sister Fernanda is now a "Caretaker" for the Railroad. Caretakers normally did not go on missions. Upon return to "Grand Central," they handled the slow, painstaking task of helping the now-free women deal with the severe trauma of their ordeal and putting their lives back together. Caretakers were part psychologists, part counselors, and part-surrogate mothers.

Sister Serena is in charge of it all as the "Conductor," the person who has the overall responsibility for the entire mission, the ultimate person in charge of everyone rescuing the slaves and getting them to safety. Sister Serena and the Twins had been rescuing slaves sporadically in Southern Mexico and Central America for years, and had gained quite a reputation. They had heard whispers of some priest in Durango doing the same thing when one day, he found them.

'Packages" or "cargo" are slaves. Their intelligence told them that they would find thirty at most, not one hundred sixty. It doesn't matter now. They have to make it work.

The original Underground Railroad still had the popular perception of being a well-coordinated system secretly helping fugitives from "station" to "station," but that was an exaggeration. There was a lot more spontaneity and luck involved. Runaways often did the escaping all on their own. Not so with their modern Railroad. Nothing is left to chance and all the best tek, equipment, intelligence, and people were used. Slaves back then were a valuable commodity. Sex slaves today are a "disposable commodity." Every means necessary had to be used to free them and get them to safety, and the slavers themselves had to be killed or they would come after the rescued slaves or simply snatch other girls, or boys, off the street to replace their lost "property."

Corporal Diaz keeps a fast walking pace through the jungle. Several members of her team stay about twenty paces ahead to clear a path as best they can for the women. Squad members flank either side with their weapons pointing out and away, and others carefully watch the rear for any signs of pursuers. Fernanda constantly circles through the rescued women to reassure them. Serena and the Twins walk behind them.

It is going to be dark soon and they will need to make camp. They not only need to keep themselves invisible from the General and his men, who will undoubtedly be watching for any light sources, but keep everyone safe from wild animals.

At dusk, Diaz stops the "train" to set up camp. Her team busily sets up a perimeter to be monitored by sensors and guarded by squad members. Fernanda divides the women into groups of ten and, after clearing the ground a bit, lays out large ponchos for them. They share other ponchos for blankets.

The air is warm and wet; that means the annoyance of mosquitoes and other insects that aren't as bad during daylight hours, but that will eat them alive without protection. Throughout the camp they set up light sticks with the anti-mosquito beam setting, glowing so dimly they can't be seen from beyond the camp perimeter. The main concern is wild animals (besides the human kind, of course): jaguars, feral dogs, snakes, and howler monkeys.

While most people call themselves "city" or "country," the Twins are "from the jungle"—the jungles of Bolivia. They disappear to forage for food for the women and the team.

Diaz's team breaks out fire-rocks for the camp. They can't set even one natural fire, let alone dozens of them, as they would be easily seen for miles around. The fire-rocks give off lots of heat to dry the ground, but only a faint blue glow.

The Twins return with giant baskets woven from leaves and filled with edible fruits. Serena smiles. Diaz cannot believe all the food the Twins have found as they pass it throughout the camp.

Serena is sad for the women; they now have food and warmth for the night, but that doesn't deal with their fear. They are lucky that Fernanda is on the mission. She'll stay up all night moving from circle to circle, making sure all the women are okay.

The Twins walk to where Serena is sitting on the ground near a fire-rock. They sit on the other side of it and give her one of the now-almost-empty leaf baskets.

Serena whispers as she grabs something that looks like a pear. "You two can make anything and find anything in the jungle. What am I eating anyway?"

One of the Twins smiles. "Don't worry, it's not poisonous."

The other Twin grins and answers, "I think you have the same word in Venezuela, a fruit."

Serena laughs quietly. "Hey, leave my country alone."

The Twins have obviously already eaten and they lie down. Their arms crossed over their chests, holding their knives, they are soon asleep.

Serena is done with her dinner and lies down too, looking up at the stars. Sister Cyclops, the Betty Boop Twins, Father Marcos, and the Mexican Underground Railroad.

Mexico City
11:02 a.m. (One Year Earlier)

Father Marcos hasn't been here in over a decade. Mexico City is a fantastic, modern tek-city seamlessly blending traditional buildings of stone with modern buildings of glass and steel. More than thirty million people live here now. But it also remains one of the top three crime capitals in the Spanish Americas. He doesn't miss it. He is a "city boy," but grew to prefer the simpler country life of Lerdo.

There are plenty of pretty, sleek smart-cars, but there are just as many ancient ones and Franken-cars, patched together with parts of all types of vehicles. He drives his black car down the busy street—

then he sees her. The one-eyed woman walks down the street to a market. *What are the odds that I could randomly run into her?*

He stops his car. Across the street, he sees another two women sitting at an outdoor café; they must be the Twins. He gets out of the car and flashes his digi-card; the nearby parking meter beeps to acknowledge payment.

As he walks after the woman, he glances at the Twins and can see that they are watching him like hawks. They don't even pretend not to notice that he is watching them too. He knows he is walking into danger, but he's run more than enough operations himself: stalking cartel-men, street thugs, and slavers; avoiding gunmen and kidnappers; and single-handedly rescuing thousands of slaves to date. To be in this business, you must have a "third eye" and see everything and everyone around you, anticipate every scenario, always have a defense, always have an escape.

He enters the market and looks around, not seeing the one-eyed women anywhere, but he doesn't expect to. She was either signaled by the Twins outside or she saw him approaching on her own. The market is very busy with customers. He is not interested in games and knows that she is here. He walks to the back of the store and simply sits down on the floor.

He takes out his e-pad from his clothes and touches the screen. The vid-game *Kill the Devil* appears on the screen and he starts playing. This was actually how he met Rodrigo. He was playing the game while he was waiting at a bus stop and the boy was fascinated: go through different levels of hell and kill the cartoon devil any way you can, with gunfire, knives, body-blows, etc., while he tries to maim or kill you in violent or disgusting ways.

From the corner of his eye…he touches the pause on the game and looks up. Serena stares down at him, the black patch covering her left eye.

Father Marcos smiles and stands. "Good morning, Ms. Harriet Tubman. My name is William Still or Levi Coffin, whichever you prefer. I run the parish in Lerdo City in Durango. Look me up when you are in the area." He pauses. "Or don't." He walks down an adjacent aisle and exits the market.

He never looks back. The Twins are somewhere out here waiting for him. He looks all around and then smiles. On the roof of one of the buildings is one of the Twins. He waves to the Twin. She grins at him and waves back with one hand. He can't see the other hand, but knows she must be holding a weapon.

He walks back to his car and gets in, and immediately notices the meter flashing red: Illegal Parking. "Damn parking Nazis!" A common trick in Mexico on those they think are outsiders is to ticket your car even though you paid the meter. As he starts the car, he sees her. The other Twin peers out from a truck parked on the side. She grins and waves at him as he drives off.

Father Marcos laughs to himself.

He would see them all again three weeks later when they were led into his main church office by Sister Maria. His northern Mexico operations would be merged with their southern Mexico operations and he would put Sister Serena in charge of the entire New Underground Railroad with Sisters Guerros, the Twins.

The famous abolitionist Harriet Tubman, born into and escaping slavery herself, rescued more than three hundred slaves.

William Still was called the "Father of the Underground Railroad" and had helped hundreds of slaves escape—as many as sixty per month, hiding them in his Philadelphia home. He kept short biographies of each one, maintained correspondence with them, and wrote and published the book *The Underground Railroad* in 1897.

Levi Coffin was first referred to as the President of the

Underground Railroad by a slave catcher who said, "There's an underground railroad going on here, and Levi's the president of it." With his wife, Catherine, Levi helped more than two thousand slaves escape.

They would later have a good laugh when Serena told him that she checked him out only because he said he had two different names and she wanted to know what fool priest doesn't even know his own name.

They kept their street names—Sister Cyclops and the Betty Boop Twins. His code name would be Archangel.

Lacandon Jungle, Chiapas, Mexico
6:05 a.m., 7 June 2094

The Squad is breaking down the camp. Corporal Diaz walks through the area, checking in with the entire team. Fernanda has the women ready to continue the trek. However, Serena and the Twins are already gone.

Fernanda asks, "How long ago did they leave?"

Diaz says, "They were up at 3 a.m."

"We can't leave without them."

"If they don't get back soon, we will. They know our departure time. They'll catch up. We have to get going."

One of the squad calls out to Diaz. Serena and the Twins are walking back into the camp. All three of them are equipped with large backpacks and high-power rifles.

Diaz says, "We were about to leave without you."

Serena says, "Good. That's what you're supposed to do. Instead of heading north toward Tabasco, move northwest to Veracruz. We need the General to think you're coming to him."

Diaz says, "I don't know how long these women can keep walking. We need air rescue, but communications are still being jammed."

Serena says, "We got an emergency SOS message out to Archangel last night. The cavalry is on its way."

Diaz is surprised. "How did you get the message out with all the jamming?"

Serena answers, "We back-tracked to another 'station' you don't know about. It has a landline."

In a world where everything is wireless, there was still a segment of the population that did not trust sending any kind of message through the digital airwaves and preferred using old physical landlines.

Diaz asks, "What's their time of arrival?"

Serena answers, "Unknown. Just get the women out of here. The Twins and I will buy you as much time as you need until pick-up."

"How far away are they?"

"Only twenty miles away at the most. Go."

Diaz motions to the squad. Fernanda wants to say something to Serena, but instead keeps her focus on the women. Serena and the Twins head back the way they came while the "train" heads northwest through the jungle.

The General and his military caravan are stopped on the other side of the jungle, facing Veracruz. With sensors, they know exactly where the slaves are heading: directly to them!

The General turns to the Tracker who is standing outside the vehicle, looking into the jungle with his own high-powered telescope. "Do you see anything?"

The Tracker says, "No, General. Not yet. But all we have to do is continue down the road and across the bridge. We'll be able to cut them off then."

"Good. Any escape routes?"

"All over, but they won't leave the women, and more than a

hundred slave women are not going to scale down cliffs or swing from tree vines like monkeys to escape. They will stay put. We'll get them. The liberators may scatter, but once we get the slaves, we can torch or machine-gun the jungle from the air."

The General is pleased. "Good. Let's get to the bridge and get the 'property' back and kill those liberators."

The narco-military reach the Grand Usumacinta Bridge in moments. It was built decades ago by the military, specifically for use in chasing cartels that were using the jungle to smuggle drugs and people. The cartels now use the bridge for their criminal activities.

The caravan stops again. Out of the twelve armored military SUVs, the General's vehicle is third from the back. The Tracker gets out of the General's vehicle again and aims his telescope into the jungle.

"I see them on the motion detectors. They're two miles out, General."

The General smiles. "Excellent." He motions to the driver. The Tracker remains outside the vehicle at the side of the cliff, still watching through his telescope.

The caravan begins across the long bridge. The view is spectacular: luscious jungle growth on the ground and surrounding mountains, the blue water of the river below.

The General's vehicle is about to drive onto the bridge when—
Boom!

The entire bridge explodes and nine of the vehicles drop more than sixty feet into the Usumacinta River. The General and his driver scream in horror. He remains in his seat, but all the men in his vehicle and the two remaining vehicles behind quickly exit to run to the edge of the cliff. There is nothing to do but watch the disaster.

The General looks to his right to see where the Tracker is, only to see the man's body fall off the cliff. *What happened?!* He looks left and is startled—his driver is lying dead on the ground, shot, outside the vehicle! He immediately jumps into the driver's side and closes the door. He jumps into the back seats of the vehicle and sees four more of his soldiers dead on the ground outside, also shot. He closes all the doors immediately and looks out the windows to the two vehicles behind him. He sees all his men on the ground.

The General realizes that he is the only surviving member of the caravan. He crawls back into the driver's seat and jumps, startled again. *Serena stares at him from outside the window with her high-powered rifle.*

He jumps again when he sees the Twins staring at him through the window of the passenger side, grinning at him with their knives tapping the glass.

He lifts his head; he hears something. It is his helicopters. "Yes!" he yells, laughing. They will kill the liberators. His smile disappears. They are not running or even moving. They continue to watch him through the windows.

The General looks up, ignoring Serena on the other side of the glass, and sees the approaching helicopters.

"Let me see you blow up my helicopters while they're in the air."

All three helicopters are blown out of the sky!

The General is in utter panic. "What's happened?! What's happened?!" He hears something else and notices from the passenger window a fleet of at least ten helicopters approaching.

He sits back in the driver's seat and closes his eyes. His entire army, his gunships, are gone in an instant, all his men dead.

The new helicopters hover directly over his vehicle. The noise and the turbulence gently rock his vehicle. The lead helicopter descends to his line of sight, all heavy guns aiming at him. He looks to either side and sees that Serena and the Twins are gone.

It's over. He opens the driver's side door slowly. The door is immediately pulled open and he's grabbed and thrown to the ground, his hands bound behind his back with rope by the Twins.

The lead helicopter lands and Father Marcos exits with four armed White Guardsmen. He walks directly to the General, whom the Twins have on his knees. Serena stands to his side.

"So this is the great slave catcher the cartels sent after us," Father Marcos says sarcastically. He leans down to look directly into the General's face. "They call you the General, but your rank is only that of a sub-lieutenant."

The General remains quiet. He is simply waiting to be shot.

Father Marcos looks at him with disgust. "*Plato o plomo*," he says. The age-old phrase to describe the almost genetic corruption within Mexico. The General is the epitome of the narco-government, its law enforcement, military, and government. "Silver and Lead" meant simply: "take our cartel bribes and work for us or end up dead, with a lead bullet to the head."

Father Marcos stands up and turns to the Twins. "Send him down to join his men."

The General is dragged to his feet by the Twins. "No! Wait! I have a 'get-out-of-jail card.'"

Father Marcos is annoyed. "You have nothing we want. You are a murderer of innocent people and a rapist-slaver of women. Go join your men at the bottom of the cliff."

The General shakes his head. "I never raped anybody." The Twins slap the back of his head. He flinches. "I'm not lying! And I do have what you want."

Father Marcos says, "You have nothing we want."

"You and the one-eyed woman can continue to save thousands of women, but with me, my help, you could save millions instead, beyond Mexico, into all the Americas, Spanish and English, from

Canada to South America. I've been working for these cartel bastards for years! I've been working military intelligence for years! I know *everything*. But you have to let me go and promise not to come after me."

Father Marcos says, "You'd say anything to save your evil life."

"I can prove it."

"First you wanted to kill us and now you want to help us."

The General glares at him. "I don't want to help you. I want to live, and if helping you means I live, then that's what I'll do. I'll give you everything, and then you will let me go and you will never see me again. The cartels killed all my men and forced me to work for them. Now you have killed all my men and I have to give you information to save my life. I will do this last thing and no one will ever see me again. I will not work for them or you ever again! You fight each other until the end of time. I want to live and die in peace. Do you want the information?"

Father Marcos stares at him for a while. "Of course, Sub-Lieutenant Lobo."

The General says, "Untie me and get me to a computer."

The evil man delivers. It would be as if during the original 19th-century Underground Railroad, they were given the intel to save not just sixty thousand or a hundred thousand slaves, but four million slaves in America or the eighty million slaves in the rest of the Spanish Americas at the time.

After he transfers the data to them, they let him go. He runs into the jungle and is never seen or heard from again by anyone who has ever known him.

The Rise of Father Marcos

"Don't be more religious than God. He didn't send an army of angels or a bolt of lightning to help you. He sent a humble priest born in scorpion country." — Sister Fernanda

Mexico City Federal Police Headquarters
8:07 a.m., 10 September 2094

Inspector Ramirez walks down the hall. Policemen, investigators, secretaries, and federal personnel pass him in every direction. He enters a private, empty hallway. He knocks on a door one time before opening it and entering.

"Inspector Ramirez." His boss motions for him to sit. Standing behind are two other men leaning against the wall. "When do you start?"

"We're leaving soon, sir. We have avoided any leaks to the press so far. I want to keep it that way. I won't set a time until we are about to leave."

"Go now."

Inspector Ramirez is puzzled. "Now? Today?"

The boss looks at his watch. "In five minutes. Now."

"Sir, most of my men are not even at the station now. I'd have to call them back—"

One of the shadow men speaks. "Your assault team is already assembled outside."

Ramirez looks at his boss. "May I ask what's going on?"

His boss looks at him directly. "This priest Marcos is growing in popularity and influence. If we don't act, politically, we may soon not be able to touch him at all."

Ramirez is indignant. "No one is above the law, sir. This priest thinks he's judge, jury, and executioner when it comes to people they unilaterally label criminals. He will be stopped and a lesson made out of him to others. They even want to make a reality show about him."

His boss cuts him off. "Ramirez, I don't give a damn about any of that. Get him today, because with the powerful friends he's making these days, he'll soon be able to make a phone call and have you and me demoted to scrubbing excrement from toilets. Get it done now." He looks at his watch again. "You have two minutes."

Lerdo City
3:04 p.m.

Ramirez rides shotgun in the armored police SUV, fifty vehicles behind it, five high-speed tanks following them, and two heavy helicopter gunships following in the air.

When he exited the police station and saw his assault team, his mouth dropped open. This was more firepower and manpower than they had ever used against the most violent cartels in Mexico. *Why is this kind of police and military power being thrown at this one priest?* He probably exaggerated a bit about Father Marcos's criminality back in the office, but this is over-kill. *Who were those men in the boss's office?*

This priest has made a lot of enemies in the Federal Police and the Ministerial Federal Police departments. Week-long exposés are still playing in the Mexican media, linking individual federal police and very high-ranking bosses with the cartel's murder for hire, slave trafficking, and drug running. The firestorm is still not over and there are rumors that future stories will also link officials in the Presidential Guard Corps and even the Presidential High Command to the cartels.

Ramirez can't worry about politics now. He has to arrest this priest without losing the lives of any of his men.

The caravan slows down as they enter the city limits of Lerdo. Ramirez hasn't been to the city in more than two years, but he can't believe his eyes. What had been empty plains is covered with houses and commercial shopping areas. It is no longer a little town, but a huge city.

Into view it comes: the splendid New Lerdo Church sitting on a hill overlooking the ever-growing city. It was apparently built by one of the super-wealthy Mexican families.

They increase their speed. He had been planning a secret night raid, but then the boss gave these crazy orders. The caravan stops.

At first they think they have reached normal congested street traffic, but Ramirez looks around. People are staring at them: the people sitting at the café, the man sitting on the steps of a store, the women watching out the window of a beauty spa, the children playing a game on the sidewalk, the old man walking back from the store; everyone stares at them with dirty looks.

Ramirez looks up, noticing that people are staring at them from second- and third-story windows. There are even people standing and watching from rooftops. Then he notices about twenty cowboys slowly approaching on horseback. All of them are carrying rifles.

The church bells ring. Ramirez has a sick feeling as he glances at his watch. It's doubtful they are having a church service at 3:27 in the afternoon on a Tuesday. It's a signal of some kind.

Ramirez is in charge of this assault team, but they are not his men. He has never worked with them before and knows nothing about them. Every assault team is different: its capabilities, personalities, idiosyncrasies.

"I bet every person knows we're coming for the priest, from here to Gomez Palacio. I'm not going to send men into serious danger."

"You're in charge, sir," the driver says. "But we can't just disobey orders."

Ramirez says, "We're the ones here. The bosses are sitting back in their air-conditioned offices. Let me try something." He dials the phone number on the dashboard screen interface. It rings twice.

"Inspector Ramirez, please hold," the woman's voice says quickly.

Ramirez and the driver look at each other.

"Inspector Ramirez, how can I help you?" The voice is familiar.

"Who is speaking?"

"This is Father Marcos. I hear you are on your way to see me, Inspector."

"Father Marcos, I have a warrant for your arrest. Will you come peacefully?"

A pause. "Ring, ring." The call disconnects.

"What does that mean?" Ramirez asks.

Another call rings in. The driver touches the button. "Yes," Ramirez says.

"Ramirez?"

He immediately recognizes the voice. "Yes boss, Ramirez here."

"The mission is canceled. Bring the team back to headquarters at once."

"But, sir. May I ask—" The call disconnects. Ramirez and the driver look at each other again. They turn the SUV around and lead the entire SUV caravan assault team back the way they had come. The high-speed tanks and helicopter gunships are already en route to base.

Ramirez shakes his head to himself, angry. At least the recall orders came from his boss so it won't be a blemish on his personal police record.

He learns later, well into the evening, that his boss was relieved of duty by Mexico City. Father Marcos was already ahead of them. He was not in the process of making the right friends with the Mexican wealthy elite, he had already done so. Señora Gustavo called the President's wife personally at the presidential residence at Los Pinos (they are on five charitable boards together). The President's wife called the Deputy Chief directly. The Deputy Chief called the Chief of Police of Durango City. The Chief of Police called Ramirez's boss directly. It was actually the Chief of Police of Durango who ordered the arrest, but someone else had to be the fall guy. It took two hours for the assault team caravan to get to Father Marcos's church in New Lerdo. It took five minutes of phone calls to stop the entire thing and have Ramirez's boss fired.

Gomez Palacio Private Residence
11:12 a.m., 3 November 2094

"Your breasts are too big," the political consultant says to Señora Pedro.

She glares at him. "They are natural and we're not paying you to comment on my mammary glands."

Señor Pedro is furious too. "I should punch you in the nose!"

The political consultant says, "No, you're paying me to win an election. To a lot of people, you will both be portrayed as Mexican-American 'carpetbaggers,' and you're a blond-haired, blue-eyed woman. If your husband was running in Mexico City or Central Mexico or any of the big cities, it would be fine. But he's not. He's running in the state of Durango, where a Mex-Am carpetbagger with a blond-haired, blue-eyed, busty Mex-Am wife won't play well. If you want to be the next Governor of Durango and you the First Lady, we need to pick up at least ten points. Shrink the breasts, dye the hair darker; win, and you can make them any size you want."

There is a group universally hated as much as the cartels and the wealthy in Mexico: Mex-Ams. Mexicans who had left for America decades ago for the economic dream of the United States, and whose Mexican-American descendants were returning to Mexico, buying up all the land, especially in the north, getting elected to local offices, and changing the laws to benefit their personal pursuits at the supposed expense of "real' Mexicans. They are looked upon as "carpetbaggers," not Mexican, but moving into the country and pretending to be so. One state even went so far as to pass a law banning "Mex-Ams" from buying land or holding any elective office, though it was later overturned in the courts. The hostility is real; they are viewed as American invaders with Spanish surnames.

And there is the old city-country rivalry. In the country, dark skin and dark hair equal real people. In the cities, it is blond hair, blue contacts, and—for women—rib-modification for an hourglass shape, breast augmentation, and calf and leg augmentation to be taller.

New Lerdo Church, Lerdo City
9:00 a.m., 2 January 2095

Father Marcos stands in front of his Sunday congregation with Señor Pedro and his wife. The crowd is even larger than usual.

"Ladies and gentleman, it seems inconceivable that there used to be a time in Mexico when the church itself was prohibited by law from participating in our great democratic process. They even prohibited us, as priests and nuns, from being in public in our religious clothes. If I stood before you and said that the "Pope said" or "Jesus said" to vote for someone, that would be wrong. The government, even today, tells us that the church cannot be involved in politics. Well, let them come and arrest me."

The crowd applauds.

"I am a voter and Mexican and with our state at a critical junction, we as Catholics have to make sure we have the right people in the Governor's mansion in our great state of Durango. I am not picking the most popular man as anointed by the media in Mexico City. I am personally supporting Señor Pedro for Governor because out of all four candidates, he is the only one who has worked with us closely when there were no cameras around, against the cartels and against the corrupt government. His wife Hermina has been a vocal and steadfast supporter of us, against the evil worldwide slave trade which has taken so many of our Mexican daughters from us. These are good people. These are the people I want to support, as the contrast between them and the other candidates is so great. I endorse Señor Pedro's candidacy and they also have this church's endorsement. I know this decision is controversial because even today, people—this very church too—feel we must stay out of politics. I respect that opinion. I agree. When the cartels and the corruption are out of our government, this church will get out of politics. But we're not there yet. Please join me in support of Señor Pedro for the Governor of Durango!"

Durango News: Latest Mexico Gallup Poll (Top 5)
Señor Calderon – 27% of likely voters
Señor Márquez – 25% of likely voters
Señor Los Santos – 11% of likely voters
Señor Pedro – 10% of likely voters

9 January 2095

After a barrage of paid media in Durango prominently featuring Father Marcos, Señor Pedro wins the special election for Governor of Durango. Señor Pedro received 55 percent of the votes; Señor Calderon, 32 percent; 13 percent for all other candidates.

Two days after Señor Pedro is sworn in as Governor of the state of Durango, Señor Ayende, the boss of Ramirez's boss, is fired.

New Lerdo Church
9:15 a.m., 13 July 2095

A long line of cars approaches: it is the Vatican people. The procession of black limousines stops at the front church entrance as members of the White Guardsman watch. Priests, dressed in black with white collars, hold the car doors open as others exit. The cardinal and bishop, dressed in red with white collars, walk into the main church entrance with their entourage of priests and bodyguards.

When they were here three years ago, they were at a meager, run-down church. Now the church is a unique, stark-white structure like the old cathedral Sacre Coeur in Paris, France before the Islamic occupation. The church is three times the size of the old one, and the parish grounds themselves are five times larger, not including the expanded living quarters and garden—all courtesy of one of the trillionaire families of Mexico.

The Vatican turned the parish over to a boy and expected him to disappear or be absorbed by the bureaucracy to become another nameless priest among thousands, never rising to any kind of distinction. They were so wrong. Father Marcos runs Durango. He got the current state Governor elected and now personally knows more of the super-elite than the President of Mexico does. Even the cartels avoid his territory.

Cardinal Cassiano has a completely different view of the rise of Father Marcos; he is Rome's Catholic superstar! The Cardinal thinks to himself how even Sister Maria is different. Before, she was a loyal, reliable, but meek woman. Now, though still humble in the world, she has a deep confidence about herself; she is the gatekeeper to Father Marcos. She leads the group—Cardinal Cassiano, Bishop Dominguez, and a third man she thinks she knows but isn't quite sure—to Father Marcos's office, which has an amazing view of the new city from its windows.

Sister Maria says, "Father Marcos will be right in. I will have the coffee brought in."

Cardinal Cassiano smiles. "Sister Maria, please, this Italian wants to have some nice Mexican alcohol. After all, this is a celebration of sorts."

Sister Maria smiles. "Tequila?"

Cardinal Cassiano touches his chest. "Ah, you do still love me, Sister."

She laughs and leaves the room. The men take their seats in the chairs but carefully study the spacious office. They notice on one side of the wall is a plaque with a quote from America's second president, Thomas Jefferson: "The Two Enemies of the People are Criminals and Government."

On another wall is an even bigger plaque:

An Armed Man is a Citizen. An Unarmed Man is a Subject.
A Gun in the Hand is Better Than a Cop on the Phone.
Know Guns, Know Peace, Know Safety. No Guns, No Peace, No Safety.
Cartels Love Gun Control; It Makes Their Jobs Safer.
Mexican Independence Would Never Have Happened With Gun Control.

Father Marcos surely isn't shy about expressing his secular philosophies. No doubt his White Guardsmen, all Texans from

America, were especially enamored with his gun-love. But the Father would probably just say, "I'll get rid of mine when the cartels get rid of theirs."

Bishop Dominguez remarks, "The people are already calling this place the Mexican Vatican." Cardinal Cassiano nods.

One of the Gray Men comes in with a tray of glasses, a small bowl of cut lemons, and tiny bottles of tequila. The elderly man puts the tray on the small table to the side.

"Ah, yes. Thank you, kind sir," Cardinal Cassiano says as he leads the other two men to the beverages. They help themselves and sit back down.

As if on cue, Father Marcos enters. The three men stand and greet him. Cardinal Cassiano gives a great bear hug. He shakes the hands of a grinning Bishop Dominguez and the third unknown man. They don't introduce him.

"I see you are an admirer of the Americans' Thomas Jefferson. Strange, considering his background," the Cardinal says.

They all sit, Father Marcos behind his desk.

Father Marcos smiles. "Like many great men and great thinkers, he had great flaws: slave owner, though he protested slavery, anti-Christian, though he claimed to be a Christian and attended church regularly. He was an extremely complex individual, but anyone who helps found one of the greatest nations in history, though much of that has been reversed in their tek-metropolises, has to be taken seriously. He was my kind of gun-toting, anti-corrupt government rabble rouser."

They all smile again.

Bishop Dominguez starts, "Father Marcos, there is so much to cover in this meeting. First, for a man as busy as the Pope himself, we thank you for being so open with your schedule to meet with us. This church is truly magnificent, a true testament to the glory of

God. I'm glad he blessed you by putting the people who helped you make it a reality in your path. We are very impressed with all the good works we hear you and your parish staff are doing for the people. When I remember back to how this area looked just two years ago and what you have accomplished in such a short time, all one can do is praise the glory of God."

Father Marcos says, "Thank you for your kind words, Bishop Dominguez. I never take credit for my accomplishments. It is only possible because of Him."

Cardinal Cassiano speaks. "Well, Father, now that we have gotten the pleasantries aside, you know that I'm the one whom God gave no diplomatic skills. This 'Cry of Lerdo.' I am told you led thousands of townspeople to kill not only every cartel-man in town, but the entire police force. And you have their dead bodies encased in some substance and publicly displayed as some kind of amusement park for tourists. How, as an ordained Roman Catholic priest, can you possibly justify these actions?"

Father Marcos takes a sip from his glass on the desk. "Cardinal, this is Mexico. We fight the Devil and devils, also known as the cartels. 'A lion seeking someone to devour' as said in 1 Peter 5:8, but our people are so unprepared to do daily battle with him. We are in a never-ending war on Earth against these devils, and as clergymen we must 'Put on the whole armor of God so that we are able to stand against the wiles of the devil,' as it says in Ephesians 6:11. Be prepared and defend ourselves, our families, our homes, and our country at all times. Either goodness rules or evil does. Hiding in a church with your nose stuck in the Bible is no longer acceptable for our great Church in the face of the daily evil in Mother Mexico."

The Cardinal interjects, "So angels must mimic the actions of the devils?"

Father Marcos's voice is very serious. "No, Cardinal, angels know you must do what is required to stop evil from doing evil again. Christians became irrelevant in America because generations were more interested in being liked by Pagans than following God. Christians became irrelevant in Mexico because generations were more interested in pretending that evil doesn't exist than in following God. I will follow God always, but I will not allow the cartels or slavers to prey on our good people. That is how you make faith relevant.

"Even so, our biggest threat has not been the cartels, it is Christian atheism. The casual Catholic, the Catholic who views Catholicism simply as synonymous with being Mexican. Goes to mass on Sunday, then sins away or is spiritually irrelevant in the world from Monday to Saturday. That is the root of our problem. How can we try to preach on Sunday when the devil's foot soldiers are killing, raping, enslaving people every other day in between? God hates evil. God hates slavery. And He doesn't want any one of His children, whether they've accepted Him or not, to suffer under the Devil's henchmen. That is my mandate. Not just talk, but do.

"There is even civil law to support it: Existence Destiny. The people have a right to exist without being murdered or brutalized, and if there is no government to protect them, then the people take that right back into their own hands. When the people are safe, then and not before are their hearts and minds open to hearing anything about God. He didn't place me in this world to perpetuate the status quo of Mexico, but to be one of His revolutionaries for change, like Noah, Moses, and Peter before me. More importantly, it is and has never been about me. I work at all times for the people and I'm always on the lookout for the devil, even in me, which is why I can look Jesus in the eye at any time. Anything else I can answer for you, Cardinal?"

The Cardinal sits quietly for a moment. Bishop Dominguez

looks at him nervously. The third man simply sits quietly with his hands clasped on his lap.

"Father Hidalgo, whom you invoked the name of—" the Cardinal begins.

"Father Hidalgo, I'm not. There will be no massacres of innocent people or skin-color wars on my watch. Keep the cartels and the corrupt government out of my city and I will be as quiet as a church mouse." Father Marcos takes another sip of his water. "But I will go anywhere on the planet to rescue slaves. I'm curious, Cardinal, what talk do you give to the hundreds of narco-priests in Mexico?"

Cardinal Cassiano smiles. "Very similar, instead of chiding them for killing cartel-men, I chide them for collaborating with them."

Father Marcos asks, "Did I pass your test?"

Cardinal Cassiano says, "I think I want to give you a good grade, but we will have to wait until the end of the school year."

"Fair enough."

"Father Marcos, you have to understand that the Church has never had a formal strategy on how to deal with cartels in the Spanish Americas. Look how long it took to deal with the sex scandals. And the resistance to action has not only been from Mexican clergy, but even from the people. They yell at us that this is how things are done in Mexico, that their work in the church should be judged separately from their collaboration with and financing of the cartels. I once had a high-ranking Bishop tell me to my face, and I admit I can be an intimidating man, 'You don't tell us about our cartels and we won't tell you about your Mafia in Rome.'" He laughs. "Mafia? I told him, 'There aren't any real Mafia left. They died off and their descendants became lazy, rich hedonists.'"

"Cardinal, I completely understand the Church's difficulty in the matter, our war in Africa not being the least of them. Overseeing the leadership of Catholics all over the world is like trying to herd cats in one direction. I understand the complexity."

Cardinal says, "Thank you, Father Marcos. I know you understand. The Church is a franchise, not a dictatorship."

"Cardinal, how long will you be staying with us?"

"We have to return to Mexico City, but we wanted to stop here first. If we went there first with all the dog-and-pony show ceremonies, who knows how long they would have delayed us. Bishop Dominguez and I will be leaving, but I did want to know if I could impose on your hospitality to put my man up for a few weeks." He points to that third man. "This is Mr. Niccolo."

Father Marcos studies him. So this is Niccolo. The Sicilian he had heard so many rumors about, but didn't know which were true. All he knew for sure is that Niccolo was part of the very inner circle of the Pope. He is a man in his late forties with green eyes and is naturally bald. Nowadays, hair can be grown and everyone in this materialistic, vain world does it except for Faithers. Who would have guessed that baldness would become one of the tell-tale signs of a religious person?

The rumors are that he is the "fixer" for the Vatican, hinting at some kind of illegal, old-Mafia-styled assassin. Others said he was the Vatican's special advisor on all matters of consequence that involved governments and heads of state. Others said he was the head of covert intelligence for the Vatican. The people who did know exactly what he did for the Pope gave him the utmost deference. Some people said he was the only person on the planet who never had to make an appointment to see the Pope.

"Nice to meet you, Mr. Niccolo."

"It is a pleasure to meet you as well, Father Marcos. I hope my strong Italian accent doesn't make my Spanish too hard to understand."

"Not at all. Your Spanish is excellent. And you will hear many accents and dialects on the streets of New Lerdo. We have Mexicans living here from all parts of the country and the continent. We'll gladly see to your accommodations."

Cardinal Cassiano says, "Good. Can you have Sister Maria take care of him now?" In other words: Father Marcos, I want to speak to you even more privately.

Father Marcos presses a button on his desk and Sister Maria appears at the door. "Sister Maria, this is Mr. Niccolo, the Cardinal's guest. He will be staying with us indefinitely."

Sister Maria nods. "Yes, Father, I will see to it." Niccolo stands and extends his hand. Father Marcos stands too and shakes his hand again. Niccolo follows Sister Maria out of the room.

Bishop Dominguez starts to leave too. "I will see you both outside." He walks out of the room and closes the door. They are now alone.

Cardinal Cassiano looks at Father Marcos and smiles. "You've done quite a lot in two years. Many in Rome are still not able to believe it. What are your long-term plans, Father? I hear you've even gotten involved in politics and you're getting people elected to high office."

Father Marcos says, "My goal is simple. Serve God."

"That can mean anything and nothing."

"A cartel-free Mexico, Cardinal, for all God's children. A Mexico free of all types of slavery, all thirty-one states."

"And what will Father Marcos do in this free Mexico in the near future?"

"The exact same thing I'm doing now. Church services by day, rescue slaves by night. Nothing else. And if I can get an ally into the Mexican Presidency, then good. Why shouldn't the Church do so? The cartels have been getting their people elected for decades."

"You do know the higher you fly, the more people will try to shoot you down from the sky?"

"Yes, Cardinal. I am a very cautious man. A sentence I know you will appreciate: I keep my friends close and my enemies even closer."

The Cardinal smiles and laughs. He pats Father Marcos on the shoulder and walks to the door. Father Marcos follows. "Well, I'm off to Mexico City. I so love to travel, but I so hate to fly."

Father Marcos says, "Do I need any special instructions on Mr. Niccolo?"

The Cardinal opens the door and turns to him. "No." He graciously shakes his hand and walks out, seeing Sister Maria. "Ah, Sister Maria, you came back for me. You are too good to me."

Father Marcos watches from the doorway. The Cardinal doesn't turn back once. Sister Maria leads him out of the main offices toward the parking area.

Why is Mr. Niccolo here in my church?

Mr. Blond is the head of all New Lerdo Church security and with his White Guardsmen are Father Marcos's own Secret Service. The joke on the street is that the soft Caucasian boys guard the Pope in Rome, but the scary Caucasian boys guard Father Marcos in Mexico.

Rodrigo, almost fifteen years old, is head of New Lerdo Church intelligence and with his Lost Boys has eyes in every corner of New Lerdo and Gomez Palacio. No person by foot, by vehicle, or by aircraft could approach the church without him knowing.

The Hammer and the Watch-Glass are their code names in Durango.

They both sit in their secure joint offices. Mr. Blond sips from his cup, a congenital chain coffee drinker. Rodrigo has a big glass of soda next to him. Mr. Blond hands him a tablet and Rodrigo flips through the photos on the screen.

They make a good team, and Rodrigo has come to respect him

as much as the Father. Mr. Blond is smart. When his White Guardsman arrived in town, he went to every home and every business and introduced himself, shook hands, and handed out his card. Country people don't like strangers, but introduce yourself and start a conversation, and you're not a stranger anymore.

For them, the cornerstone of being one step ahead of the cartels and the government is information, human intelligence, not who has the most men or the most guns or even tek. Even before Rodrigo or Blond, Father Marcos had far more operatives than the cartels did, which is why he was so good. The delivery man who saw you go into a particular café, the three-year-old across the street who saw you at a particular store, etc. That's how it is done. In the real world, by the time there is the confrontation, you have already lost because you are not in control. It's avoiding the confrontation or having it happen when *you* want it.

Rodrigo glances at the last photos. "I'll find out who they are."

"Okay."

"Foreigners."

"I know that. They're new and moving into the area."

"No." Rodrigo realizes that Spanish is not Mr. Blond's native tongue, so true meanings of words can be off. "Foreigners. Not from the Americas."

Mr. Blond looks at the pictures on the tab. "How can you possibly know that?"

Rodrigo looks up. "The same way you know when you're fighting a man, which arm he's going to try to hit you with, or which leg he's going to try to kick you with. These people are European. Most likely West-Europa area, not Islamic though."

Mr. Blond looks at the tab again. "Europeans? Then there's a lot of them."

The New Lerdo area is in the midst of a massive Mexican real estate boom. People far and near are flocking to the region to live on lands where the cartels have no control and the state government is not corrupt. People are moving in from other parts of Mexico, Central America, South America, and even the United States. Mr. Blond monitors every group moving into the region, and it is Rodrigo's job to find out exactly who they are. New people mean new potential threats.

"Should we tell the Father?" Rodrigo asks.

"We don't have anything to tell him yet."

"Yeah, but he likes to take little road trips into areas where new people are moving in."

"He's not still doing that, is he?"

Rodrigo realizes that he has revealed a secret. "I gotta go." Rodrigo bolts out of the room.

"Rodrigo, you have to discourage the Father from doing that! He must have security with him at all times!"

7:57 p.m.

On the roof outside of Father Marcos's private residence, Niccolo is dressed in all black. He sets up a myriad of sensors and then turns on a small monitor. He sees Father Marcos enter his premises, grab a tablet from the table, and leave. Niccolo will be done with his secret work in less than an hour.

**Outside of Lerdo, Mexico
9:15 a.m., 1 August 2095**

In the ancient Shakespeare play *Henry V*, King Harry would walk out among his soldiers in disguise so that he could really know what they were thinking, both their joys and their fears. Father Marcos walks through a new residential area being built twenty miles outside the city; his disguise is a big sombrero to hide most of his facial features, dark glasses, and his civilian clothes, black but no collar. He even sports a big, fake mustache and walks with a walking stick, which is really a concealed rifle.

He smiles and waves to anyone he walks past or sees in the street. Children play as the construction of new homes takes place on one side of the street; on the other side, people move into homes finished no more than a couple of weeks ago.

He nears a family talking in a language that is not Spanish. Nothing unusual, there are hundreds of languages spoken in Mexico and there are, of course, many dialects of Spanish, sometimes so distinct that a person from Brazil and a person from Southern Mexico could both be speaking Spanish and not have a clue as to what the other was saying. The family sees him approach and stops talking.

"Good morning Señor, Señora, children," he says to them.

They nod. They clearly don't even understand "hello" in Spanish. Father Marcos smiles anyway and walks past them.

Suddenly the woman says, "Good morning to you too, sir. Sorry for being rude. We've been traveling and moving all day long. It's really a paradox. The more you work, the more work there is to do." She laughs.

Father Marcos looks back at her. First they were speaking some other language, then they couldn't understand simple Spanish, and now the woman speaks not just great Spanish but is using college words like "paradox" that the average Mexican would never use.

The woman stares back now, obviously aware that he is suspicious. She smiles, nods, and walks away into the house. The man gathers the children and they, too, disappear inside.

Father Marcos looks around and notices that all the people and children he had noticed before are gone. Everyone is inside their homes. He can see curtains move in windows and from door windows; he is being watched.

He turns to head back to his car. *Niccolo!* The Sicilian waits.

"Father, good morning."

"Good morning, Niccolo." He walks to him. "I remember now."

"What is that?"

"What Italian sounds like. It's been a long time since I heard it spoken. Until now."

Niccolo says nothing.

"I don't know what you and the Cardinal are up to. But I will find out. I do not like secrets and I don't like surprises. I am a very boring man that way." Father Marcos continues past him.

"Father, there are no conspiracies against you here. These are good, simple people."

Father Marcos says, "Yes, quite the paradox."

Niccolo watches him. He hopes the Father will give him enough time to finish his work.

The Day of the Scorpion

"Behold my golden claws, my silver legs, my opal eyes, my pulsating stinger, drip-drip with venom. I look up at you from under your bed. I look down at you from above your head." — Children's scorpion song

New Lerdo Church, Mexico
2:36 p.m., 15 September 2095

"Don't get me wrong, Father," the woman says. "I really respect you and what you are doing. I wish I could support the Church as much as I support you, but they are basically sexist."

Father Marcos says, "Are you making a joke? Do you protest Mexican tele?"

The woman is unsure what to say. "What?"

"You just told me that the Church is sexist because it doesn't allow women to be priests, but when I ask you about Mexican tele, which is so sexist I don't know how they are allowed to broadcast, you don't know what I'm talking about. That seems curious. Señora, I'm so glad that you are as passionate about women's rights as I am, so can I sign you up? In fact, will you lead the group?"

The woman again does not know what to say. "Father, what group do you mean?"

Father Marcos says, "The church's Noble Catholic Women Society. It will fight against the degrading of women in the media and music. Our girls need great role models, like the female leadership of this church and working woman executives like you."

The woman says, "I guess I walked right into your trap."

Father Marcos smiles. "You were doomed from the start. Señora, you're supposed to be smart. You went to college!"

She laughs. "Shows you how bad university education is these days. Okay, Father. I'll run your group as long as it's not just me."

Father Marcos says, "Thank you, Señora Chacon. Also, if it helps your feminist ego any, my mother always said, 'The man may be the head of the household, but the woman is the neck.'"

Another woman, standing at her side, says, "Yes Father, you put my sister in her place. But Father, I just want you to know that when they allow Catholic priests to marry, call me. Everybody else can marry, even animals. It's the priests' turn now. Don't forget me, Father."

Father Marcos laughs. "Yes, Señorita, I'll let you know the moment they let me know." He walks briskly to his meeting.

The general staff meeting: Sister Maria, nuns, deacons, lay staff, and volunteers are gathered to recap the week and plan the next. At the moment, they laugh hysterically with each other. Food and juice drinks are everywhere; not too much work is getting done at the moment.

6:36 p.m.

The last meeting of the day is over and Father talks to Sister Maria in one of the general offices.

"I need your advice about Niccolo. What do you know about him? What does he do for the Vatican?"

"You've heard all the same rumors I have, Father."

"But you have the special connections in Rome."

"They never say. But I do know that the Cardinal is on our side and Niccolo is working for him. The Cardinal wouldn't do anything against us, so neither will Niccolo."

"I wonder if this is a part of a Cloyne investigation."

Sister Maria laughs. "The sex police? They made those inquiries about you a long, long time ago."

The Cloyne Report was released by pre-Islamic Ireland's government eighty-one years ago, blasting the Church with allegations of sex abuse by priests and a cover-up by the Vatican, stating that "the Vatican chose to focus on the church rather than the children abused by its clergy and shielded by its leaders." It was one of many reports issued in many countries, but this particular one was resurrected by the Church itself to atone for the refusal of Catholic clergy at the time to meet with abuse victims and an early Vatican directive that instructed bishops to keep abuse cases secret.

However, the Church went from ignoring allegations and irresponsibly dealing with these cases to such an aggressive investigation of allegations of clergy sexual abuse and monitoring of the sexual exploits of clergy that the "sex police," as many Catholics grew to call them, actually accelerated the very thing they were set up by the Vatican to stop—the dissolution of both the American and Western European Catholic Orders. In light of these anti-pedophile protocols, only the African and Mexican Catholic Orders thrived.

"I guess I passed then."

"Yes, Father, you did. You look, but you don't touch the ladies."

They laugh.

7:49 p.m.

Father Marcos walks up the stairs to his private residence; the end of a long day. He'll shower and read the Bible for a little while before going to sleep. There is a beep from the intercom. He pushes a button on his wristband. "Yes."

Sister Maria's voice: "Father, it's the Cardinal on your personal line."

He puts his ear-set in his right ear. "Yes."

"Ah, Father Marcos, I'm glad I caught you. Even the Pope doesn't keep the long hours you do." The Cardinal laughs. "I heard you ran into Niccolo today."

"Yes, Cardinal."

"Father Marcos, let me assure you that Niccolo is working on a special project for me personally. It is critical that nothing is done to impede him in any way. Please, as a favor to me, I'd like you to allow him to do what he needs to do. I cannot divulge anything further, at least at the present time."

"Understood, Cardinal. I will cooperate fully. I'm sure you will tell me everything when ready."

"Yes, Father. We will. Thank you. Have a good night." The line disconnects.

Father Marcos does trust the Cardinal, maybe because Sister Maria does. He'll ignore his suspicions for now.

12:05 a.m.

Father Marcos can't get back to sleep. It happens. The mind just doesn't want to shut down. He stares at the ceiling. The moonlight gives a nice glow to the room.

He gets out of bed and walks to the balcony door to look out. Mr. Blond hated most of the layout of the Church, and especially his residence, from a security standpoint. He never liked the Father to go out on the balcony, no matter how far it was from any possible sniper and no matter how many surveillance vid-cams watched the space. He is about to open the screen door and walk onto the balcony for the view and cool breeze, but he hears something.

He opens his bedroom door and walks down the stairs to the ground level of his residence. *Where did the sound come from?* He hears a noise again and opens the main door a crack. Outside is the long hallway to his private glass-covered patio. He always felt the residences were far too big, but when a trillionaire builds a massive church and gives it to you, you can't exactly be critical. At the hallway door he peeks out the window and opens it. Above, there is a bird fluttering madly, trying to get out but blocked by the see-through glass-domed roof.

Two of the White Guardsmen finish their inner patrol of the east part of the parish. At night they carry their guns in their hands rather than keeping them concealed in their jacket holsters. The guns are set to first shoot a stun bullet; all other shots are live rounds. They walk from the inside to the outside as one of them stops briefly to pull a cig from his pocket, put it to his lips, and inhale. He exhales a mist of pure white vapor and then starts walking again.

Neither of them notices the massive concrete wall rise without a sound, blocking off the entrance they just passed through and every window.

At the northern part of the parish complex, two other White Guardsmen walk casually on their scheduled foot patrol. The work is simple: make the foot rounds of the entire church every hour, check each door and window. Vid-cams watch every corner of the church, but Mr. Blond insists on the human touch. They are armed with machine guns.

The two of them get to the main church office building, which also leads to the parish residences, and open the main door. One of them starts to walk through, but stops suddenly. In English: "What the—!"

Mr. Blond is woken by his wife. For a security man, he sleeps so soundly that he would be undisturbed even by a bomb explosion. His wife has to literally drag him out of bed to wake him.

"They're calling you!" she yells.

He grabs the phone and listens. "Yeah? What? Christ! Have everyone waiting! I'm there!"

When Blond arrives, there are dozens of his men gathered, armed with machine guns. The lead man points his attention to the door. Blond walks up to the door; there is no entrance, but a solid concrete barrier.

"It's the same throughout the entire complex," the man says. "All the door entrances and windows are covered by concrete barriers."

Blond taps it, then pounds it. "This is not part of the building security protocols. Did you try to reset the building?"

"We're locked out completely."

Most modern residences today are smart-houses. Temperature can be programmed to remain at a constant degree or adjusted to the weather outside. Lights can be programmed to turn on automatically when you enter a room and turn off when you leave. Smart-buildings can be configured with great complexity and synced with other devices, or even robots. Some even refer to them as "alive" because the programming is so sophisticated, but no one uses the term A.I. (artificial intelligence). That phrase scared people; in too many sci-fi movies the A.I. killed people. The building is "smart" and for some unknown reason this smart-building has decided to do its own thing.

Security for the church grounds includes a wide variety of

barriers: chain-link fences, pole barricades, or solid steel barricades. Nowhere, however, are there supposed to be solid concrete barriers, so how did they get here?

Blond asks, "Vid-cams?"

"All disconnected along with all communications. We can't see in, we can't call in."

Blond asks, "Who's in the residences besides the Father?"

"He's the only one in there."

Blond yells, "Priority red! Blow the entire wall down if you have to, but get to the Father now!"

Father starts to go back inside, but then hears more sounds. He looks up at the glass dome roof of the patio. There are now three birds fluttering around. He then notices two others flying up and hears noises from others in the shadows. *Where are they coming from?*

He closes the door and almost instantly one of the birds crashes into it, startling him. Instinctively, he opens the door, expecting to see an injured bird lying on the ground. *On the ground is not a bird, but a pigeon-sized scorpion with what look to be wings!*

There are fluttering sounds coming right at him. He slams the door shut and runs just as seemingly dozens of them hit the door. Already at the end of the hallway, he slams the other door behind him.

Jumping three steps at a time, he is up the stairs. He runs down the short hall and into his bedroom, then slams its door. Something whizzes by his head and hits the balcony glass doors, disappearing behind the curtains.

Father Marcos stands there, paralyzed. One of them has followed him right back to his bedroom! As a native Duranguense, he has seen plenty of scorpions in his life. As a boy, he played the games that town boys play with them, got stung half a dozen times, and even did the traditional scavenger hunting to sell scorpions at the market. He was never scared of them. Tonight he is terrified. There were no such things as flying scorpions, but one is in his room.

There is a thud on his bedroom door: another one of the creatures. Another thud and then another and another. *This is impossible! How do they know where I am?*

He runs to his bed and reaches under the pillow. Out comes his gun and he aims it at the moving curtain. He walks closer to the balcony and freezes.

There is something outside on the balcony itself, huge and moving. It's too dark to see it clearly.

Father Marcos walks back slowly. *I have to get into the panic room now!*

Panic rooms are commonplace nowadays. A secret, secure room that a person or family could escape into, away from any kind of danger: home invaders, gangs, fire, etc.

Suddenly the external bright lights illuminate the entire balcony as if it were day and not 1:00 a.m. Father Marcos is aghast. The thing on the balcony is another scorpion—*the size of large dog with two stinger tails!* The creature is stunned by the bright light and in an instant is gone, jumping up and out of view, to the roof like a kangaroo.

He runs back to push the secret button to his panic room when he suddenly hears the glass of the balcony door shatter. He turns to see the pigeon-sized flying scorpion lying on the ground on its back, not moving. He turns back to what he was doing: extending his hand to push the panic room button. *Pop!* He yanks back his hand in excruciating pain. He's been shot.

Niccolo jumps through the balcony window and into the room. He lunges at Father Marcos. *He's trying to kill me!* Father Marcos immediately hits the open button with his other hand. The door begins to open as Niccolo grabs him by the t-shirt and pulls him close.

"Let me go!" Father Marcos yells.

Niccolo holds his face an inch from Father Marcos's. "Run with me now if you want to live!" Niccolo grabs him by the arm and faces him toward the balcony. "Run!"

The thuds hitting the door—must be a swarm of the flying scorpions—are now so loud it is as if they are going to bust down the door. From the panic room, he hears the bone-chilling scream of an animal. But it isn't any animal he has ever heard before.

Niccolo grabs Father Marcos; they run out to the balcony and jump over its wall. They don't see it behind them: large stingers dart out from the bedroom, barely missing them. A concrete barrier rises, closing off the entire bedroom.

His residence is only two stories, but the way the church is built on the hill, his room is actually at the farthest point of the complex, the steep face of the hill itself. They plunge twenty stories down.

Father Marcos was trying to think of something before, but nothing focuses the mind like jumping off a cliff without a parachute. He glances at Niccolo, who is so calm. He feels something touch his back and then it seems like two other arms wrap themselves around his waist. Scared, he tries to see what it is. Another robot jet-pack wraps its robotic arms around Niccolo. Their rapid fall slows to a hover and they softly touch down on the ground.

Mr. Blond and White Guardsmen run to them.

"Boss!" Rodrigo is among them. Niccolo removes the jet-pack from Father Marcos first before taking off his own. Father Marcos drops to the ground on his knees.

Niccolo yells, "He needs medical attention for his hand."

Rodrigo asks, "What happened to his hand?"

Niccolo answers, "I shot it. I was trying to stop him from opening the panic room."

Blond says, "Why? What's in the panic room?"

Niccolo answers, "Something that shouldn't exist."

Blond says to his men, "Let's blow a hole through the main entrance and go room by room. Kill anything that moves!" To Niccolo: "What are we dealing with?"

Niccolo answers, "Scorpions."

Blond and his men stare at him. The medic arrives and immediately starts treating the wound to the Father's hand. Blond says, "Then we'll stomp them to death."

Niccolo shakes his head and says, "Not these scorpions."

Father Marcos stands with the medic still working on his hand. Looking at Blond, he says, "Scorpions. First type: bird-sized with leathery wings, able to fly. Second type: dog-sized with two long stinger tails, able to leap at least six feet. Third type: unseen, but makes strange, unnatural screaming sounds. Assume it's some scorpion-creature too, and even deadlier since it was in my panic room."

They stare at him in disbelief. Blond asks, "Excuse me, since we're new to living in Mexico, is this for real?"

Niccolo says, "Unfortunately, yes. The creatures tried to kill us."

Father Marcos continues, "Assume the creatures are everywhere, have access to the entire parish complex. They must not be allowed to get out into the city. We have to stop them, whatever it takes. My God…" He suddenly realizes. "…that swarm of flying scorpions. If they escape into the sky…into the city…"

They all look at each other. The White Guardsmen are not afraid of anything—cartels, terrorists, gangs—but those are everyday monsters; this is something altogether different. Blond touches his ear-set. "Are you in the air?"

"Yes, I'm above the residence now." A voice booms through the speaker.

They look up to see a hovering white helicopter in silent mode. Blond says into the ear-set, "What I'm going to say to you next will seem crazy, but take every word dead serious. Start a recon pattern and what you're looking for are—"

The voice yells, "Oh my God! What's that?!"

They all look up at the helicopter again to see one of the dog-sized scorpions sailing through the air toward it. The helicopter swerves away and the scorpion-creature falls straight down toward them.

Blond yells in English, "Light that up!"

The White Guardsmen open fire with their machine guns. Niccolo pulls Father Marcos back. The creature is shot to pieces and all that hits the ground is its disembodied two tail stingers and chunks of what used to be its body.

They all stare at the remains of the scorpion-creature for what seems to be ages.

Father Marcos looks at Niccolo. "How did you know?"

"We have many sources around the world and we had reason to believe that there was a plot to kill you and destroy your new city. I was sent to uncover the plot, find out who and when. I was also to make sure you were never alone in your residences. I slept in a secret room above your bedroom. Only Mr. Blond knew. I planted sensors in and around your room: motion, infrared, night, et cetera. But it was the ultraviolet and motion-imaging sensors that showed them clear as day at around midnight. I saw them come out from deep inside the residences, from everywhere."

Blond says, "Sensors? You didn't tell me about that."

Father Marcos asks, "How long have you known about this plot?"

Niccolo says, "Nine months."

Blond to his men: "Let's move!"

"No, wait." Father Marcos looks down at the ground and seems to freeze. "It will blow like a volcano."

Blond asks, "What is that?"

Rodrigo shakes his head. "Saint San Jorge never saw monsters like this!" He refers to the patron saint protecting children against scorpions.

Father Marcos directs, "Rodrigo, evacuate everyone in the city, away from the church, at least a five-mile radius. I don't care how you do it. But if you don't, there will be a lot of dead people."

Rodrigo is shaking. He is scared enough just talking about the scorpion-creatures, but to know that there are many more is unnerving. He runs as fast as he can, already dialing his men on his e-pad.

Blond says, "Father, we have to go now. We have no idea when these barriers will release and the creatures will be free to escape into the city. I already have the entire parish complex surrounded, but we need to send teams inside."

Niccolo stares at him. "'It will blow like a volcano.' What does that mean?"

"Several months ago, we picked up a strange conversation from one of the cartel families. One of our taps. We didn't know what it meant then, but I understand the words now." Father Marcos shakes his head. "This plot is truly satanic. It's the entire hill."

Blond stares at him. "I don't understand."

Father Marcos clarifies. "The hill. The hill is an anthill. But instead of ants, it's these scorpion-creatures."

All the White Guardsmen look to the ground under their feet. Blond touches his ear-set. "Priority evacuation now! Pull back to the base of the hill! Get off the hill!" Blond and his squad create a protective circle around the Father. Everyone runs.

Gathered at the bottom of the hill, at the bottom of the church complex, the White Guard army grows as men off duty arrive with more SUVs and armored vehicles. The sky above the church fills with white helicopters.

Blond says, "This is not a plot we've ever seen before. It means this was planned a long time ago. It means the construction crew that built the church had to be part of the plot, even if they didn't personally know they were." He looks at the Father, "Do you know which cartel did this?"

"I do."

Niccolo adds, "The cartels may have done this, but another force set the plot in motion."

Father Marcos looks at him. "What outside force tells the cartels what to do?"

Niccolo intentionally ignores the question. To Blond, "Why can't you hack in and take back control of the smart-building?"

Blond answers, "We don't control the 'brain' anymore. It's an unknown foreign A.I. We can't even find an entry point, so it must be self-contained and shielded. Damn thing locked the building down with the concrete barriers, shut off all electronics, and programmed to seal Father in the building with the scorpion-creatures."

Niccolo says, "But I don't think the program is done."

Blond looks at him. "Isn't killing Father the program's mission?"

"No, it's the start of the mission. Father is supposed to be the first victim, but far from the last. The second victim is supposed to be all of you and your men, because you would inevitably go in after him. Remember, you are not supposed to know that these creatures are inside. The program believes that all you know is that the building is sealed with Father inside."

Father Marcos says, "Kill us and then the city."

Blond and the men look at him. "This is more than a cartel

assassination plot. This sounds like terrorists, but much, much more. Niccolo, you never did answer Father when he asked you about a force directing these cartels. What force?"

Niccolo says, "Let's deal with one satanic force at a time."

The concrete barrier blocking access to the main entrance explodes. The dust cloud billows everywhere and then begins to settle. A dead walker approaches, walking to the entrance through the cloud, a simple humanoid robot like those used by law enforcement, military, and security companies. In English they are just called "walkers," but in Spanish that term is used for street prostitutes. Dead walkers, equipped with real-time surveillance optics, walk into a building or any area to make sure it's safe. Another dead walker emerges, then another; several more follow, all with yellow flashlight eyes.

Other dead walker squads enter the north, the west, and the east entrances.

Blond, Niccolo, and Father Marcos watch the multiple monitors from their command center RV.

The first dead walkers walk to the Father's residence. They burst through the doors to the glass-domed patio area and instantly are enveloped by a swarm of flying scorpions. The creatures must be attracted to heat. Had they been real people, they would have been stung to death in seconds.

The dead walker squad moves forward, down the hall, up the stairs, with a swarm of flying scorpions ramming and stinging their metal frames violently. The robots push through Father's bedroom door and the first robot is hit with such force that it crashes into the wall, breaking off its head. Its eye-cam goes dead.

The remaining dead walkers can see the new scorpion-creature: it is massive, the size of a two-seater car with long tentacles ending in foot-long stingers. Its tentacles stab, crush, and whip, destroying all the remaining dead walkers.

They watch the monitors. Blond says into his ear-set, "Send all of them in now."

More dead walkers enter the church from all four entrances, all armed with flamethrowers.

The ground begins to shake. Muffled explosions are heard from within the hill. The main church begins to fall apart and the entire parish complex begins to sink into the ground. Everything disappears, crashing to the bottom of the hill from within.

A massive swarm of flying scorpions escape into the sky. Dog-sized scorpions jump out of the sinkhole and down the hill toward everyone. They then hear the sickening screams and see massive bundles of stinger tentacles reach out.

Blond yells into his ear-set in English, "Light them up napalm-style!"

The hovering helicopters spray the air with fuel mist. The main one ejects a grenade and all the helicopters jet away. The bomb explodes and the sky is set on fire. That is the first explosion. The next explosions are of every flying scorpion burning to a crisp, bursting, and falling to the ground.

The SUV gun-vehicles shoot a barrage of missiles into the center of the sinkhole. The free-standing White Guardsmen machine-gun every approaching dog scorpion. The missiles explode and the entire site is vaporized in a rapid succession of blinding orange light. It's over.

Blond says, "We need to relocate everyone to a temporary safe location and quarantine this entire area. It will take ages, but we need to survey the entire area and make sure none of the creatures survived."

Father Marcos shakes his head. "Yes, but we're not going anywhere. We're going to rebuild right here."

Blond objects. "This site is not safe, Father."

Niccolo says, "That church took fifty million and a year to build."

Father Marcos says, "Yes, and the replacement church will cost twice as much. I don't care if we have to replace every inch of dirt for ten miles around, we're rebuilding right here. Neither these scorpion-creatures, nor their devilish creators, are running us off our land.

"The people who did this will regret it. We'll unite all of Mexico in the rebuilding. They hit us with this Day of the Scorpion. We'll hit back with another Day of the Demon."

Niccolo gives him a stern look. "Don't even joke about that, Father. You know nothing about that day."

"Niccolo, I have one word for you: Russian."

The Sicilian realizes that he does know.

Father Marcos says, "Let's get our church rebuilt. Our cartel friends will be dealt with later. All that matters is that they think we can retaliate in kind. Fear will do the rest."

Mexico City, Mexico
1:32 p.m., 20 November 2095

The ruthless cartel super-boss, El Angel, sits in a conference room with men sitting around the massive table. Father Marcos did have the church rebuilt. They had flown in dirt from the birthplace of Saint Juan Diego and the Virgin of Guadalupe, of all places, with endless media coverage. New construction crews rebuilt the New Lerdo Church in sixty days, working nonstop, twenty-four hours a day.

Father Marcos used the Day of the Scorpion incident to rally all of Mexico to his cause in rebuilding the New Lerdo Church and against the cartels. Governors across the country publicly condemned the cartels and even the President gave a national address promising to wipe out the cartel "disease" of Mexico. Father Marcos is now a national cult hero.

"All we did is make him more powerful!" El Angel says with disgust.

There is a beep on the e-pad of one of his men, an email. Beeps follow on the e-pads of all the men. El Angel looks at his e-pad and clicks on the email. It is not a coincidence that they all received the same email to their super-secret numbers.

His face contorts in horror. One of the men reading his email says, "He knows it was us."

Another man jumps to feet. "The Church Man is calling the demon on us!"

The New Lerdo Church, Mexico
11:30 p.m., 21 November 2095

Father Marcos raises his glass to toast the occasion. "The most important thing in the physical world…is family. I may get the attention and accolades, but it's you, my family, that really deserves the credit, because without God, I am nothing, and without you, my family, I am nothing." His eyes tear up.

The private gathering celebrates the opening of the New Lerdo Church. Sister Serena and the Twins stand with Father Marcos and Sisters Fernanda and Angelita, while Deacon Juan Carlos stands with the three elderly gentlemen, the Gray Men. Sister Maria stands with Mona Lisa, the Gustavos, and friends (very wealthy couples) and the new Governor and his wife. Rodrigo is in the back, raising his glass of soda in a wine glass with his Lost Boy lieutenants. Blond watches from the balcony with his wife and Niccolo. Father Marcos tips his glass to them. Cowboys, Indios, other church deacons, nuns, and several select, special volunteers are in attendance as well.

Corporal Diaz arrives to join the event with a few of her squad members in black fatigues.

Father Marcos and his people told the public it was an unimaginable swarm of large scorpions that the cartels used to engulf the city; the sinister plot was not just to kill him and church workers, but the entire city. They never told the public the truth about the scorpion-creatures. The people had to be allowed to believe that monsters don't really exist.

The Day of the Demon

"The scariest monsters are the ones you can't see." – Vincent, the "Astronaut," the Mormon Order

"The scariest monsters are the ones standing right in front of you." — Inspector Cruz, survivor of the "Day of the Demon" event, Chihuahua, Mexico, 2065

City of Guadalupe Victoria, Durango, Mexico
8:05 a.m., 4 May 2064

A gray-haired, gray-bearded Father Morales listens in disbelief from his side of the confession booth. Most priests are part psychologist, trained to be hyper-non-judgmental at anything someone might say in confession. But the story told by the unseen man with the heavy Russian accent shocks the Father, who has heard confessions for some thirty years.

Father Morales ritualistically absolves the man of his sins.

"Thank you, Father," the unseen man says. "But I do not believe God will forgive me." The man exits the confessional. Father Morales sits a moment in silence.

City of Guadalupe Victoria, Durango, Mexico
6:00 p.m., 4 May 2065

It is one year exactly to the day. Father Morales stares at his phone-only. The same thick Russian accent speaks. "Father, I will not do it. You can't even comprehend what you are about to do."

Father Morales says, "You already told me the consequences. I accept them. I will freely sacrifice myself for this. This is your way to save your soul and this is my way of saving my country."

The voice says, "Your soul will burn in purgatory for this. It will not just kill you. It will rip you to pieces. You will die a slow and violent death. That's what they do."

Father Morales says, "I must save my country from these criminals! These Nazis have taken over life in Mexico. There used to be hundreds of them fighting and killing each other. Then the people could live. Now one evil man has unified all of them into a supreme cartel. He won't just devour all of Mexico, but will take over all of the Spanish Americas, from Mexico to the tip of Brazil. This is the only way. They must be stopped."

The voice pauses. "I will give you the number and I tell you this knowing that you will ignore me. It will kill them for you. It will kill all of them. But then it will find you no matter where you hide and kill you too. That is how you know it has fulfilled your murder contract. When it finds you and kills you. Once you unleash it, there is no turning back."

Father Morales replies, "I understand."

The voice says, "And if you try to commit suicide, it will kill everyone you love, everyone."

Father Morales swallows hard. "I will sacrifice myself for my country and my people."

The voice says, "I sent you the number. It is done. And Father, our friendship, as of this very instant, is terminated."

City of Nuevo Casas Grandes, Chihuahua, Mexico
7:58 a.m., 9 May 2065

El Diablo, the head of the Diablo Cartel, spent the last fifteen years killing his way to the top and then the next five years killing every other cartel boss to consolidate their gangs with his. He killed policemen, federal agents, government officials, judges, and reporters he even remotely thought posed a threat. He is now the "King of all Cartels" in Mexico.

El Diablo receives an urgent call from one of his European contacts. After the call, he is so terrified—a state that no one had ever seen him in, ever—that he immediately moves all his family, friends, and relatives to his massive super-compound in Chihuahua. He summons every last member of his cartel organization, some ten thousand men, to surround the compound for protection with orders to kill anyone, or *anything*, on sight.

2:57 p.m.

Adan carefully watches the open land. He is one of El Diablo's many gunmen and has worked eleven years for him. He loves his job, killing people, and he has been richly rewarded with money, women, and cars. He imagines he has killed at least sixty people for his boss in his career.

But this is a strange assignment. "Kill anyone or anything that approaches the compound without hesitation, or I'll kill you." The words of El Diablo still ring in his ear from their one-hour group yelling session, late last night when he was summoned.

He is about five miles from the complex. The green grass looks like a giant, never-ending golf course. Beyond his post the land is spotted with lush trees sporadically placed throughout the open space. He may be at the outermost edge of the security perimeter, but he can see anything that approaches for at least two miles away.

He looks to his left and about two hundred yards away he can see a fellow gunman doing the same thing, watching for anyone. To his right is another gunman sentry. This is all very stupid; the entire area has more sensors than the Mexican Presidential Palace. But what the boss says goes.

At 3:33 p.m. he sees the demon.

Adan stares at the approaching figure. The person is about a mile away, just a speck in the distance, too far away to see exactly who it is. He smiles to himself and pulls the compact binoculars from his pocket. "Looks like number sixty-one is walking right to me." He trains it in the direction of the person: no one is there.

He looks directly at the exact area again with his eyes and doesn't see anything at all. *Where did he go?* He walks a few steps forward, scanning the horizon. *Where the hell did he go?* His eyes stop at one of the trees about two hundred yards away.

Adan laughs out loud. The person is standing behind the tree and whoever he is, he's tall. He laughs because whoever the guy is, he's so skinny that he could have stood behind the tree and not have been seen if not for his stupid hat. The guy is wearing a wide-brim, floppy brown hat that juts out from either side of the tree. *Is he for real? He wants to play hide-and-seek?* "I see you, stupid!"

Adan raises his high-powered machine gun with laser light scope. He smiles as he aims it at Mr. Hat standing behind the tree. His actual favorite type of killing was to mow down people with machine-gun fire; he liked watching the bullets riddle through their bodies. He remembers numbers fifty-nine and sixty: a young brother and sister who rescued prostitutes, or slaves, as they put it. Adan had killed them both, cut them up, and dumped the bodies all over their town as a warning.

He aims and points the gun at the tree and looks through the gun sight. Nothing. The guy has disappeared again, twice now. He looks at the tree with his eyes. *In fact, how did the guy get from one mile away, walking down the open ground, to behind the tree without me seeing him?*

Adan suddenly bursts out laughing. *He's still behind the tree! He just took his stupid hat off his head. He wants to play hide-and-seek for real.*

Adan walks to the hiding man behind the tree. "I'm going to really enjoy machine-gunning you!" He reaches the tree. The skinny guy is doing his best to use the tree to hide himself. "Come out from behind there, Mr. Hat," Adan says. "Hide-and-seek is over."

"But I don't want to, Mister. I want to play hide-and-seek with you."

Adan is not smiling anymore. The voice of this guy isn't a male voice at all, but that of a little girl. *How could a skinny, super-tall guy like this have the voice of a little girl?* He must have one of those voice-changers, those toys you can wrap around your neck that can make you sound like you're on helium or have a squeaky voice or super deep bass or whatever.

"Okay, come out from behind there, little girl."

"I'm not a little girl, Mister. I'm a demon."

Without hesitation, Adan fires his machine gun, just missing the tree on purpose. "Get out of there now, little girl/Mr. Hat!"

"Yes sir, Mister sir," the guy says in the same little girl voice.

When the demon comes out from behind the tree, Adan at first thinks it is some kind of practical joke. The guy is well over six feet, maybe even seven feet; his skin is a very dark brown, almost black in color, with no hair at all, and his frame is super skinny but not sickly. His entire body seems almost snake-like. His long, slender arms end in long black claws and his feet end in hooves. There are slits on his head instead of normal ears and his mouth looks almost wolf-like.

The demon stares at him with shimmering, pitch-black eyes and smiles a wide smile, showing long, fanged razor teeth. "Mister, do you like what you see? I'm tired of the hide-and-seek too. I want to play the killing game now." The "little girl" voice seems absurd coming from its mouth.

Adan doesn't know how to react to the thing standing over him. *Is this a joke? Is this real?*

The demon lunges into Adan's stomach with its razor-clawed arms and rips out his innards.

The gunman sentry posted to Adan's right hears a loud scream, but the sound stops as abruptly as it starts. He immediately raises his machine gun and runs in its direction. He tries to dodge it; Adan's disemboweled upper half hits him with such force that it explodes in a mass of blood, flesh, body parts, and undigested food, killing him instantly.

The gunman sentry to Adan's left is already running toward the tree. He saw what just happened to the other sentry. He looks back at the tree to start shooting, but it's too late. The lower half of Adan hits him with equal destructive force, exploding in blood, flesh, urine, and feces.

It takes only five minutes for the sirens to start blaring at the complex. Men are running to the main gate perimeter with machine guns, followed by SUV machine-gun-turreted vehicles.

One of the men yells to another, "We've lost contact with the entire northern outer perimeter!"

The man says, "What's on the monitors?!"

"We don't know what it is. It looks like some kind of tall man."

"What do you mean, 'It looks like some kind of tall man?' Is it or isn't it a man?"

"We don't know! He looks strange."

"Lock down the entire complex!"

Large concrete barriers start to rise from the ground to block all entrances and windows. The hundreds of people inside, including El Diablo, move back from all those doors and windows.

"Everyone in the panic room now!" he yells. His family, relatives, and friends all begin to run for the basement level to the panic room: an eight-thousand-square-foot underground palatial level with its own communications center, power generator, food storage for three years, weapons arsenal lockers, swimming pool, complete weight room and sauna, inner-door track, secure Net-link, and full outside surveillance monitor bank.

The demon slithers into one of the complex windows. The concrete barriers completely shut.

Ninety minutes later.

A little girl's voice screams from every communication speaker, startling the thousands of gunmen outside the complex. "It's killing everyone! Help! Help me!"

The lead man is in horror as the gunman army follows him back to the complex.

"How do we get back in?! We can't override the system! That can be done only from inside!"

Suddenly, the concrete barriers start to lower, opening.

"They're alive and are letting us back in! Move in fast!"

The army runs into the complex with machine guns raised, fanning out in every direction. The last man enters the complex. The concrete barriers start to rise back up again—locking shut.

8:57 a.m. (Next Day)

Inspector Cruz sits in the passenger seat as the federal SUV races down the road. They are driving almost a hundred miles per hour. Some twelve other black SUVs follow at the same reckless speed.

They had been dispatched by the Mexico City Federal Director himself. The chatter on the police lines was that something happened at the palatial super-complex of cartel overlord El Diablo. They were told that a little girl was still alive inside the complex and had said that someone was killing everyone.

The federal police SUV caravan arrives at the complex main gate. Inspector Cruz jumps out even before the SUV is stopped. He directs two teams to fan out in opposite directions outside the gate and inspect the area. One team stays with the vehicles; the rest of the team follows him. All of them wear armored bulletproof vests and are armed with machine guns.

The main gate is locked, but one of his men blows the lock in seconds with a laser cutter. They run through the gate in double formation.

The Inspector notices that there's not a sound anywhere except for them. The complex is in total lockdown: all entrances are blocked by solid concrete barriers. Depending on the thickness, it could take minutes with the right explosives—or hours.

Inspector Cruz touches his ear-set, which is on two-way mode. "Central, do you still have the girl inside who made the emergency call on the line?"

Voice: "No, Inspector. She was screaming, but the line went dead. We confirmed GPS that it was from your location inside the complex."

All the men freeze when the concrete barriers begin to lower. Someone inside is letting them enter.

The Inspector is suspicious. "Everyone back to the gates!" They all turn to run away from the complex and back to the main gates. He touches his ear-set. "Central, try to connect me with that caller. We seem to have access now, but I want to verify."

"Stand by, Inspector." They all hear the line ringing and ringing.

On the third ring someone picks up. "I'm hurting, Mister."

They all look at each other as the little girl's voice comes through clearly.

Inspector Cruz says, "We're right outside, little girl. Don't worry. Can you come to the main door and open it?"

The little girl says, "I can't, Mister. I can't move my legs. Please save me. Everybody is dead. The bad people left and I'm all alone."

"Where inside are you?"

"I'm near a bedroom on the ground floor at the back. Please Mister, please save me. I'm hurting."

"Is anyone else in there with you?"

"No, Mister. I don't see anyone, but there could be other children in here, hiding like me. Will you save us, Mister?"

The Inspector says nothing. He covers the ear-set to block the sound. To the men, "Back away farther. Call Central and have them send immediate backup. Load up and let's drive back to the ridge for cover."

They all get back into their SUVs and drive away from the main gates. This is a setup and they all feel it. It could be some game that El Diablo is playing to kill or kidnap them for some reason.

They stop one hundred yards away and exit the vehicles. The Inspector points to a couple members of his team. "Keep your eyes on the main entrance." Two of the men take positions behind the SUV and aim binoculars at the complex.

From the ear-set: "Why did you go so far away, Mister? Don't you like me?"

They all look back at the complex. It is a setup!

Inspector says, "You bastard! I'm going to have the entire Mexican army here in thirty minutes. We'll see if you think this game is funny when we bomb your ass out of there! You bastard!"

The little girl says, "You're no fun, Mister. I wanted to play."

Inspector yells, "Hell with you!"

"I'll come outside to play with you."

The men look to the complex.

The demon emerges from the complex, wearing his hat. He raises his arms in the air and waves them all around, laughing hysterically.

The men on the binoculars look at the Inspector. "What is that?"

Inspector Cruz says, "It's a man. What does it look like?" He can see the binocular men are nervous.

Through the headset: "I'm not a man, Mister. I'm a demon. Do you want me to play with you or do you want me to play with your men?"

Inspector says, "Hell with you, bastard. Come closer so we can shoot you!"

"You need to choose, Mister. You or your men?"

"You'll never get near us."

"Choose."

"Me, you bastard. Hell with you!"

"Do you want to try to run or should I just come now?"

"Come now you bastard."

The demon seems to disappear.

All the men look around in panic. "Where did he go?" "Where is he?"

One of the men yells, "Inspector, go! Get in the SUV and drive!"

"No, I'm not going anywhere."

The men grab him, open the door, and push him in.

One of the men says, "If this is a game, none of us are laughing. Just drive away as far as you can until backup arrives."

The demon appears behind the last of the SUVs, towering over the two men standing there. No one else sees as it grabs them with its razor claws, cuts into their flesh to the bone, picks them up, and throws them. The men scream as they are thrown ten feet in the air toward the complex. Startled, other men automatically start firing at the two flying bodies, not realizing who they are.

Inspector yells, "Stop firing! It's our men!"

The machine gun fire stops, but too late. The two men's bodies hit the ground, dead.

The little girl voice booms through the ear-set: "Am I going to play with you or your men?"

One of his men yells, "Inspector, go!"

Inspector Cruz speeds off in the vehicle, blanketing his men in a cloud of dust. He drives fast but watches the rearview mirror. He wants to see if his men can run away or shoot whatever the thing is. The cloud starts to dissipate, but he can't see anyone.

The demon jumps on top of his SUV. The Inspector yells. He slams on the brakes. The demon flies from the roof of the SUV, but lands on its feet effortlessly.

"Leave me alone! I'm not the cartels! Leave me alone!" The Inspector is hysterical now.

Little girl voice in his ear-set: "Why didn't you say that before, Mister?" The demon turns and starts walking away from him.

Inspector Cruz sits in the SUV with his hands gripping the steering wheel so tightly in fear that he's about the rip the entire attachment from the car. He watches the demon disappear in the distance.

Little girl voice: "You have a wonderful life now, Mister. Bye-bye."

The Inspector can't move. He is paralyzed by shock.

Confidential Report / 12 May 2065

The Mexican Army arrived at the residential super-complex of cartel overlord El Diablo. The area was fully secured and a full search was conducted of the surrounding grounds. Three dead bodies were found five miles to the north of the main complex. Forensics has determined that one male was disemboweled and ripped in half by unknown "animal." Second and third males were killed by upper and lower half of first man, apparently thrown with sufficient force to kill the second and third males on impact. The three males were identified as criminal killers in the employ of the El Diablo cartel.

Inside the super-complex, forensic recovery is ongoing due to the massive numbers of deceased persons inside. Victims are adult males, adult females, and children. Inconclusive preliminary report is that victims were ripped apart and eaten by unknown animal or animals.

Two federal agents, deceased, were also attacked by animal, but were killed by friendly fire. Full investigation is in process.

Operation lead, Inspector Cruz, has been remanded to the Mexico City National Mental Institution. Facility doctors have stated that they do not know when he will be mentally stable enough to be questioned.

Of the three hundred ninety first responders to the El Diablo Massacre site, one hundred fifty-seven have resigned from the forensic criminal investigation unit, fifty-four have since died in accidents (possible suicides), twelve have committed suicide, and seven have disappeared (possible flight from Mexico or suicide).

Amended Report: Inspector Cruz has been committed permanently to the Mexico City National Mental Institution. His status will be reviewed in six months.

City of Guadalupe Victoria, Durango, Mexico
12:00 p.m., 9 May 2065

Guadalupe Victoria is a quiet, sleepy village. Its current distinction is that it is the home church of Father Morales, who has become somewhat of a national celebrity in his crusade against cartels and modern-day slavery. His services are not only attended by the local villages, but by those from surrounding villages.

The demon casually strolls into the town at 11:53 a.m. wearing his silly, wide-brim, tan hat.

Townspeople on the street stop dead in their tracks and watch it walk past them. They do not know how to react to the seven-foot, skinny demon as it walks to the church of Father Morales.

Father Morales has been monitoring the news reports on the Chihuahua and Mexico City police bands. The reports are very sketchy and fast changing, but it is apparent that something terrible has happened at the main residential complex of El Diablo.

He hears the church door open. People always asked him why he had so little security with his "celebrity" status. He always responded that he had plenty of staff: God and His angels. The truth is, he always feared attacks by the cartels, so if they did come, he would be the only one who would get attacked or killed—not some innocent parishioner, nun, or priest. But today he has sent even his small volunteer staff home for the entire day.

"Father Morales!" a little girl's voice calls out.

The Father sighs in relief. *At least I'm not in any danger*, he thinks to himself. He walks from his office down the steps to the main church area. He stops. The demon stares at him.

"Father, it is done." The little girl voice coming out of this demon is jarring to the Father.

"You know who I am?"

"Yes, Mister Holy Man, I do. You are the holy man who hired me to kill El Diablo and everyone and everything around him. I fulfilled my contract, Mister Holy Man; now it's time for you to fulfill your side of the contract or give me an option."

Father Morales is scared to death, but maintains his composure "An option? Are you suggesting that I have another option besides dying?"

"Of course, Mister Holy Man."

"Tell me then."

"Mister Holy Man, I will spare your life if you can give me a counteroffer that would please me more than killing you. Can you do it?"

Father Morales hesitates. "If you let me live, I will do such great works in Mexico now that the evils of the cartels are gone. I will work twenty-five hours a day to that end, saving souls, saving lives. It will be a Mexican Catholic Renaissance."

"Uh, Father…you do know that I'm a demon, right?"

Father Morales stares at him. *I guess the demon doesn't like my counteroffer.*

The demon lunges at Father Morales and knocks him across the hall and into the wall, knocking down the large cross in the process. Father Morales screams and looks down at his feet. The demon is eating his leg.

Tastes like chicken, the demon thinks.

The main hall of the church is designed for maximum acoustical effect. Father Morales's wild screams echo throughout the church and are heard even outside, by the entire village. People come out into the street looking at each other in fear and toward the church.

The screams do not stop until twenty agonizing minutes later. The demon exits the church, now with something of a pot belly. Everyone runs away.

The demon casually walks back down the dirt street with his stupid wide-brim hat blowing in the wind and a satisfied, fanged grin on its face.

Two nuns run to the church, obviously unaware of its presence, but stop to watch the demon walk away. They stare in disbelief at it. It continues to walk, but turns its head almost a complete one hundred eighty degrees to stare at the nuns.

Wisp the Demon turns its head back and jumps into the air. The nuns watch it literally jump over several small houses and disappear.

Word of the killing of Father Morales by the demon spread like wildfire. The expression of terror on his face, his wild screaming while he was being killed, and how he was found: three-fourths of his body eaten away.

The panic spread through country villages all over Mexico how a demon killed Satan's chief human follower, the King of Cartels, El Diablo; and God's noblest follower, Father Morales, on the same day. The day became known as the Day of the Demon: the day in Mexico when no one goes outside.

In the tek-cities, a different approach was taken: deny the event ever happened. Law enforcement purposely lied and told the public that rival gangs from Central America killed El Diablo, fearing the Mexican King of Cartels was coming after them, and that Father Morales was killed by an "animal."

Father Morales's brother collected all his belongings from his church and placed them in storage. There were a lot of old analog books, which his brother always felt was silly. Why keep five hundred antiquated physical books when you can keep a hundred fifty thousand books in your personal Net account and download them to your tablet, e-pad, or whatever device you wanted, whenever you want to? And there were his endless finger drives of classical music; again, why keep physical files when you can store them on the Net?

No one knew that he was Father Morales's brother. It was common for anyone in government, clergy, journalism, or the wealthy elite to have their identities erased so that the cartels couldn't find out who their families were.

He put everything in storage and never looked at it, as he was so traumatized by the killing of his beloved brother. He lived his life with his wife and their two children, Angelica and Marcos.

A decade later, Marcos, age ten, starts a project in school to create a full family tree. His father tells him about his deceased uncle who was a priest and who had been murdered. Little Marcos also learns of his uncle's belongings in storage.

Young Marcos spends the next year reading all of his dead uncle's books and listening to all of his music. It was on the last day that he came across Father Morales's diary, on a tablet. His uncle, a man who supposedly hated digital tek, kept a daily diary of the last thirty-five years of his fifty-five years of life. Marcos enables the device's talk-mode. It talks about his hatred of and war against the cartels, detailing specifically the people they had tortured, maimed, beaten, and killed. It talks about his hatred of slavery and his crusade to wipe it out in Mexico. It talks about his encounter with a Russian-born confessor, his later plot to "hire" a demon to wipe out the biggest cartel boss of the day, El Diablo, and the Day of the Demon. It tells the truth of how this demon wipes out more than ten thousand people on one day, and his last day on earth.

The most influential person in young Marcos's life besides Jesus was a man he never met—his murdered uncle. Father Morales gave him his purpose, his crusade against cartels and slavery, and his inspiration to become a priest. Young Marcos became Father Marcos. The Day of the Demon was the same year Father Marcos was born.

Mexico City, Mexico
1:38 p.m., 20 November 2095

El Angel deletes the email threat from Father Marcos. "I'm not going to end up being half eaten by some demonic animal. You all can stay, but I'm on the next plane out of Mexico today."

Confidential Intelligence Report: Confirmed. El Angel Cartel has left Mexico. To date, there is no significant cartel presence left in the northern states of Mexico.

There Are Many More

"They want something that is impossible—the end of evil." — Boss Gordo, crime lord

New Lerdo Church, Mexico
9:15 a.m., 21 November 2095

The Deputy Director of the Secretariat of Public Security, Señor Augustín, sits quietly in his chair. He reflects on the main plaque in Father Marcos's office, of the quote from the American President Thomas Jefferson: "The Two Enemies of the People are Criminals and Government."

Father Marcos enters and Augustín immediately stands to shake hands. "Deputy Director, it's a pleasure to meet you."

"Thanks. I thought it wise to meet you before I find myself forcibly retired," Augustín says, half joking. Father Marcos has seriously damaged the Mexican Federal Police and even the Presidency. Why else would they quickly support his rebuilding of the New Lerdo Church and publicly and loudly condemn the cartels?

"I don't think you have to worry about that, Deputy Director."

"Please call me Augustín, Father. I don't even allow my own men to call me by my title. Well, if you ever pick our next President, please put in a good word for me." He smiles again.

"What can I do for you, Señor Augustín?"

"I know you're busy, so I will confine myself to a few thoughts. First, I want to state categorically that my office is an ally."

"That seems to be an odd comment when your division was sending kill teams to my church."

"That was not my office and the individuals responsible for that act no longer have their jobs. You saw to that. But that's the past. I actually decided to come see you after a colleague of mine in Sinaloa told me that you helped them arrest some Catholic priests there, a Father Tezuma and his people. I was quite surprised since, apparently, they were fighting the cartels, as you are."

"When Hitler came to power in Germany he didn't start with the killing of Jews. He actually started with the physically and mentally disabled. This Neo-Mayan and Ne-Aztec movement of theirs, the fact that these so-called Catholic priests were fighting the cartels didn't change the fact that they were involved in evil witchcraft. They would have eventually, inevitably, moved to innocent people. I was aware of it, so I did something about it."

"I'm glad to hear that. So many times, people of a group will make excuses or even protect those in their own group when they do wrong or do evil. I'm glad to see you keep the same standards for everyone. With all that you do, I hear you still keep a daily routine of reading the Bible, preaching, and teaching."

"I always make time for the Word of God, each and every day."

"Father Marcos, the reality is that we are all the government now. We can all call each other names: the church, the rich, the government. But the welfare of this country and its people is in our hands. We don't have a choice in the matter. We must work together."

"I agree, Señor Augustín. We must work together."

"I'm glad. Call on me whenever you need to and I hope I can do the same."

"You can do so at any time, Señor Augustín."

"Thank you, Father. Also, I would like to plant the seed of another consideration with you. I would never say anything against your war with the cartels, against slave-running and drug trafficking. It is your business. You handle it your way. We have our way. Our methods don't have to be the same. However, I know of your deeply ingrained hatred of the cartels and slavery. I know this. Everyone does now. But there are many more than just one, Father. You fight these two devils, towering giants walking the lands of Mexico, but there are many more that walk the earth. If you are successful in your mission and destroy the two, make sure you don't allow the others, some even more deadly, more dangerous, more evil, to take their place. There must never be a void of power in any place you wipe free of the cartels. Not even for a day."

Father Marcos studies him carefully. *What does he mean? The number-two ranking man in Mexico's Secretariat of Public Security, the equivalent of America's Homeland Defense and Intelligence Agency, doesn't fly in from Mexico City to philosophize with me.* "What are you suggesting, Señor Augustín?"

"Mexico doesn't have the same devils walking on our lands as other countries have, that other countries have fallen to. You don't honestly think that Mexico is free of the Muslims by coincidence or luck. The government's anti-terrorist policies are pathetically just a grab-and-deport policy and it's not because of our anti-illegal-immigration border walls on our northern and southern borders."

"What are you saying then?"

"What I am saying is that the cartels do have one benefit to the country. Keeping the Muslims out. You've heard the saying many times: Mexicans and Muslims will cut your head off. Our Mexican head-cutters, the cartels, have very effectively kept the Muslim head-cutters out of Mexico. Something to keep in mind. Again, not to dissuade you from your mission, but for you to keep in mind."

He knew something of what he was saying. In the past, Muslim terrorists had tried to infiltrate the Spanish Americans, but in Mexico especially, the cartels were not having it; only they were allowed to kill Mexicans. The cartels would not allow the terrorists to succeed in attacks on Mexican soil because all that would do is make the Mexican government and military more powerful in reaction and, with that, jeopardize their criminal empires.

"Nothing will dissuade me from my war with the cartels."

"Even the Allies had to join with Stalin when they wanted to defeat Hitler. Stalin and the Communists murdered ten times more people than Hitler and the Nazis did.

"Father, I know what really happened here during the Day of the Scorpion. The Secretariat has a secret division that deals with threats of a more…unexplainable or…supernatural nature. It is top-secret and I will deny it if you ever bring it up again, but it was put in place after the Day of the Demon event some two decades ago. We know in the Division about these scorpion-creatures your people wiped out."

Father Marcos says nothing.

"Father, do you honestly believe that El Angel, the cartel boss you scared out of the country with an email, could have possibly orchestrated such an evil plan? The man is evil, but he's a buffoon. All he knows is how to count money, shoot people, and rape children. He doesn't know how to do anything else. He was the mastermind of this evil plan? I think not."

"Then who?"

"All I can say is that you need to align yourself with the Faithers in the United States. Over one hundred and sixty years ago we had the evil Mexican President Plutarco Elias Calles. America now has its own version in a man they call Galerius." Augustín pauses and lowers his voice more. "A Galerius who is the puppet master of the one we call the Bull, not the cartels and not the rich."

Father Marcos is transfixed. "Sir, you are not just suggesting, but you are outright stating, that the Office of the President of the United States—via one of the main cartels in Mexico—plotted to assassinate me with supernatural scorpion-creatures. Conspiracies of America being the root of every bad thing in Mexico is common, but you and I are sophisticated men and know better, especially as members of the Christian faith."

Augustín smiles.

President Calles ran Mexico technically for four years from 1929, but actually for eleven years. During his reign, called the *Maximato*, he founded the National Revolutionary Party and enacted the most vicious anti-religious laws against Catholics ever, desecrating and closing churches, seizing church property, denying the basic civil and political rights of clergy, allowing the raping of nuns, suspending all Catholic worship, banning clergy from going out in public, and requiring clergy to register with the government. Catholics rebelled in the Cristero War, but Calles succeeding in killing or exiling more than three thousand priests. From the viewpoint of many Faithers, the United States had a current President of a similar ilk.

Niccolo had suggested a fantastical plot, but without giving details on those really behind the Day of the Scorpion. Now a second man speaks of a fantastical plot.

Father Marcos leans forward. "Señor Augustín, so that I'm very clear: you're stating as fact, not merely suggesting, that 'Galerius,' the American President, controls the 'Bull,' the President of Mexico?"

"I am stating as fact, not merely suggesting, that Galerius controls the Bull *and* the White Lion and the Turtle."

Miles Whitehall had been the Prime Minster of Canada for two terms now. He has flowing white hair to match his sideburns and beard. His nickname is the "White Lion" in political circles. The brash Joaquim Jimenas is one of the youngest men ever elected President of Brazil. He is known for his strange fascination with turtles; the grounds of his private mansion house some sixteen species and he even named his children after different turtles.

Father Marcos leans back in his chair and says, "Can you prove this?"

"Beyond the shadow of a doubt."

"For what possible purpose, even if I did believe it?"

"If there ever were a war, America wouldn't have enough people to protect its major tek-cities, let alone the entire country. But if they could nationalize a war, create a North Americas Treaty Organization, they could create a multi-million-man army for whatever defensive or offensive purpose."

"That could never happen. Mexicans would never stand for it."

"You mean how they would never stand for cartels killing their spouses, children, and families, even though it's been happening for the last century? And if not for you, would still be happening? Every country has war plans, every one. They will do anything, create anything, to ensure victory. We the people are merely the pawns on their big chessboard. Father, you are today the only person who can derail their plans. That is why there was a Day of the Scorpion."

"What are you asking me to do, then?"

"Be the threat they fear you to be. Mexico needs a new President."

The Vatican Incident

"I had to choose between an agreement and the virtual elimination of the Catholic Church in the Reich." — Vatican Secretary of State Pacelli to the British ambassador, 1933

Every large, powerful organization has its own internal factions. The Vatican is no different. These factions are often called "Mafias" somewhat jokingly, but their constant vying for power and influence with the Pope is very serious. There is the Gay Mafia, homosexuals in the Vatican who had been rising in power, but after the disastrous affairs in America with the collapse of the Lutheran, Episcopal, and Presbyterian Churches as a result of Bishop Joe, they had been relegated to the "back of the room." The Feminist Mafia had succeeded in the first of their twin issues: getting the Church to modify its prohibition against birth control (made moot by the invention and universality of the *bio-switch*), and now focused completely on reversing Church doctrine on the ordination of women, despite Saint Pope John Paul II's *Ordinatio Sacerdotalis* near the end of the twentieth century stating that it was "a permanent teaching of the Church." However, they too had lost any influence due to cultural battles that also ended very badly for the religious in America (in this case, because of Rabbi Susan). There is the One

World Mafia that had started as an open-border faction (against all laws against illegal immigration), but had morphed into advocating for a one-world government for the betterment of all Earthers (yes, they used that term), and even wanted this new world government to be called the Federation after the science fiction series *Star Trek*. There is the Socialist Neo-Marxist Mafia wanting a "proletarian uprising against bourgeoisie power," but after the Fall of Western Europe to Islamists of the Caliphate, blamed almost exclusively on their socialistic birth-to-death welfare states, they too were pushed to the back of the back room. There is the End-of-the-World Mafia, fixated on the end of the planet and the return of Jesus, but they were viewed more as a curiosity than as a political force within the Holy See. There is the Luddite Mafia, which saw tek itself as the Devil, and the Techno Mafia, their archenemies, who were obsessed with every latest tek gadget and wanted to use the Church to spread the Word *and* technology.

But the Mafia that has the most influence is the Islamic Mafia, the faction of the Vatican that wants to create an alliance between Catholicism and Islam, and that, despite warnings and daily news stories, is not at all concerned with Muslim terrorism or aggression against non-Muslims or the Fall of Western Europe by Islamic force.

The Holy See, first under Pope Pius XI and then Pope Pius XII, entered into the *Reichskonkordat Agreement* with Nazi Germany, signed on 20 July 1933. It was considered controversial *after* World War II was over; a revisionist history of the true events was recited and spread by anti-Catholic, anti-religious, and political left-of-center circles. At the time, it was the only option available to the Pope and the Roman Curia, who wanted to ensure that the Nazis didn't destroy the Vatican City State or occupy it as they had done with Paris. They had already signed the Lateran Treaty some four years earlier with the Nazis' Fascist ally, Prime Minister of Italy

Benito Mussolini, for similar "protection."

The Islamic Mafia has achieved its greatest aspiration this day. Pope Innocent XIII will sign the Vatican-Riyadh Pact with Islamic Caliphate Emperor Al-Siddiq, establishing a permanent alliance between the two religious empires and an acceptance of the permanent neutrality and sovereignty of Rome. Even so, half the Roman Curia and Magisterium is adamantly opposed to any such alliance, and views even the signing of the Pact as a weakening of the very power of the Papacy.

The Pope feels he has no choice. The Muslim Caliphate on one side and the Russian Bloc on the other side. The Vatican has no army and must remain neutral lest one empire or the other seize the Vatican City State.

The Pact is a brilliant stroke, as Rome is often used openly and secretly as a diplomatic base on neutral soil for negotiations with either the Muslim Caliphate or the Russian Bloc separately, and between both superpowers themselves.

The Vatican, Rome Italy
1:15 p.m., June 2090

Cardinal Cassiano remembers the meeting between the Pope and the Emperor vividly. It was a secret meeting, but it was quite the ceremony: the best china, the best food, both Italian and Arabic music playing in the background.

What stuck in Cardinal Cassiano's mind was when the Emperor went to address the Pope: "Pope Chamberlain…excuse me, Pope Innocent, I and the entire Islamic people are so honored by your gracious open hand. I am honored to sign with you this treaty for long-lasting friendship between our peoples. All under the great eyes of Almighty Allah."

Cardinal Cassiano and Niccolo glance at each other. They are thinking the exact same thing as they stand quietly behind the Pope in the procession.

The Vatican, Rome Italy
5:35 p.m., December 2090

The Pope sits on his throne in a high-level ceremony with the Roman Curia and Italian government officials.

Suddenly, members of the Swiss Guard burst into the chambers and rush to the Pope from all sides. They grab him and pull him out of the chambers, into the main hallways. Pandemonium: people running and screaming everywhere.

The Pope looks to the tall arched windows as he is pushed and dragged away. All he sees are black dots in the sky. He can't make out what they are. The Swiss Guard move him quickly into a secure hallway, with cardinals and other high administrative staff following. Other Swiss Guard follow with guns drawn.

La Fine Del Cattolicesimo Romano

New Lerdo Church, Mexico
2:13 p.m., 16 December 2095

Sister Serena and the Twins stand at the wall in front of a massive vid-screen that shows a map of the Americas, from Canada to the tip of South America. All three women are in their nun habits. Seated at the conference table are Sister Fernanda and Sister Angelita.

Also at the table is their guest, the Cowboy Rabbi.

All are talking and looking at various points on the map when Father Marcos enters the office.

Cowboy Rabbi's eyes light up and he stands. "Father Marcos! The young priest who saved me!" He runs to the Father, throws his arms around him, and gives him a hug that lifts the Father off the ground.

"Rabbi, good to see you, too. It's been years."

"Father, I felt so bad from the last time. That I passed out in the car."

"Being shot can do that, Rabbi."

"But I never was able to finish my joke. No self-respecting rabbi starts a joke and doesn't finish it."

Father Marcos chuckles. "You were shot, though."

"No, no Father. That's no excuse." He pauses. "The Jew, the Christian, and the Mormon are in heaven and they see the Messiah in the distance, walking. They run to him and yell, 'Yeshua, Jesus, we must know. Did you go to Earth zero times, one time, or two times?' The Messiah looks at them and points at another group in the distance. 'Go ask the Hindus.'"

Everyone laughs. They all sit down at the table. The Cowboy Rabbi pours the Father a glass of water.

They wrap up the real meeting. Father Marcos smiles. "Rabbi, this is absolutely amazing."

By the time Father Marcos had met Sister Serena and the Twins, he had single-handedly liberated nearly five thousand slaves, mostly Mexican women and girls. Their New Mexican Underground Railroad had rescued more than seventy thousand to date, including all of Mexico and the Spanish Americas.

The Cowboy Rabbi says, "It's amazing for all of us. God put us all exactly where we were supposed to be. You built up the Mexico Underground Railroad. Sister Serena brought to you her network in Central and South America, and I'll connect you to our American network, which includes passage through all of Canada. The Underground Railroad now includes all of the Americas. We can rescue slaves from anywhere in the world, get them to any point in the Americas, and they'll be safe and free for good."

Father Marcos says, "Last time I saw you, you couldn't even speak a word of Spanish other than 'banditos.'"

The Cowboy Rabbi laughs. "Yes, but I practiced every day. Now I can tell my jokes in five languages."

Everyone laughs again.

It is almost 5:00 p.m. and Sister Maria leads Father Marcos into his offices for some special guests. Niccolo is waiting with Cardinal

Cassiano. Another man rises from his chair and Father Marcos is astonished. It is Archbishop Masai.

"Archbishop!" The two men hug.

"So good to see you, Father Marcos."

Archbishop Masai is the leader of the African Catholic Order. He is a man with humble beginnings, even more so than Father Marcos, but is credited with saving the continent of Africa, which, until he did, was considered cursed.

Shortly after Western Europe fell to the Islamic Caliphate, Islamists moved quickly to seize Africa. A continental civil war erupted, with an Islamic North and a Christian South. The Islamists were winning the war and all seemed lost when a young native-born South Sudanese Catholic priest emerged to beat them back to the North. Now, there was, in essence, a permanent stalemate at the 15th Parallel, with the Christian South controlling three-fourths of the continent and the Islamists holding onto the Northern part of Africa.

Archbishop Masai's life is truly a remarkable one. His nickname is "The Cat," as it is said he has nine lives, having survived assassination attempts, accidents (his limo drove off a cliff in the rain and flipped seven times), natural disasters (the greatest sandstorm in known African history), a stampede of elephants, a cougar attack, and a plane crash.

"When did you arrive, Archbishop?"

"I got here this morning. Sorry we couldn't tell you ahead of time, but whenever I travel I must keep the itinerary secret until the last minute."

"Yes, of course, Archbishop."

"Let us get started. Sister Maria has already gotten us refreshments."

Cardinal Cassiano says, "Sister Maria takes such good care of us." He smiles at her.

Father Marcos quickly embraces Cardinal Cassiano. The men sit back down. Father Marcos takes his seat, and Sister Maria closes the door as she leaves.

The Archbishop says, "Father Marcos, we are so deeply impressed by your work here in Mexico. We have so many Catholic leaders who see only the limitations of the Church without perceiving the greatness. You have transcended those limitations and expanded the greatness of the Church."

"I would say that of you, Archbishop. I am only doing God's work in my tiny country of Mexico. You are doing so on a continent."

The Archbishop smiles. "We are all where we are supposed to be." His expression changes from jovial to serious. "Father Marcos, what we are about to divulge must not leave this room, ever. That is essential. In fact, the four of us will now be the only people in the world who will know all in regards to the Old Catholic Order."

Father Marcos is intrigued by the phrase. "Old Catholic Order?" There is only the Catholic Order, the oldest and largest denomination of Christians in the world.

The Archbishop looks to Cardinal Cassiano, who begins to speak on cue. "I know you initially weren't all that pleased when we assigned Niccolo to you."

Father Marcos says, "That was before he saved my life from an army of scorpion-creatures."

The Archbishop smiles. "Yes, we will address that another day, but at some time in the future the Magi Order will contact you as part of their investigation."

Father Marcos asks, "The Magi Order?"

The Archbishop smiles again. "You don't know about them yet, but you will meet them one day."

Cardinal Cassiano continues. "Most people don't know what

Niccolo's function is in the Catholic Order. Even most of the Holy See didn't. I know the rumors and speculation. The best way to describe it is to think of an iceberg. The part that's above the water line isn't what sank the Titanic. It was the massive, unseen part below the waterline that sent the ship to the bottom of the sea. Niccolo's job is to know the entire iceberg, especially that unseen part. The iceberg is all the threats to the Catholic Order, and his specialty is those unseen but more dangerous threats to us. He seeks them out and deals with them. We found out about a threat to you and it was his task to uncover the plot and deal with it, to make sure you were not injured in any way."

The Archbishop says, "We do know that the late Father Morales was your uncle."

Father Marcos is surprised. "Yes." Knowing where he was going. "I would, of course, never summon that demon. Besides, the number is disconnected."

The Archbishop says, "There is a worldwide network watching for them. If they appear again, we'll know."

Cardinal Cassiano continues. "You also know that we've been moving Italians from Italy into Mexico. What you don't know is that we have been moving items, property, artwork, the library, and all archives—public and private—from the Vatican here for years. None of us could have predicted your rise to power, but we consider it providence. We joked about your New Lerdo Church being the Vatican of Mexico, but what we will be doing in secret is just that, making it the new Vatican."

Father Marcos is confused. "The new Vatican? You can't possibly be suggesting that you would move the Pope here to Mexico, all the way from Rome. Is the threat from the Islamic Caliphate that significant?"

Cardinal says, "No, Father, we're not moving the Vatican here.

We already have." He pauses for quite a while. "The Pope is dead."

Anti-Vatican talk among Catholics is natural; all Catholics do it from time to time. It is even expected in some circles, especially in extremely nationalistic countries like Mexico. But if anyone attacked the Pope, there wasn't a single Catholic who wouldn't drop everything and run, fly, drive, swim to his aid.

Father Marcos stares the Cardinal, unable to speak for seemingly an eternity. "I don't understand."

"The Pope is dead," the Cardinal repeats.

"None of us have heard this on the news," Father Marcos manages to say.

The Archbishop says, "The people who did it don't give press conferences and we are not about to announce it, either. We won't let our enemies globally try to capitalize on our perceived weakened state. The shock would be too great to Catholics. We have to keep it a secret until we've prepared everything."

Father Marcos, still dazed, says, "I'm not understanding why you're telling me all this. What do you want me to do?"

Cardinal Cassiano says, "Five years ago, Caliphate forces attacked Rome from occupied France and Germany, and seized all of northern Italy. *Operazione di esodo*, or Operation Exodus, was initiated and every Italian from Southern Italy was evacuated. We didn't feel comfortable migrating to America because of its radically anti-religious government. We kept the people on ocean liners and on the open sea all these years. Until now, when we were convinced that your rise to power was not a fluke, but a permanent state of a new Mexico."

Father Marcos sits, speechless.

Cardinal Cassiano continues. "I am the only Cardinal left from the Curia. The Pope, the entire Roman Curia, the Magistratim, the Swiss Guard, the entire Vatican laity is gone."

Archbishop Masai says, "Father Marcos, this is very cruel of us to throw at you all at once, but time is short. We had hoped to spend years breaking you into this information, but we no longer have that luxury. We also know that you were visited by Deputy Director Augustín recently. No doubt he has shared with you his findings about Mexican President Torro and others, but as disturbing as that fact is, there is no need for us to intervene other than to make sure to pick the next Mexican President, which we know you already plan to do.

"We have more pressing matters to occupy our time and energy. The iceberg is alive and is racing toward the ship. You noticed I said 'Old Catholic Order.' That is because the Catholic Order the four of us swore allegiance to no longer exists."

Father Marcos feels lightheaded. He thinks to himself, *Was this how Adam and Eve felt after they ate the fig from the Tree of Knowledge?—a painful download of information into their pure, untarnished brains, so overwhelming, so disturbing, so rapidly, all at once.* "You said you had an Operation Exodus to evacuate the people. That means you knew."

Cardinal Cassiano says, "No, but we suspected. We were not going to make the same mistake as Jewish Israel and be caught in an attack without a comprehensive plan."

Father Marcos asks, "What was the trigger for your suspicion?"

Niccolo says, "The Pope had a secret meeting with the Islamic Emperor. Cardinal Cassiano and I were there. The Emperor made an odd Freudian slip that, on reflection, we thought was a serious indicator of the true intentions of the Caliphate."

Cardinal Cassiano says, "He called the Pope 'Pope Chamberlain.'"

Father Marcos says, "I know that name, but my mind isn't working now. Who was Chamberlain?"

Cardinal Cassiano answers, "The Prime Minister of England before Winston Churchill. Neville Chamberlain signed the peace treaty with Adolf Hitler. Right after signing the Treaty, Hitler invaded Poland and World War Two began, including going to war against England. Most regard Chamberlain as a fool who was more content with a piece of paper in his hand than with the physical and military means to defend his country. They perceived the Pope as Chamberlain."

Father Marcos asks again, "What do you want me to do, then?"

Archbishop Masai says, "We need to pick a new Pope. The three of us are the new Council of Cardinals."

Father Marcos looks at him. "Surely, you will be the new Pope."

Archbishop Masai says, "No, Father. It can't be me. Africa is in a state of daily war with the Muslims. If it became public that I was the new Pope, the war in Africa would explode, with attacks from the Caliphate increasing a hundredfold, as we are right next to them. The Asian Catholic Order is in chaos, the American Catholic Order has collapsed to nothingness, the Canadian Catholic Order has been dead for ages, and what remains of the Eastern European Catholic Order is under the domination of the Russian Bloc. We are the only two free Orders. *No, it must be you.*"

Father Marcos is so stunned now that his mouth is open.

Cardinal Cassiano says, "Niccolo was also tasked with vetting you. Making sure there were no skeletons in your closet. Making sure you weren't engaging in any egregious sins. We had to make sure you were truly the virtuous man we needed for the highest honored position of Catholics everywhere."

Father Marcos feels he will faint. "First you tell me the Pope is dead. And now you tell me I'm to be the next Pope. I'm only thirty years old. I've been in charge of my parish for only three years. How can I be the leader of millions of Catholics worldwide? This is impossible. Why wouldn't the Muslims attack Mexico?"

He immediately remembers the strange meeting he had with Deputy Director Augustín.

The Archbishop says, "Logistically, it is not as easy as you would think. They would have to travel across an entire ocean to get here. All the Spanish Americas—and Mexico especially—have an established history of standing up to the Muslims, citizens and criminals alike. Father Marcos, we understand your apprehension, but this is how it must be. You have been dealing decisively with your cartel threat. I am, in essence, the Supreme Commanding General of the forces for the Catholic Order. I cannot fight the Muslims *and* be the Pope. You will rebuild the new Vatican and be the Pope. I will be the general and expand our forces because we're going to need them. It will take a few years to finalize the transformation of this city to the New Vatican. When done, we will do the transition ceremony in secret and you will be the next Pope."

Cardinal Cassiano adds, "This New Vatican must also establish formal relations with the American Christians and Jews. They have entered their post-Resistance phase and now both have created their own Continuums. The Christians have unified all their old Orders into one: the New Protestant Order. The Jews have unified all their Orders. We must move quickly to establish a greater Faither Alliance: Christians, Jews, Catholics, and the African Collective."

Archbishop Masai says, "Father Marcos, we know this is a lot to process at once, but this is how it must be. This is the division of power that must happen. The New Catholic Order will begin with your ascension to the Papacy. The Catholic Order under Rome, the Old Roman Catholic Order, is gone. The New Catholic Order, under Mexico, begins now. Speak and hear the words so that you accept them: *Father Marcos is the New Pope of the New Catholic Order.*"

Sister Maria sits at her desk outside. The man on the phone was yelling so loud. She, of course, refused to interrupt the Father's meeting with the Archbishop and the Cardinal. She may not know what the meeting is about, but she knows it is of supreme importance. She takes a message. Religious people are about the only ones who use pen and paper anymore, but the man on the phone insisted that he speak with the Father directly. The caller ID didn't show the exact number, but it did show what global region it came from: the Russian Bloc. The man on the phone spoke Spanish with a thick Russian accent. The man said he would call back in an hour, but he never did.

The New Pope would soon become aware of the Conspiracy uncovered by the American Christians and Jews. He would also learn of the return of Wisp the Demon and…his brothers.

Thirty years until the first attack of World War III. The AFTER EDEN saga continues in Book Three: *RISING LEVIATHAN*.

Thank you for reading!

Dear Reader,

I hope you enjoyed *Stars and Scorpions*.

<u>**Can You Write Me a Review?**</u>

If you enjoyed *Stars and Scorpions* (After Eden Series, Book #2), I'd greatly appreciate a review on one or more of the following sites:

Reviews are the best way for readers to discover good books. My writer's motto is simple: "Readers Rule!" Thanks so much.

Always writing,

Austin Dragon

CONTINUE THE ADVENTURE

Get Your Next *After Eden* Book!

<u>The After Eden Series (Chronological Order)</u>

Thy Kingdom Fall (After Eden Series, Book #1)
Stars and Scorpions (After Eden Series, Book #2)
Metal Flesh (After Eden Series: Tek-Fall, Episode I)
Hell's Menagerie (After Eden Series: Tek-Fall, Episode II)
Rising Leviathan (After Eden Series, Book #3)
Pure Conspiracy (After Eden Select Novel)
Red Halo (After Eden Series, Book #4) Coming Soon!

<u>The After Eden Series (Group Order)</u>

Main After Eden Series
Thy Kingdom Fall (After Eden Series, Book #1)
Stars and Scorpions (After Eden Series, Book #2)
Rising Leviathan (After Eden Series, Book #3)
Red Halo (After Eden Series, Book #4) Coming Soon!

After Eden: Tek-Fall Companion Novels
Metal Flesh (After Eden Series: Tek-Fall, Episode I)
Hell's Menagerie (After Eden Series: Tek-Fall, Episode II)

After Eden Select Novel
Pure Conspiracy (After Eden Select Novel)

Also by Austin Dragon

See all my books in science fiction, cyberpunk, mystery, horror, YA dystopia, and fantasy at: **http://www.austindragon.com/books-of-author-austin-dragon/**

ABOUT THE AUTHOR

Austin Dragon is the author of the *After Eden* **Series**, including the *After Eden: Tek-Fall* mini-series, the classic *Sleepy Hollow Horrors*, and the new cyberpunk detective series, *Liquid Cool*. He is a native New Yorker, but has called Los Angeles, California home for the last twenty years. Words to describe him, in no particular order: U.S. Army; English teacher; one-time resident of Paris; political junkie; movie buff; campaign manager and staffer of presidential and gubernatorial campaigns; Fortune 500 corporate recruiter; renaissance man; dreamer.

He is currently working on the next books in the *After Eden* Series, and new books and series in mystery, fantasy, YA dystopia, classic horror, and more science fiction!

Connect with Austin on social media at:

Website and blog:
http://www.austindragon.com

Twitter:
https://twitter.com/Austin_Dragon

Pinterest:
http://www.pinterest.com/austindragon

Google+:
https://google.com/+AustinDragonAuthor

Goodreads:
https://www.goodreads.com/ADragon

9 780988 723535